A CALAMITY WAITING TO HAPPEN

"You know, I got a real nice thank-you from your uncle in there, Tressa." Ranger Rick stepped closer. "How about you making a little nice? You are grateful for my help to your family, aren't you?"

I shuffled my feet. My association with Rick Townsend was long and complicated, often characterized by name-calling, pranks, and sparring of the verbal kind. He was way too nice-looking for his own good—and mine—which made him trouble with a big T and, quite frankly, maybe too much man for this simple cowgirl to resist.

I slid my hands lightly down one of his muscular arms and took his rather nicely-shaped hand in both of mine. I looked up and into two very dark, intense eyes and ran my tongue across my top lip for effect.

"Thank you, Ranger Townsend," I said, my voice breathless, and not at all due to my little performance. "From the bottom of my heart, I thank you." I leaned in, as if to seal my thanks with a kiss....

CALAMITY JAYNE
RIDES AGAIN

KATHLEEN BACUS

LOVE SPELL NEW YORK CITY

LOVE SPELL®

July 2006

Published by

Dorchester Publishing Co., Inc.
200 Madison Avenue
New York, NY 10016

ISBN 0-505-52669-7

The name "Love Spell" and its logo are trademarks of Dorchester Publishing Co., Inc.

Printed in the United States of America.

Visit us on the web at www.dorchesterpub.com.

For Erick, who listened to every chapter, every word, and every syllable of this manuscript, ad nauseum, last summer without one complaint when he could have been doing way more fun things. Like watching the Iowa corn grow. That's a pretty terrific son I have there. Thanks, Bubba. I appreciate it.

Thanks, too, to retired Iowa State Patrol Sergeant Charlie Black, ex-ISP 336, my first State Patrol Field Training Officer, for giving me a "behind-the-scenes" introduction to the Iowa State Fair—including an up-close-and-personal encounter with "The Great Bozo"—as a rookie trooper way back when. Those experiences proved, uh, helpful in crafting this story. I still owe you one, Chuck, you dog!

CHAPTER 1

A blonde decides to try horseback riding, even though she has had no lessons or prior experience. She mounts the horse unassisted and it immediately springs into motion. It gallops along at a steady and rhythmic pace, but the blonde begins to slip from the saddle. In terror, she grabs for the horse's mane, but cannot seem to get a firm grip. She tries to throw her arms around the horse's neck, but she slides down the side of the horse anyway. The horse gallops along, seemingly ignorant of its slipping rider. Finally giving up her frail grip, the blonde attempts to leap away from the horse and throw herself to safety. Unfortunately, her foot becomes entangled in the stirrup, and she is now at the mercy of the horse's pounding hooves as her head is struck against the ground over and over. She starts to lose consciousness, but to her great good fortune, Bob, the Wal-Mart greeter, sees her and unplugs the horse.

I know a gazillion and two dumb-blonde jokes. I began hearing them at about the same time I discovered Dr. Seuss. I laughed it up along with everyone else, only realizing later in life that I was really the butt of those jokes. Nope. Not even my own head of bleached blond hair gave me a heads-up. It took the conferring of a rather humiliating nickname for me to finally make that personal connection. Yep, that's right, a nickname. You know, like Biff, Billy Bob, Bubba, Princess, Precious, Peaches, Stormin' Norman, Slick Willy, J. Lo, Calamity Jayne . . . Uh, if you haven't already guessed, I'm Calamity Jayne.

The really frustrating thing about my particular nickname is that it has followed me into adulthood. Not too traumatic if you happen to be an Angel Eyes, Sweet Cheeks, or even a Stud Muffin, but hardly flattering when you're almost twenty-four and still saddled with a pet name that promotes the sale and use of such things as rabbits' feet and good-luck crystals, and causes folks to perform the sign of the cross when they meet you on the sidewalk.

Used to be, the nickname really gave me fits. But after the events of earlier this summer, which found yours truly in the middle of a hometown whodunit and the target of a multiple murderer, the nickname, while gaining notoriety, has actually lost some of its sting.

My real name is Tressa Turner. Tressa *Jayne* Turner. I make my home in a nice, but borrowed, doublewide mobile home adjacent to my folks' rural Iowa acreage. My father harbors "Green Acres" fantasies. My mother just wants my grandmother away from populated areas. When Gram became prone—no pun intended—to frequent falls, and seemed to be auditioning for a part on one of those I've-fallen-and-I-can't-get-up commercials, she moved in with the folks. My mom is a CPA. She has a home-based accounting and tax service. It works out well. In between debits and credits, W-2s and W-4s, she can keep tabs on the feisty, but lovable, senior citizen. Since I have two dogs, three horses, and a history of intermittent unemployment, the arrangement works for everyone.

While I'm happy to report I am at present gainfully employed at the local newspaper, the *Grandville Gazette*, the pay is not commensurate with my level of debt—or desire for frequent new shoes, horse paraphernalia, and the occasional bling. As a result, I work several jobs to supplement my income. My job at Bargain City, a discount chain, precipitated my just past odyssey of murder and mayhem. Purely by accident, you understand, I happened to drive off in the getaway car of a murderer with the still-warm murder vic stuffed in the trunk. I played hide-and-seek with the disappearing stiff (and cat and mouse with the killer) for several days before a rather, shall we say, messy confrontation with the villain, all resulting in a somewhat strained relationship with my Uncle Frank. While I won't go into the gory details—"gory" being the operative word—let me just say that Uncle Frank and I are still working through the trust issue.

As much as I would like to take full credit in the heroism department for taking down the bad guy and saving the local citizenry in my little "Murder at Silver Stone Lake" saga, sadly, I cannot. I had a little help. Okay, a lot of help. Divine intervention, as it turned out, came on the wings of the last dragon slayer I would ever choose to save this fair maiden. Rick Townsend, or "Ranger Rick," as I like to call him—among other things—is an officer for the State Department of Natural Resources. He spends his days (or nights, as the case may be) hunting down poachers, protecting the waterfowl, and enforcing boating regs. In his off-duty hours he likes to give me a hard time. Townsend and I go way back. He's been my brother's best friend since before they started wearing jock straps. Townsend is one of those guys who comes to mind when you think of the word "hott" with two t's.

Townsend and I are presently circling a relationship

like two paranoid Sumo wrestlers. We share a yo-yo past. You know: up and down, up and down. Rick Townsend first stuck me with the Calamity Jayne label, which, of course, hardly endears him to me. He has a pattern of bedeviling me that dates back to elementary school, when he wrote a mushy love note to Parker "Pig Pen" Williams and signed my name along with lots of Xs and Os. As a result, I got a big, wet, slobbery kiss from Parker at morning recess, and two days out-of-school for tying him to the jungle gym by his sweatpants.

Townsend and I made this way-over-the-top bet involving a stolen (unintentionally, I remind you!) car, a disappearing corpse, and an adorable, yet tasteful, raccoon tattoo.

After my rather dramatic rescue from probable death at the hands of a cold-blooded killer, Townsend and I initiated an uneasy truce. We've shared a few kisses and a couple of clinches kind of like the ones you see on the covers of those romance novels you'd just as soon your pastor not see you with in the checkout line. I kept my top on, though. Well, all except that one time. But that was totally Townsend's fault. Pinky-swear.

Sometimes I think since Townsend saved my cookies he believes he has the God-given right to sample them. At other times, I worry he is seeing me through damsel-in-distress eyeglasses and not focusing on the real me—the girl he's carried on a feud with that makes the Hatfields and McCoys look like kissin' cousins.

So, as you might expect, I'm making like I'm driving through a construction zone. You know: proceeding with caution. A broken heart is the last thing I need after I was almost sliced and diced with one of Uncle Frank's Ginzu knives.

In my home state of Iowa—the corn state, not the potato one—the annual state fair is a huge deal. You've heard of the musical *State Fair*; yup, that's our fair. A great state fair. Probably the best. For sure we have the best state fair cuisine anywhere. Hands down. From humongous turkey legs that you'd swear were steroid-enhanced, plate-sized charcoal-broiled burgers made only from the best Iowa corn-fed beef, to chops so thick you have to shove your bites in sideways, we've got it all. Plus, we've got anything edible you can manage to slam on a stick and deep fat fry, freeze, or both.

Food takes me to the Iowa State Fair every August. I'll go about anywhere for quality junk food, but in this case I'm the one preparing it. Okay, okay, so I eat my share, too. However, I primarily go to the fair to promote Uncle Frank's various ice cream confections. Uncle Frank's family has operated the same ice cream concessions at the same locations at the fairgrounds for more than three generations. Seniority at this event counts for a lot. And tradition. Traditionally, Uncle Frank recruits family members to man his stands annually two weeks in late summer. Traditionally, I'm one of the first tapped for service. You'll hear no complaints from me. I've always loved the fair. I was one of those cowgirls who slept with their horses in the huge, smelly horse barn while city slickers maneuvered their way around piles of horse manure reciting bad poop jokes and getting their pictures taken with horses that looked like Trigger. Once I collected my ribbons, I'd sell root beer floats and twist cones to hot, hungry fair-goers with tired feet.

Uncle Frank's fair businesses are in highly coveted places on the fairgrounds. Uncle Frank owns a modest-sized brick red ice cream parlor called—I warn you, this is bad—Barlowe's Ice Cream Emporium. It's one of the various permanent structures that were erected on the fairgrounds property years ago. It's located on the main drag, just up the hill from the Old West Town and a hop, skip, and a jump from the biggest beer tent on the fairgrounds. Talk about your location, location, location. Uncle Frank's mini-stand is on the Grand Concourse, the street that runs right down the center of the fairgrounds and supports much of the foot traffic. Every year Uncle Frank receives oodles of offers to acquire his fairgrounds concession stands. Yep, prime real estate, for sure.

I'm always drafted for set-up day due to my heavy-lifting prowess, a skill honed from years of lifting and stacking seventy-pound hay bales for my four-legged beauties. The state fair comes earlier and earlier each year. Used to be kids didn't have to worry about heading back to school until after Labor Day. Now, school resumes the second or third week of August. Since fair officials rely on schoolkids and their parents to make up a significant portion of the almost one-million folks who pass through the turnstiles at this wildly popular event, the fair begins its ten-day run the second week of August to accommodate the school starting dates. This hot, humid August day found me in the emporium dripping worse than one of Uncle Frank's triple scoopers. With the fair scheduled to open in less than twenty-four hours, my Uncle Frank was well into his "We'll never be ready! We'll never be ready!" mantra.

"That's the last of it," I said, coming out of the small, walk-in freezer where we stored the goodies. "You've got enough buckets of ice cream back there to build a respectable igloo."

"You remember what I told you about that door," Uncle Frank reminded me. "I installed a gizmo that makes it impossible for you to get locked in. You just turn it and the door opens. Okay?"

I nodded, aware that Uncle Frank was keeping a closer eye on me than those bachelors did on the bachelorette on that reality TV show. "I heard you, Uncle Frank. And I promise there won't be any trouble this year. Everything is going to run just like clockwork.

Tick-tock. Tick-tock." I performed a cash-register action. "Ka-ching. Ka-ching. Just think of all that money coming in if it stays this hot. This is one of the few air-conditioned buildings on the grounds—and the only one that offers cool treats and way cool people to dispense them. This place will be busier than the Foodmart on double-coupon Wednesday the first of the month."

"From your mouth to God's ears," Uncle Frank grumbled as he swept the reddish-brown industrial-quality tile behind the shiny clean stainless steel and glass refrigerated ice cream case. "The only thing I really care about is topping that old fart Luther Daggett's sales figures. Last year, he came too damned close for comfort. The way the economy is, people will probably stay home and suck on Freezer Pops and eat frozen Snickers bars."

Uncle Frank is always a grumblepuss just before opening day. Every year it's the same; Uncle Frank's predictions of doom and gloom are offset by my Aunt Reggie's unemotional, analytical businesswoman approach to life. Must have something to do with being a CPA's sister. Aunt Reggie is the barometer of her family. She keeps cool when Uncle Frank's temperature is in the red zone. Their only child, Frank Jr.—or "Frankfurter," as I call him—is . . . how can I put this in a nice way? A wiener. A one-hundred-percent, no-filler-added, honest-to-goodness weenie. You know, he's one of those kids who wears a suit coat and tie to the middle school band concerts, his pants just a tad short and on the Urkel side. The kid who always orders the salad and yogurt instead of the burger and fries. Who's allergic to everything you can see, smell, taste, or pet, and has the Rudolph nose to prove it.

I do feel a certain empathy for Frankfurter. He's one year older than me and still lives at home with his parents. He's trying to figure out who he is and what he wants in life. Hello. Talk about your déjà vu moments.

Uncle Frank would love to be able to retire in warmer climes and leave the ice cream businesses to Frank Jr. Sadly, Frankie shows little or no inclination to follow in his father's soft-serve footsteps. He did take an interest in the Dairee Freeze during a recent remodeling project. Frankie wanted to replace the off-white countertop with one called Shades of Southwest turquoise. He was all set to pull the entire motif together with a colorful desert dusk and turquoise border featuring delicate mauve flowers. Uncle Frank was ready to stroke out. Aunt Reggie just liked the fact that she finally had someone to go with her to look at wallpaper patterns.

"I'm out of here, Uncle Frank," I announced, snagging a chocolate bar from a display by the cash register. "I'm supposed to relieve Frankie at the mini-freeze at six, right?" I asked, referring to the much smaller Dairee Freeze location, also known as Site B, down on the concourse across from the grandstand.

"Six sharp." Uncle Frank leaned on his broom and frowned at me as I unwrapped the chocolate and began to nibble away. Have I mentioned my uncle is tighter than a pair of thigh-high hose? "You know how Frankie gets when he isn't relieved on time. He's liable to shut the place up and walk out, and we do some of our best business before the fair opens."

I nodded, familiar with my first cousin's often petulant ways. "Frankie is just a little confused, Uncle Frank," I said, wanting to somehow minimize Uncle Frank's disillusionment with his only son. I knew how it felt to be the cause of repetitive head-shaking and shushing among family and friends. "He'll come around."

Uncle Frank smiled. "Like you came around?" He put a hand to his head. "Heaven help us. I don't think my business can afford another family member's defining moment."

I giggled and gave Uncle Frank a quick peck on one whiskered cheek. "At least you can't complain of boredom when I'm around, Uncle Frank," I boasted.

"Boredom? Who has time to be bored? We'll never be ready by tomorrow!"

I left Uncle Frank shaking his head and muttering, and started down the hill, pausing to wave at other state fair fixtures along the way. The fair is like a family reunion in many respects. Once a year we all get together and catch up on what's happened during the three hundred and fifty-five days since we've last seen each other. It's like old home week.

"Well, well, well, if it isn't Calamity Jayne! Hello there, Tressa. I wondered if you would be here this year. After all that excitement, I thought maybe this old state fair would seem dull as dirt to you."

"Welcome back, Mrs. Connor," I said, pausing to greet Uncle Frank's next-door concession neighbor, Lucinda Connor, who ran a large tented souvenir stand that featured everything from mood rings to feather-trimmed tomahawks. Lucy was a decade-long transplant from the "left" coast, no doubt acquiring much of the knowledge necessary to push felt cowboy hats, multicolored Indian headdresses and plastic horse figurines from "B" Hollywood movies and trips to the racetrack-casino. "It's nice to see you again. You look younger every year," I lied. In reality, Lucy's true age was a bit dicey to gauge. She could be anywhere from thirty to fifty-five years old. Her dark, leathery skin brought to mind the texture of one of my Western saddles. The antique one. I suspected too much beach time with too little sunscreen was a contributing culprit. That and the chain smoking. This year Lucy sported a bleachy blonde 'do. In past years she'd shown up as a brunette, a redhead and a strawberry blonde. Lean and toned, Lucy kind of reminded me of what a retired aerobics instructor might look like.

"Aren't you sweet? I've been hearing the most delicious things about you," Lucy continued. "Is it really true you found four dead bodies?"

I shook my head. "Only three. One I found twice."

"I couldn't believe it when I read about it in the paper. I told all my friends, 'Why, I know that girl. I know Calamity Jayne!' Of course, they were dying to hear all about your state fair exploits. Like the time you knocked the tail off the butter cow. And when you deflated the giant beer can outside the beer tent. And there was the time you—"

"Oh, gee, I have to run." I made a point of looking at my wrist, even though I'd forgotten to put on my watch. "I have to relieve Frank Junior down at the other stand in a few minutes. Nice seeing you again."

"You're relieving Frankie? That's funny. I could swear I saw him heading out the Grand Avenue gate over an hour ago. Well, you go on now. We'll have plenty of time to catch up later."

I nodded, making a mental note to self to avoid Lucy's Trinkets and Treasures. I was trying to move away from my past faux pas. I wanted to project a new image, cultivate a new reputation. One of maturity. Common sense. Competency. Okay, so maybe I'd shoot for paying all my bills on time for six months and work from there.

I made my way to the mini-freeze via the Guess Your Weight or Age booth, thinking it might be fun if Lucy could stump the pro. I also wanted to check out how much weight I'd gained since last year. (Sorry, folks. That info is not for public dissemination.) I stopped by Tony's Taffy to say howdy-do. Of course, I had to sample each of the flavors and try this year's new offering, French Vanilla Cappuccino. (A big, but sticky, thumbs up!) I grabbed a corn dog from Carl, a lemonade from Louie, and a caramel apple from Ada. By the time I got to Uncle Frank's, I was ready for the antacid stand.

I frowned when I saw the line snaking its way down the sidewalk outside the mini-freeze. What was Frankfurter doing, anyway, the little wiener? The line was longer than the one at the Bud tent on fifty-cent draw night.

I hustled to the back of the tiny, white square building about the size of a one-half car garage, jerked the door open, and stepped inside.

"What the heck is going on, Frankie?" I asked the figure in white cotton, his back to me. "You've got customers lined up from here to the pretzel place next door. What's the deal?"

"I owe you an apology, Calamity," said the tall figure in white, struggling to construct something that resembled an ice cream cone. "These damned curlicues are not as easy to make as I thought."

I took a step back. My jaw did a trap-door motion. I gasped as the man turned and slapped a soggy, misshapen cone into my hand.

"I quit."

I looked up from the drippy mess oozing down my wrist to the kaleidoscope of color splashed across the front of the white apron across from me.

"Ranger Rick?" I stared at the gooey, ice-cream-covered man. "What are you doing here?"

"I'm splitting this pop shack," he said, pulling off his apron. "And pronto."

I shook my head, trying to process the picture of the tall, dark, and deadly handsome ranger splitting bananas and drizzling nuts.

"You look good in confections," was all I could think to say.

"Hell," he managed.

"What are you doing here?" I asked again. "Where's Frankie?"

"How should I know? I came over to get a damned dip cone and the place was unlocked, open for business, but empty as that greasy egg roll stand across the way. I figured Frankie stepped out to use the john, but I've been manning the order window for two freaking hours!" The ranger threw the apron on the counter. "I'm outta here."

"Hey! What? Where are you going?"

"Back to the comfortable and familiar world of reptiles and raptors. And as far as I'm concerned, if I never see another freaking ice cream cone it will be okay by me." He headed toward the exit.

"Hey, Mr. Ranger, sir!" I yelled. "You forgot your dip cone!"

I giggled a bit and then caught a look at the line of angry customers with facial expressions reminiscent of a group of disappointed sports fans about to tip something over. Or Democrats after their 2004 presidential election exit polls proved unreliable. I sobered. Where the devil was that Oscar Meyer cousin of mine, anyway?

CHAPTER 2

I closed up around midnight, too tired to even snitch a treat for the road. I was still royally ticked at Frankie and suspected his little disappearing act had everything to do with his campaign to show Uncle Frank he was serious about passing on the passing on of the family business. Enough complaints to the Fair Board, and they might decide not to renew Uncle Frank's business license!

I made my way in the direction of the Ice Cream Emporium. I wanted to let Uncle Frank know his son had deserted his post, and to warn Frankie to maintain a low profile where Ranger Rick Townsend was concerned—at least until the ranger defrosted a bit.

The Emporium was dark as I approached, and I frowned, thinking it was way too early for Uncle Frank to call it a night, especially on the eve of opening day. I made my way to the front door, pausing when I saw it standing open. I stood for a moment, nibbling my lip, recalling my recent past of stumbling upon dead bodies and murderers. I shook my head. Nah. Lightning didn't strike in the same place twice. I'd found my quota of stiffs. The chances of that happening again were about the same as the odds of finding a good-looking cowboy wearing nothin' but a smile and a Stetson, waiting up for me in my folks' camper.

I inched the door open. "Uncle Frank? Frankie? Hello? Anybody here?" I stepped into the ice cream parlor and reached for the light switch. "Come out, come out, wherever you are," I said, and flipped the switch.

The floor seemed to come alive. Dark shapes scurried toward the corners and under the tables. I stepped in and heard a pop and a crunch and felt a tickling on my toes. I looked down to see several large, butt-ugly cock-roaches skittering across my bare foot. I screamed and stomped my foot. *Snap, crackle, pop!*

I gazed about the room. There were hundreds of the filthy things! Several ran a race across Uncle Frank's shiny white countertop. More scrambled off the refrig-erated unit where we kept the most popular flavors for scooping.

I ran around the counter, grabbed Uncle Frank's pushbroom, and started sweeping the gross bugs up, shaking stragglers off my feet and trying not to gag. When I had a huge pile of the disgusting buggers col-lected, I swept them toward the door.

"Good God! What the hell?"

I grimaced when I recognized the person belonging to that voice.

"What is this shit?" preceded more stomping and *snap-crackle-crunch*ing.

I shook my broom over Rick Townsend's tennis shoe-clad foot. "They're cockroaches!" I said, still grossed out by that reality. "Hundreds of them. Everywhere!"

"How the hell did this many cockroaches get in here?" Townsend asked, taking mincing steps across the floor and behind the counter. "Jeezus. What an army! What's going on here?"

I shook my head. "Don't ask me. I was on my way up to the campground and decided to stop and see if Frankie had performed his mea culpas with Uncle Frank, and found the door wide open. When I switched on the lights, it was like I was the Orkin man or something!"

"Where's your uncle?" Townsend said, grabbing a state fair guidebook and flicking roaches off the counter onto the floor, popping them under his heel. Squish. Squirt. "What about Frankie? He ever show up?"

I shook my head, herding another group of invaders toward the door. "Haven't seen hide nor hair of him. You?"

Townsend kicked a roach across the room. "That little twerp knows better than to be within cow-chip tossing distance of me. Hell, I can't even face a bowl of ice cream after that experience."

"I'm worried, Townsend," I said. "First Frankie disappears without a word and now we've got cockroach central here and no Uncle Frank. He'd never go off and leave the place unlocked. Never. Lots of times he pulls an all-nighter getting ready for opening day."

I wasn't really worried about the Frankfurter. I suspected he was keeping a low profile in case Uncle Frank found out about his labor stoppage, but the icky infestation was definitely a cause for concern.

I was doing the roach rumba, jumping up and down and squealing at each bug vanquished, when soft laughter drew my attention to the door. I looked up to see Uncle Frank sashay in arm-in-arm with Lucy Connor of Lucy's Trinkets and Treasures. I stopped in mid-roach eradication and stared at the twosome in the doorway, my eyes narrowing as I took in the tall, icy cold beer I would have sold my firstborn for clutched in Uncle Frank's meaty fist.

"Where the hell have you been?" I shouted.

Uncle Frank stepped over the threshold and, *crunch*, onto a pile of recently departed insects. He looked down at his blue canvas shoe, up at me, broom in hand, and across the floor of his ice cream parlor, where die-hard bugs still zipped back and forth across the room, Townsend in hot pursuit.

The plastic cup in his hand began to jiggle. Beer erupted over the sides and down his arm. I licked my lips. Uncle Frank remained inert, unmoving, except for that thing going on with his hand. I couldn't imagine what thoughts had to be filling his head. I suddenly felt sorry for yelling at him.

"Uncle Frank?" I moved forward and touched his arm, removing the beer from his unresisting hand. I took a long swig, wiped my mouth, then took another one and belched. "Are you okay?" I asked.

He looked at the beer in my hand, then at Townsend, who was swearing and slapping the bugs zipping up and down Aunt Regina's frilly red and white checked curtains. He grabbed the beer from me, tipped his head back, and downed the remainder of the alcohol in long, successive gulps. He crushed the empty cup in his hands.

"Would someone please tell me what the hell is going on?" he said, shaking a large cockroach off his tenny. "What the hell have you done to me this time, Calamity?" he asked. "What the hell have you done to me now?"

I took a step back, a hand unconsciously moving to rest over my heart. It figured I'd get blamed for this. That was nothing new. But acknowledging the pain that came along with the finger-pointing was. I was still learning how to give voice to my true feelings, how to strip away the hedgehog prickles that protected a soft, gooey center—*my* soft, gooey center—to explore a range of emotions I'd stifled way too long. To articulate

an answer to the how-does-that-make-you-feel mantra
the TV psycho-babble gurus loved to ask their lab-rat
guests. Hmmm. Okay. Let's see. How did Uncle Frank's
accusation make me feel? Pissed off, that's what!

"Listen, Mr. Misty," I snarled, shaking a roach from
my foot. "I stopped by to see if you needed any help finishing things up, and what do I get? An insect ambush of
epic proportions, asinine accusations, and the distinct
probability that I'll never enjoy a bowl of Rice Krispies
again with the same enthusiasm." I shook a finger at
him. "Woe to you if that extends to marshmallow treats."

Uncle Frank shot me an uncertain look, and then
looked past me to Townsend in the background, doing
his own unpolished version of the roach rumba.

"What do you know about this, Townsend?" he
asked, grabbing the broom out of my hand and playing
hockey with some bugs.

"All I know is, I'm staying way the hell away from
your Dairee Freeze concessions for the remainder of the
fair, Frank," Townsend replied. "Far, far away. First I'm
left to man your other stand for hours with no help and
no prior experience in cone-top curlicues, and then I
stop by here and get caught up in a freakin' roach
round-up." He slapped at his pantleg.

"What do you mean, you manned my other stand?"
Uncle Frank asked. "Where were you, Tressa?"

"She was there," Townsend said, before I could defend myself. "Frankie wasn't. I thought he'd just
stepped out for a second and he'd be right back, but he
never showed. I was left in that damned box for hours. I
didn't know what the hell I was doing."

"I can attest to that," I remarked. "You should've seen
his apron. He looked like he'd just had a food fight with
Ben & Jerry. And lost big time."

Ranger Rick gave me a sour look. "Where the hell
was Frankie, anyway?" he asked my uncle.

"I don't know what the devil you're talking about," Uncle Frank said. "I haven't seen Frankie since early this morning up at the campgrounds. You mean, he left the other stand open and just went off?" A muscle in my uncle's jaw jumped.

"Oh, I saw Frankie earlier this afternoon," Lucy chimed in, putting a taloned hand on Uncle Frank's arm. For a while I'd forgotten she was even there. Now it occurred to me to question why she *was* there. With Uncle Frank. Sharing a beer at this time of night. "Remember, Tressa dear? I told you I'd seen Frankie leaving through the main gate when you were taking off to relieve him. I thought it was odd at the time. After all, Frank does at least ten percent of his total ice cream sales before the fair opens. Don't you, Frank?"

I looked at Uncle Frank and then back at Lucy, wondering how she would know such a thing, then realized that Uncle Frank must've discussed his sales with her—something, paranoid that he was about Luther Daggett besting him, he generally didn't share with outsiders. I looked at Lucy's hand on Uncle Frank's arm again. Maybe she wasn't as much of an outsider as I assumed. I frowned at that hand, and Lucy must've noticed, because she let it drop to her side.

"You saw Frankie leave the fairgrounds when he was supposed to be working?" Uncle Frank turned to Townsend. "You filled in for him?" He turned to me. "He never showed up later?"

I shook my head. "I haven't seen him all day. I thought maybe he would be here helping you. That's why I stopped by. To make sure you weren't too hard on him. He can get a little muddled about things sometimes."

"Pot calling the kettle, I believe," Ranger Rick interjected.

"Bug off, Townsend," I said, flicking a straggler at him from the counter.

"Confused? About what? What's that got to do with him deserting his post and telling no one?" Uncle Frank gave the broom a hard push.

"We all pretty much know how Frankie feels about the ice cream business, Uncle Frank," I pointed out. "He sees each year going by as another year of his life wasted, and he's struggling to find just where he fits into this vast picture puzzle called life. And face it, Uncle Frank—I don't think Frankie's future includes dairy. He's tried to tell you that. Maybe this was his misguided, childish way of showing you."

Uncle Frank shook his head. "You think he's trying to sabotage my business to prove a point? How crazy is that?"

I shrugged. "I think Frankie is confused, Uncle Frank. Confused, not crazy. And confused people do confusing things."

"Pot calling the kettle again," Townsend remarked.

I ignored him and moved nearer Uncle Frank, putting a hand on his. "He loves you, Uncle Frank. And Aunt Regina. You know that."

Uncle Frank squeezed my hand, then let go. "Funny way for a son to show his love. First he abandons his post and causes me untold business harm. Now he's let loose scads of the most hated bug on the planet in my business establishment, the sight of just one of which is guaranteed to send customers running in revulsion. How the hell is that love?"

I blinked. Uncle Frank thought Frankie was responsible for the roach infestation? I shook my head. No. No way. The cousin I knew might walk off in a tiff to prove a point and be too scared to face Townsend's wrath when he came to his senses, but he would never cause the kind of irreparable harm this kind of stunt could create. Still, if not Frankie, who? And why?

"You can't think Frankie did this, Uncle Frank!"

"What else am I to think?" he asked, his normally red-tinged face ashen and pale.

"Oh, Frank, this is just awful," Lucy said, this time foregoing the hand on his arm. "But we can still put things to rights. If we all pitch in, we can have this place ready to open tomorrow morning and no one will be any the wiser. I'm just going to run and get my jumbo shop-vac, and we'll have those hideous things all sucked up and disposed of in no time." She gave his cheek a pat. "Don't you worry about a thing, Frank, we'll pull this off yet."

Lucy hurried out the back door and I stared after her. She was being very helpful, I thought. Very neighborly. But maybe a tad too neighborly for my liking—and probably Aunt Reggie's. Lucy could lend a helping hand; that was cool. But I wasn't about to let her share any other trinkets or treasures with Uncle Frank.

Thirty minutes later I had to give Leather Lucy grudging credit. She had us organized and working in synchronized fashion. Townsend sucked the bugs, I held the trash bags for disposal, and Uncle Frank mopped the floor with commercial-strength cleaner. Lucy disinfected the tables, counters, and ice cream area. By three-thirty A.M. we had successfully transformed the place from Cockroach Central back to Barlow's Ice Cream Emporium.

"You ready to head up to the campgrounds, Uncle Frank?" I asked, not bothering to stifle my yawn.

He shook his head. "Nah. You go on ahead. I have a few more things to see to and I'll be along." He came over and ruffled my hair. "Thanks, kiddo. I owe you one. You, too, Rick," he added, holding out a hand for Townsend to shake. "I can't tell you how much I appreciate the help."

"Oh, I imagine I'll receive adequate compensation in the future in the form of lots of ice cream cones with perfect little curlicues on top," Townsend replied, gripping Uncle Frank's hand. "That is, when I'm back to eating ice cream without gagging. Take it easy, Frank," he said.

"Coming?" I asked Lucy, not about to leave her alone with Uncle Frank in his tired, vulnerable state. Like I said, a helping hand was one thing; holding Uncle Frank's was quite another.

Lucy looked at me, unmistakable annoyance in her face.

"Absolutely! Go on. Get out of here, Lucy," Uncle Frank said. "You must be tuckered out. I'll see that you get your shop-vac back. Go on now. Scoot!"

I followed Lucy out the door and wished her good night, looking on as she made her way back to her establishment. There she hopped into a golf cart, the fair's primary mode of transportation, and took off in the direction of the campground.

"Well, that was nice. The least she could have done was offer me a lift," I grumbled, staring at the steep, graveled incline that led to the campground.

"Can you blame her?" Townsend chuckled. "You treated her as if she was about to jump your uncle's bones. She got the hands-off message loud and clear, Calamity."

"Good," I said. "Then I won't have to bring out the big guns."

Townsend shook his head. "Big guns?"

"My Grammy," I said, and Townsend put his hands up as if in surrender.

"Right," he said. "Hannah the Hellion. Must run in the family."

"I'll take that as a compliment, Mr. Ranger, sir," I teased.

"You know, I got a real nice thank-you from your uncle in there, Tressa." He stepped closer. "How about *you* making a little nice? You are grateful for my help to your family, aren't you?"

I shuffled my feet. My association with Rick Townsend was long and complicated, often characterized by name-calling, pranks, and sparring of the verbal kind. He was way too nice-looking for his own good—and mine—which made him Trouble with a big *T* and, quite frankly, maybe too much man for this simple cowgirl to resist. That's why I'd always kept my distance in the past, keeping things on an adversarial footing. I was pretty good at mouth-to-mouth combat. I was well-armed for it. I could float like a butterfly and sting like a bee when it came to one-line putdowns and cynical comebacks. I just wasn't sure I was equally competent at the mushy love stuff—although I was certainly ready to give it the old college try, even though I was a college dropout three times over, when the right man came along. The problem was, I just wasn't certain Townsend was Mr. Right—or even Mr. Right Now. Maybe that was because I sensed from him that he didn't know either.

"Sure, I'm grateful," I said. "Of course I'm grateful. Who wouldn't be grateful?" *Nice job of verbal sparring, Tressa,* I thought with disgust.

"I think you can do better than that, T.J. Your uncle expressed his gratitude warmly and with feeling," Ranger Rick pointed out.

I thought about the pair's handshake. "You're right, Townsend," I said, wetting my lips and stepping closer to the hunky ranger. "You're absolutely right."

I slid my hands lightly down one of his muscular arms and took his rather nicely shaped hand in both of mine. I looked up and into two very dark, intense eyes and ran my tongue across my top lip for effect.

"Thank you, Ranger Townsend," I said, my voice breathless and not all due to my little performance.

"From the bottom of my heart, I thank you." I leaned in, as if to seal my thanks with a kiss . . . then suddenly gripped his elbow with one hand and started pumping his hand with the other in an energetic down-home handshake, the kind politicians give prospective voters in the reception lines or CEOs trade when they announce a beneficial business deal.

Townsend's mouth flew open. I laughed and broke the handshake and skipped off toward the campground. I stopped and blew him a kiss, then took off as fast as my tired old dogs would carry me.

Ain't I a little stinker?

CHAPTER 3

My sandaled toe caught in loose rock at the base of the incline leading to the campground that, from my weary world view, seemed as daunting as the seven-mile climb to the top of the Snow Bowl near Flagstaff, Arizona, where a branch of our family tree had taken root.

I grimaced and wished for one of those way convenient state fair trolleys pulled by the big green tractors and designed to transport pooped-out fair-goers to the campground. Unfortunately for my tired tootsies, I'd teed off Lucy, and the trolley had long ago called it a night. I gave a long, considering look at a bench near the campground gate, thinking maybe I should give my feet a rest before I hoofed it up the hill. I slapped at a buzzing near my left ear, and decided that sore feet beat West Nile virus any day. I took a deep breath and sucked it up before setting my aching arches in motion.

Every year the entire Turner-Shaw-Barlowe clan sets up camp, literally, at the state fair campgrounds in assorted RVs, campers, motor homes, and tents. Camping spaces at the fairgrounds are as cherished as a lock of

Elvis's hair to an Elvis fanatic. Or immunity to a *Survivor* contestant. People have been known to bequeath these prized rectangles of grass to family members in their last wills and testaments.

I can see it now: *To our son, Craig, we leave Dad's truck and the family home. To our daughter, Taylor, we leave the sixty adjoining acres and our Buick Regal. To Tressa Jayne, we leave the critters, the Allis Chalmers, Grandma Turner in the event she is still living, the RV, and our state fair campsite.*

Craig and Taylor are my brother and sister. Both, major overachievers. At least compared to yours truly. Especially Taylor, a full-ride scholarship recipient studying psychology in her second year at the University of Iowa. She's also gorgeous enough to be on the front of magazines that have nothing whatsoever in common with *Psychology Today* and everything to do with perfect teeth, perfect hair, and perfect hooters. Deep sigh.

I'm not really envious. At least, not as much as I used to be when I pretended I wasn't. How can I explain it? I'm like the scrawny freshman who'd really rather hide in the locker room than be a skin in a game of shirts-and-skins with guys who have six-packs. Of course, said scrawny freshman doesn't want to admit such insecurity. So the scrawny freshman volunteers to be a skin and proceeds to act like an outlandish ass to prove he doesn't feel inadequate at all. Is this clear as chocolate syrup or what?

Really, guys, I love my little sis. I do. I just try to avoid being in the same area code as much as possible. And I'm kind of afraid that once she gets a few more psych courses under her belt she'll figure I'd make a wonderful research project.

I slapped at a few more pesky skeeters and wished for a jug of Deet. The campground was hushed and quiet due to the late hour. Many of the campers would be up in three hours and eager for that first cup of coffee and bag of fresh, hot mini donuts—a personal favorite of mine as well.

I headed for my folks' Jayco travel trailer, which is capable of sleeping five people in various stages of discomfort. I always get stuck in the coffin. You know, the bed that hugs the ceiling and forces you to slide in and out sideways? I always feel like Dracula at rest. Or, in my case, I suppose, Akasha, Queen of the Damned—without the impressive set of jugs, of course. I'd never fit in the coffin with anything bigger than a B-cup.

This night, however, I would have the queen-sized bed all to myself—unless, of course, that hunky cowboy I'd daydreamed about earlier decided to make my wildest cowgirl dreams come true. I yawned, realizing that even a naked cowboy couldn't keep me awake tonight. Jeesh, was I in bad shape or what?

Uncle Frank's big tan RV, parked in an adjacent space, was dark. My folks and Aunt Reggie would arrive the next morning with my grandma in tow. I rapped on the nearest window, figuring Frankie was inside pretending to be asleep so he wouldn't get a butt-chewing from Uncle Frank in the wee hours.

"Frankie?" I said in a low voice, so as not to rouse the interest and ire of the neighbors. "Frankie?" I went to another window and rapped again. "Frankie?" I tried the door, but it was locked.

Bone-tired, I shuffled next door to my parents' trailer, opened the door, and switched on the lights, half expecting to see more brazen bugs skitter to safety. I moved through the tiny living room area, switched on the air conditioner, then shut off the light and headed back to the bedroom. I collapsed onto the bed, facedown, and let out a long groan. Man, oh, man, was I beat.

I kicked off my sandals and lay there a couple minutes, savoring the soft pillow and mattress, reveling in the pure delight of being off my feet. I rolled over on my side, reached for an extra pillow to be my hunky cowboy surrogate . . . and grabbed hold of a nose—a long one, if touch counted for anything.

A squeal sounded, but I wasn't sure if it was from me or the nose. I rolled off the opposite side of the bed, switched on the light, and gasped.

"Frankie?"

"I think you broke by doze!" my cousin's muffled, nasally voice responded.

Whoa there, Nellie. Don't blame me for the nose twang. Frankie's always had a nasal thing going. I've actually gotten used to it. Others find it a bit off-putting. It sounds like he's perpetually whining.

"What are you doing here, Frankie?" I asked, my erotic dreams of the Marlboro man cruelly dispelled by the stark contrast of my nerdy cousin reclining on the bed holding a pink tissue to his nose.

"Is it bleeding?" he asked, dabbing at his nostrils. I suddenly knew how Dorothy felt when she'd slapped the Cowardly Lion.

"Of course not," I said, parroting Dorothy's response, if not feeling the same level of remorse.

"You twisted my dose and yanked!" he accused, still checking the tissue for telltale signs of injury.

"And you scared the peewadden out of me!" I countered. "What the heck are you doing here, Frankie? And where have you been all day? We've been looking everywhere for you."

He sniffed and dabbed. "I've been . . . busy," he said.

I gave an eye roll and crossed my arms. "Busy? *Busy?* Is that what you call running off and leaving an ice cream establishment in the hands of a guy who regularly handles reptiles for a living? What were you thinking, Frankie?"

He blew his nose, and I winced. "All right, all right. So, I was trying to prove a point," he said, sniffling. "I figured if I stayed away log enough for the line to get log, people would complain, and maybe Dad would fidally get the point. I do not want to be Mr. Dairee Freeze after my dad retires. Ed of story."

"What *do* you want to be, Frankie?" I asked.

Another sniffle. "That's the problem. I don't know, cous. I really don't know."

I looked at the pale, red-nosed, tousle-haired goofball and felt instant empathy. I knew what it felt like to be chasing the wrong end of somebody else's dream just for the hell of it. I knew what it felt like to be running furiously to catch up with everyone else, only to discover you were headed in the wrong direction. And although I didn't have everything figured out in the career department, the events of earlier this summer had given me a not-so-gentle kick in the seat to get the ball in play, headed toward the right goal line this time, and to continue that forward progress no matter the opposition.

I sat down on the foot of the bed. "As you know, Frankie, I can speak with some authority on this subject," I said, and patted one of his rather large feet. "And the best advice I can give you is to get real with yourself." Frankie made a someone-tooted face at my Dr. Phil remix, but I went on, determined to impart life lessons I'd learned in Finding Tressa 101. "Discover what you're really passionate about. Identify your talents and gifts. Learn all you can about related opportunities. List them all and then cross off the ones that don't trip your trigger. Experiment. Down deep, I think you have a general idea of what you want to do with your life." I grabbed hold of his big toe and pulled. "Sometimes you just need to stir things up a bit before the answer bubbles to the surface."

He finally met my eyes. "Ya think?" he said, a touch of humor now apparent in the look he gave me.

I grinned. "Turner's Law," I said with a wink.

Frankie crumpled up the tissue in his hand and tossed it into a nearby wastebasket. "Dad'll never forgive me," he said, sobering. "I let him down. Embarrassed him in front of all his friends. Competitors, even. I bet Luther Daggett was in wunderbar heaven. His sales probably skyrocketed as a result."

I shrugged my shoulders. "So Daggett got off to an early lead in the sales department this year. Big deal. We'll get him in the end."

"But Dad's gonna chew my butt big-time," Frankie said. "And I guess I can't blame him. I do the dumbest things sometimes."

I put a hand to my chest. In that moment I felt closer to Frankie than ever before.

"That's why God invented 'do-overs,'" I told him. "So we can fix what we screw up. Again, speaking from experience. Or perhaps I need to introduce myself again. Calamity Jayne Turner," I said, holding out a hand. "Finder of dead bodies. Corrupter of senior citizens. Bail bondsman for bikers," I reminded him. "I'm sure we've met before."

Frankie gave a half-hearted laugh. "Dad's still gonna be pissed, though, isn't he?"

"Oh, buddy. Will Gramma Turner insist on wearing hot-pink flowered flip-flops tomorrow and complain about her bunions all day? Will Ranger Rick make you pay for his dairy disaster in spades? Hello: Your dad is totally pee-ohhed. And the roach rumpus didn't help matters. I expect Uncle Frank will be on a medium-to-high simmer for a while. But I think I managed to convince him that you weren't the one responsible for the bug brouhaha." I paused and squinted at Frankie. "You weren't, were you?" I asked.

Frankie's smile disappeared. "Bug brouhaha? What are you talking about?"

I proceeded to fill Frankie in on the major health code violations we'd avoided by our little midnight roach round-up.

Frankie slowly got to his feet. "You're saying someone let a bunch of cockroaches loose in the Emporium and Dad thinks I'm the culprit?" he asked.

"Not anymore," I assured him. "At least I don't think so. I mean, he wasn't threatening to hang you from the flagpole by your apron strings when I left, so that's a good sign. Isn't it? Uncle Frank will get over it. Remember how he was after the incident at the Dairee Freeze back home? It took a while, but he came around."

"There was glass inside the colored sprinkle containers and blood all over the order window," Frankie kindly pointed out. "Not to mention the fact that one whole side of the place was missing."

"Yeah, but Uncle Frank really needed to modernize," I insisted. "You know, update the place. That Beaver Cleaver look just didn't cut it anymore. Besides, there was no structural damage. And afterwards, Uncle Frank had customers by the droves. The place was packed. So, I figure I did him a favor."

"Oh, so you put his business on the map. And what, I'm trying to put him out of business?" Frankie put a hand through his hair. The brown strands stuck out like a scarecrow's bad hair day.

I stood up and walked over to Frankie and put a hand on his arm. "You have to understand: Your dad had just walked into his eating establishment and found a carpet of cockroaches. When he learned you'd walked off the job in a very cool, calculating way, what was he to think? You yourself said you tried to prove a point by delivering a low blow to his business," I reminded him.

He shook my hand off his arm. "I meant to go back. Honest. But when I saw Rick Townsend in there kicking the candy condiments and cursing the confections, I panicked and bolted. And the longer I stayed away, the harder it was to face up to what I'd done." He turned and bent down to stick his feet in a long pair of dirty sneakers. "And now Dad thinks I roached the joint. He'll never forgive me. Ever. I'm outta here."

Frankie hurried out of the bedroom, with me trailing along behind him. "What are you doing, Frankie?" I asked, shadowing him. "Where are you going?"

"To find *my* destiny, cous," he announced. "And, hopefully, find myself in the process." He pushed the door open and was gone amid a community of cracker box trailers and four-wheel-drive vehicles.

"Frankie!" I yelled. "Come back here! Frankie!"

I shook my head. "Oh, Frankie—what are you doing man?" I said to myself.

"I wonder if we'd better knock first. She might have someone in there with her, you know. It could happen. Not likely, but it could."

I was still in bed, watching early morning sunlight peek in at me from the window at the head of the bed and wishing for a few more hours of sleep before the bedlam of opening day at the Iowa State Fair.

"What if she's not alone? What if she and that hunky ranger are lying in that bed in there right now, naked limbs intertwined, bodies slick and sweaty, their breathing rapid and shallow?"

I jumped off the bed.

"You read too many romance novels, Hannah," my mother responded.

"Maybe she doesn't read enough. If she did, she'd know just what to do with that boy," my grandma continued. I put a hand to one cheek. My face felt warm as a car hood in the state fair parking lot in midafternoon. I raced to the front door and opened it. *Hey, like I had a choice here, guys.*

"Greetings, loved ones!" I welcomed.

"Is it safe to come in?" Gram inquired after she had already entered the trailer and checked out the bedroom and bath.

"Of course, why wouldn't it be?" I asked, and followed her back to the bedroom, playing dumb, thinking that was the smart choice. See how my brain works?

"We just thought you might have had a friend sleep over," Gramma remarked, walking over to the bed and examining the sheets like a CSI analyst, minus the penlight.

"As a matter of fact, I did have a visitor last night," I replied, pulling the sheets up and making the bed. "Or should I say, early this morning," I added with a wink at my mother in the bedroom doorway.

"Was this a male or female visitor?" Gram asked, sitting on a padded chair in the corner.

"Oh, very much male. Tall, darkish hair. Big brown eyes."

"And what time did this tall, dark male leave, my dear?" Gramma asked. "Or is he hiding under the bed?"

"He left around four A.M., Gram. We were both exhausted."

My grandma raised an eyebrow. "I see. And may we assume you harbor deep feelings for this brown-eyed fellow?"

I nodded, casting a look at my feet to hide my smile. "I love him, Gram," I replied, my voice soft and a bit breathless.

"Love?"

I nodded again. "And I'm pretty sure he returns that sentiment."

My mother stepped into the room and gave me her version of the Luuuccy-you've-got-some-'splaining-to-do look. To be honest though, it's kind of hard to tell one look from another with my mom. CPAs don't tend to need that many different facial expressions.

"Are we talking wedding bells here?" Gram asked. "Or just immoral cohabitation?"

"I'm fairly certain one is illegal and the other just plain yeeesch," I replied with an all-over, body-length shiver.

"Huh?"

"Well, it is illegal to marry your first cousin," I said with a grin. "Isn't it?"

"Cousin?"

"Frankie."

"Frankie? You were talking about Frankie?"

"Of course. Who did you think I was talking about?"

"Oh, you are such a pip," Gram said, shaking a finger at me. "You get that from your mother's side of the family, you know."

"Yeah, right, Hellion Hannah." I shook my finger back at her. "Right."

"So what was Frankie doing here that late?" my mother asked. She tends to get right to the point.

"He was, uh, well, hiding out, I guess you could say," I told her.

"Hiding out? From what?"

"Who," I said. "And the answer is Uncle Frank. They'd had a bit of a problem earlier in the evening. Frankie thought he'd wait here until Uncle Frank cooled off a bit."

"That Frankie," Gramma snickered. "What'd the boy do this time? Change the color scheme for the ice cream

parlor from red and white to pomegranate and puce?"
While Gramma isn't related to Frankie by blood, she'd
seen enough of him while he was growing up to take on
the role of surrogate grandma. I was all in favor of that.
The more of us there were, the less time and energy she
had to focus on us individually.

"Frankie was trying to make a point with Uncle
Frank but did it rather, uh, clumsily, I'm afraid," I said.

"What did Frankie do?" my mother asked.

I hesitated, not really wanting to rat Frankie out a second time. I was saved the necessity of a reply. A door
slammed and heavy footsteps moved toward our location at the back of the trailer.

"Okay. Where is he?" boomed Uncle Frank, his wide
body filling the narrow bedroom door. "Where is my
son?"

I stared at Uncle Frank. "What do you mean?" I
asked. "Frankie never came home?"

"Hell, no! I waited up all night for that little bird turd
and he never showed. What the hell is going on with
that kid?"

A feeling a lot like the one you get after you've just
made a New Year's resolution to give up chocolate so
you can fit into your bikini for spring break and then
the Cadbury Creme Eggs go on sale came over me. I
looked over at Uncle Frank, who was proceeding to fill
my grandma and mother in on the previous night's exciting extermination extravaganza.

I frowned. Opening day at the fair and a six-foot
Frankfurter had gone missing.

CHAPTER 4

I disappeared into the tiny bathroom and did about half a dozen cockeyed twirls in the eensie-weensie shower, trying to expose as much of my body to the weak, wussie spray as possible. I'm used to taking fast showers—probably because I'm always running late. I washed, rinsed, then pulled my hair back into a tight ponytail and gelled up, donned khaki shorts and a navy tank, and shoved my feet into my comfy Soft Spots sandals. I emerged from my hasty cleanup to find Aunt Reggie and Uncle Frank arguing about Frankie, my mother setting up her laptop and printer, Gram painting her toenails black, and my dad nowhere to be found. Wise man, my father. He generally drops his wife and mother off at the campground, then hightails it back to Grandville and his job with the phone company and a week of peace and quiet. He sometimes visits on the weekend, but he's not a big fair fan. Seen one, you've seen 'em all: That's my dad's position.

"I can't believe you think Frankie is responsible for

those roaches," my Aunt Reggie was saying. "My god, Frank, he's your son."

"Some son," my uncle said, shoving a hand over his smooth razor-cut gray head and staring out the front door. "He spits in my face when I offer him a business I've spent my whole life building. He embarrasses me with my competitors. He disappears on the eve of opening day, just when I need him the most. Why the hell wouldn't I be suspicious? That kid has a lot to answer for. If he ever has the guts to show up again," he added.

"Where does a person get cockroaches anyway?" Gram asked, looking up from her toes. "Do you go to the landfill and start flipping over garbage? Do you get 'em from those guys at the universities who study bugs? Maybe you breed them. I wonder if there's a stud fee for roaches. You know what? I bet you can buy 'em online. You can buy anything online. Some guy auctioned off a kidney online. Made a tidy sum!"

"That's illegal, Hannah," my mother informed her from the modest dining area.

"You can live with only one kidney, you know," Gramma went on. "Lots of people do."

"Hannah," my mother said.

"You can even buy Viagra online," Gramma continued. My eyebrows went north.

"Viagra's for men, Gram," I told her.

"That's what you think, missy," she replied with a wink. "That's what you think."

I could only stare. "Have you got the schedule worked out yet, Mom?" I asked, wanting to get the heck out of Dodge before Grandma's little piggies dried and she recruited me to escort her to the fairgrounds. "When and where do I next report?"

My mother made a few clicks with the mouse. "You're scheduled at Site B from eight to one, with Frankie relieving you, then Site A from five 'til close."

My mother referred to Uncle Frank's mini-freeze and emporium that way, as Site A and Site B. Must be that accountant thing again. She added, "We may have to make adjustments for Frankie." Looking over at my aunt and uncle, she saw they were still in a heated discussion over their only child. "We'll just have to play that by ear."

I nodded. "Who's going to pick up Taylor? I asked. "With Frankie possibly a scratch, we'll need her here ASAP."

My mother's fingers flew over the keyboard. "Oh, Rick offered to collect her. He had to make a trip back home early this morning to get a few more specimens for the DNR exhibit. He said he'd swing by and pick her up on the way. There wouldn't be any place for her to park her car here anyway."

"By specimens, you mean snakes," I clarified. Despite the stuffy trailer, I shivered at the thought. Who in their right mind kept snakes as pets? Okay, so being petrified of the slithering serpents I'm hardly impartial—and rather inclined to stay that way.

"That was very considerate," I observed, "to volunteer his reptile-mobile to transport Taylor. I hope she's suitably cautious and keeps her eyes peeled for anything that slinks, wiggles, twists, and squirms. Including the good ranger," I added, telling myself the unpleasant sensations in my gut were hunger pangs. Certainly they weren't jealousy twinges.

My mother shook her head. "Oh, Tressa. Really. Rick is doing our family a favor, not putting the moves on your sister."

I snorted. "Oh, really? What? You don't think a big red four-by-four filled with snakes makes a good chick pickup vehicle?"

"That ranger don't need no fancy wheels to attract females," my grandma interjected, looking up from her goth toenails. "He's a regular chick magnet. At least for any gal whose magnetic field is in working order."

I wrinkled my nose, aware that Gramma thought I was moving slower with Ranger Rick than the line at the grandstand restroom during a Faith Hill/Tim Mc-Graw concert. Still, the idea of a Taylor Turner/Ranger Rick match was hardly a new concept. Earlier in the summer there had been an all-out campaign to shove the toothsome twosome together. I had watched with a cynical eye and a bellyful of bile. It wasn't that I had any particular designs on Rick Townsend, I told myself; I just didn't want Taylor putting her mark on him before I figured out just why I cared one way or the other who Ranger Rick ended up with.

"My magnetic field is humming away just fine," I said. "In fact, it's pointing me in the direction of a large order of fresh-from-the-deep-fat-fryer, sugared mini donuts. So, dear family, if you will excuse me, I'll be off to Dottie's for a bag of baked heaven, a cup of coffee, and to loiter alongside her concession stand until I smell just like a bag of lovely, warm donuts. So sorry your toenails aren't dry, Gammy, or I'd let you tag along. Toodles!" I waved and headed out the front door.

"We've got donuts and coffee at the emporium, too, you know!" Uncle Frank called out.

"Give me a break! Those are dry as Frankie's nasal passages in midwinter," I said. "Get some donuts that won't work double duty as door stops or hockey pucks and I'll be first in line!" I yelled. Then I skedaddled before Uncle Frank could come in hot pursuit.

I headed down the gravel road that led to the gate from the campground, inhaling deeply with each step that brought me closer to Dottie's Donuts. I love the various food fragrances of the fair on opening day. Donuts, funnel cakes, and cotton candy—all meld with the smell of turkey legs, hot dogs, pizza, and every type of

beef product imaginable. Add to these the odors ema-
nating from the livestock barns and pavilions, and you
have quite the olfactory odyssey. But the midway—well
now, that's a horse of a different aroma. Let's just say
that, after a week of hot, humid August weather, you
don't want to walk through the midway without Vicks
stuck up your nose—you know, like those TV morgue
guys do who have to post a floater. It can get really ripe
between rains. A daily hosing down of the black-topped
ground does little to dampen the pungent aroma of the
massive numbers of hot, sweaty people meandering
along the narrow walkways, mixing with the smell of
Technicolor hurls from the poor souls who feasted on
funnel cakes or corn dogs before stepping up to brave
the galleon or whirl around one time too many in a tiny
teacup. No, the midway is definitely not one of your
scratch-and-sniff moments.

As I walked, I thought about Uncle Frank and Aunt
Reggie and the fight over Frankie. While the sudden
roach infestation at the emporium was no accident, I
still didn't believe my discontented yet harmless cousin
had set the filthy bugs loose in his dad's business. But if
not Frankie, then who? (Or is that whom? I never can
decide.) One thing was certain: I needed a donut jump-
start followed by a caffeine chaser.

I hurried to Dottie's Donuts, my mouth watering the
closer I got. I rounded the corner and bit back a bad
word when I saw the length of the line. Dottie's is always the most popular early morning concession stand.
The wait never seems to bother most of her patrons,
though. The donuts are worth it.

I took my place in line, trying to tell myself that a
medium bag of donuts would do, but knowing on a bad
day I could put away two large bags with nary a
thought for my thighs. This morning I convinced myself that, considering my previous night's good deed at

the emporium and the fact that my hunky dream cowboy had been cruelly replaced by a dorky cousin with a deviated septum, I deserved the jumbo bag. I was about to step up and place my order when fingers gripped my shoulder and squeezed.

"Two jumbo bags of mini donuts and two large coffees," I heard over my shoulder. I felt my sphincter muscles contract. I stood mimelike and did my best hear-no-evil routine.

"That'll be seven dollars," Dottie, whose real name is Mervin, since Dottie had been dead for the last three years, barked. He reminded me of that soup guy on *Seinfeld*. He didn't have to be polite to keep the customers coming back. His—or would that be her—donuts did that.

"I'll get that." A bony hand reached around me and handed Mervin a ten-dollar bill, then accepted the change and the bags of donuts. I grabbed the two coffees and followed the tantalizing bouquet of cinnamon and sugar and hot donut batter like the Wimpy character follows hamburgers in the old Popeye cartoons.

My baked-goods benefactor deposited the goodies on a nearby picnic table, parked his arthritic rear, then brought a jumbo bag of donuts to his nostrils to breathe deeply—one of those long, drawn-out, nostril-narrowing thingies you do when you're out in cold weather and your nose starts to run and you've got no tissue, so you inhale hard enough to suck the snot back up into your nostrils so you don't gross anyone out. Oops, sorry to ruin your appetite, there.

"Whoo-wee, do I remember that smell!" the sly senior with an insider's knowledge of my sweet tooth exclaimed. His eyes closed and he sucked in so hard I wouldn't have been surprised to see a donut do a disappearing act up his nose. "First thing I eat at the fair every year," he said, and patted the bench seat next to him. He slid one jumbo bag of donuts in my direction. "Here, take a sniff."

I hesitated, wavering between walking off empty-handed and empty-stomached or snapping the old guy's suspenders, grabbing the goodies, and hauling ass away from the scene.

"Come on now." It was temptation in the form of a seventy-four-year-old guy in knee-length khaki belted shorts, white socks and hiking boots, and a neon green windbreaker. He coaxed, waving the donut back and forth in front of me like a hypnotic charm. "You know you want it."

I wiped the perspiration from my upper lip and stared. Damn, he was good.

I shook my head, set the coffee on the table, and took a step back. "No, I can't. I won't." I took another step back to escape the confection's impossible power.

The donut dangler waved the treat before me like a red flag. "Come on, take it. You know that's what you want to do."

I took another smaller step back. "I can't. I'm not supposed to see you," I said. "Or talk to you. Or come within a hundred feet of your geriatric behind."

"Well, if you insist." The guy, who looked like he was dressed to audition for *Croc Hunter III*, started to bring the donut to his mouth with much fanfare when suddenly I lunged forward, snatched it from his fingers, and popped it into my mouth. I chewed the still-warm sweet dough with my eyes closed, savoring each delectable moment.

"Have a seat. There's more where that came from, girlie."

I gave the old fella a grave look before my eyes came to rest on his bag of donuts. "Bad things happen when we get together, Joe," I reminded him.

Joe Townsend had played a prominent role in my small-town thriller earlier in the summer, much to the distinct displeasure of his grandson, Ranger Rick. In fact, Joe, or "The Green Hornet," as he liked to be called, had been harder to get rid of than Uncle Frank's latest product—"mud pies." Don't ask. You don't want to know. Trust me.

"What could happen?" he asked.

I rolled my eyes. "Oh, only little ole things like tailing murder suspects and losing car keys. Or losing hand-guns and finding dead bodies. Or using pepper spray on jumbo-sized bikers and—"

"The fair only comes once a year," my tormentor reminded me. "And Dottie's donuts are only available for a limited time."

Like Shamrock Shakes, Cadbury Creme Eggs, and marshmallow snowmen, I thought.

My ex-partner in crime-fighting removed the lid to his coffee, picked up a donut, dipped it once, twice, into his steamy brew, and then brought it to his lips. Oh so slowly, he took it into his mouth and chewed, making more of a production out of it than my grandma does with the one candy bar she is allowed every week. (The one my mom knows about, that is.) He washed the remains of the donut down with a noisy swallow of his coffee.

"Hmmm. Better than I remember," he said, reaching for another mini donut. I sucked in air, calling on any and all reserves of willpower I had left.

"Your grandson will kill me," I said, inching closer to the table.

"What he doesn't know won't hurt him."

"You'll blab."

"I'll be silent as the Open Bible congregation on Commitment Sunday," Joe swore. "Besides, Rick threatened me, too, you know. And personally I like having someone else do the driving when I have to have my ye.. colonoscopy."

I took a couple of hesitant steps forward, wanting to appear I was fighting the good fight, but in reality I knew there was an invisible white flag above my head waving for all it was worth. Knowing me way too well for my own good, the smooth operator cinched the deal. "They're getting cold," he warned.

"All right! All right!" I said, and raised my hands in an I-give-up pose. "By the way," I said, taking a seat across from Joe, "for your information, you had me at 'donut.'" I snatched the bag from him, placing it over my nose and mouth like an oxygen mask. "Aaaagh." I took a nice long sniff, then dug in.

"As good as you remember?" Joe asked.

"Even better," I said. "'Cause you paid."

He grinned. "Figured you wouldn't have much spending money."

I acknowledged his remark without rancor. His assumption was right on the nose. I was always a day late and a dollar short.

"How's your Grandma Hannah doing?" Joe asked, and I paused in my scientific study of how many donuts you can dunk, then swallow, in three minutes or less, and looked over at the man from Gram's past.

"Same as ever," I said, looking around for a napkin to wipe my mouth. "Why do you ask?"

"Oh, just curious," he said. "Has she arrived at the fair yet? I was thinking she said she'd be up this morning bright and early."

I tried not to smile. Joe and my Grandma Hannah shared a complicated history. His father had been mayor of our hometown at the same time my great-grandfather had been police chief, and the two had feuded for years. As a result, whatever feelings Gram and Joe harbored for each other had never been allowed to develop. By the time Joe Townsend got back home from the service, Gram had married Paw Paw Will, and a few years later Joe Townsend tied the knot with a local girl he'd met upon his return. I always got a little teary-eyed when I considered the circumstances that had kept the young people apart, despite their assurances later in life that they had both been content with their choices. Recently, the two had started to show up at the same events on a semi-regular basis. It was kind of cute in a scary way. Considering the seniors involved, I wondered if some sort of public safety announcement should be made. You know, something along the lines of "When these personalities interact, results could be unpredictable."

I nodded. "Gram arrived in top form this morning. She was primping when I left the trailer," I said, declining to mention the nail polish color she'd chosen. Let Joe get a load of her toes himself. Knowing him, though, he was probably into the goth look. Or he would be shortly.

"Mom was finalizing the work schedule, trying to cover for a possible no-show on Frankie's part." As soon as the words were out of my mouth, I wished them back. I took a large gulp of coffee and stuffed a couple of donuts into my jumbo-sized mouth.

"No-show? Frankie? Is the boy still AWOL?" Joe asked.

I coughed, and coffee sprayed across the picnic table. "How'd you know about Frankie?" I asked, wiping the table off with a wad of napkins.

"Rick told me this morning before he left," Joe explained. "Said Frankie went off and left the stand unmanned and he'd spent two hours filling in. That boy was still steaming this morning. But he did mention he had a new appreciation for what you've accomplished."

I felt a warm sensation in my chest. Ranger Rick appreciated my accomplishments? I frowned. Just what accomplishments was he talking about?

"Yep, Rick said you could peel and split a banana in record time. And I think he admires your dancing abilities."

I looked over at Joe, puzzled. "What makes you say that?" Line dancing and the two-step were about it for my repertoire.

"He said you tap dance around your feelings better than Shirley Temple, and your side-stepping is Ginger Rogers quality. And there was some reference to a roach rumba, whatever that is."

I felt my lip curl. So Ranger Rick didn't care for my fancy footwork, huh? Well, too freakin' bad. Ginger here was going to keep dancing as fast as she could.

I snorted. "Your grandson is a legend in his own mind," I said, licking the cinnamon and sugar from my fingers.

"Funny. That's just what he says about you," Joe replied, sucking on his own sticky digits.

"Hardy har har," I said. I'd been smart to take it nice and easy with Ranger Rick. Well, okay . . . so I was still working on the *nice* part. Considering our history of gorilla warfare (yeah, *gorilla*) I was finding that as awkward as conversation at family reunions. You know what I mean. When you're a kid, adults can get away with saying, "You're growing like a weed," if they haven't seen you in a while and can't come up with anything else to say. That almost always works. However, one can't use the same lines back. Often, those people have either shrunk in size due to osteoporosis or gained a ton of weight. Even a generic, "My how you've changed!" won't work in those situations. That's why I generally just stick pretty close to the food tables.

Yeah, right, Tressa, you're thinking. Uh-huh. *That's* why. I can't pull a thing over on you guys, can I?

"So, when do you clock in?" Joe asked, looking at his large sports watch with all the bells and whistles strapped on the outside of his windbreaker. "It's a quarter to eight now."

I took another gulp of coffee and wiped my mouth. "I guess I better be hoofin' it, then. I have to be at the mini-freeze at eight to open up and get things going."

"Your Uncle Frank got that bet going with Luther Daggett again this year?" Joe asked.

For the last thirty years, Uncle Frank and Daggett's Cone Connection concessions had competed for top sales at the state fair, with the loser expected to donate something to beautify the state fairgrounds in the name of the winner. There are nice new park benches all over the fairgrounds with Uncle Frank's and Aunt Reggie's names prominently displayed on a gold nameplate. There's a new butterfly garden along the stairs to Exhibition Hill that proclaims Uncle Frank as the benevolent benefactor. One small gazebo, two purple gazing balls, three wood sculptures, four trolley signs, and a partridge in a pear tree—sorry, I got carried away there—such items are a testament to Uncle Frank's record of successes when it comes to soft-serve sales at the fair. The first year Luther Daggett managed to beat Uncle Frank was the very first year they competed. That year the loser took the winner out to dinner. Cheapskate that he is, Uncle Frank catered the meal himself, serving chili dogs, shakes, and fries. The only other time Uncle Frank suffered defeat was when straight-line winds whipped through the fairgrounds in '93 and the poor unfortunate mini-freeze ended up on the porch of the old administration building. Apart from that, Uncle Frank has retained his soft-serve king title.

This year a new horseshoe-pitching venue was scheduled to be erected before the next fair. Devotees of the sport, both Uncle Frank and Luther Daggett wanted dibs on the project as this year's ultimate prize—and to see their name front and center on the new and much improved horseshoe pitching facility. Uncle Frank had talked of nothing else for weeks.

"We can't let our guard down for a minute, people," he had stressed at a church picnic three weeks earlier. "That Luther Daggett will do anything to take the prize this year," he said. "Anything. That guy has a set on him the size of those coconut-covered pink marshmallow snowballs Tressa likes so much." Unfortunately for Uncle Frank, the minister had chosen that moment to stroll by, leaving Uncle Frank in the unique position of trying to convince the good reverend he'd been discussing a set of new frozen taste treats.

I thought about that conversation, and about how it might relate to the cockroach caper at the emporium the night before. What better way to sway the contest in your favor in a bug way—I mean *big* way—than to contaminate the competitor's premises with hordes of hideous, dirty, disgusting, business-busting bugs? So there was another person besides Frankie who stood to benefit from a dramatic dip in Uncle Frank's cone sales: Luther Daggett d/b/a Cone Connection.

"You okay?" Joe's question brought me out of my mental musings. "A donut didn't go down cockeyed, did it? The way you were wolfing them down, it's no wonder."

I shook my head. "Just thinking," I said.

"Ah, that explains it," Joe responded. I gave him one of my often-practiced but never mastered one-eyebrow-raised looks and he went on. "The slightly wrinkled brow. The somewhat pained expression—like the one I get when I haven't included enough fiber in my diet."

I winced. I reckoned my intense concentration look needed some work.

"So, is the bet on again this year?" Joe asked. I nodded.

"And the stakes are higher than ever," I said. The knot in my stomach had almost nothing to do with a large coffee and a jumbo order of mini donuts.

CHAPTER 5

I left Joe finishing up his donuts and coffee and trying to figure out where he'd have the best chance of running into my grandma by accident. This was so cute, I thought; what modern-day romance needed was less in-your-face aggression and more sneaky subterfuge.

"Stay put," I told Joe, sharing the benefit of my vast experience in the matter. "I guarantee she'll hit Dottie's first thing. That is, if she's clever enough to lose her assigned keeper for the day." My bets were on Hellion Hannah all the way. My grandma has an independent streak so big it can be seen by the astronauts in space. And the lure of Dottie's donuts among my family was legend.

"I reckon we'll be down your way for a cold refresher later on," Joe warned me. "And between the two of us we could mind the store if you wanted to take a little break."

I hoped he didn't detect the sudden dilation of my pupils or the hoarseness in my voice as I bid him adieu.

Just the thought of the dynamic duo doling out dairy gave me acid reflux.

I jogged the last block to the ice cream stand, the coffee sloshing around in my stomach with each step. I gave myself a mental head slap. Why had I swilled all that coffee when I was about to be cooped up for five hours selling root beer and soda pop?

I hurried up to the Dairee Freeze satellite stand and stopped when I saw the side door ajar. I frowned. I'd locked that door last night. I knew I had. I'd taken special care to do so once I figured how grumpy Uncle Frank would be when he found out about Frankie. I didn't want to give him additional cause to chew this cowgirl's be-hind.

"Frankie?" I called out, moving to pull the door open. "Uncle Frank?"

The moment I stepped over the threshold, I caught a sour smell ten times worse than the chronic projectile spit-up of the Parker twins I used to babysit in my teens. The unmistakable done-gone-bad odor nearly knocked me over. I put a hand over my nose. Whatever it was, something had exceeded its expiration date—by a good month, easy. I took a step inside. Make that two months.

I took another step, felt my sandaled foot slide out from under me and grabbed wildly to gain my balance, putting a hand on the freezer to right myself. I checked out the floor to see what I'd slipped on, and a nervous little pulse started to throb in my neck. My gaze followed a gooey, sticky pattern of light browns, off-whites, and pinks that turned the floor into a modern art project. You know—where the artist tells you what he painted and you have to take his word for it? I reached out and patted the front of the freezer with the palm of one hand, then slid both hands along the sides of the upright. The pulsing in my neck had turned to a full-fledged tom-tom beat. I took another look at the floor.

"Holy shite, what now?" I said, grabbing hold of the freezer door handle and opening it just a tig-tag and with the same level of enthusiasm with which I opened my mouth at the dentist. Or my legs for a Pap smear.

The smell had told the true story. I took a deep breath (through the mouth—not the nose) and threw open the freezer door. When I saw all the sad little sunken tubs of ice cream, all the depressed little plastic novelty bags and lonely little Popsicle sticks, I wanted to cry. All of Uncle Frank's Dairee delights were downright deflated!

I examined the temperature gauge inside the freezer. It was set on the right temperature. I shook my head. Talk about your bad luck: to have a freezer just stop running like this. I prepared to close the door again to save my nostrils from further abuse when I noticed the thick, gray cord that ran from the freezer to the plug-in, a cord that normally was never in sight. I slid over the sticky surface to the electric outlet at eye level and gasped. The freezer wasn't even plugged in! I stood there for a moment, trying to figure out how the cord could have become unplugged and knowing for certain it had not been that way when I left the previous night. I did an Ice Capades move over to the soft-serve dispenser, my eyes narrowing when I saw that it, too, had been tampered with. I pulled on the twist ice cream lever and rancid, baby-pookie-brown ice cream soup dribbled out. I quickly turned the lever to the OFF position and stared at the melting mess around me, one thought first and foremost in my head:

At least I won't be blamed for this one.

I quickly sobered when I realized who would be taking the heat.

Can you say "weenie roast"?

* * *

"So the door was open and everything unplugged when you got here?"

"Huh?" I seemed to be having difficulty following the conversation. Of course, it had absolutely nothing to do with the totally hunky state trooper who'd arrived to take the incident report on the latest mischief directed at Uncle Frank's concession stands.

The trooper looked up from his notepad. "The door. Open? Right?"

I nodded, wishing he would take his sunglasses off so I could get a peek at his peepers. You can tell so much about a person from their eyes, you know. Like, if they are looking at you or not. "Yeah," I replied, "it was standing ajar."

"And you're sure you locked it up last night?"

My eyes narrowed. My reputation couldn't have preceded me this quickly. Could it?

"It was locked tighter than Uncle Frank's grip on his wallet," I said. I elaborated for the trooper's benefit, "We're talking lug-nut tight. And everything was plugged in, turned on, and in working order," I added, anticipating his next question.

"And you left at what time?"

I paused, trying to recall what time I had left Uncle Frank's smaller establishment and started playing shuffleboard with that collection of cockroaches. "Well, I left here around ten-thirty or so, I'd say. I discovered the insect infestation at the emporium around eleven or thereabouts."

I felt a heavy pressure on my toes and looked down to see Uncle Frank's white tennie on top of my foot. Uh-oh. I guessed that information was like my grammy's age: limited to family members, her personal physician, and the Social Security Administration.

The dishy trooper finally removed his shades, tucking them into the flap at the top of his uniform. I almost

swooned when two beautiful, clear, sky-blue eyes settled their intent gaze on little ole me.

"Insect infestation? You had some difficulty last
night, as well?" he asked.

Uncle Frank increased the pressure on my wee little
piggies.

"Nothing significant," Uncle Frank interjected.
"Someone's idea of a joke. Just a few unwelcome visitors was all. We had the place spic and span and back to
rights in no time." Uncle Frank slapped me on the back
with a robust motion. If I hadn't been anchored by his
fat foot, I would've fallen forward, face-first. "No big
deal, right, Tressa?" he asked.

The trooper's eyes never left my face. I was wishing
I'd taken more time with my makeup. And hair. And
clothing. And choice of kin.

I looked up at Uncle Frank. "I think we should level
with him, Uncle Frank," I said. "After all, we want to
find out who's behind the monkey business, don't we?"

Uncle Frank removed his foot from mine and ran a
hand over his buzz cut, then looked at me. "Do we?" he
said.

My mouth did an open-closed-open movement.
(Please note: My mouth tends to always end in the open
position. What? You'd already noticed?)

"You can't believe Frankie had anything to do with
this . . . this malicious mischief!" I said, surprised that
Uncle Frank could still entertain the idea. "He's your
son! He wouldn't do something like this, Uncle Frank,
even though he despises the ice cream business and
would rather be poked in the eye repeatedly with a
sharp stick while listening to Rosie O'Donnell sing the
National Anthem than take over from you!"

The trooper's eyebrows raised. I rewound those last
words in my head and slapped a hand over my loose-
lips-sink-cousins mouth. I bit my tongue when the

trooper started scribbling in his notebook. I knew from past personal experience this was not a good thing.

"Ugh, what are you writing, exactly?" I stepped toward the trooper, trying to get a peek at his pad. He closed it with a quick flip of the cover.

"So you suspect your son had something to do with this and the insignificant little incident that may or may not have been a major health code violation the other night?" the trooper asked Uncle Frank.

I shifted my weight back and forth, wondering why Dr. Phil had never done a show on foot-in-mouth disorder. I needed a cure. Real bad.

"I assure you, Trooper . . . Trooper . . ." I looked at the silver nameplate above his left front pocket. "Trooper P. D. Dawkins. My cousin Frankie had nothing whatsoever to do with any of this."

"I'm certain you're right, Miss T. J. Turner," the trooper responded. I caught my breath. Great looks, a sense of humor, and no wedding ring. What were the odds?

"And I'm sure I'll feel the same as you do once I've heard it from your cousin Frankie himself," the trooper continued. "If you'd be so kind as to tell me where I might find him, I'm sure we'll have this cleared up in no time."

I looked over at Uncle Frank. He looked at me. He had the same look in his eyes as he did when he saw Ranger Rick and me waging battle against invading forces in the emporium the night before.

"Is that a problem?" Trooper P. D. Dawkins asked.

"Of course it's not a problem," I said, looking to Uncle Frank for help. "Is it, Uncle Frank?" He gave no indication he heard me. "It's just that Frankie can't be reached at present," I said. "He's, uh, out of town."

"Out of town?" The trooper rubbed his perfect jaw.

"But he was here yesterday, right? At least long enough to give your uncle, here, the idea he might have had something to do with the vandalism he's experienced. So, where is he?"

I shot Uncle Frank my own version of the look-what-you-did-now look that is usually directed toward me and turned back to the trooper, who was looking less and less taken with me each minute.

"Well, you see, he—uh—had, uh—"

"The boy took off," Uncle Frank announced. "Split. Took a powder. Flew the coop. Got the heck outta Dodge."

"Now we don't know that for sure, Uncle Frank. You know how Frankie is. I'm sure he's just off somewhere sulking. He'll show up. I know he will."

"When was the last time anyone saw your son, Mr. Barlowe?" Trooper Dawkins questioned, snapping his little pad open again.

"That would be Tressa here. She saw him up at the campgrounds after we'd finished cleaning the emporium. About what time was that, Tressa?"

I wanted to shush Uncle Frank but couldn't figure how to do it without the trooper seeing. And my foot didn't bear as much weight as his.

"Around four A.M. I guess," I said, shuffling my feet, not only because I was nervous but because the tall coffee I'd consumed earlier was making its presence known. Big time.

"And what was he doing the last time you saw him?" the peace officer inquired, his blue eyes prepared to miss nothing about my delivery.

"Tell him, Tressa," Uncle Frank instructed. "Just tell him."

I looked over at Uncle Frank and tried to spin it the best way I could for Frankie.

"He was running as fast as his long, skinny, bird legs would carry him," I said, and winced. Note to self: You suck at spin.

"And why was he running, Miss Turner?" the trooper asked.

I hesitated. How could I explain to this young police officer who had so obviously known what he wanted to do from an early age how hard it was to try to find out just where you belonged, what you were meant to be and do, when you were a square peg trying so hard to fit in somebody else's round hole?

"I think he's on a vision quest, Trooper P.D. Dawkins," I said. "You know, to seek his path, find his destiny, live the life he was born to live." The "huh?" look on the officer's handsome face was one I'd seen often enough to describe to a sketch artist. "Or maybe he's just lost," I finished on a lame note.

The trooper handed a card to Uncle Frank and one to me.

"You will give me a call when you hear from Frankie, won't you?" he asked, tipping his brown Smokey Bear hat with two tanned fingers. "I'll leave you to your cleanup. Mr. Barlowe. Miss T. J. Turner."

I watched the trooper walk off, admiring the cut of his dark tan pants, which hugged his muscular legs and tight rear.

Uncle Frank snapped his fingers in front of my face. "Snap out of it, Calamity," he said. "We've got work to do."

I nodded, taking one more look at the trooper's hindquarters, trying to convince myself that his derriere was no better than the average bear's.

Yeah, right, Yogi.

CHAPTER 6

Cleanup took a little longer than it had the night before, mainly because I did it with a clothespin pinching my nostrils and had to stop and release the pressure every so often. Aunt Reggie had the insurance agent on the phone, had a claim filed, and had arranged for a new shipment of frozen ice cream treats and hot dogs before the polish on Gram's toes had dried, all while covering the Emporium. I stand in awe of such organization. Most days I have trouble finding two socks that match.

While Uncle Frank helped unload the new inventory, I ran a damp mop over the floor for the ninth time. We were back in business shortly before the lunch rush.

I was sitting on a stool letting the fan blow on me while reading the latest copy of *People* and the article "What Were They Thinking?" that featured the worst dresses worn to the Emmy Awards (female category) and wondering how Oprah continued to keep the weight off for this long when I caught a whiff of something good and greasy.

"You like egg roll? Nice and hot. Fresh from cooker. No peanut oil. Veggie oil."

I looked up and recognized the short, slight, Oriental gentleman from Li's Asian Express booth, which was located down by the john. He waved a small cardboard container of egg rolls in my face. "Hot and fresh. No gristle. You take. Eat."

I smiled and started to shake my head, and then realized that, despite the donuts, hot dog, root beer float, and chocolate chip cookie ice cream sandwich I'd consumed, I was still hungry. And this little guy knew it.

The egg rolls passed by my nose again and Mr. Asian Express smiled, displaying two missing teeth. "Going once. Going twice," he said. "G—!" I grabbed an egg roll in midair and gobbled half of it before he could say "Egg roll gone." Grease dribbled from the corner of my mouth and I dabbed at it with a napkin. Mmmm. Good egg roll.

"You like," he said; not a question, but an affirmation. "You like."

"I like," I managed through the cabbage and pork in my mouth. "I like a lot. Thanks. You in the mood for a root beer?" I offered. Comping was a way of life for fair concessionaires. We all sampled each other's wares free of charge. I just sampled more, uh, robustly than most. "Root beer?" I asked again and picked up a tall foam cup and jiggled it. "Nice and cold. No peanut oil," I added.

He laughed but shook his head. "Flat," he said, and I blinked.

"Egg roll today. Tomorrow crab rangoon. Full of crab. Lots of cream cheese. Hot and good."

I could feel my mouth watering already. Stop it, Tressa, I scolded myself. At the rate I was eating, they'd need a rendering truck to haul my carcass out of the campground in two weeks.

"That's okay, Mr. Li," I said. "I'm on a diet."

He slapped the counter and gave a long laugh. "Diet. Good one," he said. "You like working fair, serving the customers the ice cream from tiny shack?" he asked out of the blue. My brain struggled to process the quick subject change.

I shrugged. "Sure. Yeah. Why not? I love the fair."

"And Uncle Frank? He love fair? Like to sell the ice cream?"

I scratched my forehead. I wasn't sure if Uncle Frank loved the fair or not. I'd never thought to ask. For that matter, I had no clue if he enjoyed his job, period. In a family business, one didn't always have a say in their career track. I thought about that for a second and felt my brow crinkle. I'd never even considered whether Uncle Frank felt fulfilled at what he did for a living or if he liked his work. Heck, who likes work? Now I had to wonder if Uncle Frank had been given any choice in the matter and, if not, how that factored into the father/son dynamic currently playing out.

"Uncle Frank's not one to share his innermost thoughts," I said. "But I guess if he didn't like the fair and the ice cream business, he'd sell."

Mr. Li's eyes grew big. "Uncle Frank sell? No more Dairee Freeze? No more hot dog? No more takey business? I buy! I buy! Be on main drag! No more smell of toilet. No customer hold noses in line. I buy! I buy!"

I winced and shook my head. Geez, the little guy was jiggling up and down like I did after I'd polished off two large gulps of diet cola from the Get'n'Go.

I stood. "I didn't say Uncle Frank *was* selling, Mr. Li. I said if he wasn't happy, he would probably sell. As far as I know, he's content with his business." If not with his only child.

"I buy! I make good offer. I pay! I give egg rolls and crab rangoon for life!"

My eyes widened. "Lo mein, too?" I heard myself saying.

Mr. Li laughed, and a torrent of speech in an unrecognizable dialect poured out. He pumped my hand and jogged away, his short, skinny legs barely touching the ground.

I frowned. I didn't just sell the Dairee Freeze. Did I?

"Still no sign of Frankfurter?" Gram sat across from me at a round umbrella-topped table, gnawing on a super-sized turkey leg. "That boy ought to be strung up by his Buster Browns," she said. "The family is in an uproar. Why, poor Regina is worried sick."

I nodded, still too full from my earlier overindulgences to consider a leg of anything. "She did look a bit tense when she relieved me," I said. "I wish there was something I could do to help."

"Kids these days are spoiled," Gram went on. "All this crap about how spanking is bad for the child and damages their self-esteem: hogwash. I had my share of lickin's growing up, and I turned out just fine," Gram said. "And I got plenty of self-esteem."

"And some to spare," I teased.

"Kids are coddled too much," she went on. "In my day there was none of that how-does-that-make-you-feel bull hockey. Nobody gave a damn how you felt. We were too busy trying to survive, to make enough money to squeak through another day."

"Your father was the police chief, Gram. Your uncle ran the hardware store and Paw Paw Will worked for him."

"Times were hard, missy, and no mistaking that. A person had to be tough. Resilient. We aren't doing these kids any favors these days by smoothing all the bumps in the road for them. They need to stub a toe now and then, fall flat on their faces, pick up a few splinters in their tongues and see what the view is like from floor level. That's the only way they can learn to pick themselves up and get moving again."

I had to admit, Gram was a tough old bird. She'd surprised me numerous times over the years with her pluckiness and determination. And while she'd adapted with the times, she'd never changed her opinion when it came to personal responsibility. Or Lawrence Welk, whom she still considered a hottie.

"Frankie's not a kid anymore, Gram," I pointed out. "He's an adult."

"Exactly. And he needs to start acting like one. Get a backbone or quit moping, that's my advice to Frankie. And that's what I plan to tell him first thing if he ever shows his face again."

I watched as Gram ripped into her turkey leg. No fatted calf for this prodigal son's return, I thought, with a twinge of sympathy. Frankie would be lucky if he merited a complimentary corn dog.

"So, did Taylor make it up okay?" I asked.

"Taylor? She's around. Saw her over at the DNR exhibit earlier. I think she was helping Rick with his serpents."

Despite the heat of the late afternoon, I shivered. Assisting the ranger with his snake collection was not something I could ever volunteer to do. Never ever. Not even if I spent several hours and tons of money I didn't have imbibing in the beer tent could I ingest enough liquid courage to handle Ranger Rick's legless lovelies. But apparently my little sister was up to the task. Of course, Taylor had never interacted with the species up close and personal as I often did during hay-baling season. I was fairly certain she'd never experienced the sensation of having a surprise visitor slither out between her legs while she rested on a square bale.

Gram dropped her poultry leg on her plate and looked over at me. "You plannin' to be an old maid all your life?" she asked suddenly, a barbecue-sauce mustache making it hard to take her seriously. "Some shriveled-up old lady like Abigail Winegardner?"

Abigail Winegardner was Joe Townsend's neighbor and, according to Joe, Miss Winegardner had it bad for him. I'd sampled many of the goodies she'd prepared for Joe, and I had to say, she seemed like a keeper to me.

"Times have changed, Gram," I said. "Women who don't marry aren't considered old maids anymore."

"No, they're just considered lesbians," Gram countered with her usual directness.

"I'm not gay, Gram," I said. "I'm just selective."

"We aren't talking about choosing a pot roast at the meat counter at the Meat Market," Gram said. "We're talking about a life partner, girl. Someone to share the good times and the bad with. Someone to be there for you through thick and thin. Someone to have safe sex with on a regular basis!"

I heard a throat clear and looked up to find Rick Townsend holding a turkey leg in a large white napkin in one hand and a soda in the other, grinning down at me.

"Well, fan me with a brick, Rick! We were just talking about you!" Gram said, and I wanted to kick her under the table—but I remembered Gram kicked back. Hard.

"No we weren't, Grammy," I said. "We were talking about Frankie."

Townsend set his food on the table and pulled up a chair beside me. Even in his kaa-kaa—I mean, khaki—uniform shirt, he looked way too sexy for his own good. And mine.

"So, who is Frankie not having safe sex with these days?" Ranger Rick asked with a teasing twinkle in his eye.

"Don't people think girls without boyfriends are lesbians?" Gram asked in a too-loud voice for the subject matter. "It's just a fact."

"Old Lady Winegardner never married, and no one thinks she's gay," I pointed out. "You say she's been after Joe for years."

"That's 'cause she's a slut," Gram said matter-of-factly.

Townsend coughed and soda sprayed the table. He wiped it up with his napkin and chuckled. "You slay me, Hannah," he said. "You shoulda been a stand-up comedienne. You could have been famous."

"Maybe I will be yet," she said with a lift to her chin. "Maybe I'll go on one of them reality TV shows where they pick the next great comic or superstar. Maybe even *Big Brother*. Why, I'd be a shoo-in on *Big Brother* if they didn't have the women wear them skimpy outfits and bathing suits all the time. Now, in my day, I'da put them all to shame. Now? Well, now I'd just put them into a fit of laughter. Or have them running for an available toilet. But believe me, fifty years ago I would have given these young actresses a run for their money and you, young man, you'da been standing there with your tongue hanging out like all the rest."

Rick patted Gram's hand. "I believe you, Hannah. Pops tells me you were one foxy chick. And he has the photos to prove it."

Gram beamed, and in that moment I saw a glimpse of the girl she used to be on the outside and apparently still felt like on the inside. Growing old really sucks.

"He still has pictures of me?" Gram asked, putting a hand to her head and patting her blue curls. "I had no idea."

I smiled. Right.

"Where is your grandfather, by the way?" Gram asked and I marveled at how she looked like she could care less. I'm not one of those tell-us-how-you-really-feel-Tressa people, I'm afraid. My feelings are easier to read than a *See Jane Run* book.

"I thought for sure Joe would be at Dottie's first thing

this morning," Gram went on, "but I was late getting there. Chipped a couple of toenails and had to reapply my polish." She held up a hot-pink flip-flop to show off her newly polished tootsies.

"I think he stopped over at the first-aid station to have his blood pressure checked."

"Blood pressure?" Townsend had Gram's full attention now. "He's not having difficulty, is he?"

Townsend pulled off a length of turkey meat and popped it in his mouth, then shook his head. "Naw. There's a volunteer up there he likes to visit first thing every year," he said, washing his turkey down with a swig of pop. "I guess she's newly widowed or something, and he just wanted to pop in and check up on her."

Gram shot to her feet faster than the Space Shot ride on the midway. "I've been needing my blood pressure checked, too," she said, hitching up her hot-pink fanny pack and light pink shorts. "I think I'll mosey up that way just to make sure I'm in the normal range."

I grinned, thinking that if she was in the normal range, it would be a first. "You want some company?" I offered.

"Don't be silly." She waved me off. "You stay and visit with Rick. If I hurry, I can just catch the next shuttle up the hill. Toodles," she said, and was gone, a pink splotch of color in a jungle of whites and blues and greens.

"Oh, you are sooo bad," I said to Townsend, doing the naughty-naughty sign with my index fingers.

"What?" he responded with his palms up. "What did I do?"

I shook my head. "You manipulated my Grammy, that's what. Shame on you, Townsend. She's a frail, feeble old woman."

"Frail, my fanny," Townsend chuckled. "I've come up

against seasoned, serious poachers who aren't nearly as crafty or feisty as Hannah Turner," he replied.

I nodded, then slid Gram's unfinished turkey leg across the table, picked it up, and began to eat. I can't stand to see good food go to waste.

"So, I hear there was some more excitement at Frank's concession stand last night," Townsend said. "Something about the freezers being unplugged."

"I didn't do it!" I yelled before he asked the obvious. With my background, folks tend to assume a lot of things about me. Okay, so sometimes those assumptions are accurate. Except in this case, I was innocent. Blameless. Not gonna be the fall gal.

"I know, I know. Sounds like a deliberate act," Townsend said, wiping his mouth and throwing his napkin on the table. "Very cold and calculating. Designed to hit Frank where it hurts. In other words . . . personal."

I stopped chewing and set my—Gram's—drumstick down. "You don't think it was Frankie, too, do you?" I asked. "Whoever roached the emporium and nuked our ice cream inventory had to be desperate—" I stopped and chewed my lip. How desperate was Frankie? How hopeless did he feel about his life? About his future? Just how angry was he with Uncle Frank for expecting him to follow lockstep in the family soft-serve business with nary a whimper of dissent? I sighed. If someone had told me I was expected to follow after my mother in her accounting and tax business, I'd have let loose with a whole lot more than a collection of cockroaches!

"I know it looks bad for Frankie," I said. "And I know he's not your favorite person after last night at the mini-freeze, but do you really think Frankie would go to these lengths rather than just tell Uncle Frank, 'Hey, Dad, I quit'?"

Townsend shrugged. "Your Uncle Frank can be pretty

intimidating, Tressa," he said. "And there's also the fact that Frankie doesn't want to disappoint his folks, particularly his mother. People can do irrational things when they are despondent or depressed."

I rubbed my temples. I didn't want to think about missing Frankfurters, or rancid ice cream, or crunchy cockroaches anymore. I wanted to enjoy my time at the fair. Especially the time I wasn't chained to a hot concession stand.

"So, get the reptiles relocated?" I said, deciding to change the subject. "Taylor didn't go all squeamish on you, did she?"

Townsend shook his head. "Nope. She didn't pull a Tressa on me, if that's what you mean. Most women can't stand snakes, but Taylor got right in there and down and dirty with the little guys. It was beautiful," he said with a grin.

I made a face. "How nice for you," I said. "A match made in herpophile heaven. Where is Taylor, anyway?"

"She pulls the next shift at the emporium. You relieve her at six, right?"

I nodded. "At least it's air-conditioned," I said, fanning myself with Gram's half-eaten drumstick. "Sometimes the mini-freeze gets hotter than that ugly, inflatable, bouncing moonwalk attraction on the midway. Plus, at the emporium, there's always the bonus of that short walk to the beer tent after closing."

Townsend wrapped his drumstick in his napkin and pushed it away. "You planning to stop in for a cold one after you close?" he asked. "Maybe I'll see you there."

"Only if you're really, really, really lucky, Ranger Rick," I said, cocking a pleasantly surprised brow. So there, Gram, I thought, unaccountably eager to tip back a few frosty cold ones with the only man on the planet who made every nerve in my body hum and the only person who could make me seriously consider trying to conquer my fear of snakes. Who's the lesbian now, Grammy? I thought. Who's the lesbian now?

"Well, well, well, if it isn't Ms. T. J. Turner. We meet again!"

I saw Rick's head snap to the left and followed the line of his gaze to discover Trooper P. D. Dawkins staring down at me, no question this time as his glasses were off and his vibrant blue eyes locked on mine in a well-hello-there gaze.

"Oh, uh, hey again," I said, feeling warmth pool in my cheeks and hoping I was tan enough to hide the telltale blush. When Townsend raised an eyebrow in my direction, I knew that I wasn't.

"So, has your vanishing cousin reappeared yet?" Trooper Dawkins asked. "I dropped by the stand to check, but your uncle was busy and I didn't want to bother him." He nodded to Rick, who rose from his seat and gripped the trooper's offered hand. I stared at the two uniformed men, comparing the trooper's dark brown shirt and tannish pants to Townsend's tan shirt and dark pants and marveling at how they both filled out their togs so splendidly.

"Rick Townsend," Ranger Rick supplied, "DNR."

Too late I realized that, rather than space off in my visual study of the two attractive men, courtesy dictated I perform the intro myself. Dumb, dumb, dumb.

"Rick is from my hometown," I said, for some reason feeling the need to explain why the two of us were together and not understanding at all why I felt compelled to do so. "Trooper Dawkins took the report on the mischief at the mini-freeze this morning," I said, feeling the same need to explain away Trooper Dawkins for an entirely different reason. I think.

"Nice to meet you," Trooper Dawkins said. "I saw

you over at the DNR exhibit earlier with a dark-haired young lady. For snake handling, she looked like she was having a pretty good time."

I turned to Ranger Rick and caught a fleeting look I couldn't recognize.

"That would be my sister, Taylor," I said, turning back to the trooper. "She's into things reptilian."

"So, about your cousin . . . He find his way home yet?" the trooper asked.

I shook my head. "Still MIA," I said. "But I'm sure he'll turn up soon. He's never been the independent sort." Truth be told, Frankie had never done his own laundry, probably never cleaned a toilet in his life, and still had his mommy help him with the hospital corners on his beddy-bye.

The trooper nodded. "I hope you're right. You'll let him know I'd like a word with him, if . . . when he shows up, won't you, Ms. T. J. Turner?"

I made a goofy salute. "Yesss, sir, Trooper P.D. Dawkins," I said.

He smiled, and I found myself smiling back. "Rick," he said, shaking Townsend's hand again. "And I'll see you around—Calamity," he added with a wink and strolled away. My mouth popped open like the zipper on my favorite Levi's when I ate too much.

"Of all the nerve!" I sputtered. "How the devil? Where does he come off?" I looked over at Rick, who stood there, arms crossed and foot tapping.

"What?" I yelled. "What?"

Townsend unfolded his arms slowly and reached out to me—not in a warm, comforting, now-there gesture—but one, I imagined, of a darker nature and focused on the area around my throat. He stopped, shook his head, and walked away, leaving me to wonder what the devil I'd missed this time.

CHAPTER 7

"And I told you, I don't know what the hell you're talking about, Li!"

I had stopped by the mini-freeze to pick up the keys I'd left there by mistake and heard Uncle Frank's bellow from the cinnamon roll place a good six stalls down. Don't ask why I was near the cinnamon roll stand. Please, just let it pass.

"You agree sell. You want sell. You retire. See sights. Visit Hawaii. No selly the ice cream. Relax. Enjoy life."

I considered a quiet retreat—hey, there's no shame in avoiding conflict—but ultimately decided that Uncle Frank had enough on his plate without having to confront a hostile takeover initiated, in part, based on my motor mouth. I came around the corner of the mini-freeze to see Uncle Frank rubbing the back of his neck and addressing the tiny Mr. Li, flanked by his twin sons, Tai and Chai. I never can tell the two apart.

"I told you, Mr. Li, I have no plans to sell," Uncle Frank repeated. "No selly the ice cream business."

Mr. Li's head bobbed up and down. "Right. Right. No

selly the ice cream anymore. Retire. Enjoy wife. Play golf."

"I don't play golf," Uncle Frank said, appearing more perturbed by the second. "And I enjoy my wife as much as the next guy."

I winced, glad Aunt Reggie wasn't around to hear the way that one came out.

"You old. You retire. Son no want selly the ice cream. Frankie no like. Frankie leave because no want to selly the ice cream anymore."

"Just a cotton-pickin' minute there," Uncle Frank growled. "What makes you the authority on what my son does or doesn't like? And I'm not old!"

Seeing the two men were drawing an interested crowd, I hurried over. "Uh, I think there's been a misunderstanding here, gentlemen," I said, inserting myself in between the heavy bulk of my Uncle Frank and the diminutive but wiry physique of Mr. Li. "Now, it has been my experience most disagreements can be resolved by unemotional, well-reasoned, and clearly articulated dialogue," I said, remembering the catchphrases from a past episode of my main man, Dr. Phil. Or was that Dr. Laura? I shrugged. "As calm, rational individuals who respect and value the opinions of others, we should be able to find a common ground for discussion and mediation of our conflicts," I said, figuring I'd earned As on both style and presentation.

Uncle Frank and Mr. Li both looked at me as if I'd suggested we all drop our drawers and jump into the bubbling hot tub on display at the Varied Industries building au naturelle.

"So, what say you, gentlemen?" I asked, in my most grown-up, adult voice. "Who will be the better man?"

"She's the one!" Mr. Li suddenly screamed and began hopping up and down again. "Calamity Jayne! She say you sell. She say Uncle Frank not happy. She the one.

No more egg rolls. Calamity Jayne takey egg rolls under false pretenses!"

I stared at Uncle Frank's fellow concessionaire in shock. "Why, you, you, you fibber!" I said. "You forced those grease-filled egg rolls on me. I was merely being polite by eating them."

"All six of them? Ha, ha, ha, real polite."

"Why, you little—"

The Li twins stepped forward in defense of their father.

"Is there a problem here, folks?" Hunky trooper P. D. Dawkins, this time with a female partner in tow, stepped into the fray. "Anything I should know about?" he asked me in particular.

Uncle Frank shook his head. "Just a simple misunderstanding," he said. "Nothing that can't be resolved through 'well-reasoned and clearly articulated dialogue,'" he said. "Right, Li?"

I was so proud in that moment. Something I'd said had made a real impact on these two gentlemen. I looked at Mr. Li for confirmation and agreement.

"Screw you!" he said, and stomped off. Tai and Chai, or was it Chai and Tai, gave me dual dirty looks before following.

Well, one out of two wasn't bad.

I retrieved my keys and used Uncle Frank's cell phone to call Mom and assure her I was on my way to relieve Taylor just in case Taylor called all bent out of shape and they sent the posse out looking for me.

How can I describe Taylor? She's way smarter than I am. (Oh, I see. You'd imagined that, already? Nice.) She's also tons more diplomatic than I am, but I'm really working on it. Hey, remember my attempt at mediation between Uncle Frank and Mr. Li? That was almost a success story.

Taylor is brilliant, beautiful, and level-headed. But she

has no sense of humor and, as a result, is not a laugh riot to be around. I suddenly recalled Trooper Dawkins's comment about Taylor having so much fun with Ranger Rick and hesitated in my trek up the hill to the Emporium. Maybe it was just around me that Taylor's sense of humor eroded. Maybe, I told myself, she was actually in awe of her older sister's zest for life and thirst for adventure. Yeah. And maybe I'm scheduled to be on the next season of "The Apprentice."

My younger sister isn't the outdoorsy girl I am and that's a fact. She prefers more . . . cerebral pursuits. While she enjoyed photographing our horse family and eventually did learn to ride, she never developed the passion for the equine species that I did. And although she tolerated my two hairy golden labs, Butch and Sundance, she never got down on all fours and made growling sounds at them like I often do. Or dressed up in a Halloween mask and sneaked up on them. Or bundled them into the car in the dead of winter and drove to the capital city and sneaked them into the warm botanical center. (Uh-oh. Just kidding there. I didn't do that. Of course, I wouldn't do that. That would be against the rules.)

Perhaps I was being unfair to Taylor. Maybe her tastes ran more to scaly creatures than four-legged, furry, huggable critters. Or *owners* of scaly creatures maybe. Hmm.

Over the years I've often wished for a closer relationship with my sister, but finding common ground between us is like trying to find a back for your pierced earring when you're late for church. (BTW, I've ended up sticking pencil erasers on in a pinch, so keep that one in mind, ladies!) Or trying to locate which level you parked your car on after Christmas shopping at four malls in the same day.

I hate the distance between us, the loving yet some-what snippy, superficial nature of our relationship, but have never found a way to breach the great divide. I sus-pect lots of folks think I'm envious of my smart, talented, gorgeous baby sister, but honestly, guys, those qualities were never that important to me. Oh, don't get me wrong: There were times I wanted to grab a pair of scissors and make a midnight visit to my sister and shear her billiard-ball bald, cursing the hair gods who'd blessed her with silky, shiny, healthy, rich brown hair while they'd gifted me with the Bozo look without Bozo's color. It was only the last several months, with Taylor beginning to show an interest in a certain ranger, that I had begun to cast a more critical eye on our differences, and to feel that I, too, often and in too many ways, came up short. The old Tressa would never have acknowledged she gave a flip. The new, and hopefully improved, Tressa was more in touch with her feelings. And guess what? It bit the big one! For once I wanted to be the smarter, sexier sister. I wanted to have the Pantene hair, the dark, seductive eyes, and the full, pouty lips. Natural, not collagen-enhanced. I wanted to be the one noticed first when we walked into a room together, and not because I was trailing toilet paper from my heel. I wanted to have someone, anyone, ask *my* advice for a change. And then actually consider it. I wanted what every normal, healthy, twenty-three-year-old girl wants—hooters you don't need a magnifying glass to find! (Whew, let me catch my breath here a sec-ond. Rabid envy run amok takes a lot out of you!)

I traversed the final distance to the Emporium, hurry-ing past Lucy's Trinkets with my head down, one hand hiding my profile. I didn't feel like hearing episode two from "Calamity Jayne Does the State Fair" right now. I hurried to the front door, eager to get in out of the heat in the air-conditioned comfort of Barlow's Emporium.

On a hot, humid evening like this the place would be packed with folks resting their weary feet and enjoying a respite from the steam.

I opened the door and walked smack dab into a wall of hot, stifling air and an empty Emporium. Empty, that is, except for Taylor, who stood fanning herself with a newspaper, her hair pinned to the top of her head. How she still managed to look Cover Girl–ready is anybody's guess. I'd only been in the place forty-five seconds and already I could feel my gelled-back hair breaking free of its stiff confines and beginning to frizz around my face.

"Why is it so hot in here?" I asked, and hurried over to the ancient but reliable window air conditioner and began flipping switches.

"Uh, I tried that already, Tressa," Taylor said, annoyance evident in her tone. "I went to turn it on around noon and nothing. I checked the cord and it was fine. I guess it's just seen its day."

I flipped a few more switches, pulled the cord, plugged it back in, flipped a few more switches, and then gave the unit a rather hard tap.

"I think it's a DNR," Taylor said.

"Huh?" I asked, wondering what Rick Townsend's employer had to do with a window air conditioner that probably came over on the Mayflower.

"DNR. Do Not Resuscitate."

I nodded. "Oh, yeah. Good one," I said. "Did you notify the next of kin?"

Taylor nodded. "I called Aunt Reggie right away. She said Uncle Frank wanted to take a look at it before we called the official TOD."

I gave her another "huh?" look.

"TOD. Time of Death."

I nodded. Taylor was getting scary. Maybe it was all those behavioral psych classes. Or the liberal-leaning institution of higher learning she was attending.

"I don't suppose you've been very busy then," I said, grabbing a napkin from the nearest table and mopping my face.

Taylor shook her head. "That door opened over a hundred times, but once the customers stepped inside and felt the heat, they turned around and walked out. I celebrated every time the door opened; it was the only ventilation I had. I was afraid to open the coolers out front for fear the ice cream would begin to melt, but I did go stand in the freezer a couple of times just to cool off. When is Uncle Frank going to come fix the AC, anyway?"

I shrugged. "Beats me. This is all he needs right now. First Frankie pulls a Houdini, then there was the trouble here last night, and the meltdown at the mini-freeze this morning. Now this. When Uncle Frank sees the sales figures, or no-sales figures, he'll freak out! I already had to pull him off Mr. Li of Li's Asian Express earlier before things got ugly," I said, enhancing the elements of the story just slightly for effect. "Somehow Mr. Li got the impression that Uncle Frank was selling his fair business and wasn't too pleased when he found out it wasn't so."

Taylor walked around the counter, still fanning her face. "I can't imagine what gave him such an idea. Uncle Frank loves the ice cream business. This fair is part of who he is."

"Oh? Is it, Taylor?" I said, ticked that my kid sister again seemed to have all the answers—or thought she did. "Is it really? How do you know Uncle Frank loves the ice cream business? Did he confide in you? Spill his guts? E-mail all his secret thoughts to you clear over in Iowa City? How do you know Uncle Frank is happy, Taylor?"

Taylor finally stopped fanning. "What is your problem, Tressa?" she said. "You're being very passive-aggressive here."

I wasn't exactly sure what passive-aggressive involved, but the aggressive part was right on the money.

"Problem?" I batted my baby blues and tossed my head, feeling new curls spring forth. "I don't have a problem. I'm just wondering how you know so much about a man you've only spent, oh, say three hours with in the last nine months."

Her eyes narrowed. "Is that what this is all about? My not spending enough time at home? I'm sorry, Tressa, but college is hard work. It's very demanding. I can't just clock out and run home whenever I want," she said. "There are expectations. Deadlines."

"I have deadlines, too," I said, referring to my on-again, off-again reporting job at the *Grandville Gazette*. I'd been let go after I'd mislabeled an obituary photo identifying the publisher's wife's dear, departed Aunt Deanie as the dear, departed Mr. Stubby P. Burkholder. We re-established our professional relationship during my role in the events of last June. I was still on probation but determined to make the job work. I'd even convinced Stan, my boss at the *Gazette*, that if he provided a digital camera, I'd provide him feature material from the fair. I made a face. I'd totally forgotten to think up a feature for the preview. Great start, ace cub reporter.

"You work part-time for a small-town weekly newspaper, Tressa. I have legitimate assignments that require my full attention. This is my future we're talking about."

"Mine, too, Taylor," I said, and realized for the first time how self-absorbed Taylor sounded. "Mine, too."

"Can I go now?" she asked, pulling off her apron and setting it on the counter. "I need to take a nice, long shower."

"Good luck with that," I said. "With the spray from that showerhead, you'll be lucky to get your entire body wet."

"Yeah." Taylor stood at the door for a second, as if she

wanted to say more. "Bye, Tressa," she said and was gone.

"So much for sisterhood," I said to the slamming door.

By ten o'clock, I'd read the fair program seven times and visited the walk-in freezer seventeen times, where I closed my eyes and pretended I was standing at the top of a ski slope in Tahoe, ready to zig-zag down the hill. In my winter wonderland fantasy, however, Ashton Kutcher races past me and runs into a tree. I save his life, and as a result of the unfortunate accident, he has amnesia and only remembers the beautiful, heroic young woman who pulled him down the frozen mountainside to safety. *Tough break, Demi.*

I'd also had the opportunity to make my way through half of Uncle Frank's ice cream flavors, one dip at a time, purely out of boredom (honest) and still no Uncle Frank. I'd listened all evening to the laughter, shouts, and midway music outside my sweathouse lodge, but inside the stifling confines of Barlowe's Emporium, neither Uncle Frank's business nor my long-acting deodorant stick were faring well.

I did a last-minute spot check of the place, grabbed my digital camera from the back room, locked up, and left, deciding I didn't give a cowgirl's yee-haw how bad I'd feel once the cold beer met and mixed with the Rocky Road, Tin Roof, Fudge Ripple, Chocolate Bon Bon (okay, so I'm partial to chocolate), and assorted other ice cream flavors currently taking up space in my tummy. I needed a cold beer!

I sniffed an armpit, wondering if anyone would notice that the twenty-four-hour roll-on that promised to keep a marathon runner desert-dry and non-offensive had left the race four hours earlier. I shrugged. Chances were there'd be smellier folks than me hankering for a cold one.

I'm a regular at the Bottoms Up beer tent. No, I'm not a lush or anything, although I do enjoy the occasional lite beer, like most good ole girls. I go mostly to watch people cut loose and have a down-home good time. Lots of concessionaires stop in for a cold draw before they call it a night, so it's like old-home week. This particular night, however, I also needed to snap a few pictures to send with a short article about opening day at the fair. Since most of the venues were closed other than the beer tents and the midway (and no way was I going near that with a belly full of dairy), the beer tent was the natural choice. I figured I could snap some shots, add a couple of lines about the hot weather, the great food, and speculate (as everyone did yearly) if we would break the attendance record this year or not. This heartland hoedown attracts a million visitors annually. Much depends, of course, on the weather. Weather is always an important topic of conversation among folks whose living depends on Mother Nature. If all else failed, I could always go with the weather.

I entered the beer tent and found the Good Ole Boys Band in the middle of a boot-scooting set that had couples out on the rectangular dance floor Texas two-stepping while single gals without a dancing partner did a simple line dance along the edge.

The smells of beer, popcorn, hot-and-spicy chicken wings, and body odor met and mingled in a country sunshine kind of way. I smiled and nodded to acquaintances but didn't make prolonged eye contact with anyone, and made a beeline for the bar.

"Well, it's about time!" Rhonda Gable, a longtime fair fixture at Bottoms Up greeted me. "Folks were laying bets that you would be a no-show this year. I told 'em, naw, nothing keeps Calamity Jayne from the Bottoms Up on opening night. So, how's the ice cream cone business, kiddo? I hear Frank's been having a run of bad luck. Frankie running off. The freezer fiasco. The Emporium turning into a sauna. I gotta tell you, kid, early betting gives Luther Daggett four-to-one odds to take the prize this year."

Rhonda handed me a lite draw and I took a long swallow. "Ah, just as good as I remember," I said, wiping my mouth. "Thanks, Ronnie."

She smiled. "Beer don't change all that much," she said. "But I guess the same can't be said of you. What's all this I hear about you helping expose a murderer? Weren't you scared shitless?"

I nodded. "That about sizes it up. But I was so peeohed I think that helped." I took another long drink. "So, where'd you hear about Uncle Frank's, uh, series of unfortunate events?" I asked.

"Why, from Frank himself, of course."

That took my attention away from my beer. "Uncle Frank was in here?" I said, torqued that Uncle Frank had decided to stop and smell the roses—or the beer nuts—while I was stuck in the fiery furnace of his Ice Cream Emporium.

Ronnie shook her head. "*Is* in here."

"Huh?"

"Your Uncle Frank's been here for a couple of hours now."

"Uncle Frank? Here?"

Ronnie nodded toward a darkened corner of the establishment. "He's over there. And he's not alone." She performed an inquiring-minds-want-to-know eyebrow thingy.

Still confused, I turned in the direction she'd indicated and, sure enough, there was Uncle Frank, all cozied up in the corner and appearing to take great interest in Lucy's trinkets or treasures. Or both.

"What the heck—?"

"They came in together about eight or so. Been sitting back there ever since."

My eyes never left the couple. "What's he drinking?" I asked.

"Same as you. Lite beer. A pitcher an hour, tops. No chug-a-lugging there."

I nodded. "That's good," I said, wondering why Uncle Frank was sharing a cold beer and a table in the back with Lucy when he should have been taking care of business up the hill a piece and saving his nieces from dehydration.

Ronnie picked up the digital camera I'd put on the counter. "What's the camera for?" she asked. "Oh, this is one of those digital numbers, isn't it? You can see your picture immediately. I keep telling Jack he's gotta get one of these. How does it work?"

Ronnie turned on the camera and held it up. "How do you set it so you can see what you're shooting on this little black screen?" she asked. I monkeyed with it for a second, then handed it back to her.

"You can see what you're taking right there," I said. "And all you do is push the button on top."

Click. Flash.

"Well, looky here. Don't that beat all? There's the picture I just took! I've gotta get me one of these!" She snapped a couple more before I could get the camera away from her.

"That is just awesome. You can just delete the stinkers," she said.

I nodded. "And you know what that means," I said.

Ronnie shook her head.

"No more blackmail pictures!" I said, pointing at the camera. "No more threats of sending around pictures where you look like you've just completed your thirtieth night on 'Survivor.' No more closed eyes and open mouths. No more slipping bra straps showing or thigh spreads that make it look like you can't get your knees together anymore. A truly miraculous piece of technology," I said, and bowed my head in mock reverence.

"Fill 'er up, Ronnie," I heard over my left shoulder and turned to see Ranger Rick holding an empty cup in each hand. It was a photo op I couldn't pass up. I snapped a picture and received the added bonus of the ranger's open mouth.

"Ah, the two-fisted style, I see," I said, motioning at his beer cups needing refills. "Hitting it kinda hard there, aren't you, Mr. Ranger, sir?" I added. "What's the deal? One of your prehistoric pets didn't tolerate the transport well? Or did you just learn you have to bunk up with your gramps in the ole RV? Do tell."

Townsend grinned and placed the cups on the counter. "Actually, only one of these is mine. The other is for your sister over there." He cocked his head toward the patio area and I followed his nod. My little sis sat perched on a long-legged, wrought-iron stool at one of several tall white tables, surrounded by a gaggle of cute guys. I immediately got a picture in my head of a young queen and her court. Jesters, I told myself. Jesters. "She is twenty-one now and legal," Townsend continued.

I hoped the reaction I felt wasn't translating into all kinds of little crinkles on my forehead.

"This isn't usually Taylor's scene," I said, annoyed that my sister was encroaching on my territory. And I wasn't just talking about Townsend here. "She usually goes for more, uh, higher-level activities. You know, like reading and studying psychotherapy."

"She's been under a lot of stress lately," Townsend said, pulling a wad of bills out of his jeans pocket and placing several on the counter. "Maybe she just wants to unwind a bit. No harm in that."

Oh, so Ranger Rick was now Taylor's confidant. And what stress was Taylor under? I was the one who probably held the record at the IRS for largest number of employers in one tax season and, as a result, was no doubt on some government watch list somewhere high up. I was the one who'd found three corpses in a week's time and ended up in the cross-hairs of a murdering psycho and an irate ranger. I was the one who had lived in the shadow of two do-no-wrong siblings, acting the fool (okay, so I didn't need Academy Award–quality acting ability to assume the role) and being labeled Calamity Jayne, the cockeyed cowgirl of Knox County, since before puberty. Compared to my life, the little princess hadn't even broken a good sweat.

I couldn't think of a sufficiently snarky comeback, decided it was because I hadn't had enough to drink, and grabbed my beer to take several long, successive gulps. I swept my hand across my mouth and let out a lusty belch.

"Shouldn't you be getting that beer back to your date?" I said. "You can't impress someone who hasn't acquired a taste for beer with a warm drink. It tastes too much like cow piss—or so I've heard," I added.

"It's not a damned date, Tressa," Rick said. "Just a bunch of friends hanging out." I could almost hear his teeth grinding. "You're planning to join us, aren't you?"

I took another look at Taylor, who had showered, didn't smell like the big boar down at the Avenue of Breeds, and had reapplied makeup to a face that didn't need it. Yeah, right. Who wouldn't want to join the group under those circumstances?

"Uh, actually, I still need to put a quick piece together for Stan the Man at the *Gazette* before I call it a night," I said. Hey, I have my pride. "You run along and keep Taylor's jesters—I mean *courtiers* in line. And remember, she's not used to drinking, so keep an eye on her. Hear?"

What was I saying? The last thing I wanted was for Rick Townsend to keep an eye on Taylor. Or anything else, for that matter.

He hesitated for a second, then shrugged. "Have it your way, Calamity," he said. "Have it your way."

I watched him walk away, tempted to take a shot of his nicely sculpted fanny, but settled for zooming in on Taylor and her group of admirers and clicking off a couple of pictures, figuring I could use Taylor and Townsend in my fair piece and wouldn't have to worry about someone getting bent out of shape over having their photo in the paper.

I picked up what was left of my beer and headed over to the couple in the corner I'd wondered about earlier.

"Hey, Uncle Frank." I stood at the table and looked down on the twosome sharing a still half-full pitcher of beer. "Where've you been? Taylor and I were both sweltering in that incinerator you call an Ice Cream Emporium. I thought you were going to fix the AC."

Uncle Frank looked up at me. He looked a little sheepish, I thought. Of course, maybe he just had to pee.

"Oh, howdy, Tressa," Uncle Frank said. "As a matter of fact, I was just on my way up there and stopped in to have a quick drink since it's so sweltering."

"Sweltering?" I said, surprised that Uncle Frank felt the need to play fast and loose with the truth. "Try sitting cooped up in a brick building with refrigerated units running, no ventilation, and no air conditioning. It got so hot in there, I had to wring out my underwear. Twice. Ronnie says you've been in here for over two hours."

"Nosy old—"

"Uncle Frank!"

"Your uncle has had a long day, Tressa," Lucy Connor spoke up. "I'm sure you agree there's nothing wrong with knocking back a couple after a long day's work. After all, you're here for the same reason, aren't you?"

As much as I hated to admit it, Lucy had a point. It just occurred to me that Uncle Frank shouldn't be knocking back anything with any woman other than my Aunt Reggie. Okay, so maybe I'm a bit old-fashioned when it comes to things like wedding rings and marriage licenses. Until yours is legally proclaimed null and void, you best limit socializing to the guys or the little woman.

"Yeah, well, opening night at old B.U. here is a bit of a tradition," I said. "One that Uncle Frank has studiously avoided. Until today, that is," I added.

Uncle Frank's uncomfortable look grew more intense. Major bladder pressure, I thought.

"Tressa's right, Lucy," Uncle Frank said, and got up. "I've got to hit the trail. I need to check out that cooling unit and see if I can rehabilitate it. Then I need to get on up to the campgrounds and get a little shut-eye."

Lucy gave me a smile frostier than a fresh pitcher of beer and got to her feet. "I'm ready to take off, too, Frank," she said, grabbing her pack of cigarettes and lighter from the table. "Good night, Tressa," she said.

"Night, Mrs. Connor," I said, opting for a more formal reply. "Do you need any help, Uncle Frank?" I asked.

My uncle turned and gave me a long look. "If you happen to see Frankie," he said, "tell him—" He stopped. "Never mind," he said, and left the beer tent, little Miz Lucy at his side.

I sat down at the table and considered the beer still left in the pitcher. Thrift was a virtue, I told myself. Waste not, want not. I filled my glass and raised it.

"Where ever you are, Frankie," I said, "this Bud's for you!"

CHAPTER 8

"Stan Rodgers e-mailed. He wants to know where your fair article is. He says you're holding up the presses."

I struggled to open one eye, succeeded, but decided it was way too early and way too bright to expose my other eyeball to the harsh realities of morning. I covered my head with the sheet. Due to my cramped quarters, I'd slept like I was in the chrysalis stage, my sheet tucked tightly in around me so I couldn't thrash about and bump my noggin, bruise a kneecap, or roll off the bed and onto the floor. Still, it was better than bunking with my grandmother.

Fortunately for me, Taylor had drawn the shorter straw and was sharing the pull-out in the living room with the dear lady, who usually embraced sleeping "as God intended." Except, with woolly socks. I get it that God originally intended us to be happily oblivious to our—nakedness—but once Eve suckered Adam into taking that forbidden first bite—well, the rose-colored glasses came off and the fig leaves went on quicker than I put the CLOSED sign up on a Saturday night at the

Dairee Freeze back home. Still, you gotta wonder why the first couple were so ashamed of their bodies. After all, Eve didn't have a Mae West or Dolly Parton to compete with. And there sure weren't any *Playgirl* centerfolds running around to intimidate a poor, inadequate Adam, so what was the big deal?

"Did you hear me, girl?" my grandma hounded. "You're holding up the news. If you need some help, I've got a tidbit or two about opening day I'd be glad to write up for you. The things you pick up at the AARP booth."

Despite a head slightly fuzzy from too much beer and too many trips to the potty in the night, Gram's comment brought me out of my cocoon in a hurry. "Ouch!" I rubbed my head where I'd clobbered it. I recovered, slid out sideways, and stretched to my full body length with a deep sigh.

"That's okay, Gram," I said, cracking my neck a good half dozen times. "I've got it covered. I'm just going to write up a piece about the weather and attendance figures from last year and estimates on this year's attendance and e-mail the digital pics I took last night. That should do the job."

"If you want to put your readers to sleep," she remarked, slathering cream cheese on a bagel. "Now, I heard talk of a couple of long-time concessionaires who were having a good old-fashioned fair fling. 'Course I didn't get any names yet, but give me time and I'll not only have names, I'll have dates, times, locations, and number of climaxes."

"Hannah, really," my mother scolded from the kitchen table, where she sat in front of her laptop. "That isn't appropriate material for a local paper."

"Seems to me it would spice up the rag a bit. I'm sick to death of reading obituaries," Gram replied. She smiled and chuckled. "Sick to death. Get it, Tressa? Sick to death of reading obituaries? See, I could write an entertaining piece for the paper. I've got a million of them like that."

Yeah, bless her heart. And I'd heard all of them.

"Thanks, Gram. I'll keep you in mind if I'm stuck for a topic. And I hope that's the light cream cheese you're pasting on that bagel," I added, knowing full well she'd pilfered the good stuff.

"Hannah!" My mother reached over and took the bagel. "You know that's not good for your cholesterol. I buy the low-fat brand especially for you." She handed my grammy another bagel and the no-fun cream cheese. "I think your son needs to have another talk with you. I can only imagine what you're eating when our backs are turned."

Gram shoved the bagel away and looked at her watch. "Oh, my goodness, look at the time. I promised to meet Joe at the trolley stop ten minutes ago."

"You two seem to be seeing a lot of each other lately," I observed. "Care to divulge any details? I promise I won't splash it all over the *Gazette*," I teased.

"What's the point, then?" Gram said. "Besides, there's nothing to report. We're just enjoying each other's company. Hanging out. Killin' time."

I hoped time was the only casualty of their cockamamie courtship.

"Slow and easy is good," I agreed.

" 'Course, I don't have all the time in the world either," Gram said. "So who knows? Reckon that's what they call 'sexual tension?' " she asked. She got to her feet, stuck a straw hat with a wide brim and red and white bandanna trim on her blue curls, hitched up her white elastic-waist shorts, adjusted her bright red top, and fastened her fanny pack. "You're at the Emporium beginning at three, right, dear?"

I looked over at my mom, who nodded. "Taylor took

the early shift at the mini-freeze until Craig and Kimberly take over. Frank and Reggie are at the Emporium."

My brother Craig is two years older than me and sells cars for the local dealer. His wife, Kimmie, is employed at the county courthouse in the clerk's office. They've been married for three years and Kimmie thinks it's time for them to start a family. Craig has yet to be persuaded, but I have faith that Kimmie will somehow convince him he's ready. Or else. I think it would be a hoot to be an aunt. Auntie Tressa; that has a certain ring to it. Hmmm. Maybe I needed to work on Craig, too.

"Joe and I'll be by for a little pick-me-up this afternoon, then," Gram said. "See you both later."

She flip-flopped to the door and was gone.

"She's heading straight for Dottie's Donuts, isn't she?" Mom asked.

I nodded. "Hello. Do Uncle Frank's cones leak?" I responded.

My mother shook her head. "As if I don't have enough to worry about, I have to police my mother-in-law's eating habits and bedtime. Last night she didn't get in until after midnight. And your father is no help. He hates friction."

I looked at my mom and for the first time noted the dark smudges under her eyes and the tiny lines crinkling the corners. Not, I suspected, laugh lines. My mother always seems so very much in control, so untiring and—what's the word?—indefatigable. (How's that for a big, literary word? Okay, so I typed *unflagging* into the thesaurus and saw indefatigable. I'm still expanding my vocab. Jeesh.) Mom always makes everything look so easy. And she never breaks a sweat. I'd never stopped to wonder the cost to her own well-being and happiness. It was something I found myself thinking a lot about these days. With Frankie. Uncle Frank. Aunt Reggie. My mom. Me.

I put a hand on her shoulder. "You okay, Mom?" I asked, not at all comfortable with the role of comforter but concerned enough to give it a shot.

She patted my hand. "Of course. It's just the situation with Frankie and everyone having to work longer hours to cover. It's hard. That's all."

I pulled out the chair Gram had vacated and sat down. I picked up the caloric cream cheese bagel and cut it in half, handing one portion to my mother and taking a nice, big bite out of the other half.

"What do you think about Frankie, Mom?" I asked through the wad of bagel in my mouth. "You don't think he's the one responsible for all the monkey business at Uncle Frank's eateries, do you?"

I watched as she seemed to contemplate her words more carefully than I did a shoe purchase.

"I don't know what to think about Frankie, Tressa," she said finally. "But one thing I do know: his behavior is taking a big toll on my sister's marriage. Regina and Frank are hardly speaking to each other. I've never seen them so distant. So at odds. And it worries me, Tressa. It worries me a lot. And now there's all this vandalism at Frank's. He seems to think someone tampered with the air conditioner at the Emporium now."

I saw my usually stoic mother's eyes grow moist and thought about Uncle Frank and Lucy Connor and the cozy corner table, and decided now was not the time to tell where her brother-in-law had been last night when he should have been getting the air back on in the Emporium.

"I'm sure everything will work out," I said, suddenly not as sure as I was when I'd woke up that morning. "Frankie will probably show up today, and once Trooper P. D. Dawkins talks to him, I'm positive he will no longer be considered a suspect."

My mother dropped her half bagel. "The police want

to question Frankie about the trouble? Does Frank know?"

I put down my bagel, my appetite eroded, and nodded. "The state trooper spoke to Uncle Frank yesterday. He wants us to let him know when Frankie turns up again. But like I said, that's routine, just to rule Frankie out. Then they can find out who really has it in for Uncle Frank."

And at the top of my list was none other than long-time loser, Cone Connection's Luther Daggett.

"I hope you're right, Tressa," my mother said. "I hope you're right." She clicked her mouse a couple of times, grabbed her cell phone and key ring, and stood. "I've got to get to the Emporium and talk to Frank. You better get that article sent off to Stan. He's got a deadline, dear, and he's not known for his patience."

Didn't I know it? It had been harder to convince Stan to give me a second chance—all right, *third* chance—than it was convincing my dad to let me drive his brand-new Chevy pickup truck. I sure didn't want to cripple my journalistic career before it even got out of the starting gate.

I stood and gave my mom another awkward shoulder pat. I know. I'm pathetic. I'm just not much of a hugger.

"Things will work out," I told her. "Between Aunt Reggie and Uncle Frank. And for Frankie, too. You'll see."

She smiled. "Are you predicting the future now, in addition to fighting crime?" she asked.

I shook my head. "That was a one-shot deal. I'm very content to resume my boring little existence, thank you very much."

"Speaking of boring, you'd better get something off to the *Gazette*," she reminded me, and I smiled at her uncharacteristic quip. "Lock up when you leave and don't forget your keys," she told me, again all business.

"Ten-four," I said, hoping that meant affirmative.

Mom waved and left. I polished off the bagel remnants and washed them down with orange juice—not a compelling taste combo—then sat my butt down in front of the laptop. Thirty minutes (and two more e-mails from Stan) later, I had a decent, somewhat generic, opening-day article. I hurriedly uploaded the digital photographs and e-mailed them to Stan, telling him he could select the one he wanted to run, then signed off and hit the shower.

Half an hour later, dressed in navy blue shorts, white tank top, and white and navy Skechers, I went in search of something more substantial than bagels and a fair weather report.

What would be compelling and of interest to the hometown crowd? I wondered, acknowledging my grammy wasn't too far off the mark with her gossip column concept. People loved to be titillated. I sighed, thinking the trouble at Uncle Frank's fair establishments would be newsworthy but knowing I'd be running from Uncle Frank if I ran with that story.

It was still fairly early, not yet ten, but the mugginess of the morning promised a hot time at the old fair today. I made my way down the graveled hill, opting not to take advantage of the fair trolley when I saw that the line of seniors waiting for the next transport was longer than those waiting for flu shots when there's a shortage of flu vaccine. Besides, I didn't want to look like a complete wimp by being the only one out of adolescence and under retirement age to bum a ride.

I watched my stride—too long to be ladylike—and admired the way my shoes matched my outfit. Definitely cool and trendy. I checked out my legs and decided I needed a few days sunbathing to even out my tan. Swimsuit tan lines are one thing; a farmer tan with sock lines is quite another.

I purposely avoided the area around Dottie's Donuts, as hard as that was, and tried to figure out what sounded good that I hadn't already tasted this season. The choices were limited and it was only day two of the fair. I was as bad as my grammy. Ultimately, I decided to go the healthy route. (Okay, you can stop laughing now.) I made my way to the Fruit by the Foot booth where you can buy a twelve-inch slice of watermelon for a buck. And they have cute little spittoons at various locations in case you feel inclined to try your seed-spittin' aim. I'm actually quite good. Due to years of practice, you know. I polished off my section of melon, ordered another one, and had it up to my mouth, gobbling away, when a horn blast sounded in my right ear. I jumped the height of a stalk of corn in midsummer and pivoted, my watermelon dropping to the dirty ground at my feet, narrowly missing my shoes.

The horn sounded again, this time several toots in succession. I looked up to see a painted clown face just inches away from my own.

"I have a message for your Uncle Frank," the clown with neon green hair and gigantic red sunglasses whispered. "Tell him it's time to retire. Tell him he needs to take a nice, long permanent vacation. You know: travel. See the sights. Spend some time with the wife. Got that, sister?"

I stared at the clown, taking in the baggy yellow polka-dotted pants and God-awful orange shirt and frowned. Apparently, judging from his apparel, this particular clown had been getting clothing tips from Joe Townsend.

I have always hated clowns. Despised them, in fact. I think it goes back to the obnoxious rodeo clowns I've tangled with in the past. Every clown I've come into contact with seems to pick up on my dislike for them and home in on that negativity like flies on you-know-what. While other kids were having Freddy Krueger nightmares, I was fighting mutant clowns from Mars in my dreams.

"Wh-what?" I tried to reply, but I'd bitten off more than I could chew in the watermelon department and felt several seeds start to slide down the back of my throat. I began to gag and choke.

"This way nobody gets hurt," my painted-faced friend went on. "Nice and clean. Good for everybody. Got the message?"

I finally managed to spit and/or swallow the remains of my melon and realized that Uncle Frank's bug benefactor and the supplier of the soured ice-milk stood before me—unrecognizable in clown paint—and could only shake my head. This joker had the judgment of Michael Jackson to select me as the conduit for his coercion.

"Huh?" I got out, thinking the dude obviously didn't know me very well, or he'd never have chosen me to carry his goofy greeting to Uncle Frank. Heck, I can hardly remember my own social security number most of the time. Add to that the fact that I was presently scared watermelon-seed spitless and it didn't bode well for this clown's caper.

"Just deliver the message," he said and turned to leave.

"Hey, wait!" I finally regained the ability to speak— something I'm sure you folks never for a moment thought I was in serious jeopardy of losing for any length of time—and grabbed at the clown's large, poofy sleeve. "Hey!"

The clown was faster than he should have been, given the long, ridiculously wide shoes he was wearing, or I had eaten way more at the fair than my thighs could handle. The crafty comedian was out of the Fruit by the Foot stand before I'd gotten to my feet.

Not about to let the two-legged proof of Frankie's innocence get away, I tore after the clown, dodging fair patrons and vendors as I struggled to keep the clown in sight and the watermelon in my stomach. A little better than fifty yards ahead of me and increasing the distance between us, the clown blew past the Foot Long stand and around the Pizza by the Slice booth. I called on calve muscles too long ignored and vowed I was going to start a fitness program just as soon as the fair was over. For sure before the Christmas-time wedding of my best friend, Kari. I'd be lean and mean by then, I decided. And Townsend better not try any of his lame jokes on me, either. He'd ruined my brother's wedding for me. This time, I'd take no prisoners. I'd be a fightin' machine. A regular G. I. Jayne.

I passed the grinder booth and sucked in the smell of grinder sausage as I ran by. Around the corner of the administration building and by the old clock on the Grand Concourse, I inched closer, thankful I wasn't wearing my black flip-flops or darling white Mootsie Tootsies with the two-inch heels, hoping against hope that the damned clown on the run was getting blisters from his stupid clown shoes. We both were beginning to generate a lot of attention from fair-goers. Heads jerked up in our wake and fingers pointed. Sad to say, I'm used to this kind of reaction.

We blew past Mike's Mexican, clipped past Candy's Candies, and slowed to a brisk plod by the time we got to the Pork People. I pinched the stitch in my side, cursing at having inherited the junk food gene from my grandma.

Reminding myself I had also inherited her grit and love for John Wayne movies, I pumped my legs faster and harder than I could ever remember. Well, except for that one time that we won't talk about. I saw the clown look back with an angry, frustrated look in my direction. I'm used to these facial expressions, too, and have learned to read them with pinpoint accuracy. I gathered all the remaining air in my lungs and kicked it up a notch more, feeling victory at hand as I closed in on the conniving clown.

He saw the trolley pulling away and beginning its ascent to the campground at the same time I did, but identified it as a getaway vehicle way before I realized he was actually desperate enough to attempt to board the moving object—big, flopping clown feet and all.

"Stop that clown!" I yelled when his intent became evident. "Stop the clown!" I ran as fast as my too-many-tacoed thighs could carry me. "Stop that clown!"

I looked on as the brazen Bozo, hellbent on escape, lengthened his stride visibly and reached out to grab hold of the rail at the back of the trolley. He seemed to hang in midair for a time; then I saw him grab hold with his other hand and pull himself up and over the rail and into the trolley to a chorus of cheers from the crowd and trolley occupants, who apparently thought the clown and I were part of some traveling fair attraction. I slowed to a jog, zero hope of being able to repeat the clown's feat—or feet. The clown waved at the crowd, bowed, then turned his attention back to me. He put his fingers in his ears and wiggled them, stuck his tongue out, and made "she's nuts" gestures at his head with his index finger. Then, in an ultimate clown up-yours, he raised his obnoxious little horn in my direction and sounded a succession of bested-you blasts. I did what any self-respecting cowgirl would do: I gave him the finger.

Have I mentioned I hate clowns?

CHAPTER 9

"And this . . . this horn-blowing Bozo escaped on the fair trolley?"

I had the attention of five family members, one Jackie Chan relic, one skeptical ranger-type, and a good half dozen customers in the Emporium when I reported for duty shortly before three.

I gave Townsend a bite-me look, followed by a vigorous nod for the benefit of the others. "That's right."

"I saw the whole thing!" piped in a rotund little guy with a shiny bald head who had, according to Uncle Frank, been camped out in the Emporium sipping a Diet Coke off and on since he'd yanked the old air conditioner and stuck a brand-new one in its place. "I've never seen anything like it. This tall, gangly clown with neon green hair about the color of your T-shirt there"—he pointed to Joe Townsend—"with big clodhopper shoes and pants so baggy I thought they would fall any minute, running for that trolley car as if a pack of Rottweilers was on his tail. Turns out it was only blondie here, but she was closin' in. And she'da caught him, too, if that derned trolley hadn't been pulling out."

I flashed a smug grin that I hoped said, "I'm all that," and smiled at the Emporium customer. "I sure tried to catch that varmint," I said in my best Yosemite Sam–speak.

"For curiosity's sake, what would you have done if you'd caught him?" Ranger Rick asked, arms crossed, showing off his tanned, muscular biceps to best advantage.

"Done?" I repeated, thinking that was either a really stupid question or actually quite brilliant. Hmmm. Let's see. What *would* I have done?

"Yes, done. Once you apprehended the crazy and possibly dangerous clown-type? What would you have done next?" Townsend pressed.

I thought about it a second. "Well, unmask him, of course."

"Oh. I see. And he's just going to lie there and let you have your way with him?" Townsend continued.

"I would have thought of something," I said, defending my somewhat impulsive action. "Besides, everywhere you look there's always a trooper. I've seen brown shirts in my dreams," I said.

"I'm sure you have," Townsend murmured, his reference to Trooper Dawkins not escaping me.

"Considering the circumstances, I think I handled the situation very well," I told my audience, who had gone from impressed interest to she's-at-it-again eye-rolling, give or take an occasional nervous tic.

"Yeah, especially the part where she flipped the clown off," the roly-poly customer said, his body a prototype of things to come for me if I didn't lay off the fast food pronto. I gave him my back-off-buddy look, and he went back to pretending to read his newspaper.

"The opportunity to clear Frankie's name presented itself and I had to pursue it," I said. "That's all."

"How do you know the clown wasn't Frankie?"

I turned and stared at the person who'd uttered those words. "Aunt Reggie?" I said, shocked that such an idea could come from her of all people. "You can't mean that," I said. "Not you, too."

She shrugged, a barely perceptible lifting of weary shoulders. "You can't rule it out, Tressa. None of us can. Face it, my son is not himself. He's going through some identity crisis or something. I hardly know him anymore."

I looked around the room. My mother patted her sister's shoulder, a lot like I'd done earlier and only slightly less awkwardly. In between making goo-goo eyes at each other when they thought no one was looking, Gramma and Joe Townsend shared a banana split at the counter. And Townsend? Townsend had me fixed in his sights.

"I know that clown character wasn't Frankie," I said. "It's like, the guy is allergic to practically everything. Do you really think he'd slather himself up with face paint, drape himself in hot clothes, and don an itchy green wig designed to give you a heat rash? Give me a break. We're talking about Frankie here. The guy has allergic reactions to water, for crying out loud. Come on, people."

After a moment Aunt Reggie smiled at me. "You're right, of course, Tressa," she said. "Frankie wouldn't be caught dead in a clown suit. I don't know what I was thinking. I just wish he would come back so we could sit down and work things out."

"I'm sure he will, Aunt Reggie," I said. "In his own good time and in his own way, he'll find his way back to us."

I sure hoped I wasn't whistlin' in the wind here. For

Uncle Frank and Aunt Reggie's sake, as well as for one skinny, bunless Frankfurter.

Around ten that evening I finished up the nightly routine, wiping down the counter one last time, then pulling off my candy-stripe apron and hanging it on the stainless steel coat tree near the back door. Uncle Frank should be very pleased; business had really picked up once the temperature and humidity rose and word got around that the AC in the Emporium was belting out cold air guaranteed to give you icicles on your whiskers—if you had whiskers, that is. My mother had remained at the Emporium until eight and then called it a night.

Craig and Kimmie were closing up the mini-freeze. Knowing Taylor, she was probably in front of her laptop at the trailer working on some psychology summer course relating to overachievers and the people who put up with them.

I retrieved my keys and the cell phone Mom had left, turned the air conditioner off, checked all the plugs-ins and windows and doors, locked up, and left.

It was a hot, humid night. Just the right kind of night for a nice cold dip in a hotel pool. A hotel where one could return to a luxurious room after a swim and take a nice, long, leisurely shower in a bathroom where a certain grandmother wouldn't barge in and flush while you were shampooing. Where one could snuggle up on a king-sized bed with Ashton Kutcher (hey, at least I'm monogamous in my fantasy world) and order room service and Pay Per View all night. Ah. That's the life.

I shook my head to erase the picture of Ashton reclining on my bed clad in a pair of low-riding boxers. Sigh.

I decided to check out the Bottoms Up beer tent. I wanted to make sure Uncle Frank wasn't engaged in another rendezvous with little Miz Lucy. Okay, so the idea of a beer on this hot night was as tempting to me as a carrot on a stick was to Bugs Bunny. I waved to Rhonda from the doorway and she hoisted an empty cup in the air, raising a fill-'er-up? eyebrow at me. I nodded in response, and she slipped the cup under the lite beer tap and turned on the nozzle. Don't you just love non-verbal communication?

I slapped a five on the counter and took the proffered tall one. "Hey, Ronnie. How's it goin'?"

"So far it's been a lollapalooza couple days," she said. "With it being so warm, folks have been coming in for beer in droves. If the weather holds, we could be lookin' at a record-breaking beer year."

"Congratulations," I said, sipping my ice-cold drink. "We were pretty swamped at the Emporium today, too. Hot weather makes for great ice cream sales, you know." I set down my beer and leaned across the counter. "Have you, uh, by any chance heard anything via fair chatter about who might be responsible for all the antics directed at Uncle Frank this year?" I asked, knowing that if it was being said, Ronnie would have heard it. Bottoms Up was the central clearinghouse for fair news and Ronnie was the equivalent of town crier.

She hesitated, not wanting to make eye contact.

"Ronnie?" I said. "If you've heard something, you've got to tell me," I urged, and regaled her with a recitation of my run-in with the bad, bad clown. Of course, it was already old news to Ronnie.

"Only you would chase down a loco clown on the Grand Concourse in ninety-degree heat," she said, shaking her head. And yes, I've heard . . . scuttlebutt about the trouble Frank has been having. But you might not want to hear what the consensus is, kiddo."

"Folks think Frankie's the one, don't they?" I asked, already predicting her response.

She nodded. "Now, I'm not sayin' Frankie's to

blame," she said. "That's just what the word on the vine is. Personally, I think Frankie lacks the gumption—no offense intended, of course. I just can't see him fiddling with cockroaches, tampering with air conditioners, and vaulting onto moving conveyances wearing a clown costume. Frankie's not what you'd call a risk-taker. On the other hand, you, Calamity Jayne . . ." She trailed off.

"I see," I said. "Well, here's more fodder for the fair watch that you can pass along. Frankie is not the bad guy here. Plain and simple. And I intend to prove it. There's your scoop."

Okay, I'm pausing here for a moment so someone can explain how I consistently fit my size nine foot in my mouth—and with relative ease. Dang.

Ronnie put her elbows on the counter. "Oh yeah? Well, when you can prove it, Calamity, get back to me and I'll spread the word. By the way, that back table is sure popular with your clan this fair," Ronnie said, wiping away the wet ring of condensation left by my glass.

"Are you kidding? Again?" I said, expecting to turn and find Uncle Frank and his far-too-neighborly neighbor sipping drinks together.

I looked around, ready to chew big-time uncle butt, even at my own peril, when I saw an entirely different combo at the cozy table in question. They were laughing and talking and appearing to have a terrific time.

"I thought you and that hunky DNR fella had an understanding," she said, somewhat more tactfully than she was known for. "Is there something I should know—and pass on?" she asked.

I took another drink and turned my back on my sister and her new friend. "Just that I'm out to vindicate my cousin Frankie, and expose the real bird turd in this little campaign of intimidation against my Uncle Frank. And that is hot off the presses," I said. I pulled out another five-dollar bill. "Oh, and send another pitcher to the corner table," I added. "With my compliments." I tapped the counter. "Take it easy, Ronnie," I said and walked out.

Let's see: I could have stomped up to the table and thrown my beer in Townsend's face. No, that's no good. He might think I really cared. I could have doused Taylor. Naw. Too cat-fighty for me. Besides, why waste good beer? I might have waltzed on over, slid next to Ranger Rick, and planted a great big, long, wet, beer kiss on him. I considered that for a moment and shook my head. Too slutty. No, I handled it just right.

I walked along the midway, finishing off what was left of my beer, ticking off all the shoulda, coulda, woulda options at my disposal for dealing with a ranger who obviously didn't care enough to give me time to make up my mind about if there even should be an us, and a little sister who, despite just turning twenty-one, was way too young and way too naïve to be testing her wings with the likes of Rick Townsend.

"Do you always talk to yourself, or is it the beer talking?" a voice, emitting hot breath on the back of my neck, questioned. Remembering the clown, I whirled around, ready to "sing" (solar plexus, instep, nose, groin—I've watched *Miss Congeniality* a time or two) before he had time to toot his evil horn in my ear.

I had just raised my right fist to deliver a gut punch when I recognized Trooper P. D.'s breathtaking baby blues. He'd lost the Smokey Bear ensemble and was wearing a white Cyclone T-shirt and khaki shorts, Nikes, and short socks. Smart fellow, I thought. I try to avoid wearing sandals or flip-flops on the midway. You never know what you might step in.

"I almost didn't recognize you without your clothes on," I said with a grin, easing off my *Charlie's Angels* stance.

Trooper Dawkins grinned back. "Do I look more approachable in my civvies?" he asked, cocking his head to one side. "Less a keeper of the peace and more human?"

I blinked. The guy looked this-cowgirl's-about-to-drool-worse-than-her-two-happy-tongued-puppies sexy.

"You still stand like a trooper," I said. "With or without the brown shirt and badge."

He studied me with a critical eye.

"What?" I said. "What?"

"I'm just trying to decide if that's a good thing or a bad thing," he responded. "How does a trooper stand, anyway?"

Hmmm. How to explain without offending? "The cops I know—and I do know a few—stand as if they have a metal rod stuck . . . down their shirt and along their tailbone into their pants," I finally said, choosing my words carefully. "Real stiff and rigid and upright. You know. Like the Tin Man in *The Wizard of Oz*," I explained.

He rubbed his chin. "I'm still wondering if that's a good thing or a bad thing. A tin man isn't very, uh, approachable."

"But isn't that the idea?" I asked. "Don't cops have to project a stern, harsh exterior to convey to the public that they're ready to handle any situation that comes their way at any given time? I imagine that kind of bearing could cut some fracases off at the pass, before they start. One look at a straight-backed trooper and bad guys think better of giving the cop a hard time. So, I imagine it's a good thing for you guys, even if it's a bit intimidating for those who are easily put off by what may appear as conceit, arrogance, or delusions of godhood," I finished, somewhat embarrassed by my lengthy analysis of police posture.

The trooper chuckled. "Now tell me what you really think, Miss Turner," he teased.

I started to walk and he joined me. We continued a piece in silence.

"I suppose I walk like a trooper," he finally said.

I cast an eye at his long, purposeful yet natural gait. "I'd call it more a swagger," I said. "Not quite to the strut stage. More a self-confident, non-cocky swagger."

"Thanks. I think," he added with that compelling twinkle in his eye. "Do you want to know what you walk like?" he asked.

I looked down at my own strides, which almost matched the trooper's. "Uh, no, thanks," I responded. "Some things are better left to the imagination."

We strolled along the midway beneath strings of multicolored lights and gaily decorated carnival games such as the Pop Bottle Ring Toss, the Ping-Pong Throw, where the prize is a gold fish in a glass bowl—a big come-on for little tykes who love the idea of a pet of any kind—and the ever-popular Inflate the Balloon with a Squirt Gun game. All vendors hawked the promise of awarding a prize every time through a rather loud bullhorn. Which is true, I suppose, if you count tiny inflatable pillows and plastic gold fishies as prizes. For the unseasoned, the midway games are a tourist trap of epic proportions. For a veteran like me who knows the secrets to beating the games and have a respectable collection of stuffed animals and overstuffed pillows to prove it, the games are not the challenge they once were. And since the carneys knew I was a pro at their games of chance, they generally ignored me when I went by.

An intriguing thought occurred to me, and I looked over at Trooper Dawkins, who appeared to be in danger of catching that infamous Macho, Macho Man bug that guys accompanying a girl on the midway invariably come down with.

"So, how do you like fair duty?" I asked. "Been doing

it long? I'm here every year, and I don't recall seeing you in years past." I batted my eyes at him. "And believe me, I would've remembered."

Trooper Dawkins laughed. "Actually this is my first fair," he replied, and I felt the bad little Tressa on my left shoulder jab me with her tiny, but sharp, pitchfork. "Oh, I've been to fairs before," the unsuspecting trooper went on, "but having been born and raised in the western part of Iowa, we didn't get to the state fair all that much."

Even better, that naughty little devil whispered in my ear.

"Oh, wow! Look at that giant Nemo!" I exclaimed, pointing at the large, overstuffed fish with bulging eyes and wide black mouth hanging above progressively smaller Nemos. Orange balloons were inflated and fastened to a white board along the back of the booth. "I just love Nemo, don't you?" I grabbed the trooper's elbow.

"Who the hell is Nemo?" he said. I gasped.

"You don't know Nemo? Shame on you, Trooper P. D. Dawkins," I said, and grabbed him by the elbow and pulled him over to the stand. "That"—I pointed to the huge orange plush toy above us—"is Nemo. Just the coolest fish ever!" I performed a long, loud, wistful sigh. "What I wouldn't give to win one of those," I said.

Trooper Dawkins looked the game over carefully. "You know these games are rigged, don't you?" he said. "It's almost impossible to win."

I stuck out my lower lip in a pout and crossed my arms. "I didn't say you had to win one for me, Mr. Smokey Bear. But you could try. Just once, couldn't you?" I put my hands together in a prayerful pose. "Pretty please?"

He smiled and put his hand in his pocket. Over his bent head, the game operator, Billy, a long-time carnival worker, gave me a big wink, which I returned with relish. The trooper handed Billy a five-dollar bill in exchange for three darts.

"We have a brave young feller here hoping to win this here young lady a Nemo, folks," Billy barked into his bullhorn. "Step up and see a winner. Everybody takes away a prize. Step right up."

"This ought to be a piece of cake for a trooper," I told Dawkins as he was lining up his first throw. "After all, don't your people have to qualify with firearms regularly?" The trooper looked over at me and then returned his concentration to his aim.

"I bet you're one of those sharpshooters, aren't you?" I continued, interrupting his concentration again. "I can tell. You're one of those SWAT guys. You know, that tactical team where they kick in doors and storm the building?"

He smiled, his amusement a little less genuine than it had been previously, and focused his attention on his target and threw.

Fifteen dollars, nine darts, and three little plastic Nemos later, I was beginning to feel really guilty. The guy was bound and determined to win me the grand prize. See if I ever listened to the temptress on my left shoulder again.

"It's okay," I told the totally torqued trooper. "I've had second thoughts. That orange would really clash with my bedroom decor," I told him.

"No, no," he argued. "I want you to have Nimrod there."

"Uh, it's Nemo, and that's okay. The bulging eyes would probably give me nightmares anyway."

"Just three more darts," he said, and I could see that he wasn't about to let go of his pursuit of the huge fish. It was Hemingway's Old Man, the Sea, and a giant marlin all over again.

"What if I threw the darts this time?" I suggested. "Then, win or lose, we're done. Deal?" I asked.

The trooper looked at Billy, back at the orange balloons, up at the huge Nimrods—I mean Nemos—then over at me.

"Go for it," he said.

I nodded at Billy, and he handed me three darts. A respectable crowd had gathered once Billy announced to the world that a trooper was throwing. I planted my feet a good twelve inches apart, zeroed in on my target, and BOOM! The first balloon popped like the backfire of my old Plymouth Reliant. I saw the surprised trooper glance in my direction. I braced myself, set, and threw. BOOM! Balloon number two bought the farm. I could feel the intensity of the trooper's eyes on me as I adjusted my stance for the last shot.

"Could I do the honors?" Dawkins reached out and gently removed the last remaining dart from my hand.

I looked over at him and watched as he let the last dart fly. KABOOM! A chorus of claps and cheers erupted at Billy's Big Fish stand.

"And we have a winner!" Billy screamed into the megaphone. "And that's how it's done, folks, and by none other than Calamity Jayne and Smokey the Bear! Step right up and try your luck! A winner every time!"

Billy took a long hook and unfastened a giant Nemo from his collection and handed it to the trooper. Dawkins raised it over his head and gave a he-man holler. The crowd erupted. He then handed it to me.

"Your Nimrod, your ladyship," he said with a courtly bow.

"It's Nemo," I said, and reached out and took the large orange fish with a shaky hand.

"Uh, no. This particular fish is hereinafter to be referred to as Nimrod," he said. "Which is what you think

I am if you think I didn't see that shyster hand you a new set of darts," he added.

I stared at him.

"And now I intend to trounce you soundly at the baseball toss, the whack-a-mole, and the frog launch. What do you have to say to that, Miz Calamity?"

I grinned at the now cocky copper.

"Let the games begin, Smokey," I said. "Let the games begin."

"Okay, I think you've proven your point," the heavily laden trooper said, his flushed face peeking out from behind several Simpsons collectible beer mugs and crystal cake platters courtesy of the dime toss (where the secret is to toss the dime up into the air in a high arc so it drops directly onto a plate); an adorably ugly little brown mole from the whack-a-mole game (the secret? Practice makes perfect); and a long-limbed amphibian a rather nauseating shade of green from the frog launch game, where the trick is not to aim for the nearest lily pads as rank amateurs do, but instead launch that puppy—or froggie—as high into the air as possible with absolutely no regard for the location of the lily pads. The position of the frog to be launched is also key. When placing your frog on the catapult, fold the legs under its stomach, just like the little feller would likely sit if he were actually alive.

"Just one more," I said, not ashamed to admit I'd caught a bit of the gambling bug. Okay, so in my case it wasn't as much of a gamble—but I was sure enjoying the heck out of impressing this dishy peace officer.

"That one looks like a piece of cake," Dawkins said, pointing to the baseball toss with one of the frog's front legs.

I shook my head. "That's a flat joint," I told him, and he gave me a puzzled look. "Flat-out impossible to win," I explained. "The vendor has been known to hide springs in the baskets after the state inspectors have done their pre-opening day walk-through." I gave the carnival worker my best hello-slimeball look as we passed.

"Well, well, well. Look what we have here. Calamity Jayne finds Nemo."

I felt my lip curl involuntarily, and turned to find not only the biggest hemorrhoid on the midway, but my sister, Taylor, beside him. I shoved one of Dawkins's little plastic Nemos at Rick Townsend. "Pompous ass finds a bathtub buddy?" I asked.

Townsend barely gave mini-Nemo a look. "Cute," he said, handing it to Taylor. "Looks like your friend here hit the jackpot." I seethed, knowing he likely knew I'd done most of the winning. "Very impressive."

I raised an eyebrow. "Isn't it, though? Uh—P. D. here is a member of the state SWAT team," I told Townsend, realizing I didn't even know the trooper's first name. "He's a real crackpot," I said, catching my mistake only after it tumbled off my lips. Townsend always gets me flustered.

"Uh, don't you mean crack *shot?*" Rick asked, not bothering to hide his mirth. He reached out to shake the trooper's hand, which was occupied by critters, so he ended up shaking the frog's ugly green leg.

"You know what I mean," I snapped. "What are you two doing on the midway? You planning to win a few toys for my baby sister there?" I asked, hoping he got the not-so-subtle implication that I thought he was too old for Taylor.

"I think I'm a little past the toy stage, Tressa," Taylor interjected. "Besides, who has the bed full of Beanie Babies?"

"They're collectibles," I snapped. "That Princess Di bear is worth a small fortune." I wish. "Well, it's been fun and all, but we were about to leave, so we'll catch you later."

"Ah, that's too bad. I thought maybe we could hold a friendly competition here," Townsend said. "Losers buy a round of drinks."

I frowned at Townsend and looked over at Taylor. "Haven't you been to the Bottoms Up once already?" I asked her.

"I ordered a cola," Taylor replied. "And, by the way, you're not my mother."

I gave her a closer look. That kind of comment was more like me than my good-natured sis.

"Okay. Whatever," I said.

"Since it appears your sister and her new friend—" Townsend said to Taylor, then stopped and looked at me, eyebrows raised, expecting me to supply a name I didn't know.

"Patrick," Dawkins said, managing to hold out a hand to Taylor. "Patrick Dawkins, ISP two-three-two."

"As in Iowa State Patrol," I translated.

"Nice to meet you, Patrick." Taylor shook his hand, causing the froggie to fall to the dirty pavement. I retrieved and tucked him under the trooper's arm.

"Since it appears Tressa and Patrick are not confident enough in their gaming abilities to take us on, I guess we'll move along," Townsend continued.

Foolish man. He knew I was the undisputed queen of the midway and would step up to defend any challenge to my title.

"I think we have time for one more game. Right, Patrick?" I said, grabbing hold of his arm, causing the poor froggie to plop again to the hard surface below. I scooped him up and stuffed his long, lanky legs in the waistband of my shorts.

"What's it to be, T?" Townsend asked, his eyes bright at the prospect of getting the best of me.

In his neverland dreams, I thought.

"Name your poison," he said.

"Whazz-up," I replied with a you're-dead-meat look, referring to the group game where each player is given a joystick that controls a pitcher and the object is to keep that pitcher under a moving beer tap that spouts water. Whoever fills their pitcher first is the winner.

"So be it," Townsend said. "And may the best pitcher-filler win."

Patrick and I left our assorted prizes in the care of Billy at the Big Fish booth and plopped down three bucks each, a bargain to be able to put a conceited ranger in his place. Pitchers four and eight, I knew, moved with the greatest ease and since my lucky number was eight, I chose that one. I raised my eyebrows when I saw Townsend select number four. No other contestants anted up as we took our positions. I looked over at Taylor and gave her my funeral face. To Townsend I presented a prepare-to-eat-dirt smirk. The bell rang and the race was on.

"And the winner is . . . number four!"

I stared at the pitchers in frustration. Townsend had beaten me by mere drops.

"How about a rematch?" I suggested, unwilling to end the night a loser.

Townsend stretched his well-shaped arms and rotated his head in a circular fashion. "That's it for me. Besides, I don't want to have to carry any more heavy prizes out to the parking lot," he said. "Admit it, T. I beat you fair and square."

I wasn't so certain about that, but since I had no way to prove it, I let his comment pass.

"Whatever," I said my usual response when I don't want to acknowledge the possibility that someone else could be right. Especially when that someone was Rick Townsend.

"Guess we owe you a beer," Patrick said, showing himself a gracious loser.

"Since it's so late, you'll give us a raincheck on that beer, won't you, Patrick?" Ranger Rick asked, so conciliatory it made me want to hurl. "Monday night at ten at Bottoms Up?"

"Sure. Sounds great," Dawkins replied.

"Don't forget your prize there, Rick," the Whazz-up operator reminded Townsend. My eyes narrowed. "Rick," was it now? Something was rotten in carneyland, me thought. I looked on as Rick surveyed the available prizes. He hesitated and looked over at me. I stood, tapping my toe, thinking he was making more of a production of this than they did for Superbowl commercials.

"Sometime today would be nice," I said.

Rick turned back to the assorted animals, and I cursed under my breath when I saw him select a long purple snake with green spots and a yellow underbelly.

He brought the reptile to where Taylor, Patrick, and I stood. He walked behind me, and I felt him drape the length of the serpent over my shoulders and around my neck. A warmth poured over me that had nothing to do with the humidity of the night or my feverish efforts to best him earlier. For some reason, I felt his bestowing his snake on me was some kind of symbol, a sign that we were bound together. A primitive staking of a claim, if you will. I bit my lip to keep from misting up, only to have Townsend grab the snake's head and pretend to sink its huge, hideous red fangs into my neck with a hiss, then slide the snake from around my neck and place it, like a royal cloak, over my sister's shapely shoulders.

I felt tears coming in earnest now, and was so determined the wretched ranger not see them that I grabbed poor Patrick by the arm so hard, he dropped a crystal glass plate. It shattered into a gazillion pieces.

"I'm so sorry, Patrick," I said.

Patrick grinned. "Truth be told, I'm glad you did it. I wasn't looking forward to walking to my patrol car holding a damned cake plate."

I managed to laugh, grateful for the trooper's nicely timed humor.

"Didja hear about the blond coyote who got stuck in a trap, chewed off three legs, and was still stuck?" a voice rang out.

My head snapped back. Any time I hear a blonde joke, I have that reaction. But this time, the blonde joke was broadcast over a very distorted loudspeaker. I looked around, confused. "What the—?"

"What do you call a really smart blonde? A golden retriever. Why do blondes have square breasts? They forget to take the tissues out of the box. How can you tell if a blonde's been using the computer? There's Whiteout on the screen. How can you tell if another blonde's been using the computer? There's writing on the Whiteout. What's a blonde behind the wheel called? An airbag. Two blondes in a car? Dual airbags."

I searched for the source of the insults, somehow feeling they were directed straight at me. A crowd was gathering around a dunk tank in the northeast corner of the midway. I read the sign above the enclosure. "Bobo the insult clown," I read.

The crowd parted, and I caught a look at the insult-spouting Bobo. I blinked several times, rubbing my eyes with one of froggie's feet. I stared at the clown sitting on the board over the water tank. The red shirt, the yellow polka-dot pants, neon green hair . . . I felt the corners of my mouth curl upward in a smile.

Bobo, the psycho clown, was trapped in a chain link prison and there was no way out except through one hunky trooper, Nimrod, and me.

CHAPTER 10

"Hmm. Sounds like the clown *has* met you before, Calamity. Sure you didn't date him at one time?"

Under other circumstances, Townsend's remark would have prompted a carefully chosen comeback, but my delight at finding the clown at a distinct disadvantage and with a certified member of the law enforcement community by my side, convinced me to let it pass.

"High and dry! The great Bobo! I'm high and dry! Yoohoo! Blondie! Why do blondes put their hair in ponytails? To cover up the valve stem!"

I took a tentative step forward. The clown appeared to be looking right at me, but it was hard to tell, since he was wearing those absurd red sunglasses.

"Yeah, you, blondie. The one with the hair you need a curry comb to get through. You ever heard of Frizz Ease?"

The crowd responded with laughs. Several folks pointed in my direction.

I put a self-conscious hand to my hair, discovering

springy curls that had broken free of their gelatinous prison. The damned clown was taunting me.

"Why can't blondes put in light bulbs?" the clown continued. "They keep breaking them with the hammer."

The crowd went crazy with that one, slapping their sides and looking to see how I was taking the ribbing.

"Yep. Definitely an old boyfriend," Townsend remarked, and I turned to him.

"Oh, really, Einstein? So, you don't notice anything about that particular clown that's out of the ordinary? Nothing at all?"

Townsend studied me. "Don't tell me; let me guess. He's the clown you say accosted you this morning. The one who used a trolley pulled by a John Deere as his getaway vehicle."

I nodded. "That's right, it's him. Down to the same dopey face paint, polka-dot pants, and green wig."

Patrick Dawkins gave me a puzzled look. "What's all this about a clown?" he asked. I hurriedly explained.

"So you see, it's not Frankie after all. Someone else wants Uncle Frank to sell out," I told them. "And that clown was their messenger."

"And you're absolutely certain this clown is not your cousin?" the trooper asked.

"Absolutely positively," I assured the peace officer.

"I'm high and dry here! The great Bobo. High and dry! Hey, blondie, why'd the blonde leave a coat hanger in the back seat of her car? In case she locks her keys in the car. The great Bobo is high and dry! Why did the blonde drive into the ditch? To turn the blinker off."

I took a couple more steps toward the clown cage, and the crowd parted to provide a direct path from me to the red-and-white bull's-eye fastened to the front of the chain link enclosure. I felt like Moses in that *Ten Commandments* movie, minus the staff. And the beard, of course.

"High and dry and gonna stay that way. Hey there, blondie. Step right up and defend blondes everywhere. Or are you scared?"

This huckster was using all my buzzwords to best advantage.

"Just ignore him, Tressa," Taylor said. "You don't want to make a scene here."

I considered my baby sister's advice—for about a tenth of a millisecond.

"Tressa," Townsend warned. I shoved Nimrod into his arms and advanced on the impertinent clown.

"You have a problem with blondes?" I asked. "Or just this blonde in particular?"

"I'm high and dry! The great Bobo! What's black and fuzzy and hangs from the ceiling? A blonde electrician!"

I'd finally taken all of this clown's particular brand of non-humor I could hack.

"Two cannibals are eating a clown," I yelled. "One turns to the other and says, 'Does this taste funny to you?'"

"Oooh," the crowd emoted.

"Tressa, what are you doing?" Taylor asked.

"Just having a little harmless fun with the clown here," I replied. Before I moved in for the kill, that is.

"How'd the blonde break her leg raking leaves? She fell out of the tree."

"What do you have when there are fifty clowns buried up to their necks in horse manure?" I countered. "Not enough manure!" The crowd cheered, and I kept my pace steady as I walked toward the cage.

"What did the blonde customer say to the buxom waitress after reading her nametag?" The clown stopped, put a hand on his chin, and cocked his head to one side. " 'Debbie,' " he continued in a Valley Girl voice. "'That's cute. Like, what did you name the other one?'"

Judging from the boos and hisses, the crowd was starting to turn my way.

I advanced on the clown cage. "If three clowns jumped from the double Ferris wheel at the same time, who would hit the ground first?" I hollered.

"WHO CARES!!!" the crowd roared. I suddenly understood the rush Leno and Letterman felt nightly.

I was now less than a yard away from the front of the cage.

"Hey, blondie!" Bobo was obviously not done. "Do you know why most blondes don't breastfeed? It hurts too much to boil their nipples."

"That's it! Drown the sucker, blondie!" I heard a woman—obviously also blonde—yell.

I reached in my pocket and pulled out a five-dollar bill, then moved close enough to the chain link to touch it with my nose. I slid my hands up the side of the fence, grabbed hold, and stuck the bill through the wire. "Did you hear about the clown who messed with Calamity Jayne?" I whispered. The clown and I stared at each other.

"They found his legs over there," I continued in a soft, nasty voice, "his arms over there, and his balls . . ." I hesitated. "His balls were found in bucket number three."

I saw Bobo's Adam's apple bob up and down several times in succession. I dropped the five bucks in the cage, raised my hand and punched the bull's-eye with a closed fist. Down went the great Bobo into the murky depths of his watery trough.

The crowd went wild.

I looked on as the clown floundered, seeking his footing and struggling to stand. He finally managed to get to his feet, and something about the way he moved, the shape of his hands, the size of his ears—real, not fake—made the breath hitch in my throat. I found myself blocking out the hurrahs of the crowd and focused, instead, on the saturated soul slipping about in front of me.

When he turned his head, his oversized sunglasses now floating on the top of the water, I found myself looking directly into two sad, wet brown eyes. At least I hoped it was water trickling from the corners. I felt like I'd just been gut-kicked by my Appaloosa quarter.

"Holy shite, Frankie," I whispered. "Is that you?"

The clown turned away from me and fumbled around, resetting his precarious perch above the water.

"Frankie?"

He climbed back on his board, water dripping from his face and streaming from his clothes, and stuck his soaked sunglasses back on his nose.

"We can't talk now," he hissed, covering the microphone fastened to the side of his cage. "You'll blow my cover. If you haven't already." He drew his head back and sneezed.

"Cover? What's going on, Frankie? Why are you dressed up like a carnival clown, and why did you threaten me earlier?"

He sneezed again. "What are you talking about? I haven't seen you since that first night in the trailer. That's why, when I saw you on the midway, I had to get your attention. So, I started telling the blonde jokes. I knew that was sure to get a reaction. I know what's been going on with Dad's businesses," he said. "And don't think I don't know everyone believes I'm responsible. I hear the cops are even looking for me. That's why I'm dressed as a clown. It's the perfect disguise to go deep undercover at a fair. They're always on the lookout for temporary Bobos, so they don't ask a lot of questions. There's a quick turnover in this job. I can already see why."

I raised a brow.

"Swimmer's ear and general crotch discomfort," Frankie explained. I made a face. "But you wouldn't believe all the stuff I've heard. Still, we can't talk here. We've already attracted too much attention. I just hope Taylor and Townsend haven't recognized me."

"Or mentioned it to the trooper on Taylor's right, who's holding an assortment of fair prizes and has been on the lookout for you since yesterday," I agreed.

Frankie's Adam's apple did another up-down number. "Trooper? You're dating the trooper who wants to run me in?"

I shook my head. "We're not dating," I explained. "Just hanging out. Frankie, bud, we've got to talk. Your mom's worried sick, and your dad is more bent out of shape than those balloons clowns twist into animals." I looked at him. "You haven't learned to do that yet, have you?" I asked, thinking balloon animals were the only cool thing about clowns.

"No! And we can't talk now. Meet me at the sky glider. Nine sharp. Come alone. No cops. Now get out of here!" Frankie urged, sounding like an actor in some hokey gangster flick.

"But, Frankie—"

"Now!" my cousin said in a strangled voice. "They're coming this way!"

I turned to look and, sure enough, Townsend, Taylor, and Patrick were making their way in my direction. The former two looked pee-ohed, big time. The latter was merely confused. Why do I have that effect on men so frequently?

"What are we gonna do?" Frankie asked, and sneezed again.

I watched as Townsend elbowed his way through the crowd, Nimrod in his arms.

"Think, think!" Frankie urged.

I looked at Frankie and back at Townsend, who was getting closer and closer. Thinking under pressure was not my strong suit. (All right, all right. Thinking *period*. Geez, you guys are a tough audience.)

"Ah—ah—"

Before Frankie could "choo!" I punched the bull's-eye lever. Townsend stepped up beside me. Over Townsend's shoulder I saw a submerged Frankie, who apparently planned to remain that way until I left or water filled his burning lungs, whichever came first. I grabbed Nimrod from Townsend and clamped a hand around his arm, dragging him away from the dunk tank and over to where Patrick and Taylor were waiting.

I released Townsend and observed three pairs of eyes fixed on me with what-the-hell-just-happened? expressions.

"Uh, gee, sorry about that, guys," I said with a sheepish grin. "Wrong clown."

Bleary-eyed but fortified by a large coffee and an extra-large bag of Dottie's donuts—hey, don't judge me—I headed to Frankie's designated meeting place the next morning, feeling nothing like Woodward or Bernstein.

I was sipping coffee and chewing my tenth donut (though, who's counting?) when I observed a character sliding along the Channel 8 stage off to the left of the Sky Ride. I stared. The guy looked like he'd walked straight off the set of a Roy Rogers rerun. Dressed in a red-and-white-checked Western shirt with an open collar and a red bandanna fastened around his neck, his up-to-his-armpit jeans were stuck into a pair of tall, tan cowboy boots. A white Stetson with a rather large feather trim sat atop dark blue-black hair that fell to his shoulders. The cockeyed cowboy looked first one way, then the other, before darting across the gravel road in my direction.

"Good," he panted. "You came alone. I had to be sure."

I stared. "Frankie?"

He placed his fingers on the brim of his hat. "Ma'am," he said.

"What's with the get-up?" I asked, noticing he'd even taken the time to fashion a braid on either side of his face.

"I can't wear the Bobo face all the time. I'm beginning to break out."

"Don't you know the idea of undercover is to blend in?" I asked. "Not shout, 'Look at me, I'm a freak of nature!'"

He took a look down at his clothing. "What do you mean? This is Western attire. We live in Iowa. You know. Cows. Horses. You wear a cowboy hat all the time."

"When I'm riding a horse," I told him. "As I recall, the last time you were on a horse you got dizzy and had to be helped down by the fire department."

"I had a severe ear infection complicated by inner ear syndrome caused by allergic rhinitis," he said. "Besides, that's the idea. Who's gonna expect to see *me* dressed as a cowboy?"

"Cowboy? You look like one of those guys featured on a how-to-learn-line-dance video," I replied. "For goodness sake, Frankie, at least untuck your pants," I said, bending down to yank his pants out of his boots.

"Call me Garth," he said, and I stopped.

"Huh?"

"Call me Garth. That's my undercover cowboy name."

I finished with "Garth's" boots and started on his waistline. "You're taking this undercover stuff way too seriously, bud," I said, yanking his trousers down to a less nerdy level.

"My pants are dragging the ground now," Frankie complained.

"Exactly," I replied.

"Let's go," he said, and I looked at him.

"Go where?"

"On the Sky Ride, of course. It's the only place we can talk without the possibility of being overheard. Besides, who would be looking for me on a ski lift ride?"

I shook my head. "I dunno, Frankfurter—I mean Garth," I substituted when I saw his peeved look. "Aren't you afraid of heights?"

"I'll be fine as long as it keeps moving," he said. "Now come on. We're burning daylight."

"Okay, but don't say I didn't warn you, Garth," I said. "And make sure if you hurl, you don't hit anyone below. I guarantee you *that* would get someone's attention in a hurry."

Frankie handed the operator fare for two round-trips, and we waited as the ride came in behind us and scooped us off the ground. We appeared to be the only early morning customers. Everyone else was either in bed, eating breakfast and reading the Sunday paper, or attending the nondenominational church service held in the pavilion. Gram enjoyed attending the service every year. I usually accompanied her. Following the service, we were generally first in line for the Methodist Church pancake-and-egg breakfast. Okay, so Gram always got a coughing spell that forced us to leave the service a bit early so we could be first in line for the pancake breakfast. I figured being a senior, she was entitled to a good place in line. And as her devoted granddaughter who accompanied her when I could have slept in, I deserved a perk, too.

"So, did the trooper seem suspicious last night? Did he have questions?" Frankie asked.

"Just about my sanity," I told him. "But I gotta tell you, Frankie, I'm more than a little concerned about *you*. You've gone way off the deep end here," I said, then added, "no pun intended. What do you hope to accomplish by this little game of hide and seek—or maybe I should say 'trick or treat'—you're playing?"

"Do you think this is a game? I'm fighting for my good name! To convince everyone I'm not who they think I am. Seems to me that's something you of all people should understand, Tressa," he said.

I sighed. Hard to argue with that kind of logic. I'd been on a campaign to gain some credibility since I figured out that acting the dumb blonde isn't cute; it's just dumb.

"You're right, Fr—Garth," I said, feeling foolish but willing to play along because of my own history. "And I do understand. I do. Not too long ago I was trying to convince folks I'd found a stiff in my trunk and was met with more than a little skepticism. And I admit I resorted to some rather creative means to accomplish my objective. But I hate seeing what this is doing to your folks, Frankie—uh, Garth. They're really worried. If you're innocent, why not come out of hiding and say so?"

He shook his head, and a braid slapped against his cheek.

"You know why. No one will believe me unless I have hard evidence," he said. "And I'm learning some very interesting stuff. Like, did you know that Luther Daggett has already drawn up plans for the horseshoe-pitching renovations? Word is, they're very pricey. You don't think he'd invest more than the minimum necessary if my dad's name is going to end up on that 'donated by' plaque, do you? He's thinking he's got this competition locked up. You gotta wonder why. And from what I hear, the Lis of Li's Asian Express are out to increase their presence here at the fair, and to get away from their present location near the toilets."

"Are they planning to add lo mein to the menu?" I asked Frankie. He just looked at me. I shrugged and launched into an account of my little misunderstanding with Mr. Li. "He called me a liar—right to my face! Can you believe that? And I was just being polite when I ate those egg rolls," I added. "They were barely edible."

Frankie looked down at his hands and my eyes followed. Poor guy, I thought; he still bit his nails.

"So that leaves us Luther Daggett and Mr. Li as possible suspects," he said.

"Plus every other concessionaire on the fairgrounds," I pointed out. "Your dad has prime spots, which translates to big business. Gotta be any number of folks who'd love to have him sell out to them."

"But who wants the real estate badly enough to go roach collecting?"

"And knows enough to frame you in the process?" I added.

"And how far will they go to get what they want?" Frankie asked.

I shivered. The roaches had been nasty and the meltdown at the mini-freeze a royal pain, but nothing had reached a level of actually being harmful to anything but Uncle Frank's business. Just how far these bad guys would go to achieve their goal was anyone's guess.

"So, what's your plan?" I asked Frankie, still a bit unclear on how he thought he could expose the evildoers while spouting insults from a dunk tank.

"The way I figure it, we have to run surveillance on both ice cream locations. Then we're sure to nab the culprit the next time he strikes."

I did a double take. "Uh, whatdya mean 'we,' paleface?" I asked, using the punchline from an old Lone Ranger joke.

"Well, I can't very well be two places at once," he said. "Can I?"

"Well, no."

"And I can't risk coming forward now, or we may never find out who's behind the treachery. The only way the bad guys can continue to conduct their nefarious business as usual is if I remain missing. That way they can put the blame on me. If I show up, the pranks will stop."

"Isn't that what we want, Frankie?" I asked. "For it to be over?"

He gave a long, loud sigh. "Yeah," he said finally. "And I could end it here and now. I could get off this Sky Ride, walk over to the trooper headquarters, and turn myself in, and the pranks would probably end. And a lot of folks, probably including my own parents, will think I was responsible for the mischief. And there'd be no way for me to prove I wasn't. Ever. I don't know if I could handle that, Tressa," Frankie said. "Having people think I could do something that low to my own family. . . ."

I thought about what Frankie said and realized he was right. I, more than most folks, should understand the dynamics at play that drove Frankie to go underground in a clown costume and garb himself in hot, scratchy Levi's and heavy boots. I'd once tailed a murder suspect to a marina in the dead of night with only an ancient amateur sleuth who harbored delusions of Chan-hood as back-up to rehabilitate my rocky reputation. How, then, could I deny Frankie his opportunity to establish his innocence?

"Okay, Kemosabe," I said. "Count me in."

We approached the departure point for the halfway portion of the Sky Ride.

"We could get off now, if you like," I told him.

He appeared to seriously consider for a moment, then took a shaky breath and flashed our return tickets at the operator.

"We'd better finalize our plans," he said.

"No prying eyes at a hundred feet up, right?" I said, and he drew a finger across a beaded upper lip.

"A hundred feet?" he repeated.

I nodded. "Thereabouts. But you're okay. No inner ear malady to make you dizzy today. Right?"

He nodded but, I noted, scrupulously avoided looking down.

First we agreed on a method of communication, deciding to leave notes for each other under a poster on the large bulletin board in the horse barn. Then we set up our surveillance schedule, with Frankie taking the Emporium and me the mini-freeze. Frankie figured he could sneak in and out the back door of the larger establishment without anyone seeing him, and could bunk down on the floor behind the counter for some shut-eye. He reminded me to make sure I doubly disinfected the floor before I left each night.

I would watch the mini-freeze from two to five A.M. each morning. Since everyone was pretty much in for the night after two and folks were already starting to rouse at five, we figured those would most likely be the times the mischief-makers would strike. I'd catch a few z's after five in the trailer and whenever I had a break throughout the day. Good thing I was the type to sleep pretty much anywhere. (Hey now, don't take that the wrong way there, pilgrims. Bring that mind up outta the gutter, ya hear?)

"So, what exactly am I supposed to do if I catch someone in the act?" I asked, recalling Townsend had inquired the same thing when I'd been in hot pursuit of the clown. Having no plan wasn't as big a deal with hundreds of thousands of fair-goers milling about. But at two A.M., help on the way would come with an indefinite time delay. Like, enough time for the bad guy to hurt me. Bad.

"Well, I don't want you to make a citizen's arrest or anything that foolish," Frankie said. "By the way, you wouldn't do anything that foolish, would you?"

I grabbed Frankie's nose and gave it a twist. "Don't

tell me what you don't want me to do, tell me what you *want* me to do. And remember, there may not be a trooper every hundred feet at that time of the night," I reminded him.

"You'll have your digital camera. It has a setting for night photos, right?"

I nodded.

"Then, snap a couple of pictures and run away. Scream 'Fire!' if you have to. Don't yell 'Help,' people are guaranteed to ignore you. Yell 'Fire.'"

I shook my head. "How sad is that?"

He ignored me. "Remember, you have to be real careful not to be seen while letting yourself back into the mini-freeze," Frankie advised. "Maybe you should wear a disguise, too."

I gave him a you've-got-to-be-kidding look. "I think I'll pass on that, Frankie," I said. "Besides, you've already taken all the fun fair disguises."

He shook his head, unwilling to let me escape his plan. "You'll have to dress as someone who wouldn't seem out of place in that area of the fairgrounds at that time of the morning," he said. "A clown or a cowboy would stick out like a sore thumb."

As if he himself didn't stick out like an extra digit.

"What did you have in mind?" I asked, not certain I wanted to find out.

He hesitated, and I knew it was going to be bad. "You'll have to be a sanitation worker," he said.

"Get outta here," I exclaimed. "A garbage man? No way!"

"A refuse technician," he politically corrected me. "They're the only people free to roam the fairgrounds that late who won't draw undue suspicion. You'll have to be a sanitary worker. Do you have a short-sleeved khaki shirt?" he asked.

I gave him a get-real glance. "After wearing khaki at

Bargain City for two years, I've sworn off khaki," I informed him.

"Well, I'm sure you can scare something up," he said after a moment. "And buy a couple of fair patches and baste them to the sleeves. They won't match, but no one will be able to tell in the dark."

"Baste? Baste? Isn't that something you do to a turkey?" I asked.

"Sew!" Frankie practically shrieked. "Basting is temporary hand-sewing with large stitches," he explained, way too much in the know for my comfort level. "And many machines have a baste stitch on them."

I shook my head. "Frankie, ole man," I said, "we gotta talk."

"Oh, just Super Glue the damned things on," he said, and I took a closer look at him. He looked a bit green around the gills.

"Are you all right, Frankie?" I asked, concerned.

He put a hand to his bandanna, untied it, and began to mop his face.

"Uh, Frankie?"

"I'll be fine," he snapped. "We've only got a few minutes left. Right?"

I nodded. "Sure, we're almost there." Which wasn't entirely correct, since we were only halfway up the hill and looking down on the tops of trees.

"So, Frankie, how'd you come up with all those dumb-blonde jokes on the fly?" I asked, trying to keep his mind off the ground far below for the remaining few minutes of the ride. "You rattled those suckers off faster than I rattle off Gram's and my takeout orders from the China Buffet."

That got his attention. He turned to me. "Oh, yeah? Well, what about your clown jokes?" he asked. "Where'd you dig up all those? I couldn't believe it when you started hurling them back at me. I mean, who'd write such nasty jokes about clowns? Everyone loves clowns. Right?"

Keep telling yourself that, Garth, I thought, deciding that now was not the time to inform Frankie about the wehateclowns.com website I'd discovered.

We'd reached the highest point on the ride back up the hill when all of a sudden the ride stopped. Just stopped. I saw Frankie grab the bar in front of us like I used to hug the dashboard when my Grammy still had her driver's license and insisted on driving me to town.

"Uh, what's going on?" he asked. "Why have we stopped?"

I turned around to check out how many other stranded travelers were behind us when Frankie grabbed my arm.

"Don't move! You're rocking the lift! Stay completely still." Frankie was an uglier green than the froggie toy I'd won the night before, and his eyes were bigger than Nimrod's.

"I just want to take a look and see what's going on," I told him, twisting around to look back, "but I'm sure they'll have us up and running in no time."

The ride bobbed up and down.

"Please! Don't move!" he repeated. "I'm not kidding, Tressa!"

"For heaven's sake, Frankie," I said. "What do you think is gonna happen? We'll dump out onto the concrete below, our heads splitting like the pumpkins I squashed—uh, some pranksters squashed—at Townsend's house a year or so back?"

His face turned from avocado green to apple red. "I'm burning up," he said. "I need air."

"Well, if you weren't wearing that long-sleeved shirt and those hot denim pants, you wouldn't be so uncomfortable," I snapped. "It's already practically ninety in the shade. You know, if our heads did hit that pavement below, our brains would be sizzling in no time."

"You're not helping, Tressa!" Frankie told me, unbuttoning his fancy Western shirt to expose a white undershirt.

"Ye gods, Frankie. No wonder you're broiling! And I bet anything you're wearing hot, sticky briefs rather than cool, airy boxers."

It didn't take a mind reader to come to this conclusion. The fully cooked frankfurter beside me was presently pulling at his crotch and trying hard not to rock the boat—or the lift. Oh, you know.

"Oh, look! There's my grammy and Joe!" I said, spotting the twosome below us. "I bet they're on their way to church." I leaned over the front of the ride's rail. "Hello, Joe! Hey, Gramma! I'm up here! On the Sky Ride!" I waved energetically, and the ski lift shook and bounced. "Yoo-hoo! Gram! Joe! Up here!"

"Stop that bouncing!" Frankie said. "I'm gonna lose my boots."

I looked over at Frankie. "Your boots? Don't you mean your your lunch or breakfast?" I asked.

He shook his head. (Well, it wasn't actually his head he shook, it was more like his pupils.) "The boots are too big. I guess I didn't think about that when I chose the Sky Ride as our meeting place."

"Too big? Where'd you get those boots, anyway?" I asked, knowing that the Little Mermaid would be far more likely to own a pair of cowboy boots than Frankie.

He wiped his face again. "From the horse barn. I borrowed them from a napping cowboy," he said.

"You stole some sleeping cowpoke's boots?" I said. "Are you insane? That's a hangin' offense in these parts, mister." I hoped my clueless cousin didn't run into the bootless cowboy before he returned the footwear.

"I was desperate!" he replied. "I needed a new disguise, and the shirt, pants, and hat were hanging there—"

"You took his clothes, too?" I made a quick sign of the

cross, even though I'm not Catholic. "And his hat? Talk about taking your life in your hands. I just hope you don't meet up with that naked, barefoot cowboy," I said.

Frankie nodded. "Me, too," he agreed. " 'Cause I sure as shoot couldn't outrun him."

I nodded.

"Uh-oh, it's slipping! My boot is slipping!" Frankie suddenly shrieked.

"Scrunch your toes up!" I yelled. "And it's not *your* boot!"

"It's not working! I can't hold it!"

"Grab the top!" I yelled. "Grab the top of your boot with your hands!"

"I can't lean over. I'll get sick."

I winced, thinking that wouldn't be a pretty sight to see from any angle. "Oh, for heaven's sake, I've got it," I said. And I took hold of the top of his left boot.

"That's not the one!" Frankie yelled. "Look out! There it goes!" he screamed, and I stuck my head over the rail to watch one huge brown boot plunge to earth.

"What the hell?" I heard from below us.

I saw Joe motion upward. Gram put up a hand to shade her eyes and followed his gesture.

"Oh, hello, Gram . . . Joe," I called down to the surprised seniors, relieved they had managed to dodge the object from above. "Uh, everybody okay down there?"

"Tressa! Is that you?" my grammy asked. "What on earth are you doing up there? Why are you stopped? And who the devil is that long-haired cowboy next to you?" she asked.

Hunched over the side of the ride, Frankie managed to tip his hat—or the now naked cowboy's hat—to my grandmother. "Garth, ma'am," he yelled down, in a Woody-Allen-goes-country kind of voice. "Garth Wayne."

I shrugged. Every family tree has several interesting members who occasionally swing from the branches and pelt folks below with banana peels or cowboy boots, right? (I said, right? Oh, okay, so our family tree looks like the freakin' indoor exercise facility for orangutans at the metro zoo. Give us credit for diversity.)

"Well, looky here, Frankie," I said, noticing the emergency equipment heading in our direction. "This should bring back memories for you," I told him, recalling his rather celebrated dismount from a horse called Thunder. "I wonder if it's the same fireman."

"I think you're enjoying this," my cousin accused.

"I think you're right on the money there, Garth," I responded.

"It was the frizz joke, wasn't it?"

"Give that cowpoke a big cee-gar," I agreed, leaning back to wait my turn at rescue. With my luck, Frankie's firefighter would look like Orlando Bloom. And mine? I was bettin' mine would look more like Gram's circa 1970s heartthrob, and present-day Branson, Missouri, entertainer, Tony Orlando.

CHAPTER 11

We were ably brought back down to earth by the capable men and women of the Des Moines Fire Department. Turns out they even train for emergencies like this. Frankie's biggest concern was that his wig would fall off and blow his cover. My biggest fear had more to do with becoming a human pancake, an ironic metaphor—or is that simile?—because I had been denied my traditional Methodist Church brunch (and hadn't had a bacon fix in well over a week).

I had the foresight to send my digital camera down with Frankie so he could snap a couple of pictures of my extrication and rescue. What a totally kick-ass addition to my fair feature! But once he slapped the camera in my hand and retrieved the boot that would fit Shaquille O'Neal, he was gone. The last glimpse I caught of him, he was hitching his jeans back up to midchest level. Hello. Hadn't the guy heard of rolling up his pantlegs?

"Where'd your cowboy friend run off to?" Gram asked, once my teeth had stopped chattering and my knees were no longer knocking together. Funny how I'd been a pillar of strength while stranded one hundred feet up in a glorified tin can with a nervous Nellie, but the ladder descent in the strong arms of a veteran fire-fighter had me saying Hail Marys. And I wasn't even Catholic. I guess I figured, knowing my luck, the most likely time for me to go "splat" would be during the rescue attempt.

"He sure didn't look like no cowboy I've ever seen," Gram observed. "The fellow was walking clean out of his boots. And I'm sorry to tell you this, Tressa, but he was pulling at the front of his pants like he had one of them ferrets or some other critter stuck down there. Do you suppose he wasn't wearing underwear?" She added, "Some men don't," giving Joe an assessing look.

"Well, I'm not one of them," the old man said when he caught her gaze. "Been wearing boxers for over thirty years. Briefs don't give you proper ventilation," he explained. "I was having to pour cornstarch in my pants to avoid chafing. Eventually got tired of the billowing white cloud that formed whenever I sat, so I switched." I decided that this was way too much information.

"My Will used to wear briefs," Gram said. "I expect that's why we just had the two children. They say briefs can lower the sperm count. You remember that, Tressa: You want a man who wears boxers. Got it?"

I nodded, feeling a little light-headed from lack of food and so much oxygen.

"Now your Paw Paw Will would wear boxers to bed as night shorts. I hear some girls do that, too. You do that, Joe? Do you wear your boxers as night shorts?" she asked.

"Uh, don't you think that's a bit personal, Gram?" I asked.

She snorted. "Personal? That's not personal. Personal would be telling Joe, here, that I like to sleep nekkid.

That would be personal." My grammy always pronounces *naked* as nekkid. It's so cute.

I saw Joe's eyebrows rise almost to his hairline—or where his hairline would be if he had one. "I wear boxers during warm months, but I need something a bit more substantial during an Iowa winter," he managed to respond. "I usually wear sweatpants during the winter. I can't wear the ones with the elastic 'round the bottom, though. Cuts off my circulation."

Gram nodded. "I have velour sweats I wear during the winter around the house. They keep me nice and toasty."

I felt like I'd been transported to the senior citizen center. There, if you were lucky, the topics of the day were politics, the weather, and court TV shows. If you were unlucky, it was detailed descriptions of specific ailments, doctors' visits (and evaluation of treatments), and Michael Jackson.

"With all this excitement, we missed church," Gram said. "And for sure we missed first place in line at the Methodist Church breakfast."

"There's always Dottie's." Joe gave me a wink.

"I think I need something more traditional," I said, my hankering for bacon and eggs, a fluffy ham and cheese omelet, or a country skillet breakfast jumpstarting my salivatory glands.

"Come to think of it, I could go for one of those omelets stuffed with hash browns, grilled onions, green peppers, and ham and smothered in cheese sauce myself," Joe said, pulling out his cell phone. "I'll just call Rick and ask the boy to drive us to that family restaurant up by the freeway. The one with the big flag."

"I *love* that place," Gram said. "What about you, Tressa?"

My mouth was already watering, but I wasn't sure I wanted to eat across the table from Ranger Rick this morning. I was way too tired and hungry to spar.

"You don't report to the mini-freeze until three today, isn't that right?" Gram asked. "So you should be okay. Go ahead and ring up your grandson, Joe," Gram told him. "We'll make it a foursome."

Joe punched a button and shortly after began to speak into his phone.

"This is not a double date, you understand, Gram," I hissed, as Joe arranged for Townsend to pick us up at the Grand Avenue gate. "I just really want that skillet breakfast." She made no reply.

Half an hour later, Townsend pulled alongside the curb at the main gate in his shiny red four-by-four pickup truck. I always look at shiny red vehicles with a smidgen of envy. Okay, a smidgen the size of a Mack truck. I drive a white Plymouth Reliant that rolled off the assembly line during Ronald Reagan's first term in office. I'm always a tad wistful when I see a nice set of wheels. My vintage transport had served a rather pivotal role in the thriller that had played out earlier in the summer—but that's an entirely different story.

I squeezed into the back of the extended crew cab pickup, moving a stack of Townsend's uniform shirts and trousers to one side. Joe helped Gram in and climbed in after her.

"Gonna be another hot one," Joe said, pulling off his Hawkeye cap and wiping a hand across his forehead. "We need a good storm to break the heat."

"Looks like that's on tap for later in the week," Townsend said. "May get severe."

"I hope we don't get any high winds like we did in 'ninety-three," Gram said, amazing me at how she could remember dates like this and forget to take her daily fiber supplement. "We had to haul our fannies down to the Emporium and hide in the freezer," she said. "That's the year Frank's mini-freeze blew away.

That was sure an exciting time. Oh, and speaking of excitement, did you hear about my granddaughter's thrilling Sky Ride adventure?" she added.

I poked a foot under the seat and jabbed upward. Townsend jerked. "Wrong seat," he growled, his eyes meeting mine in the rearview mirror.

"She got stuck on the Sky Ride, didn't she, Joe?" Gram said. "Joe and I were just walking by and there she was, stranded in midair on a swing, and with a rather, shall we say, questionable character right beside her. Anything could have happened. What was that cowboy's name again?"

I saw Townsend give his attention to the traffic and then back at me in the mirror. "Cowboy?" he asked. "You sure it wasn't a state trooper, Hannah? They wear those big-brimmed hats, too."

"How do you know Gram's not talking about Taylor?" I asked Townsend. "After all, she has more than one granddaughter."

Townsend shook his head. "But only one who would get stranded in a ski-lift ride on a Sunday morning," he said.

"Kindly tell your grandson that I know the difference between a cowboy and a trooper," Gram snapped at Joe. "And what was that cowpoke's name? The one whose boot fell off and nearly maimed you. The one who wore no underpants."

I put my head in my hands. Hash browns or not, no breakfast was worth this.

"Garth," Joe supplied. "Garth Wayne was his name. And a very suspicious character he was, too. Fabio hair down to *here*." He motioned to his shoulder. "A black mustache Groucho Marx wouldn't be caught dead wearing. You know, I wouldn't be surprised if he was in the system," Joe said.

"System?" I asked. "What system?"

"You know. NCIC. CODIS. VICAP. The FBI's MOST WANTED. The sexual offender registry. You could run him, couldn't you, Rick?" Joe leaned forward to look at his grandson. "Run him through the system for hits. It's Garth. G-A-R—"

"I know how to spell it, Pops," he said, "but ideally you need at least a date of birth plus a legitimate reason to run someone. And, sadly, going sky-riding without underwear isn't sufficient grounds." He looked at me again. "Besides, if he's a friend of Tressa here, surely she can vouch for him."

"Today was the first time I've seen this particular cowboy," I said, which was technically true. "We just happened to share a rather harrowing experience a hundred feet off the ground—but we didn't exchange DOBs or phone numbers, if that's what you're asking," I added.

"Well, I'll tell you one thing," Joe said. "If I see him again, I'm gonna recommend a smaller boot size. He could have given me a skull fracture. I could be in a coma right this minute."

I grunted. "You're way too hard-headed to worry about traumatic head injuries, Joe," I told him. "An anvil falling from the Giant Slide wouldn't put a dent in your head."

"Well, if I see that cowboy again, I'm gonna tell him to get a shave, a haircut, and a couple of packages of boxers," Gram added.

I shook my head. "Are we there yet?" I asked Townsend. He smiled, his eyes crinkling in the mirror. My insides immediately turned to melted butter. Damn, the man was all that! And knew it!

We pulled into the busy restaurant, parked, and several minutes later were seated at a corner booth. Gram and Joe strategically arranged themselves on the same side of the booth. Well, actually, Joe shoved me aside and slid in beside my grammy before I had time to react. Or complain. That meant I had to brush thighs with Townsend all through breakfast. And we were both wearing shorts. I wondered inanely if Townsend had on boxers or briefs. Or nothing at all. Down, Tressa. Down, girl.

We'd just been brought our water when Grandma started in.

"Frankie Barlowe is a disgrace to this family," she said.

I looked at her over the top of my menu. "Whose family?" I asked, not going to remind Gram that technically she wasn't related to Frankie. It was convenient having Gram consider Frankie one of her own: It took some of the pressure off me when there was another screw-up to share the spotlight with.

"Our family. If I had ten minutes with that young man, I'd set him straight pronto," my five-foot-five-inch grammy stated. "And he knows it. That's why he won't be seen within a city block of me anytime soon. I can't think what's gotten into that boy. He's causing a lot of friction between his mama and papa." She paused and opened her menu. "I do hope he's all right, though. So I can wring his neck when he finally does show up!"

I had to hide a smile behind my menu on that one. Her answer depended on whether you thought dressing up like a smart-alecky midway clown or a bad impression of Roy Rogers and skulking around the fairgrounds was being "all right." And not ninety minutes earlier, he'd been close enough to get a whiff of Gram's Ben Gay (called Gay Ben by everyone under the age of requiring it) and White Diamonds, an oughta-be-a-law-against-it fragrance combo that could easily knock the boots right off your feet at a hundred paces.

"I'm sure he's fine, Gram," I said, wishing I could put her mind at ease—*all* of their minds at ease—and tell them what Frankie was really up to. How he was trying to protect his family and win their respect at the same time. A been-there-done-that moment of sentimentality struck me and I felt my eyes grow moist.

"You aren't crying, are you, girlie?" Joe asked.

"Of course not," I told him. "It's Townsend's cologne."

A chesty brunette came over to take our orders. Her mouth dropped when she caught a look at the tanned, toned Ranger Rick.

"What are you having, Pops?" Townsend asked his grandfather.

"I'm having the country omelet stuffed with hash brown taters, with a short stack on the side," Joe answered.

I caught myself before I drooled on the table. "Oooh, I could go for one of those," I decided.

"They have a fifty-five-plus menu," Townsend said, "with egg substitutes. Why don't you take a look at that?"

Both Joe and I frowned. "I came to eat, son," Joe said. "And my cholesterol level is twenty points below the at-risk guidelines," he pointed out. "Besides, I have this rapid—"

"I know, I know. Rapid-fire metabolism," Rick responded. He turned to me. "I give up."

"Two country omelets with short stacks," the waitress managed to tear her eyes away from Townsend to write.

"What looks good to you, Gram?" I asked.

"I'm going to have the strawberry Belgian waffles," she said.

I licked my lips. "Oooh, that sounds yummy, too," I said, rethinking my order. "Maybe I'll have that, instead. With bacon on the side."

The waitress gave me a pained look. "You want to change your order?" she asked.

I smiled my best the-customer-is-always-right smile. I know this expression intimately from my own retail work. I'm just usually on the receiving end. It was nice to play the role of always-right customer for once. "If it's not too much trouble," I said.

She crossed out my previous order and looked at Townsend. Out came the white-toothed smile, a not-so-subtle puffing of the chest, and an accompanying see-anything-you-like? look.

"Now, sir, what can I get you?" the amply endowed waitress asked. She gave a whole new meaning to the phrase "short stack."

I looked at her nameplate. Toni, it read, and I caught myself thinking about the blonde joke Frankie had told about the buxom waitress, Debbie. I felt a giggle work its way up and out my throat.

"What's so funny?" Gram asked. "What did I miss? Did I toot or something?"

I shook my head, the desire to laugh almost overpowering. "No, Gram," I managed. "I'm just thinking of a certain waitress joke I recently heard."

"Tressa!" Townsend jabbed me.

I motioned to Toni, determined not to look at her nametag again. "Please, go on," I said.

"I'll have the Heartland Omelet," Townsend said, giving me a sidelong look and another jab to the ribs. He started to hand his menu to Toni. "Fruit, no cakes," he said, but I grabbed the menu out of his hands before Toni could take it.

"What's in a Heartland Omelet exactly?" I asked, trying to find it in the menu.

I'm sure Toni was giving me a disgruntled look, but I couldn't risk looking at her again or, sure as my grammy would pass gas at the table before we were done, I'd be off in a fit of laughter beyond my control.

"Diced ham, bacon, sausage, and sharp American cheese, topped with diced tomatoes and more cheese." The monotone response told me this waitress did not believe this particular customer was *ever* right. "I suppose you want to change your order again?" I heard her ask, still not taking the chance of looking at her.

"I'm sorry," I said, feeling a bit guilty at my inability to make up my mind. But it had been so long since I'd been out to eat where someone waited on me for a change; where I didn't have to wait at a window to pick up my order. I wanted the perfect dining experience— which, of course, required the perfect order. "Uh, no fruit, though. I'd like the cakes. Uh, if you wouldn't mind?"

She gave a loud sigh and reached out a hand to take the menu. The menu flipped open and I caught a look at an item I'd missed.

"Whoa! Just a minute there," I said, turning my head upside down to try to read. "Does that say 'Double-bacon Benedict'?" I asked, craning my head to see if such a magnificent, mouthwatering item actually existed. "Double bacon, as in twice as much?"

"Don't tell me," the waitress said. "Let me guess: You want the double-bacon Benedict now."

I nodded, never so sure of anything else in my life. "Yes. Definitely. Double eggs Benedict is my final selection," I said.

Toni crossed out my order, rolling her big brown eyes in the process. She picked up the remaining menus and turned to go.

"Come to think of it, that double-bacon Benedict thing don't sound half bad," Gram said. "Switch my order to that, too," she said.

I finally braved a peek at Toni. Her eyes were crossed.

She wrote the order down like the zombielike Lurch in *The Addams Family* would—snapping her pencil in the process. In slow motion, she turned to go.

"Oh, and dear, make sure we get the senior discount, won't you?" Gram asked. "I know we don't look like we qualify," she continued, "but we do. Barely," she added.

Toni backed away from the table.

"She seems nice," I remarked.

"And now she's gone," Joe said. "Now let's hear that waitress joke, girlie."

A few seconds later three-fourths of our table were wiping their eyes or blowing their noses. I'll let you guess who the party pooper was. Hmmm. Is that your final answer? Woo-hoo! Ding, ding, ding! We've got a winner!

Townsend and I sat in his pickup truck outside a Des Moines department store waiting for his grandfather and my grandmother. My grammy had convinced Townsend to stop on the way back to the fairgrounds, as she wanted to buy a pair of hot-pink Capri pants to wear with her Passionately Pink nail polish. She had assured us that it would only take a minute, but knowing my grammy's penchant for shopping was second only to her passion for *Judge Judy* and *Entertainment Tonight*, I knew we were in for a long wait.

I sighed from the cramped quarters of the back seat.

"You can move up front, you know," Townsend offered for the third time. I figured it was safer being behind him than beside him. His proximity in the restaurant and the frequent brushing of thighs had actually diverted my attention from my breakfast several times. Usually it takes a natural disaster or a case of the flu to get my focus off a meal. Especially one that includes bacon.

"I'm good," I said again, my fidgets belying my words.

"You're stubborn," Townsend said. "You are, without a doubt, the most stubborn female I have ever met. Or maybe *contrary* is a better word."

"Why? Because I don't want to get out and walk around and climb in the front of the pickup when, at any moment, I'll just have to turn around, get out, and climb into the back again? I think that's called economy of effort," I said. In my case, it was just plain self-interest. With the amount of food I'd consumed, there was a good chance my shorts would split if I tried to bend my body out of the back of the pickup. Besides, I'd spent enough time sucking in my breath whenever Townsend and I accidentally brushed arms or legs.

Townsend turned around and placed a deeply tanned, very toned arm across the length of the seat-back between us and looked at me. "So, you liked the clown's blonde jokes the other night after all?" he asked. "That's a first. You usually want to punch some-one's lights out when they tell 'em around you." He rubbed his chin. "Hmm. I wonder what it was about this clown—the wrong clown, as you called him—that reversed a lifetime of anti-blonde joke activism. And, for the record, I thought you hated clowns," he said.

I avoided eye contact, instead playing with the patch on one of Townsend's uniform shirts. "Hate is a very strong word, Rick. I'd say intensely dislike."

"But this clown was different? More likeable?"

I pulled at a thread on his sleeve. "I suppose you could put it that way. He just didn't annoy me as much as others have in the past. Or maybe I'm just mellowing out a bit. Keeping things light. Upbeat," I finished.

Townsend nodded. "Upbeat," he echoed. "Don't you mean 'beat up'? You looked like you were ready to play a little game of clobber the clown," he said. "Until you dunked him. After that, you just walked off and ignored the guy. Explain that."

"Dunker's remorse?" I replied with a wide-eyed and what I hoped was innocent look on my face.

Townsend blew a long, noisy raspberry. "How the hell gullible do you think I am, Tressa?" he asked, grabbing one of my shoulders and forcing me to look at him. "Tell me. What kind of fool do you think I am?"

I stared at him, not sure what he wanted from me.

"Do you really think I didn't know that Bobo the clown was your cousin Frankie? Geez, give me some credit. Those ears alone gave him away. Not to mention the pimples."

My mouth flew open. "You knew? All along you knew? And you didn't say a word?"

Townsend's lips thinned into a politician's smile— the kind they give when they're shaking your hand with one hand and shaking you down with the other. "How does it feel, Tressa, to have someone deliberately withhold information from you? Someone you really wished would trust you and open up. Tell me, how does it feel? Or do you give a shit at all?"

I waited for inspiration to strike, for my usual ready response to leap forth and be heard. But this time I didn't have a made-for-the-occasion quip or rejoinder. I had nothing. How could I explain that the problem wasn't a lack of feeling on my part but a lack of confidence. In me. In my own appeal. That I was still too uncertain to step forward in faith, but still too optimistic to step back. So I remained frozen in place, safe and secure in Tressa's limboland, my own low-risk version of Neverland, where to dare nothing in the relationship realm was to keep the evil forces of heartbreak at bay.

"So, is this about the clown?" I asked, still not willing to breach a vast chasm hewn by years of deft dueling and feigned animosity. I wasn't yet ready for what I might—or might not—encounter on the other side.

Townsend ran a hand through his hair and cursed, then reached out and touched my cheek. "Someday, Calamity, you'll have to confront your true feelings, get up close and personal with them. I just hope we all have the stamina to hang in there 'til then." He dropped his hand. "Now, tell me what the hell Frankie is up to."

I quickly filled Townsend in on Frankie's theory that Luther Daggett or Mr. Li of Li's Asian Express could be behind the acts targeting Uncle Frank. I also informed Townsend that the cowboy on the Sky Ride had been Frankie in another outrageous outfit, but skipped the part about our planned dual surveillance. I knew Townsend would blow the whistle on us pronto, and I still believed Frankie deserved the chance to clear his name.

I skipped over the details, too, knowing I couldn't discuss it in front of the Mac and Myer for Hire when they returned from their shopping.

"Frankie is bent on staying under wraps until he has the goods on the bad guys," I told Townsend. "And I promised him I wouldn't tell anyone, not even his folks, what he was up to. He thinks if anyone else knows, it will tip off the bad guy and the pranks will stop and he'll never be able to prove it wasn't him. So, you can't tell a soul, Townsend," I stressed. "Not a soul. Please. I promised."

Townsend let out a long, loud breath and shook his head. "Okay. I'll keep this to myself for now," he said.

"Thank you!" I put my arms around his neck and hugged.

Townsend drew back and looked at me. "I hope you're not bettin' on the wrong horse here, Calamity," he said.

I let my arms drop. "What's that supposed to mean?" I asked, the ranger's tone transmitting a signal I didn't think I wanted to pick up on.

"The clown on the trolley. How sure are you that behind the clown paint and large, fake nose that wasn't dear ole cousin Frankie?" he asked. "Just how sure are you?"

I winced. I'd better be pretty darned sure, 'cause I was bettin' the farm that this weenie wouldn't roast.

CHAPTER 12

Gram and Joe finally finished their shopping and found their way back to Townsend's pickup. Joe handed me several large shopping bags and I stuck them on the floor behind the front seat.

"Hope we didn't take too long," Gram said as she slid in beside Townsend. Joe crawled in behind her. "They had a sale, and they had so many colors I couldn't make up my mind. I had to try the ones I picked on. Used to be, I could go into a store, pick my size, and walk out knowing it would fit. Now, the sizes are so screwy, I don't know what size I am from one day to another. Or one store to the next."

I took a peek in Gram's bag to see what she'd ended up with. A kaleidoscope of peach, lavender, and hot pink blinded me. I reached in and pulled out a package of men's boxers. "Who are these for?" I asked.

"Me. I figured I might as well see how they work as pajama bottoms," Gram said. "Seems your sister had a bit of an objection to sharing a bed with me the other night, so I thought these might help matters."

I shoved the shorts back and took a peek in Joe's bag to discover another package of boxers, some breath mints, and the latest *Rush Hour* DVD.

On the way back to the campgrounds, I tuned out the chatter in the front seat—a heated discussion over whether a soap opera character who'd just returned from the dead had undergone collagen injections in her lips, which, Gram swore, looked like those of an Ubangi tribeswoman. I found myself wondering what on earth I'd been thinking when I'd agreed to play detective and keep tabs on the mini-freeze in the dead of night. I suddenly remembered that I hadn't come up with an appropriate shirt to wear. I gave myself a mental head slap. I should have purchased a shirt while Gram was shopping. It sure would have saved me a rather uncomfortable conversation with Townsend.

I shifted position on the narrow seat, and one of Townsend's uniform shirts slid to the floor. I bent over and retrieved it, smoothing the wrinkles out of the fabric. I stroked the light tan-colored material and ran my fingers over the DNR patch on the short sleeve. I stared at the patch, then at the shirt in my hands. I looked over and noted two other shirts wrapped in plastic.

No. I couldn't. I shouldn't. He'd throttle me.

He'd never know, I told myself. I'd slip the shirt back in his granddad's RV and Ranger Rick would never miss it. I slipped the shirt on the bottom of Gram's sack, rearranging her orange flip-flops and matching nail polish neatly on the top and sat back, thinking maybe this security guard detail might work out after all.

Townsend dropped us off at the campground. I mumbled a thank-you to Townsend for the ride (and the use of his shirt) grabbed Gram's bag, and held the door for her as we entered the trailer.

"I'll just go lay your Capris out on the bed so they don't wrinkle more," I said, heading for the bedroom, trying to figure out where I could safely stash Townsend's shirt and retrieve it later without rousing the sleeping occupants of the trailer. I finally decided my bunk was the only place no one would go near, and I folded the uniform shirt up and stuck it down the front of my shorts. I left the bedroom and walked across the tiny living area. Gram sat on the couch and watched.

Dang. How was I going to pull the shirt out of my pants with her sitting there? I walked to the kitchen and got a drink of water. "You might want to check that I laid those Capri pants out all right, Grammy," I called out to her. "You know how you always say I look like an unmade bed. I can't fold. That's why."

"It can wait for a bit. I'm reading *People*. Did you know that Paris Hilton was engaged to a feller named Paris? If he took her last name, they'd both be Paris Hilton. Paris Hilton. Do you suppose that's how they answer the phone in France at the Hilton Hotel? 'Hello, Paris Hilton.' I wonder why they named her Paris. Or him, for that matter. Do you reckon they were conceived during a hot, steamy affair in gay Paree?" she said. " 'Course they coulda been named after the faucets, too, I suppose."

I pounded my head against the tiny built-in microwave. I drank my water, rinsed the cup, stuck it in the drainer and returned to the living area.

"I think I'll take a short nap," I said, looking at the time and figuring I had a good two hours before I had to report to the mini-freeze. "You gonna be around to wake me at two-thirty?" I asked, preparing to pull myself up into the crypt.

"You know, a short catnap doesn't sound too bad," she replied. "I'll use the big bed and set the alarm. You can take the couch." She rose. "You know, dear, you might want to take it easy on the double bacon for a while." She motioned to my bulging abdomen. "You're getting quite a paunch there."

I nodded. "Thanks for the tip, Gram," I said. "I'll watch it."

She moved to the bedroom, and I pulled the now wrinkled uniform shirt from the front of my shorts and secreted it under the pillow in my bunk, staring at a stomach that was still way too Buddhalike for my peace of mind. I rubbed my tummy and belched hollandaise sauce. Grammy was right; I did have a paunch. Instead of sacking out on the sofa, I should be doing sit-ups or going for a jog.

Somehow my feet found their way to the sofa anyway, and my head hit the pillowed arm shortly thereafter.

I stared at the ceiling, detecting the sound of Gram's snores from the bedroom. My eyelids grew heavy. The last thought I had was that someone could make a killing if they'd invent a pill that sucked the body fat from you while you slept. Hey, it could happen. Who'd have thought they'd come up with a pill that causes eight-hour erections?

"Does this make me look fat?"

I wiped the sleep out of my eyes and was sorry I did.

Britney Spears fifty years down a rather long, bumpy road stood over me in peach Capris, matching flip-flops, and long, dangly orange earrings that nearly reached her shoulders.

"What's that?" I asked.

"Do these pants make me look fat?"

I sat up, my girlish dreams shattered. I'd fantasized that the time would come when womankind every-where would never feel the need to let such a query fall from their collective lips ever again. I shook my head. If a woman who'd raised a family, survived menopause, and outlived a husband of forty years still lamented her body shape, all was lost.

"You look wonderful," I told her, thinking she made an adorable, if somewhat pear-shaped, peach. I suspected Joe would think so, too. And there, I knew, lay the root of Gram's sudden anxiety over her appearance.

"What time is it?" I asked, rolling to my feet.

"A quarter 'til three," she answered.

"Gram! I told you to wake me at two-thirty!" I exclaimed, running to the bathroom to check out how bad a case of bed-head (or couch-head) I had. I screamed, yanked the scrunchy from my ponytail, and began salvage operations. I squirted some spray gel on, pulled my hair back so tight I gave myself an instant face-lift, then secured it. Pulling up my T-shirt, I rolled on some deodorant, then slathered cocoa butter lotion on my arms, gave my hair a final squirt to be safe, and headed out. I strapped on my cheapo watch, grabbed my khaki visor, keys, and camera on my way out the door.

"Bye, Grammy!" I called. "Stop by the mini-freeze if you're out and about. You could drop that *People* magazine off if you're done with it, too," I said. Sometimes it gets really boring whipping up ice cream, especially on a Sunday evening.

I checked the time again, and a naughty word escaped me. I caught an episode of *Oprah* some time ago that featured folks giving up their bad habits, so I decided, What the heck, I'm in. The hardest part was picking which of my bad habits I needed to break the most. After I got Popsicle sticks glued to my fingers during craft time at Vacation Bible School last summer and an uh-oh word slipped past my lips in front of the youth pastor, I decided language usage should be at the top of the list. I've been doing a pretty decent job of self-monitoring. I still have slips occasionally, but those are mostly under my breath and those don't count, do they?

Joe Townsend saw the same *Oprah*, and he stopped trimming his toenails in the living room. At least that's what he says. I haven't checked his living room for toenail clippings. And don't ever intend to.

Noting the time again, I jogged the last two-twenty, wondering how much I would have to run to get rid of the double-bacon breakfast I'd consumed earlier. Probably a 25K marathon. In hundred-degree heat. With Joe Townsend strapped on my back.

I was thirty minutes late when I reached the door of the mini-freeze. I opened it and rushed in with a very detailed excuse prepared. I would blame it all on my grammy.

"I am so sorry, Kimmie," I said, grabbing an apron and pulling it over my head and securing it around my waist. "Gram overdid it a little in the bacon department at breakfast, and she went in to lie down, and I really didn't feel comfortable leaving until she was up and I knew she was okay. Man, it's hot out there. Townsend says we've got thunderstorms on the way for later in the week. I bet the midway is already getting a little ripe, don't you?" I stopped and finally looked at Kimmie.

Normally Kimmie is clothed to the nines. She reminds me a lot of Hilary Duff, but Kimmie's hair is darker. Her hair and makeup always look just right, and she has a knack for coordinating clothes. In other words, she has the skill sets I don't. This Kimmie, however, looked like she'd been chopping onions for the burn-your-innards salsa Uncle Frank put up each summer. Tears streamed down her face much like the water had trickled down Bobo's—I mean Frankie's—face after his abrupt introduction to the dunk tank. Kimmie's eyes were redder than I imagined my cheeks were from having hoofed it to the mini-freeze.

"Oh, Kimmie, I'm sorry I was late. Honest, it won't happen again." I patted her arm. "Next time that old lady is on her own," I said. "I swear."

I looked around the tiny stand. "Where's Craig?" I asked. Craig and Kimmie always work together as a team, since Kimmie is relatively new to the ice cream business, only having three years under her belt. Besides, they're new enough in the wedded bliss department that they still enjoy each other's company. "Call of nature?" I asked.

"He's gone!" Kimmie wailed, grabbing a wad of napkins from the dispenser and blowing her nose loudly. "He walked out!"

I looked at her, wondering what it was about the mini-freeze that prompted people to disappear.

"Come again?" I asked.

"We got into a major fight," she announced, wiping her eyes and discarding wet napkins for dry ones. "And he left."

"My brother is a selfish ass," I said, suspecting that what they'd been fighting over was his readiness to become a father. Craig said he wasn't sure. Kimmie assured him he was, even if he didn't know it yet. I'd kept out of the brewing storm so far, but seeing how upset Kimmie was and coming to realize how cool it would be to have a little niece or nephew to totally screw up, I was ready to join her campaign against my own flesh and blood.

Kimmie blew her nose again. "He's not really a selfish ass," she said, not quite able, it appeared, to stop herself from defending him. "He's more an immature ass. A six-foot, adolescent ass."

I shoved her gently onto a stool and took the other one. "So, this is about baby Turner?" I asked, thinking that on any number of levels men can be adolescent, immature asses.

She nodded. "He still says, 'What's the hurry? We're both young. We have plenty of time. Blah, blah, blah, blah.' That's easy for him to say. He's not the one who has to carry and deliver a baby. I'll be twenty-seven years old in September," Kimmie went on. "If I conceive now, I'll be nearly twenty-eight when I give birth. That will make me forty-six when my first child graduates from high school. Forty-six! That's eight years away from AARP and senior discounts!"

"My grammy says that if men could have babies and couples took turns, every couple in the world would have only three children—providing the woman had the first one, that is," I said. "Men are totally clueless when it comes to pregnancy and motherhood." I reckoned I was, too, but decided not to point that fact out to Kimmie.

"I told him he needed to quit spending so much time with his buddies and their toys and games. If it isn't boating, it's snowmobiling. If it isn't fishing, it's hunting. If it isn't football, it's basketball. If it isn't rec sports, it's TV sports. It it isn't pro, it's college. I just want to scream, 'Grow up!'" Kimmie's voice rose, and several folks on the sidewalk outside the stand stopped and looked over at us.

"Excuse me: We're having a conversation here," I said. "Do you mind? Listen, Kimmie, if you'd like, I could have a talk with Craig—you know, try to get him to see your point of view on the matter. I could even bring along some of those 'Your Pregnancy' flyers they have at the doctor's office, with the pictures of babies in various stages of fetal development," I offered.

Kimmie shook her head. "My luck, he'll see them and throw up," she said. "But maybe it would be a good thing to have someone in his own family talk to him."

She stood and patted my shoulder. "Thanks, Tressa," she said, pulling off her apron.

"No problem," I said, thinking I was getting better at this touchy-feely family stuff.

"I'll see if Taylor can talk to him. She's a psych major, so that should help." Kimmie reached down and gave me a quick hug. "Thanks again, T!" she said, and was gone.

I stared after her and shook my head. Taylor?!! What had just happened here?

I shook my head. It was the same old, same old, dumb blonde shuffle, that's what. Two steps forward and three steps back. What the devil did it take to overhaul a reputation, anyway? Mr. freakin' Goodwrench?

I pushed the button on my Bargain City cheapo glow-in-the-dark watch to quiet the alarm and, through eyelids that refused to open beyond a slit, read the time. One forty-five. I sighed and buried my face back in my pillow, wondering what it was about me that made it impossible to verbalize the teensy-tiny, insignificant itty-bitty word *No*. Or why I had such a hard time accepting that little word from others. The alarm sounded again, and I shoved my chirping wrist under the pillow to silence it.

I finally roused myself enough to crawl out of my hole in the wall and stand beside my bunk, my head resting on the bedcovers. When I felt my eyes crossing and my mouth pop open, I shook myself and remembered the mission I was on—to catch the Dairee Freeze saboteur in the act and exonerate my cousin before he permanently joined a freak show. (Mission impossible, you're thinking, right? I see how your minds work.)

I pulled up a pair of blue jeans over my navy blue bikini undies, and grabbed Townsend's uniform shirt from underneath my pillow and put it over the white tank top I'd worn to bed. I slipped my feet into a pair of white New Balance walking shoes with navy blue stripes, grabbed my grammy's pink fanny pack, and stuffed it with keys, camera, and cell phone. (Oh, just so you know, if you plan on telling anyone I wore a hot pink fanny pack, I'll deny it to the death.) I stuck a navy blue Cubbies baseball hat on my head and left the RV, careful not to disturb the occupants of the sofa pullout. It was fortunate my grammy got up so much in the night; everyone in the trailer expected to hear someone awake and about every couple of hours.

The night felt cool after the heat of my bunk. I was glad for the warmth of Townsend's shirt. On impulse, I sniffed the sleeve, half-expecting to detect the smell of Townsend's cologne. Or the scent of Townsend himself, maybe. I thought about Rick, wondering if he was enjoying a good night's rest with his grandpappy, wondering if Joe was wearing his boxers this night, wondering if Townsend slept in the buff like my grammy. I pinched myself, right along the waistline, where your love handles like to hide, and where it hurts really bad when someone pinches you. I did not need to be thinking about Townsend in bed nekkid when I should be thinking of how I was going to pretend to be a sanitation worker sanitizing the same section of fairgrounds for a three-hour period.

I moved past the Emporium, wondering if Frankie was asleep on the floor behind the counter and proclaiming myself all kinds of stupid that I hadn't called dibs on that place first. *I* could be the one sacked out in there, dreaming sweet dreams of Rick Townsend dumping his snake menagerie and promptly professing his undying love. What? For me, of course.

I continued down the hill, my arms swinging at my

side, and decided a fanny pack wasn't all that hideous a fashion accessory after all—if worn between the hours of two A.M. and five A.M. and only on dark, deserted fairgrounds, that is. Or as part of a Halloween costume.

The Grand Concourse was deserted as I approached the mini-freeze. I tried the door and it was secure, so I moseyed around the stand to check the exterior. In stakeout talk, I reckon that would be called doing a sweep of the perimeter. Either way, all appeared copacetic. Figuring I'd have a better chance of getting decent pictures of the perp if I put some distance between me and the staked-out premises, I headed across the wide paved street, foregoing Frankie's trash-collecting suggestion, deciding that a corner of the small stage just outside the main gate to the grandstand would work fine for my purposes. It was doubtful anyone walking down Grand would see me curled up in the dark corner of the stage, and almost impossible for someone coming behind the stage to see me at all. I drew my shirt—Townsend's shirt—around me and hunkered down for a three-hour marathon that was sure to drag on worse than a lousy grandstand opening act.

I should've brought my CD player, I thought, settling down for an uncomfortable and boring hundred and eighty minutes. And why hadn't I thought of snacks? I called myself ten kinds of stupid. I should've brought snacks. Quiet ones, though. Nothing that crunched, crackled, or required slurping of any kind and/or resulted in burps, the need to urinate, or suck on antacids afterward. Since I was already bored, I muddled over possible choices.

Let's see, what snack items didn't make noise or promote some urgent bodily reaction? Donuts, I thought, then discarded the idea. I'd eaten way too many donuts already and, frankly, the thrill was gone, even if consumed at two A.M. and trailing crumbs down Townsend's DNR shirt. Twinkies, I decided, then shook my head. The wrapper was too noisy. A corn dog was quiet, I decided, but, unfortunately, also unavailable at this hour. Ice cream? Too cold. Plus, I'd want a cup of coffee afterwards, and the coffee would make me have to whiz. Yogurt? Too healthy. Pixie Stix, I decided. It had to be Pixie Stix. They were quiet. You just tore off the end of the straw, tilted it upside down over your tongue, and started pouring. Yummy.

I frowned. Ah, that wouldn't work either. I usually choked myself by getting the sugar too far back in my throat. I shook my head and drew Townsend's shirt closer around me. Selecting surveillance fare wasn't as easy as it sounded, and I decided to switch to something a bit less challenging.

I was reciting the alphabet backward in my head for the eighth time when I noticed a shadow move along the corner of the Varied Industries building, which sat roughly fifty feet back behind the rows of concession stands that ran the length of the concourse. I was stuck on *R* anyway, so I sat up and trained my eyes on the spot where I'd observed movement. I carefully removed the digital camera from my grammy's fanny pack (yes, the same fanny pack I'll never admit to wearing) and held my breath, waiting for the soft-serve saboteur to show himself.

I caught a quick peek at a denim-clad leg, and a few seconds later, a full torso and head came into view. My gosh, the Frankfurter had been right: His stakeout plan was working!

This shady character, however, was much shorter than the horn-blowing clown. He wore a dark baseball cap and a black T-shirt. Obviously, the person was trying to blend in—something I had strived a lifetime for but never seriously achieved. The figure moved to the door of the Dairee Freeze, looked around briefly, then grabbed the doorknob. I raised my camera, poised to snap a photojournalistic caught-in-the-act front-page pic. The persistent perp twisted the doorknob, and it squeaked and he stopped and looked around again. I switched on the camera, adjusted for night photography and zoom capabilities, and brought the camera to a ready position.

The doorknob rattled again, but the door didn't open. The perp tried once more, placing a hand, palm down, on the door, quietly rapping against the wood. He then placed an ear against the door, and I picked up a hushed inquiry. What was he doing, chanting "Open sesame" to Uncle Frank's mini-freeze door?

A few more low queries and the figure moved around the corner of the white building and out of my line of sight. I got to my feet, not about to give someone the opportunity to wreak more havoc on my aunt and uncle's livelihood. Plus, I loved working the fair, and if Uncle Frank sold out, where would that leave me? I'd be forever relegated to paying regular price for fair admission plus all that food. Not to mention no sneaking in free to grandstand shows.

The injustice of it all—including the sobering reality of having to pay full price for donuts for the rest of my life—got me revved up quicker than my horse, Black Jack, gets before a barrel race. I sprang out of my crouch like an unleashed tiger—or a Jerry Springer guest confronted by her boyfriend's ho who happens to be a him, and propelled myself off the end like some demented superhero in khaki.

I flew across the concourse, my fun new sneakers proving to be more than adequate for running and worth the investment I'd recently made but couldn't afford. I approached the corner of the Dairee Freeze, slowing up to surprise the mischief-maker with a photo, and then run like hell just like Frankie had advised. A momentary sense of doom settled over me like the hot-pink knit hand-crocheted poncho I'd bought to wear with my hot-pink-and-turquoise cowgirl boots I hoped soon to be able to afford. (Hey, the poncho was marked down 50 percent. That's a deal!)

I crept to the corner of the mini-freeze, my body pressed against the building like you see on cop shows. I eased toward the edge, sidestepping a little at a time. The only thing missing was a service revolver held securely in my shaking hands. Oh, and a badge. And legal authority to be doing what I was doing.

I heard heavy breathing and held my breath. Nothing. I let my breath out, listened for a moment, and heard the breathing again. I sucked in my breath again and waited. Nothing. After I'd held my breath a good half a dozen times, I finally figured out it was me making like Darth Vader with a respiratory infection. I shook my head. Some sleuth.

I straightened my spine, thankful it hadn't deserted me, and jumped out from the corner in a really retarded Kung Phooey move I'd seen Joe Townsend execute with only slightly less panache. I frowned. No one was there. I adjusted my ball cap and wiped my perspiring brow. Okay, so where was the phantom of the fairgrounds anyway?

I took a tentative step forward—and felt a sharp object jab me between the shoulder blades.

"Don't move," a voice commanded. As if I was capable of anything but keeping myself from tinkling down my leg.

"Raise your hands."

I complied, thinking no matter who was behind me, I was screwed. Big time.

"So, what do you have to say for yourself?" the voice at the back of my head asked.

"I'm about to urinate?" I said, wishing I could do the gotta-go-right-now dance but afraid to make any sudden moves that might be misconstrued. Especially with that unidentified object still making a painful indentation in my back.

"About the Dairee Freeze. Why'd you do it?"

I shook my head. "Do what?" I asked.

"Don't play dumb with me." I rolled my eyes. As if I haven't heard that one before. "What's that you've got on you? A weapon?"

I shook my head. "Digital camera, keys, and cell phone," I said. "And I think there might be some Passionate Pink lip color, too, but it's not mine. It's my grandma's. I go more for the natural look, you know, more of a pouty gloss with just a hint of mauve." I have a tendency to chatter when I'm nervous. Remember?

"Turn around slowly."

"I'm not sure I want to," I said, my voice pathetically wimpy even to my own ears.

"I said, turn around!"

I decided I'd better comply, so I whirled around, bringing my camera down to eye level. As I turned, I hit the button on top, flashing a momentary blinding light in my assailant's face. I clicked two more pictures in double action before I lunged for the jean-clad knees opposite me and tackled the as-yet-unidentified individual to the ground. I prayed when I opened my eyes I wouldn't be staring at a badge or down the barrel of a handgun.

"Get off me!" I heard, and the voice sounded vaguely familiar and vaguely feminine. "Get off!"

I opened my eyes and focused on a face that said that if looks could kill, I'd be laid out in Ferguson's Funeral Home with folks filing past saying things like, "I knew all that junk food would catch up to her eventually." Or "She'd just die if she saw how they did her hair." Or "This is the only time I've seen her with her mouth closed." Sniff. Sniff.

"Dixie Daggett," I said, recognizing Luther Daggett's daughter's short, puggish nose and rather liberal eyebrows. I mean eyebrow.

"Tressa Turner," she responded in kind, a definite edge to her voice that, when translated, meant I was not one of her favorite people. "Figures. You mind getting off me now? Those thunder thighs of yours should be registered as deadly weapons," she growled, giving me a shove with her upper body.

I frowned. My God, had those donuts already settled on my thighs? I sat up. "I'll have you know muscle weighs more than fat," I told her. "It's in all the fitness books."

"How much does cellulite weigh, then?" she asked. I winced. Nice one.

"Not more than that unibrow thing you got goin'," I shot back. "What are you doing lurking around outside my Uncle Frank's mini-freeze?" I asked, my eyes narrowing in much the same way, I suspected, that my dad's did in his trademark explain-yourself-young-lady look.

"I might ask you the same question," Dixie replied.

"I'm doing a good deed," I said. "You?"

"Ditto," she said.

"By that, I take it you mean you're doing a good deed for good old dad?" I asked. "As in a he-can't-win-a-bet-against-Uncle-Frank-fair-and-square-so-he-puts-his-daughter-up-to-nuking-the-competition good deed."

"I think you've found one too many dead bodies," Dixie snapped, sitting up and brushing herself off, picking up the long black keychain she'd jabbed me with earlier. "You're inventing cockamamie conspiracies."

"Oh, really? Well those cockamamie cockroaches at the Emporium looked pretty real to me," I said, picking myself up off the ground. "But you wouldn't know anything about that, now would you, Dix?" I asked.

"That's right, I wouldn't," she agreed, getting to her feet. "And you still haven't said what good deed brings you out at this hour of the morning." She blinked. "Is that a hot-pink fanny pack you're wearing?" she added.

I crossed my arms, covering Gram's fanny pack, and decided to throw down the gauntlet. To put my cards on the table. To let it all hang out—in a manner of speaking.

"I'm conducting my own investigation," I told her. "To prove that my cousin Frankie is not to blame for all the incidents that are happening to the Dairee Freeze concessions. Hence, the stakeout. I figured if I could catch the culprit in the act, I could clear Frankie's name." I looked at Dixie. "It appears I was right." Well, actually, Frankie was right, but since I was the one in the line of fire, I felt I deserved the kudos.

I retrieved my camera and punched the review button. "Well, would you look at that! What do we have here? Why, I think I done caught me a Daggett," I said, not really looking at the pictures all that closely. "I expect we'd better mosey on down to the state patrol headquarters and have a little discussion with the brown shirts down there, don't you, Ms. Daggett? I'm sure they would be fascinated to hear you explain what you were doing outside my uncle's concession stand at three-thirty in the morning."

Dixie Daggett shook her head. "Give the 'Nancy Drew Does *Legally Blonde*' act a rest, Turner. You're embarrassing yourself." She frowned again. "And why are you wearing a DNR shirt? Townsend give you the shirt off his back?" she asked with a sneer. "Or did you rip it off?"

"I'm working undercover as a groundsperson," I explained. "And I'm not kidding about Frankie, Dixie," I said. "This is serious. He's taking the heat for someone else's mayhem, and this kind of thing could ruin his life. I'm really worried about him."

Big fat tears welled up in Dixie's eyes, shocking me. Her lower lip quivered. "Me, too!" she whimpered. "Me, too!" I felt like I was witnessing a metamorphosis more startling than that *American Werewolf in London* transformation. Way scarier, too. I looked at her fat little fingers wiping fat little tears from her fat little cheeks, and could only stare.

I'd always thought Dixie Daggett incapable of any deep emotion, our interactions often characterized by sarcasm, rabid animosity, or blatant belligerence. But seeing this soft side exposed was, well, unsettling. And frankly, faintly nauseating.

"Dixie?" I asked, taking a step closer to make sure I wasn't mistaken. Or dreaming. Or hallucinating. "Are you *crying*?"

"Go to hell, Turner!" she said, and then she tore off on a mad dash down the concourse into the darkness.

"Tsk, tsk." I shook my head. "Back to blatant belligerence. And we were making such progress."

"Hold it right there!" a voice shouted.

I turned slowly. Two tall troopers, one old, one younger, had slipped up behind me from the brick restroom down by Li's Asian Express.

"Hello there, officers," I said, bending over and pretending to tidy up the area. Wouldn't you know I'd pick an area as pristine as the White House lawn? I headed for the nearest waste receptacle and tossed in a cigarette butt I'd managed to find, and made a big show of rearranging the garbage can. "Guess that's it," I said. "I've got this piece of ground looking mighty tidy, if I do say so myself. Pity folks have to litter like they do, isn't it, officers? Of course, if they didn't, I'd be out of a job. Right? Well, good night then." I turned to leave.

"Just a second, miss."

I paused. "Is there a problem, officers?"

"Well, miss, if you're planning to try and convince us you're fair maintenance when you just so happen to be wearin' a Department of Natural Resources uniform, then yeah, I think it's safe to assume we've got ourselves a little problem," the older, obviously veteran, trooper said.

I crossed my arms slowly. "What if I tried to convince you I was a DNR officer? Would we have a problem then?" I asked.

"It's against the law to impersonate a certified law enforcement officer, miss," the trooper responded.

I nodded. "Then I'm a refuse technician," I decided. "But I do aspire to greater things."

"You got any ID on you, Ms. Refuse Technician?" the brown shirt with arms as big around as my pre-fair thighs asked me.

I patted my pockets and made a big deal of looking through Gram's fanny pack. "I must've left it back at the campgrounds. By the way, just so you know, this is not my fanny pack," I told the officers. They looked at each other.

"You stole a bright pink fanny pack?" the younger trooper asked.

I shook my head. "It belongs to my grandma. I only borrowed it so I could have my hands free in case I got in trouble."

"You *are* in trouble, miss," the big trooper said. "Let's go." He took my elbow.

"Shouldn't you read me my rights or something?" I asked the burly trooper with, I now noticed, sergeant's stripes. "I was questioned by the police several times back in June during a murder investigation, so I do know something about the law."

Two pairs of trooper eyebrows disappeared underneath the brims of their Smokey Bear hats.

I bit my tongue and winced. Maybe there was an online support group for runaway blabbermouths. I'd check it out first thing in the morning—if I wasn't in the pokey, that is. County lock-up probably didn't come with Internet access.

CHAPTER 13

The cop shop at the fairgrounds, a modest, old brick building located near the main gate, was not a hub of activity on this night. Nor was it the most modern (or cleanest) example of professional law enforcement I'd ever seen. However, the give-me-a-cup-and-I'll-give-you-my-firstborn aroma of freshly brewed coffee that hit me when I entered the establishment negated all criticisms of the stark and outdated decor.

A long counter ran along one end of the room we entered, and behind it were two desks, outfitted with laptops, facing each other. A blond trooper was seated at one, clicking the mouse. Solitaire, I thought. Or maybe Free Cell. His eyes bounced between me and the monitor for a second, then his head snapped up. Apparently I now had his undivided attention. I reckoned that had more to do with the DNR shirt I had on than any allure on my part, given my lack of sleep, no makeup, and with my hair sticking out the back of my ball cap in a tangled mess.

He looked over at the sarge.

"Hey, Pete. What's up? Drunk and disorderly?"

"Drunk and disorderly? Who? Me?" I asked, not pleased to hear possible charges being bandied about.

The sergeant moved around the counter to stand directly across from me. "Naw. Criminal trespass maybe."

"Criminal trespass? Who? Me?" I sounded like those twenty-four-hour cable news networks where they repeat themselves so many times you want to throw a Walter Cronkite book at the TV. That's why I get my news from more efficient outlets. Like my grammy.

"Well, what would you call wandering the fairgrounds at three-thirty in the morning, miss?" Sergeant Sanders asked. (I finally read his nametag) "Wait, don't tell me: You're a refuse technician. You were . . . what, removing refuse from the fairgrounds? While wearing a Department of Natural Resources uniform shirt?"

"I did pick up several pieces of trash," I defended. "People really are so environmentally lazy, aren't they? Like, they can't walk an extra ten feet to the waste receptacle to toss their cotton candy sticks or taffy wrappers. It really is sad." I shook my head forlornly.

"About your ID?" the officer asked, taking a clipboard and sticking an official-looking document underneath the shiny metal clasp. He pulled out a pen.

"Are you really sure we need to go to all this trouble, Sergeant?" I asked, giving the two younger troopers my best come-hither look. I wished I could take my hat off and let a curtain of silky blond hair fall to my shoulders like you see in the movies, but the hair underneath my hat was probably plastered to my scalp like a hair net, and my ponytail would require my dogs' wire brush and a gallon of No More Tangles hair potion to get the knots out.

He nodded. "It's procedure, miss," he answered.

I leaned across the table. "Do you always go by the book, Sergeant?" I asked. "A big, strong officer like you,

you probably have the authority to, shall we say, color outside the lines occasionally," I said.

"I leave that to my three-year-old grandson, miss," he said. "Name?"

I frowned and considered giving my sister Taylor's name, but knew there was definitely a law on the books about providing false information to a police officer. Besides, I was trying to establish a bond of trust with my little sister. Having her name penciled in on an arrest record probably wouldn't do much to promote that.

"My name is Turner. Tressa Jayne Turner," I supplied.

"Well, I'll be damned. It's Calamity!" the trooper on the computer exclaimed. I stared at him.

"You know me?" I asked, thinking he must've heard some of the hoopla that surrounded the criminal investigation back in Knox County several months earlier. I raised my chin. I guess I needed to get used to being a celebrity.

"Sure, I know you. I've heard all about you. You're almost a legend."

I resisted the urge to ask if he wanted my autograph. Okay, so stardom is all very new to me. "I wouldn't actually consider myself the stuff legends are made of, Officer," I said, wishing I'd had the chance to put on some of Gram's Passionate Pink lip color before I met my public.

"Don't kid yourself, Calamity," he said, getting out of his chair and walking to the counter. "You're larger than life here at the fair."

I tensed, recalling Dixie Daggett's thunder thighs comment, and then relaxed when I realized the trooper couldn't see my thighs from behind the counter. "That's very kind of you—"

"Did you really shovel horse shit on the feet of one of our senators?" he asked.

YES! ☐

Sign me up for the **Historical Romance Book Club** and send my TWO FREE BOOKS! If I choose to stay in the club, I will pay only $8.50* each month, a savings of $5.48!

YES! ☐

Sign me up for the **Love Spell Book Club** and send my TWO FREE BOOKS! If I choose to stay in the club, I will pay only $8.50* each month, a savings of $5.48!

NAME: _____

ADDRESS: _____

_____

TELEPHONE: _____

E-MAIL: _____

☐ **I WANT TO PAY BY CREDIT CARD.**

☐ VISA ☐ MasterCard ☐ DISCOVER

ACCOUNT #: _____

EXPIRATION DATE: _____

SIGNATURE: _____

Send this card along with $2.00 shipping & handling for each club you wish to join, to:

Romance Book Clubs
20 Academy Street
Norwalk, CT 06850-4032

Or fax (must include credit card information!) to: 610.995.9274.
You can also sign up online at www.dorchesterpub.com.

*Plus $2.00 for shipping. Offer open to residents of the U.S. and Canada only.
Canadian residents please call 1.800.481.9191 for pricing information.
If under 18, a parent or guardian must sign. Terms, prices and conditions subject to change. Subscription subject
to acceptance. Dorchester Publishing reserves the right to reject any order or cancel any subscription.

JOIN NOW!

I'd gone from superstar to village idiot so quickly I got whiplash.

"How was I to know he was standing in the doorway of Jack's stall?" I asked. "And horses are people, too. They have urgent bodily functions that include the elimination of waste products."

"And there was that hypnotist!" the trooper recalled. "Folks say you were clucking and scratching and pecking up on that stage for all you were worth."

I gave him a sour look. "That was a number of years ago. Besides, I wasn't the only one who was doing goofy things on that stage. He was a hypnotist. That's the idea."

"Yeah, but you were the only one who tried to lay an egg."

I closed my eyes, trying to blot out the horrible memories of an incident that, even though I'd been spared the humiliation at the time, had been recorded on more camcorders than first haircuts. "I was under hypnosis at the time, so clearly I wasn't responsible for my actions," I growled, adding an angry tilt to my chin.

The trooper gave me an intense look. A look of challenge. A gotcha look.

"What about the monkey?" he asked, each word slowly and carefully articulated for full effect.

I gasped. Only one other person knew about that damned monkey.

"Townsend," I managed through gritted teeth. "That no-good, lying blankety-blank-blank-blank!"

Half an hour later, the three officers had verified I was who I said I was by means of my driver's license photo. As if anyone else would pretend to be me—especially with that mugshot. I look like I'm trying to pass a kidney stone. Seriously, it's not a Kodak moment you want to carry with you for six years. In no time the officers knew my life story, had made the connection to the Knox County crime spree earlier in the year, and had exchanged their thoughts on that.

The uber-efficient officers also ran me through the system, all their little crime databases known only by cute little acronyms. Apparently, I checked out okay: "No wants, no warrants." Phew.

"So, you still work your uncle's ice cream concessions each year?" Sgt. Sanders asked.

I nodded. "It's sort of a family tradition," I said. "Well, more like an obligation, really, but I'm cool with it. I love the fair."

"I see from our reports that your uncle has been having some difficulties this year with pranksters causing damage to his establishments," the sergeant went on. "Is that right?"

"Yeah, someone is definitely screwing with Uncle Frank," I agreed. "Or his business. That's for sure."

"I understand that Mr. Barlowe's son, Frank Junior, may know more about the incidents," the sergeant went on, "but he seems to have disappeared without a trace. Am I right about that, too, Miss Turner?" he asked.

I pondered my answer. Frankie didn't know any more about the stunts than I did. At least, that was the position I was taking. And as for disappearing without a trace, well, while that wasn't strictly true; the officer would have no way of knowing I'd had contact with said person. If all was going according to plan, Frankie was dreaming peaceful dreams in air-conditioned comfort in the Emporium.

"I wish I could help you out, Officer," I said, congratulating myself on the slipperiness of my response, "but I can't. I do know my cousin is innocent of all charges," I maintained.

"He hasn't been charged with anything, miss," the sergeant responded.

"I just wanted it a matter of record. You wrote it down there, didn't you? Just write 'Tressa Turner says Frankie Barlowe Junior is innocent of any charges and will be exonerated.' You got that?"

He gave me a tired look. "You ought to be more concerned about what charges we might file on you," he said. He put down his pencil and ran a hand through his short black and white hair. "I have a piece of advice for you, Ms. Turner," he said. "And I hope you take it: Leave the policework to the professionals. Forget your little one-woman stakeouts and delusions of crime fighting. The fairgrounds can be a dangerous place for a woman on her own late at night. Keep that in mind. Patrol officers can't be everywhere."

"That's not what my dad says," I told him. "He says whenever he goes a little bit over the speed limit, one of you guys is right there."

The sergeant smiled. "You must have an interesting family," he said.

I nodded. "You have no idea."

"For curiosity's sake, just what did you hope to accomplish playing private eye out there, Miss Turner?"

"Why, to catch the bad guy in the act, of course! And it worked!" I whipped my camera out of the fanny pack and plunked it on the counter. "Voilà! The unidentified subject—or UNSUB, as you law enforcers like to say—is no longer unidentified!"

The sergeant gave me another tired look.

"I've got pictures!" I told them. "Digitals! Of the person sneaking around my uncle's concession stand in the dead of night with intent to wreak malicious damage on his property and irrevocably harm his business."

All three troopers were now leaning on the counter with various degrees of interest—or lethargy, depending on the peace officer.

"You have pictures," the sergeant echoed.

"Does Donald Trump need a hair makeover?" I asked. Turning the camera on, I pushed the review button with an index finger. "These ought to break your case wide open," I told the skeptical officers. "This is eyewitness stuff. Very compelling. Very indisputable. There!" I showed the first picture to the officers, who were now all behind the counter. "There's your proof!"

"What is that, anyway?" one of the policemen asked. "It looks like an eyebrow."

"Huh?" I turned the camera around and sure enough, I'd only caught the top right corner of Dixie Daggett's forehead and a portion of her thick eyebrow. "Okay, so the first one didn't turn out. I have more," I said, hitting the review button to look at the next.

"What's that? It looks like a belly button."

"What?"

"Yep, someone's navel for sure."

I checked out the picture, cursing under my breath as I caught a glimpse of a not very attractive belly button. How had I totally muffed the pictures?

"Too bad the belly button didn't have a piercing, or we could have used that to get a positive ID match," the blond trooper joked. "Might be kinda fun to have a belly button line-up."

"You'd like that sort of thing, wouldn't you, trooper?" I asked, sensing the direction in which our interaction was heading. "Of course, you'd have to get off your duff and away from your computer solitaire and do a little bit of po-licework."

His smile disappeared quicker than tortilla chips and salsa on a Sunday afternoon during pro-football season.

"I tell you, that is Dixie Daggett's belly button! And this is her eyebrow!" I insisted. "How many girls have eyebrows that look like long, woolly caterpillars?" I asked. "Her father, Luther Daggett, is out to beat my

Uncle Frank's sales this year by hook or by crook, and he's not above using his daughter to do it."

"Or maybe someone just wants us to believe that," the blond trooper suggested. "Someone who wants to shift the focus away from a member of their own family maybe?"

It didn't take Mapquest to figure out where this guy was headed.

"Like I said before, Miss Turner, it's generally best to leave the law enforcement to the pros," the sergeant reminded me.

"Oh, but if I'd done that in Knox County, I wouldn't be here today to meet you fine officers," I said with a touch of sarcasm. Okay, so it was more than a touch. More along the lines of the filled-to-overflowing manure hauler out back of the livestock barns.

"We need to make a few phone calls, Miss Turner," the direct but polite sergeant said. "If you would be so kind as to have a seat over there." He motioned toward a small bench beside a couple of what looked to be . . . porta cells. You know, like porta potties, only for people in temporary custody. Holding cells. That's the term I'm looking for.

"Do I need to make a phone call of my own?" I asked.

"Just have a seat, Miss Turner, and I'll be back with you shortly," Sergeant Sanders said.

I grabbed my camera and stuck it in my fanny pack, then headed in the direction he'd indicated. As I approached the first cell, I noticed the far one was occupied by a hulk of a man. He was standing at the front, his bear-sized paws gripping the chain link. I intended to avert my eyes and walk slowly past the incarcerated giant without drawing undue attention, but I had just walked past the figure in shadow when I heard, "Hey, Barbie doll—what you in for?"

My feet got tangled and I stumbled. I knew that

voice. I'd first heard it back in June when, in the midst of trying to prove myself equal to Xena, the warrior princess, I'd posted bail for the massive biker who looked like The Rock's younger but much larger brother in return for a helpful tip.

I turned. "Manny?"

"Yo, Barbie. Whazz up?"

I moved to the door of the temporary cell, looking at the structure and wondering if it could possibly hold this incredible hulk if he decided to turn big and green.

"What are you doing here, Manny?" I said. "And what have you done with your hair?" The last time I'd seen Manny, he'd been bald as some of my favorite country-western male vocalists under their cowboy hats. Now, he had a short growth of very dark and very attractive hair.

He smiled, and his teeth were really white against the dark interior of the cell and his black biker's shirt and pants. "Contempt of cop," he said, giving a grin as if his words explained everything. "You, Barbie doll?"

I grimaced. "Operating mouth with both feet fully inserted," I answered.

Manny laughed. "Same ole Barbie doll," he said.

"Same old Manny," I replied, and proceeded to hit the high points of the fair fiascos so far. ". . . And a belly button doesn't constitute positive ID, I guess," I summed up. "Although I have heard of certain celebrities who can be identified by certain unusual physical characteristics—"

"Turner!"

I jumped.

"You have a visitor."

"Who is it?" I whispered to Manny, my hands clenched around the wires that separated us.

"Rick the dick," Manny said, not exactly a member of

the Rick Townsend Fan Club. The feeling was, for Townsend, mutual.

I made a my-gooseberry-pie-needs-more-sugar face.

"Does he look angry?" I asked.

Manny shrugged. "Hard to tell."

"Does his face look like he just had multiple Botox injections and they paralyzed him?"

Manny nodded. "Sounds about right."

I let out a long, loud sigh. "I'm in for it now," I said. I turned to face my accuser.

"Uh, by the way, Barbie, if someone should ask, the name's Manny DeMarco," Manny said.

"Huh?"

"DeMarco, not Dishman, Barbie. Got it?"

"Not really," I told him, "but nice meeting you, Mr. DeMarco," I added, for the benefit of the assembled representatives of the law enforcement community. I had to wonder what the devil Manny was up to now.

I hurried over toward Townsend before he spotted Manny.

"I can explain everything, Rick," I said. "Once I get done, everything will make perfect sense," I assured him.

"You're free to go, Miss Turner," the sergeant told me. "Officer Townsend here has decided not to file theft charges."

"Theft! Are you for real?" I asked Townsend. "I intended to return the shirt when I was done with it. I was even planning to have it dry cleaned."

"Let's go, Tressa," Rick said, and he took hold of my hand. "It's late. I'm tired. I'm pissed. Let's just go."

I let him drag me off, taking a second to look back and wave at Manny. He flashed me the peace sign as Townsend pulled me out of the tiny cop shop.

I struggled to keep up with Townsend's long strides. He didn't say a word, but I could tell from the way his heels hit the pavement that everything wasn't kosher. We were approaching the Emporium on the way back to the campgrounds, and he still hadn't uttered a word to me.

"Aren't you going to say anything?" I asked, about as comfortable with the silent treatment as I am wearing bridesmaid's dresses and old lady underwear. "Aren't you going to rip into me? Chew me a new one? Lecture me?"

Rick stopped in midstep, looked at me, put his hands out in front of him, palms open, as if searching for the right words, then dropped them back to his sides and started walking again. I trotted to catch up.

"Okay, okay, so what do you want me to say? That I'm sorry I borrowed your shirt? All right: I'm sorry. Okay? I shouldn't have taken it. I apologize," I huffed.

Townsend stopped again suddenly. "Don't you get it? It's not about the damned shirt, Tressa," he said, running a hand through his hair, leaving it tousled yet sexy. I've often wished I could run my fingers through my hair, but they always get stuck in the tangles. I've lost combs in my hair before and, believe me, it's not a pretty extrication process.

"Well, what *is* it about, then?" I asked, crossing my arms.

"Are you sure you want to know?" he asked.

Did I? The realist in me (yes, there is such a critter) knew that if Rick Townsend and I were ever to have the opportunity to draw closer, I had to figure out how to hog-tie the commitment-phobic part of me that kept pushing him away. The part of me that just wasn't ready to risk a Texas-sized heartbreak. And the horny little devil in me just wanted to jump Townsend's bones and damn the consequences. With so many conflicting feelings and insecurities vying for ultimate survivor status, it was a miracle I could walk and chew gum at the same time. (What's that? I can, too! Except when I wear three-inch stilettos. It takes all my concentration to walk in those. I usually end up swallowing any gum I'm chewing.)

"What do *you* think it's about?" I asked, deciding this was both a fair question and a safe response.

Townsend sighed and rubbed the back of his head. "You wanna know what I think? I think you've created a monster, Dr. Frankenstein. A long time ago, for whatever reason, you decided it was safer to hide under a mop of blond hair and an I'm-clueless-and-proud banner. It worked for you. Or so you think. You made it through on a set of dimples, big blue eyes, and a cocky cowgirl attitude. But now? Now you have so much invested in that persona, you can't give it up. Or won't. Maybe you've nurtured it so long it's become part of you. Maybe it's still a safe place to hide—a nowhere land where little is required and even less dared. But catering to a lackadaisical lifestyle that was low risk when you had a family safety net to catch you, Tressa, is putting you at great risk of harm as an adult. Don't you see that?" He paused to see if I was paying attention. And boy, was I ever!

"Proceed," I said.

"Being reckless and rash and hard-headed and stubborn—hell, Francis the Talking Mule has nothing on you in the stubborn department—can be downright dangerous in a world where some people are motivated by darker passions and emotions," he went on. "And unfortunately, rapists, criminals, and serial killers don't come with 'Hi, I'm Psycho Cy' nametags for easy identification," he finished, pinching the bridge of his nose with a thumb and index finger like I did when I had a sinus headache coming on.

I was thrown off-balance. Wow, this guy couldn't have nailed me better if he'd had a Craftsman heavy-duty deluxe nail gun and twelve-penny stainless-steel nails. It was incredibly insightful, and so unexpected I wanted to yell "Hallelujah, he gets me!" Either that or scream "He sees right through me!" and run as fast as my shoes with the comfy gel insoles would carry me.

"Is there anything you *do* like about me?" I finally asked, looking down at my feet, wondering if he suspected his next words had the power to eviscerate.

Townsend seemed to be having trouble knowing what to say. This is something I can't relate to, as I usually just blurt out what's in my head. No wonder I'm in it up to my rhinestone belt and horseshoe buckle so frequently.

"Too many to name," Townsend said. "That's the problem. The same things I want to strangle you for are many of the same things I like about you." He shook his head. "I sound almost as goofy as you," he said, with a smile that made me forget the insult.

"What kind of things?" I asked, feeling if I didn't ask now I might never know for sure. And I wasn't about to let pass by an opportunity to hear it straight from the horse's mouth.

Townsend hesitated. "This probably isn't a good time—"

I grabbed his hand. "What things?" I urged. Seeing him wince, I retracted my fingernails from his palm.

"Just . . . things," he said. "Like your enthusiasm and energy."

I frowned. He obviously hadn't seen me after a double shift at the Dairee Freeze followed by a regular night shift at Bargain City.

"Go on."

"And your quirky sense of humor. Sometimes I bite the inside of my mouth to keep from laughing. Later, though, when I think about it, the laughs come."

Oh, great, I was a source of amusement. Roseanne Barr without the facelift. Every girl's dream come true.

"Despite a reputation for being dumb, I've always

had a smart mouth," I told him, thinking this conversation was going nowhere fast.

He nodded. "You do have quite a mouth on you, that's for sure," he said, and I sensed a subtle change in his tone. Maybe it was the slight movement of his body in my direction. Or the look in his eyes as they moved over me, coming to rest on my mouth. All I know is that my body heat rose faster than my credit card balance at a buy-one-get-one-half-off shoe sale.

"You know what else I like?" he asked, and I ran my tongue across lips suddenly so dry they made Gram's heels seem smooth as silk. "Your lips," he said. "I like them a lot."

Damn, I knew I should have slapped some of Gram's lip color on.

"What exactly do you like about them?" I asked, always having thought them pretty ordinary. As long as they covered my teeth, didn't have a bunch of creases around them for lipstick to find its way into, and remained free of cold sores, I was happy.

Townsend moved closer, insinuating one long, short-clad leg between my two much shorter ones. I was thankful I'd shaved my legs, thighs included, the day before. Hey, I admit it: Sometimes I only shave so far up when the prospect of anyone seeing me above the knees is remote. Ah, come on, women, get real. You've done it, too, and you know it.

Townsend placed a hand on either side of my face and moved closer. "I like them because they belong to you," he said, hitting the what-every-woman-wants-to-hear ball clean out of the park.

"What?" I said, wondering at the last time I'd had my hearing checked by a certified audiologist.

"Your lips," he said. "They intrigue me. I've watched them enough in the last fifteen years to be somewhat of an authority on them, you know."

"Is that right?" was all I could get out, since I was now very much aware of how closely he was looking at my mouth. I just hoped to heck I didn't have something stuck to a tooth or breath from the leftover garlic bread I'd consumed before I'd crawled into bed.

He nodded. "There's just one thing I haven't had an adequate opportunity to analyze," he said. "One area that needs more research."

"Yes?" I croaked, thinking how really unfair it was to be looking like a skank just when the guy you've had a secret crush on since you were twelve and discovered that *National Geographic* and anatomy books made for very interesting reading, was finally showing an interest in you beyond arm-wrestling and wars of words.

"I need more hands-on experience to make an overall assessment, though," he said, taking his thumb and trailing it ever so gently and slowly across my bottom lip. I shivered despite the warmth of the night.

"Cold?" he asked, and I shook my head, liking the touch of him on my mouth.

"You were saying something about hands-on experience," I reminded him, unable to resist the naughty impulse to flick his thumb with my tongue.

He took a noisy breath. "I think this is going to require something a bit more intensive," he said. "More along the lines of lips-on experience." He put his arms around me and drew me close. I could feel my heart thumping in my chest and wondered if he felt it, too. I knew my eyes reflected my conflicting emotions. Nervous anticipation versus enter-at-your-own-peril warning sirens blared in my head. Should I or shouldn't I? There they were again, the saint and the sinner sitting on my shoulder, one saying, "Don't you dare," the other saying, "I double-dog dare ya."

I was still debating which advice to listen to when Townsend dipped his head and took my lips in a kiss so hot it was guaranteed to have the little devil on my shoulder dancing with glee and the saint cooling off with a tub of Haagen-Daaz and a big spoon.

We kissed and stroked and caressed for a while, enjoying those activities that might fall under the category of foreplay. (Use your imagination here, ladies. I'm blushing just thinking about it. If I actually wrote it down—well, how could I face the congregation at Open Bible next Sunday? Besides, you guys can no doubt spice it up more than I ever could.)

I moaned into Townsend's mouth, figuring my breath must be okay or he wouldn't keep kissing me.

"Do you have a key?" Townsend asked.

"Key?"

"To the emporium." He nodded toward the front door beside us.

"Uh, yeah," I said. "You want ice cream at this hour?" I said, initially wondering how he could think of food at a time like this, then realizing I often thought of food at inopportune moments as well. Like, stopping at a fast-food drive-up while tailing a murder suspect. Or eating tacos on the floor in the back seat of a car while hiding from the cops.

He shook his head. "I want to be alone," he said. "With you."

I wasn't sure I didn't want the same thing, but I did know the Emporium didn't afford the opportunity for privacy that Townsend was looking for. Not with my cousin Frankie sacked out on the floor and waiting to catch him a bad guy. No telling what he would do if we walked in and started making out. Knowing Frankie, I didn't want to find out.

Townsend looked at me. "Is there a problem, Tressa?"

There was. A six-foot-two-inch, gangly, scruffy cowboy/clown problem, but I wasn't sure I wanted to tell Townsend that. Not when we'd just been getting along so well. Besides, I wasn't altogether certain I was ready to be somewhere alone and private with Townsend. Not until he exposed more. As in, *confided* more. Geez, you guys take things so literally.

The truth was, I needed him to share more. More about his true feelings for me. More than "You're more stubborn than Francis the Mule, but I like your lips." Okay, okay, I hear what you're saying: *What is she doing? She's too dumb to live.* Yeah, like I haven't heard that one before either. But, trust me on this. A cowgirl knows when her stallion is ready.

"It's pretty late," I said. "I probably need to get back to the campgrounds."

Townsend squeezed my shoulders and put his forehead next to mine. "Give me strength," he muttered and started to pull away.

Some crazy impulse, or maybe a natural impulse—I'm a healthy woman with urges—made me reach for him and pull his mouth down to mine. I kissed him, pouring all my conflicted feelings for him, all my confusion about myself, all my desires as a woman into that kiss, and just wanted it to go on and on.

The sound of shattering glass ripped through the night. I didn't understand the significance until Townsend had taken back custody of his tongue, yelled at me to stay put (as if!), and run across the street toward the emporium, me on his heels. Before we got there we heard more glass breaking and picked up the pace. Townsend made it around the corner of the brick ice cream establishment just before I did. I stared at the back of Uncle Frank's Emporium. Two windows had been shattered, shards of glass still hanging from the panes.

"Hey, you! Stop!" Townsend yelled. I turned and saw a clown peeking out from behind a kettle-corn stand.

"Frankie!" I yelled, forgetting that Frankie had told

me he'd had to lay off the clown costume for a while due to zits. "Frankie?"

The clown suddenly took off running, and Townsend took off in hot pursuit after him. I quickly unlocked the Emporium and went inside.

"Frankie!" I called. "Frankie?"

I turned on the lights and hurried around the counter. "Frankie?" No sign of Frankie on the floor, or in the Emporium at all.

I grabbed my cell and called the cops, giving them as good a description of the clown as I could, advising them Townsend was in pursuit, and waited for Townsend to return and the cops to show up.

"Dammit, I lost him!" Rick said, rushing back into the Emporium and looking around. "For a big guy in clown gear, he can sure motate. You okay, Tressa?" he asked, no doubt noticing I'd spaced out and was looking at an object sitting on the counter.

I stared at it, trying to figure out how a horn could have ended up inside the emporium. A horn just like the one the psycho clown had blown in my ear at the watermelon stand. A horn that had no reason to be here. No reason at all.

Unless . . .

"Tressa?" Townsend came up behind me and put a hand on my shoulder. "Was that clown Frankie?" he asked.

I laid my cheek against Townsend's hand and, for once—and mark this on your calendars, folks—for once, words escaped me.

CHAPTER 14

"Two men have been very important to you. I see one shrouded in shadow and the other—"

"Cloaked in green neon?" I asked, earning a "Shush" and a poke in the ribs from my gramma and a dirty look from Sonya the Seer, midway psychic extraordinaire.

"I see romance on the high seas in your future," Sonya continued, stroking Gram's liver-spotted hand with fingers that had nails so long they rivaled Freddy Krueger's steel devices of death.

"You plan on buying a Jacuzzi, Gram?" I asked.

"I cannot do the reading in this atmosphere of skepticism," Sonya said, waving a hand about her in frustration. "It's not conducive to the flow of positive energy."

Gram pinched me on the arm. "You hear that? You're disturbing her energy flow. Hush up! I paid good money for this reading."

Every year my grammy dragged me to a new attraction. One year it was the infamous hypnotist encounter. She'd begged me to volunteer to be one of the subjects and, doubter that I am, I thought I could resist the hypnotic suggestion. You know, like some people think they can beat the box when the cops ask them to take a polygraph. Turns out, I was the first one under and the most entertaining chicken of all. Some claim to fame.

This year it was psychic Sonya's turn. I didn't recognize Sonya from past years and wondered if she was a last-minute replacement for Flavia the Fortune-Teller, who'd been our resident reader for several fairs.

"I sense turmoil in your family. A dark cloud of suspicion. Betrayal, perhaps. Does this make sense to you?" pyschic Sonya asked.

I looked at Gram and shook my head.

"Maybe," she said. "Go on."

"I foresee heartbreak and a family torn asunder if change does not occur soon. Only a fresh start can avert the turmoil ahead."

Gram sat up in her chair. "You picking up any names by any chance?" she asked. "Distinguishing features?"

Sonya shook her head. Draped in a loose-fitting, red silk jacket with lots of shiny spangles and beads, her black hair was streaked with gray strands and scraped back tighter than mine was into a tight bun on the top of her head. Long black sticks with fake crystals stuck out of the bun, resembling insect feelers. "It doesn't work that way, my good woman," she said. "I pick up impressions only, feelings that I interpret through my gift."

For a not-so-modest fee, I thought.

"What about this romance thing? When do you see that happening? I'm not getting any younger, so I haven't got much time left." Gram paused. "Or do I?" she asked.

Sonya shook her head. "I don't get into end-of-life issues, but rather dwell on one's quality of life while one yet lives."

"Well, you hit the family turmoil dead-on," Gram said. "This family's got issues right now."

I poked my grammy this time. "You're not supposed to offer information, Gram. The psychic is supposed to enlighten you, not the other way around."

"I was just letting her know she's on the right track. With all the hoopla surrounding Frank's business, his missing son, and certain rumors I continue to pick up, well, 'turmoil' just don't cover it."

"Gram, stop blabbing personal family business!" I scolded, at the same time acknowledging that loose lips were genetic. Although they had skipped a generation in my dad's case; I'd apparently been bequeathed his portion.

"I do feel that there is hope for this family. I feel that the answer lies with a patriarchal personality. If he can embrace change and diversity, all will be well."

Gram turned to me. "See there? She's talking about your Uncle Frank."

"Gram!"

"What else do you see?" Gram asked. "You know, about my love life?"

"I see you going on a trip," Sonya said. "Somewhere very warm and sunny. And I see a large ship and many people who appear . . . larger than life. I hear music and laughter. There's dancing."

"What about sex? You see any sex?" my grammy asked.

"Gram!"

"It's a valid question. What about my granddaughter here? You see any sex in her future? She's in a bit of a slump, but you probably know that already, since you're psychic."

"Gram!" I put my head on the black tablecloth.

"There is an extra charge for an additional reading," Sonya said.

I jumped up. "Well, it's been real," I said. "But we've

got to go. You ready, Gram? You don't want to be late for the husband-calling contest. Plus, I need more pictures for my fair feature," I reminded her.

"I remember the year I took first place in that contest," Gram said. "I coulda won it every year running but decided that was just plain greedy. Besides, once I got my tonsils out, I never could yell quite the same. Here." She handed Sonya money. "Let's hear what you got for Tressa, here."

"Really, I'd rather not—"

"Sit, girl!" Gram pointed to the chair I'd just vacated and I dropped into it and folded my arms.

"This is such a waste."

"I sense hostility," Sonya said.

"Gee, ya think?" I responded. "What else you got in that bag of tricks, Felix?" I asked.

Sonya gave me a tight smile. "Ah, a comic," she remarked. Grabbing my hands firmly in both of hers, she shut her eyes. A frown created furrows in her forehead and crinkles collected at the corners of her eyes. "You have been in great danger," she said, opening her eyes and looking at me. "Death has visited you in the recent past."

I looked over at Gram, whose eyes were big as donut holes. "Anybody who picked up a paper in the last couple months would know that," I pointed out.

"Chaos often walks in your wake," Sonya continued, and now I was the one frowning. "You lead a life that invites mayhem, courts calamity."

I jumped to my feet. "Okay. Who blabbed?" I asked Sonya, figuring someone had divulged my nickname and colorful history to the seer.

"I don't know what you mean," the woman responded.

"You mean to tell me you didn't know about my nickname?" I asked. "You know, Calamity Jayne."

The psychic shook her head. "What does a character from the Old West have to do with you?" she asked, and I gave her credit for a pretty good job of acting.

"This is hooey," I told Gram. "Let's go. I'm thinking a caramel apple right about now sounds good."

"I can't eat a caramel apple with an upper plate. I'd need a knife to slice it," Gram argued.

"A grinder, then. Have you had a grinder yet?" I asked.

"I sense much confusion," Sonya interjected.

"We're always ambivalent when it comes to food," I said, preparing to vamoose.

"I also sense great sexual conflict," she continued, and now I found myself sliding back into my seat. She looked at me. "You have deep feelings for a man, yet you keep a tight rein on them. You wish desperately to let go of those burdensome reins, kick free of the stirrups, and embrace that wild ride—yet you hold back, keep your feelings in check, waiting . . . for something." She paused. "A sign, perhaps. An assurance or possibly reassurance. Your greatest fear will always be not of physical harm but of irreparable emotional harm. But I'm getting a feeling that all is not safe for you even yet. In both realms. All is not as it should be."

I felt a chill and rubbed my arms.

"You never answered my question," Gram said. "Do you see sex in her future?"

Sonya smiled. "The stronger the sexual tension, the more powerful the climax," she said. "At least, that's the way it is in romance novels," she added.

My face grew warm. "Let's go, Gram. It's getting hot in here."

I took my gramma's hand and helped her out of the dark tent. She snorted. "I get a big boat with lots of large, laughing people, and you get steamy sexual tension and promises of powerful climaxes," she grumbled. "I want your fortune," she said, as if we could exchange them like fortune cookies. "Let's trade."

"Deal," I agreed, shaking her hand. Right about now, the idea of boarding a boat and heading out to sea to enjoy music and dancing with a ship full of strangers didn't sound too bad at all.

Anchors away!

It was coming on noon when I dropped Gram off at the Tooterville Trolley for her ride back to the campground and a bit of rest. She'd opted out of the grinder and decided, instead, to have mozzarella sticks and a foot-long with sauerkraut. I joined her, purely because I know she doesn't like to eat alone. She'd handed me a couple of peppermint candies wrapped in plastic just in case my tummy began to hurt later. I was already sucking on the last mint.

I needed to leave a note for Frankie at our predetermined location to let him know that my cover at the mini-freeze had been blown and that we needed to switch surveillance duties. I also wanted to set up a face-to-face meeting with Frankie—not face-to-clown or -cowboy—to get a few things straight between us. Like, why wasn't Frankie at the Emporium last night, as he was scheduled to be? And how had that stupid clown horn come to be in the Emporium?

I headed down the paved street in my Chestnut Dingo Hornback slouch boots, a pair of denim shorts, and a pale blue T-shirt with a gorgeous cowgirl mounted on a perfect Palomino rounding a red, white, and blue barrel with the words, YOU WISH YOU COULD RIDE LIKE A GIRL. I figured I would attract less attention in the horse barn if I looked the part. Besides, I'd really missed my boots.

The minute I walked into the horse barn and smelled the hay, the poop, and general aromas of horse, a wave of horse-sickness swept over me. I missed my babies so much. With everything that had been going on the last couple of months, I'd neglected my animals. I looked forward to spending some quality time with the gang when I got home. Frankly, sometimes people wear me out. I'm sure I wear other folks out, too. Heck, lots of times I wear myself out.

I headed to the bulletin board, checking out the latest postings on horses for sale. I'm always in the market for a new horse. Unfortunately, with my budget and the current price of grain and hay, the only additional horses I can afford either come in boxes for display purposes or have a stick rammed into their necks.

I found the poster Frankie had mentioned and pulled it up. You've got no mail, I thought, and thumbtacked my note requesting the stakeout change underneath. Replacing the poster, I went to a picnic table outside the horse barn near Charley's Coney Shoppe and wondered what I should do with myself until my next shift at the Emporium at three. I decided to mosey over to the outdoor pavilion and watch the 4H-ers compete in the pee-wee division and snap a few pictures. The peewees are so cute. They look like dwarf cowboys and cowgirls. I sat in the stands and remembered bygone days when I'd competed, garnering first-place ribbons and hoorays from my family. Taking my victory trot. Ripping my pants and having Rick Townsend broadcast it from the announcer's table. Ah, childhood.

I felt the bleachers behind me drop and detected a knee in my back.

I scooted as far up as I could, but the knee kept jabbing me. I turned around.

"Do you mind? Your knee is—" I stopped when I saw that the knee in question belonged to one of the Li twins. "Uh, hullo," I said, turning away from Tai and Chai and trying to focus on the peewees about to compete. I moved up one bleacher seat and was not pleased when I felt another sharp jab in my back.

I turned and gave the pair a dark look. "Is there a problem?" I asked.

"Yeah," Tai—or was it Chai?—answered. "You shined our dad on."

I looked at them, not quite sure what they were accusing me of. "What do you mean?" I asked.

"Shining. Led him, spirited him on."

"Huh?" I asked, still not getting a clear picture of what I'd done that was sticking in their craw.

"You told him your uncle was gonna sell out, just so you could get free eggrolls," one of the twins accused. "That's toad, man. Real toad."

I wasn't totally tuned in to "toad," but I got the gist of the rest. "I most certainly did not tell him any such thing," I told them. "Your father misunderstood—"

"That's low, man. Low. To get an old man's dreams up and then shoot him down. And all for crab rangoon and lo mein."

I shook my head. "There was no lo mein. And the crab rangoon never materialized either. And for the last time, I did not tell your dad that Uncle Frank was going to sell. As far as I know he hasn't considered selling, although he always has plenty of offers."

"He's had offers?" Tai/Chai said. "We want first dibs."

I wanted to scream. These guys were as delusional as their pop. "There are no dibs, because there are no offers," I told them.

"You just said that your uncle had plenty of offers," the twins pointed out. "What's he doin'? Holding out for the highest one?"

"Well, naturally when someone sells something they first consider the best offer," I said. "But Uncle Frank has shown no—"

"So he *is* considering offers."

I was ready to get out a pad and pencil and write "Unkey Frank no sella the ice cream concessions," but remembered how that conversation had gone with Mr. Li.

"No!" I said. "No sale!"

Tai and Chai frowned at me fiercely. "We know what this is all about," one of them said. "This is racially motivated. A case of discrimination. You don't want to sell to an ethnic food franchise. You want everything to remain Americanized."

I stared at them. "I love ethnic food. All kinds and colors and textures. I even have my own booth at the China Express back home!"

Tai and Chai put their faces close to mine. "It would be advisable if you would use what influence you have with your uncle to get him to see the benefits of retirement while encouraging small business entrepreneurship among the Asian community," they said. I swallowed, the sound loud even to my ears.

"I'm a big fan of entrepreneurs," I told them. "Especially ethnic entrepreneurs. But I don't see Uncle Frank selling—"

"Your Uncle Frank has had a run of real bad luck lately, hasn't he?" the Li twosome reminded me. Not necessary, of course; I'd had a front-row seat. "It would be too bad if that run continued all through the fair. That could really be a business buster," they said.

"Business buster?"

"Not to mention the possibility of people getting hurt if these little incidents continue to happen."

I tried to swallow again, but was unable to do so due to insufficient spit. "Meaning?"

They shook their heads. "Well, if it gets out to the Asian community that your uncle is opposed to diversity . . ." The twins' shoulders raised in unison. (How do they do that?) "Well, we can't be responsible for what might happen in response to that cultural insensitivity."

"Uh, is that a threat?" I asked, figuring no way were they going to admit it, but I wanted it on record that it had come across that way. " 'Cause I don't think Uncle Frank is the kind to take to threats very well. He was in the service, too, so you better remember that." Actually, Uncle Frank had served his time in the kitchen or mess, or whatever they call it in the military, but these two didn't need to know that.

"I thought he was a cook," one of the twins said, and I nodded.

"Yeah, right. If that's a code word for a very covert operative. He saw some very dangerous duty," I told them. "You know, CIA stuff. Very hush-hush." Okay, so I was winging it here, but I figured if we were going to face the Asian mini-Mafia, I was going to make sure we had a covert operator or merc in our camp. Or at least a couple of pretend ones.

"Right," the two said, getting to their feet together as if someone had said, "Please stand." "Just remember what we said: *Retirement can be a wonderful thing.*"

They jumped down off the bleachers and walked away.

A Navy SEAL could be a wonderful thing, too, I was thinking. Now all I had to do was find one.

CHAPTER 15

It was half past three that afternoon, the glazier had just left the Emporium, and we were clearing up the accompanying mess. We were basically your bummed out bunch. Bummed by the recurring vandalism, by the declining sales figures, and by the obvious tension that existed between Uncle Frank and Aunt Reggie whenever they were in a room together—and we're not talking sexual tension here, psychic Sonya.

Lucy Connor had offered the use of her shop-vac again, and was presently sitting at the counter enjoying a complimentary strawberry sundae and reading the metro paper.

"Anyone want to place a bet on what's gonna happen to Frank's place next?" my gramma asked, refreshed by her catnap and now sharing a table by the jukebox with Joe Townsend. "Something else *is* gonna happen. That psychic lady told us so, didn't she, Tressa?" Gram asked. I acted like there was a really stubborn stain on the counter that needed my total attention. "She foresaw turmoil and a family ripped apart. Isn't that right,

Tressa? Of course, she also saw Tressa maybe having sex, so who knows how good a psychic she is."

"Gram!"

That got Joe Townsend in on the act.

"Who'd she see her having sex with?" he asked. "Was he in uniform? Did he have dark hair and a good job?"

Gram shook her head. "I tried to pin her down, but Sonya said it don't work that way. No names. No descriptions. Nothing. Just impressions."

Joe reached out and took my grandma's hand. "Did she give you the impression she saw any hot sex in *your* future, Hannah?" he asked with a wink.

"I'll never tell," she said.

"Well, I will!" I burst in, coming around the counter faster than I had on Blackjack when we'd competed in the pavilion. "Sonya the Seer saw Gram, here, on a boat with music and dancing and laughter."

"Don't that sound just like *The Love Boat* to you?" Gram said to Joe.

"My Ruthie loved that show. Always wanted me to take her on a cruise. I was makin' plans to go when she fell sick. Sure wish I'd done it earlier." I saw Gram squeeze Joe's hand, and felt my throat thicken.

"I never liked that butterball Captain Stuebing or that goofy first mate," Gram said. "What was his name? Some kind of rodent. Gopher! That was it. But I did like that perky cruise director," Gram added.

"Julie," Joe chimed in. "Her name was Julie."

Gram nodded. "The show went downhill after Julie left. Kinda hard to draw viewers with a fat captain and a dorky first mate."

"I don't know," Joe said. "*Gilligan's Island* did pretty well. Although . . . that Ginger, rrrreeowrrr!" He rolled his tongue and roared like a big jungle cat. "By the way, you get yourself into another jam last night, girl?" he asked me. "Something about staking out the mini-freeze and photographing belly buttons?"

From across the room I felt Uncle Frank snap to attention.

"Pipe down, would you?" I said. "I don't want the world knowing my business."

"You know, if you were gonna do more undercover work, you shoulda called me. I have experience," he complained. "I know how to fade into the background. Disappear."

I took a look at his camouflage shorts and army green T-shirt, and thought he maybe had a point. "I was in enough trouble borrowing your grandson's shirt. If I'd borrowed his grandfather, I'd probably have to disappear myself."

"Like Frankie," Gram said with a frown. I sobered.

"No, not like Frankie. He hasn't disappeared. He's just taking a long break."

"Rick told me what happened with you and that Daggett girl. You know, Hannah, the one with the mustache. Rick says Tressa and she had a set-to last night. I hope you got the upper hand, Blondie. She may look like a man, but you can take her."

I wondered if there was anything Townsend didn't tell his grandfather. Remembering the passionate embraces we'd shared, I hoped to heck the ranger had at least had the decency not to kiss and tell. I felt my ears grow warm.

"We didn't have a fist fight, Joe," I said. "But I do have to admit to being curious as to why Dixie Daggett was at the mini-freeze at that hour of the morning."

"What's that about Dixie Daggett?" I jumped sky-high when Uncle Frank appeared at my right shoulder.

"Tressa, here, caught Dixie Daggett up to no good at the mini-freeze last night. Snapped pictures with the camera she got, too, but only got a belly button," Joe said. "Now, if I'd been there, you can guarantee I'd have gotten more than a belly button."

"I got an eyebrow, too!" I said. "And I still maintain you can make a positive ID from an eyebrow. Especially one that looks like it's never been introduced to a tweezer or wax."

"Dixie Daggett was sneaking around my stand last night?" Uncle Frank asked. "Interesting."

"Not to the police," I said. "They said that didn't prove anything. That my pictures were inconclusive, and since there wasn't any damage—"

"Police? What police?"

"Tressa got picked up for impersonating a DNR officer," Joe supplied. I turned to him.

"Do you mind if I tell the story? After all, you were up dreaming sweet dreams of Jackie Chan at the time."

"Only because you left me out of the loop," Joe snapped.

"Me, too!" Gram chimed in. "Why am I always the last to know?"

I shook my head. "Oh, please. You know who dies in town before the ink is dry on the death certificate."

She smiled. "It's a gift," she said.

"So, tell your story," Uncle Frank instructed, and I gave a somewhat truncated version of events, omitting any reference to an organized stakeout, the cousin who'd put me up to it, and those mushy moments with a certain ranger.

"And you caught her in the act?" he asked.

"Well, I caught her poking around the stand, but she didn't actually do anything," I said. "It was sure suspicious, though."

"Isn't it?" Uncle Frank said. "Highly supicious. And beginning to make a lot of sense."

The bell on the top of the front door tinkled, and we all looked up.

"What the hell are you doing in here, Daggett?" Uncle Frank greeted the newcomer with a snarl.

Once you saw Luther Daggett, you understood where his daughter, Dixie, got her looks. What you noticed first were the two—well, actually one—bushy black eyebrow that stretched across his forehead, and a nose that seemed to have met with blunt-force trauma before it was done growing. I'd seen noses like that before. On bulldogs. He was short and stocky, another trait bequeathed to his unfortunate offspring.

"I heard you had some more trouble here last night. I just wanted to let you know you can forfeit our bet now if you want. You know, save some face when we start tallying sales figures."

Noticing the sudden tic in Uncle Frank's jaw and the bulge in his neck, I took an involuntary step back. Lucy Connor, however, pivoted on her stool and moved to stand by Uncle Frank's left shoulder.

"You'd like that, wouldn't you, Daggett?" Uncle Frank asked. "Then you wouldn't have to come up with any more ways to tank my business. But a man has to be pretty low to recruit his own daughter to break the law just to win a God-damned bet."

Luther Daggett's neck did some bulging of its own. "What the hell are you trying to imply? My daughter has nothing to do with this."

Uncle Frank crossed his arms. "Oh, yeah? Well, then, why was she skulking around the mini-freeze last night after everyone closed up for the night?"

"What are you talking about?" Daggett asked.

"My niece, here, caught her before she could follow through on whatever she had in mind. Didn't you, Tressa?"

Seeing Daggett's bushy brow and dark eyes turn in my direction, I'd just as soon Uncle Frank had left me out of it.

"You saw my daughter last night?" Daggett asked.

"Well, actually, it was this morning," I said.

"And she was at Barlowe's mini-stand?"

I nodded.

"What was she doing?"

I frowned, not sure how to answer because at the time I hadn't been sure what she *was* doing. "Uh, it looked like she was talking to the door," I said, remembering.

"How's that?" Uncle Frank asked.

"She was tapping on the door and seemed to be saying something," I told them. "But I couldn't make it out from where I was."

"Are you sure it was Dixie?" Daggett asked.

"She's got pictures!" Joe piped up. "'Course they aren't very good. And all belly buttons look pretty much the same, don't they?"

"Not really, Joe," Gram said. "Some folks have innies and some have outties."

"Was this an innie or an outtie?"

"I don't know. Tressa, was the belly button an innie or an outtie?" Gram asked.

"I'd be interested in the answer to that, too," Luther Daggett said, his eyebrows lifting in anticipation.

"Oh, for heaven's sake. It was an outtie. Okay?"

"Like this good lady pointed out, lots of folks have outties," Luther Daggett said. "What does that prove?"

"What about the eyebrow?" Uncle Frank asked. "Not just everyone has a Daggett eyebrow. Besides, my niece saw her there."

"And I seem to recall your niece having some credibility problems in the past."

I was now beginning to wish Uncle Frank would punch Luther in the kisser. Or let me do it.

"I think it's your daughter's actions that are at issue here, Daggett, not my niece's," Uncle Frank stated, unfolding his arms.

"And you've got no proof my daughter's done anything. Besides, you think I'm the only one who believes you're an arrogant son of a bitch?" Luther asked. "There must be a list longer than Santa's Christmas one of folks who have had it up to here with the Barlowe family lording it over the rest of us just because they've been here longer than dirt."

Uncle Frank cracked his knuckles, and Lucy put a hand on his shoulder. "Frank," she cautioned.

Just then the door opened and Aunt Reggie walked in. I saw her eyes widen when she saw Luther Daggett and her husband toe-to-toe with Lucy and me flanking them. "What's going on here, Frank?" Aunt Reggie asked.

"It's okay, Reggie," Uncle Frank said. He turned back to Daggett. "I don't know anyone who has any issues with me other than you, Daggett," Frank said.

"What about Li? He says you backed out on an agreement to sell your smaller stand."

Uncle Frank turned to look at me, then back at his not-so-friendly competitor. "Li's loco," he replied. "He's wrapped one too many wontons."

"And what about Frankie?" Daggett asked. "Talk is, the police think he may be responsible for the trouble, but they haven't been able to speak to him." Daggett craned his neck. "Seems he's disappeared. 'Course I knew that couldn't be right. A son wouldn't take a powder and split just when his father needs him the most. Where is the boy, by the way? I'd like to say howdy."

Uncle Frank's face turned redder than the ketchup dispenser on the counter. It crossed my mind to wonder if the first-aid station just up the hill had one of those defibrillators on hand just in case Uncle Frank needed a jump-start.

"My son has nothing to do with the problems I'm having," Uncle Frank said. "And I'd appreciate it if you would leave him out of it."

Luther Daggett took a small step toward Uncle Frank. "Ditto for my daughter, Barlowe," he said, wagging a finger at my uncle. "Ditto for Dixie. And you'd best remember that." Daggett turned on his heel, nodded curtly to Aunt Reggie, opened the door, and left, the little bell above the door bouncing wildly.

"Well, don't that beat all?" Gram said. "He might as well a come out and *accused* Frankie of being the bad guy. I hate it when folks mealy-mouth around an issue. Spit it out, I say, or don't bring it up in the first place. So, whatdya think, Frank? Is Frankie guilty?"

"Frank?" Aunt Reggie said, looking at her husband, and Lucy's hand as it dropped from his shoulder. "What are you thinking? Or are you thinking at all?"

Uncle Frank looked at her. "You want to know what I'm thinking?" he asked. "I'm thinking I need a drink," he said. And ripping the door open, he went through and slammed it shut, exposing the poor little bell above to more abuse.

"You know what I think?" Gram echoed.

"What, Hannah?" my aunt just had to ask.

"I think Frank's gonna get shit-faced."

Aunt Reggie looked as if she wanted to cry. I probably looked like I wanted to snap the old lady's neck. Instead, Aunt Reggie whirled around and escaped to the kitchen. Lucy escaped out the front door.

"Gram!" I scolded, when Aunt Reggie was out of earshot. "Aunt Reggie doesn't need to hear that right now. She needs Uncle Frank to open up to her—not a tall, cold one. She needs some understanding. Some sensitivity."

"She needs to have her head removed from her rear end," Gram argued, "so she sees what's goin' on around her. Speakin' of hind ends, mine's gettin' numb. Come on, Joe. I need to walk a spell."

"Sounds like a plan," Joe agreed, standing and then

helping my gramma to her feet. He looked at me. "Aren't you missing something?" he asked.

I shook my head. "I don't think so."

"Something bright pink that fastens around your waist maybe?" he added.

I could feel my eyes narrow to slits. "That big jerk!" I said.

Joe chuckled. "You include me in your next stakeout and I won't tell a soul," he whispered.

"That's blackmail, Joe!" I accused. "Besides, I'll just deny ever wearing it."

"You gonna deny making out with my grandson?" he asked.

"That pig!" I yelled. "How dare he divulge something personal like that!"

Joe smiled and patted my shoulder. "He didn't. I was just playing a hunch. But now you see why you need my help. My hunches are always dead-on." He placed a piece of paper in my hand and closed my fingers around it. "Here's my cell phone number. I always carry it with me. Even in the john."

I winced.

"Call me," Joe said.

"You comin', Joe?" Gram asked, and Joe put a finger to his lips and gave me a big wink.

"Just our little secret," he said, and opened the door for my grandma. "By the way, Hannah, I do like that hot-pink fanny pack you're wearing. It's very stunning." He gave me a grin as he left.

I watched the door close and listened to the cheerful chime of the tiny bell, thinking that maybe Frankie had the right idea. As a child I'd often wanted to run off and join the rodeo circuit. As things stood now, the circus seemed a more fitting choice.

CHAPTER 16

Aunt Reggie and I did a brisk business Monday afternoon. I had to keep my mouth full of various Emporium offerings so as not to break down and reassure my aunt that her only child had not met with a criminal or tragic end, and decided the next time I saw Frankie I was going to insist on getting his okay to tell his family what he was up to. Well, maybe everyone except my grammy. I've already alerted you to my grandma's inability to keep a secret, haven't I?

I could tell Aunt Reggie was stressed out. Her movements were robotic. Twice she dropped food, and got orders wrong right and left, and my Aunt Reggie rarely gets an order wrong.

"Why don't you take off, Aunt Reg?" I told her at nine-thirty. "I can handle the stragglers." I was also thinking I might stay open just a teensy bit beyond the hour we were supposed to close to give Uncle Frank that little edge over Luther Daggett.

Aunt Reggie looked weary but undecided. "To tell you the truth, Tressa," she said, taking a seat at the counter, "I'm not really looking forward to going back to the trailer all that much. Things have been rather strained between your uncle and I, although you probably didn't need me to tell you that."

I nodded, filling the napkin dispensers while we talked. "Gram says every marriage has its ups and downs," I told her. "I was just thinking about it, but I don't believe I've ever heard you and Uncle Frank have a disagreement before, so I gotta think there's some kind of midlife crisis thing goin' on. And all the crud that's been happening to the business—well, it's no wonder things are a teensy tense right now. I'm sure once the fair is over and we're all back in Grandville, everything will return to normal." Or what counts as normal in our family.

Aunt Reggie forced a smile. "Why is it always the man who is allowed to have the midlife crisis?" she asked. "Why can't, for once, the woman be the one to go out and have the tummy tuck, get the gray covered, get a new wardrobe or hot new sports car?"

"Or a hot new babe," I added before my brain could stop my tongue. I need one of those five-second-delay mechanisms. You know, like they use on live TV programs so they can edit out the naughty words. I could attach it to my mouth so my lips wouldn't move until they'd received the all-clear signal from my brain. "But you don't have to worry about that with Uncle Frank, Aunt Reggie," I told her, trying to backpedal. "You can trust Uncle Frank," I said, thinking there couldn't be all that many women even willing to have a mad fling with him—but deciding it was probably wise not to use the logic to reassure her.

"I used to believe that, Tressa," she said, playing with her wedding band. "But I'm not so sure anymore. I'm not sure of a lot of things." She stood. "If you're sure you can handle the close," she said, "I think I will head for the barn."

I nodded. "I've got it under control."

Business picked up again after she left, folks figuring if they wanted something to eat, they'd better get it or they'd be out of luck. I had a steady stream of customers well past ten-thirty, when I finally prepared to hang the CLOSED sign on the door. I was doing that when someone knocked, and I peeked through the curtains and saw Trooper Dawkins grinning back at me. He wore an off-white cowboy hat that looked like the real thing. I opened the door, and the trooper-turned-wrangler stepped in wearing a pair of cowboy boots that looked pricey, too.

"Well, well, well, to what do I owe this transformation?" I asked.

"It's not really that much of a stretch," Dawkins said, easing onto a bar stool. "My grandparents owned a farm and I spent summers there."

The trooper looked good enough to be the cover model for *Cowboys and the Cowgirls Who Love Them*.

I looked down at my apron. It looked as if a bunch of preschoolers had finger-painted it with various menu items, and I wished I'd thought to take it off before I came out from behind the counter.

"So, what brings you here this evening, Trooper P.D.?" I asked. "Looking for a late-night cool treat?" I asked, thinking he looked pretty sweet as he was in a pair of blue jeans and a Packers T-shirt. (Well, all except for the Green Bay shirt. I'm a die-hard Vikings fan, even if they can never win the big ones.)

"No thanks. I was worried when you didn't show up at Bottoms Up to pay up on our little bet with your sister and her friend."

I slapped a hand to my mouth. "Ohmigosh, I forgot

all about that!" I said, thinking I had been working way too hard if I'd forgotten a date with a handsome keeper of the peace. "Are Taylor and Townsend still there?" I asked.

"They were when I left," Dawkins said, "but Rick was clearly annoyed."

"That's hardly breaking news where the good ranger and I are concerned," I said. "I'll just check everything one last time before we go. You can't be too careful, you know," I said, pulling off my hideous mess of an apron and tossing it in the laundry bag.

"Yeah, I heard about the run-by bricking by the clown," he said. "I wish we'd get to the bottom of this for you and your sister's sake—and your uncle's, too, of course."

I gave the trooper a closer look. Had Taylor made yet another conquest so soon? He must have seen my face and decided an explanation was in order.

"We both got to Bottoms Up early, so we had a chance to talk. She's very concerned about what's happening. And about your cousin, of course."

The bad Tressa got a sick thrill out of knowing Frankie had entrusted me with his secrets rather than my saintly sister. The good Tressa still wanted to give Taylor the benefit of the doubt.

"It's nice to have Taylor involved with family affairs for a change," I told the trooper. "It's so hard to keep close when you see your dentist more frequently than you do your family."

P. D. gave me a long look. "I know how you feel,' he said. "With me it was an overachieving big brother."

"How could that be?" I asked him. "You're a state trooper! That's like up there with God here in Iowa."

He laughed. "My brother was an NFL all-pro line-man. He was injured several seasons back and is now a defensive coach for—"

"Don't tell me; let me guess. The Green Bay Packers! Now I know who I have to thank for the Vikings not making it to the playoffs last year," I added.

P. D. grinned. "Now, be fair. You can't blame my bro's defense if your offensive line tumbled like a stack of dominoes."

"No, but I can blame him for those two blitzes that caused our guy to fumble twice," I said.

"Fair enough," Dawkins acknowledged. "So, are we good to go?" he asked, taking my hand. I suddenly felt like I was cheating on Townsend. It wasn't altogether such a bad feeling. Oh, boy; there goes bad little Tressa again!

I locked up and we hurried down the hill to the hangout. The country-western band wasn't half bad, and my booted toe was already tappin' by the time we got to the door. There was a respectable crowd for a Monday night, and I waved to Rhonda from the doorway.

"Noisy bunch!" Patrick yelled in my ear.

"You call this noisy?" I asked. "You should see the place after the rock-and-roll reunion and the tractor pulls. Wall-to-wall folks trying to reconnect with their youth."

"That's strange; I don't see your sister or Rick," P. D. said.

I looked around and couldn't spot them either. Usually my ranger radar homes right in on Rick Townsend. "Let's ask Ronnie. She can tell us where they are and, if they left, pinpoint the exact time to the second."

We made our way to the bar, where Ronnie was barely keeping up with the draw orders. Like the veteran barmaid she was, she anticipated our orders and handed us each a lite beer as we elbowed our way to the counter.

"Have you seen Tressa's sister around?" Patrick asked. "She was here with Rick Townsend when I left to hunt Tressa down," Patrick told her.

Ronnie looked at me, and I nodded. "They left about five minutes ago," she said, and I flashed an I-told-you-so look at Patrick. "Townsend looked pissed, and your sister was upset."

"Townsend has that effect on women," I replied.

"Taylor looked fine when I left her," Patrick assured me.

"It wasn't Townsend who upset her," Ronnie told us. "It was Dixie Daggett."

I blinked. "Dixie Daggett? Why would anything Dixie Daggett said or did upset Taylor?" Unless she'd been telling Taylor and Townsend what a total headcase I am. And that wouldn't make Taylor upset. Eager to add to her psych file on me, maybe. "Did Dixie leave, too?" I asked.

Rhonda shook her head. "I wish. I was just getting ready to have someone go get her father," she said. "Dixie has had a little too much to drink."

"How can you tell?" I asked.

"She's tried to go up on stage and sing with the band four times already, and we had to haul her down from a table twice," Ronnie explained.

"Dixie Daggett?" I clarified, and put a hand out to about shoulder level. "Short, stocky gal? Black hair and mustache? Personality of a Popsicle stick?"

Ronnie nodded. "That's the one. Uh-oh. I'd better get over there. She's on stage again and has custody of the microphone. She's probably so drunk she thinks she's in a karaoke bar." Ronnie prepared to step out from behind the counter.

"Let's go talk to her," I heard myself say.

Next to me, Dawkins choked on his beer. "Uh, warn me next time before you volunteer to handle a ten-fifty-six on my off-duty time, would you?" Seeing my confused look he explained: "Drunk pedestrian."

I nodded. "Consider yourself warned," I told him.

"Besides, this would be a good time to question her about last night and why she was at the mini-freeze. She's too drunk to lie. Or do you trooper types just write tickets?" I asked, using my baby blue eyes to best advantage.

"You know what, Turner? You've got more balls than the National Football League," he said.

I batted my eyes again. "Why, Trooper Dawkins, I bet you say that to all the girls!" I took his arm. "Come along, cowboy. And don't drag your feet so. I promise this won't hurt a bit."

"But I'm gonna regret it in the morning, aren't I?" he asked Ronnie.

She shrugged and grinned. "Depends on how you feel about free beer for a lifetime," she said. "Well, my lifetime, at least," she amended.

Trooper Dawkins gave us each a you-better-deliver look. "Lead on, Calamity," he said, "but be gentle."

We made our way through the throng of folks visiting, dancing, propositioning, and chug-a-lugging, and stopped about six feet from the stage, where Dixie Daggett was massacring one of my favorite songs. You may know it; it's the one about how the singer shoulda been a cowboy. That tune always gets me thinkin' that in another life I had to be a wrangler or a ramrod. Or the original Calamity Jane. I dunno. I still feel like I was probably some lowly but content old cowpoke singing lullabies to the cattle on a starlit summer night while smoking a cheroot and quietly passing gas brought on by a meal of beans at the chuckwagon. See? I can wax poetic.

"Well, look who we have here!" Dixie said, spotting me. "A star!"

I looked around for the local weather guy or a politician who took a wrong turn, but found everyone else looking at me.

"It's Calamity Jayne, Iowa State Fair's own down-home celebrity! Did ya'll know she sees dead people? How about it, Calamity? Come on up and take a bow. If ya reckon you can get up here without splitting those tight shorts, that is. Isn't she just adorable, folks, with her cute little cowgirl boots and Pippi Longstocking hair?"

I put a hand to my head, felt the frizz, and ripped the cowboy hat from Patrick's head and stuck it on my collection of curls. To my chagrin, it fit.

"Now ain't that a purty picture, ladies and gentlemen?" Dixie went on. "Doesn't she just look like *Shirley Freakin' Temple Does Dallas?* How about it, Calamity? You wanna come on up and give us a little good ship lollipop?" Dixie asked. "Come on, folks, give her a nice round of applause and let's get her up here."

To my amazement some folks in the crowd actually clapped. I looked at Patrick. He held up his hands. "You're on your own, Calamity," he said. "I have an image to uphold that isn't consistent with tap dancing on stage at the Bottoms Up with an inebriated patron and a crusading cowgirl, no matter how cute she is."

The *cute* part didn't escape me and did a lot for my confidence as I made my way to the stage to end Dixie's fledgling career before the crowd started throwing beer nuts. (Real cowboys never throw beer. That's tantamount to sacrilege.)

"Let's go for a walk, Dixie," I urged, putting a hand out to her. "Get some air."

"I don't need no stinkin' air!" she yelled. "I want to perform. To act!"

She was acting, all right. Like an *American Idol* reject gone screwy.

"I don't think your father would approve—"

She started giggling, with a really unattractive snort thrown in. "That's a good one, Calamity. I think you missed your calling. Maybe you should be doing stand-up. Folks, would you believe this girl is the only person who has been hit by not one, but two, cow chips during the chip-throwing contest? In the same year!" The crowd started to warm up to Dixie. "And didja know she is permanently banned from her local car wash for leaving horse shit in the wash bay? Or that she was goin' at it hot and heavy with a certain member of the law enforcement community last night? Didn't think anyone saw, huh, did you, Calamity?" she said when she saw my face, which I imagine was about the color of Gram's fanny pack. I looked back to see how Patrick was taking the news. He looked like he'd just swallowed a handful of red hot chili peppers with a tequila chaser.

"That's it," I said. "She's fixin' to be an angel." I stepped onto the stage to the hoots and hollers of the crowd. I reached out to take the microphone away.

"Let's call it a night, okay, Dix?" I asked.

"Call it a night? The night is young! I thought you were gonna perform for us. If you won't, I will." She grabbed the mike back from me. "'On the good ship lollipop,'" she started, and the crowd began to get antsy.

"Throw the oinker off the stage!" someone yelled.

"Get the hook!" another one called.

No, neither person was yours truly, although I did have a few choice words to share with little Miss Dixie when she was sober enough to understand them—and when I wasn't pee-ohed enough to want to kick her chunky you-know-what into the next county.

"I said, show's over, Dixie." I yanked the microphone out of her hand and placed it back on the stand. "You've made a fool of me enough for one day," I told her. "And I don't like it one damn bit, 'cause that's usually my job."

She looked at me and squinted. "You're not as dumb as everyone makes you out to be," she said. "Are you?"

I shook my head. "You're not as mean and ornery as you make yourself out to be, are you?" I replied.

"The hell I'm not."

I took hold of her arm and helped her off the stage. She suddenly put a hand to her mouth.

"I'm gonna be sick!" she warned.

"Oh, no, you're not," I said. "Not on my Dingo Horn-back slouch boots that took me six months to save for." I grabbed her waist and gave a hard pinch, and she squealed. Pain usually takes a person's mind off their pukeyness. At least temporarily. "I'd really have to kick your ass if you did that," I told her.

"You could try," she said.

I smiled. "Do or do not," I told her. "There is no try."

She smiled a goofy smile. "I really am gonna be sick, you know."

Patrick and I carried her out of the bar.

"Boy, you cowgirls sure do know how to show a guy a good time, Tressa," Patrick said, as we stood watching Dixie retch in a nearby trash receptacle. I was just glad I didn't have sanitation duty that night.

"Stick around, buckaroo," I said, removing his hat and placing it back on his head. "You ain't seen nothin' yet."

"You all right, miss?" P. D. eased back into his peace-officer persona like a great character actor takes on his next role. "You need to sit for a second?" he asked Dixie.

She wiped her mouth and nodded, and we helped her over to a nearby bench. Dixie jumped back as if she'd hit an electric fence.

"I can't sit there," she said, staring at the bench like it was fixin' to take a bite out of her.

"Why not?" I asked.

She pointed to the bronze plate screwed to the back of the seat. It read DONATED BY FRANK AND REGINA BAR-LOWE & FAMILY.

"It would be disloyal," she said.

"Sitting on a bench is disloyal?" P. D. asked.

She nodded. "To the family. Do you know how many benches I have to walk by before I find one I can sit on? And the butterfly garden? I've never seen it. I have to cross to the other side of the street when I pass."

"Isn't that a bit anal?" I asked, wishing I had Taylor's handle on the psychological stuff.

"That's easy to say when you're always a winner," she said. "You don't know what it's like to be a loser all your life."

I looked at her then. Who the heck did she think she was talking to? I'd been handed a raw deal so many times, it was a wonder I didn't have E. coli.

"I've got a pretty good idea," I said. "Rather than waving at me, folks in my hometown flash the big *L* sign. Either that or they point to their heads and make little circles with their index fingers."

"At least they acknowledge you," Dixie replied. "Try being invisible."

"I tried that last night. We both know how that worked out," I told her. "Speaking of last night, what were you doing at the mini-freeze?" I asked, hoping she was still drunk enough to admit what she'd been up to.

"I'm feeling woozy again," she said, and I looked at Patrick, who shook his head.

"Let's get you to bed," he said, and I glared at him.

"Did you go to the mini-freeze last night to cause an-other snafu for Uncle Frank, Dixie?" I pressed. "Have you been helping your father behind the scenes? Do you know a clown named Bobo?"

Patrick shook his head at me again. "These questions

can wait for another time," he said. "I think Dixie needs to get tucked in for the night."

I rolled my eyes. Just my luck: a compassionate cop. Where was a do-you-feel-lucky-punk type when I needed him?

"All right, all right," I said. "I'll see Dixie gets home," I told Patrick. "Her folks have an RV down the road a piece from us, so I'll drop her off on the way."

Patrick gave me a doubtful look and then nodded. "Behave yourself," he warned, and I snapped to attention.

"Yessir!"

He smiled and shook his head. "Catch you later," he said.

I nodded. "Roger that!" I told him.

"Come on, Dix, let's call it a day," I said, pulling her along behind me. "If you need to stop and hurl, give me adequate warning, would ya?" I told her. She mumbled something that I took as agreement, but I decided to change positions and walk behind her just in case.

Three-quarters of the way to her folks' campsite, Dixie became more talkative. I figured the alcohol in her system was still working on those inhibitions.

"I wish I could wear cute boots," Dixie said, "but my legs are so short, I'd look like a potted plant. I'm built like my dad's side of the family. I look at my grandma and shudder, thinking: Is that what I'm gonna be like in fifty years?"

I looked at her. Holy moley, another looking-glass moment. I'd often wondered—okay, worried—whether my own grammy embodied the vision of the Tressa to come.

"You know, I'm not exactly turned on by the ice cream business either," Dixie said. "Let's face it, dispensing fattening food all day is far from glamorous. And how do you think I got this weight? Boredom," she told me. "Sheer boredom."

"Why do you do it, then?" I asked her.

She shrugged. " 'Cause it's safe, I guess," she explained, and I again felt the connection I'd experienced earlier, surprised by how many people there were out there living their lives in such a way that they didn't make any ripples in the depths around them. Some because they didn't want to disturb the still waters of others' lives, and others so they could drift along unnoticed and just get by.

My life made the wave pool at Waterworld look like a home whirlpool. I now realized I kept the waters churning because I'd craved attention but didn't feel I could earn it the conventional way. Not when I had an honors grad setting the standard ahead of me and a beautiful genius bringing up the rear.

We'd just rounded another bend when Dixie suddenly stopped and I ran into the back of her.

"Is that a clown?" Dixie asked, pointing to a figure standing smack-dab in the middle of the gravel road ahead. "Or am I still drunk?"

"Yes to both questions," I told her, stepping around to get a better look at the clown.

"That looks like Booboo," Dixie said. "What's Booboo doing in the campgrounds?" she wanted to know.

I was curious about that myself. "That's Bobo," I said. "Stay here." I walked toward the clown, not about to let the slippery varmint get away this time. He advanced on me. I felt like Gary Cooper in *High Noon*—well, except there wasn't a clown in the movie showdown and Coop was pretty much on his own. I did have a tipsy back-up who, from a distance, could pass for a short man. Okay, so Dixie could pass for a man at closer range, too. She had.

We stopped about ten feet apart, and the phrase, "This fair ain't big enough for the both of us, Bobo" played in my head. I'd always wanted an opportunity to say something so classically, heroically cowboy as that.

"Bobo," I said, flexing my fingers at waist level, as if I really did have a six-gun on my hip and wasn't afraid to use it.

"Calamity," the clown responded, with a similar stance and terse nod. Of course, with his clownish shoes and pants and made-up face, any dramatic effect was lost.

"You got business with me today, Bobo?" I asked, thinking we probably looked more like a Mel Brooks parody of *High Noon*.

"Who's that with you?" the clown asked, his voice low and hoarse.

"A hapless drunk," I answered.

"Yoohoo! Booboo!" Apparently, after emptying her stomach's contents, Dixie was feelin' good again. I heard gravel fly up behind me but didn't take my eyes off the clown for a minute. "What are you doing here? Shouldn't you be resting up for your next round of dunking?" Dixie asked.

Sensing that Dixie had distracted the clown character, I decided that the moment had come to act. I lowered my shoulder like Dawkins's ex-lineman brother would and hurled myself at the clown, coming in low like he was a football dummy, "taking him completely out of the play" like the football broadcasters like to say. Once he was good and down, I piled all one hundred and blankety-blank pounds, including thighs strengthened by years on the back of a horse, on the stunned carnival comedian.

"Okay, buster, the jig is up," I said, managing to keep the struggling jester in check.

"Ouch, let go of me! What are you doing!"

"Frankie?"

"Frankie!"

Dixie's shocked gasp got my attention.

I eased up on the prone prankster.

"Frankie, is that you?" Dixie asked.

"Dixie?"

I looked from Dixie's stunned face to the clown's ridiculous one.

"Frankie!"

I was shoved aside and fell to the graveled road like a discarded pizza crust. You know, the crust that isn't stuffed with cheese.

"Oh, my God, Frankie, I was so worried!" Dixie tilted her head to one side. "What on earth are you doing dressed up like a clown? And why hasn't anyone seen hide nor hair of you? Oh, Frankie!"

I looked on, dazed, as Dixie the drunk embraced Frankie the fool. I was even more amazed when the clown hugged the ten-fifty-six back. (That's cop code for an intoxicated person, remember? See, I learned something and applied it! Aren't you proud?)

I got to my feet, brushing the dirt from my rear and extracting bits of gravel from my thighs. I looked down on the kissing couple, who appeared totally oblivious to my presence. Lacking a garden hose and the requisite cold water, I kicked some gravel in the duo's direction to get their attention.

"Frankie? Dixie?" I said. "You two like each other?" I asked, thinking under the circumstances, and considering they were rolling around together in the middle of the road, it was about the dumbest thing I could have said.

"Worse," Frankie said, his hands on Dixie's shoulders. "We're in love."

I stared at the odd couple. Luther Daggett's daughter and Frank Barlowe's son? And they both hated the ice cream business. These two had about as much of a chance surviving their courtship as a snapping turtle has of crossing the lanes on the mile-long bridge back home.

In other words, we were looking at some imminent road kill.

CHAPTER 17

"Tressa! Hello!" My best friend, Kari Carter, waved to me as she marched up the gravel road that ran through the campground. "Yoohoo!"

I waved back from the picnic table where I was sipping French vanilla cappuccino (instant, but not bad at all) with Gram and Aunt Reggie, and trying to keep my eyes open while trying to put all the various pieces of the great fair puzzle together.

Frankie and Dixie. Dixie and Frankie. No matter how I considered it or how many times I said it, the idea still seemed like one of those jokes that leaves you shaking your head going, "I just don't get it." (Yeah, I know. I *do* say that a lot.)

I was still confused over what role, if any, Dixie had played in the campaign to force Uncle Frank out of business and into retirement. Why had she been scoping out the mini-freeze the other night, and why did she get foxed the next? Had her father's plan backfired and Dixie's guilt over having the bulk of the blame laid at her beloved's door been too much for her to deal with?

Why hadn't Frankie let on before about his relationship with Dixie Daggett? I thought back over everything I'd said about her in front of Frankie and had one possible answer: I could be such a clueless ass sometimes.

I also had to wonder why Frankie was still wearing the Bobo costume. He'd told me earlier he had to abandon it due to pimple problems, but I hadn't seen any more bumps than usual when I tackled him, and believe me, when it comes to pore care, I'm on top of things. In light of this new romantic angle and a mutual dislike of their family businesses, it occurred to me that it would be in both Frankie's and Dixie's best interests if Uncle Frank threw in the towel and retired, leaving Frankie free to pursue his destiny, guilt-free.

I'd left the newly reunited couple together after making sure Frankie had received my note regarding the assignment changes, adding that if he needed further information as to why, he should ask Dixie. I'd caught a couple of hours of sleep at the trailer and bedded down again from two to five at the Emporium, but all was quiet. I'd managed to climb the hill and jump into my bunk before anyone noticed I'd been gone. The dark circles under my eyes from lack of sleep? They were on their own.

"Whew! That's quite a climb," Kari said, taking a seat on the picnic bench across from me. "Good thing I had my breakfast of champions this morning!"

My best friend, Kari, will soon be starting her second year as a middle school teacher. She teaches Language Arts to sixth graders. I know, I know: you're wondering how a college graduate and educator of impressionable young minds and a multivocational, college dropout got to be best buds. Frankly, I'm still trying to figure that one out, too.

Kari and I have been fast friends since that day in fourth grade when we first met and discovered a mutual fondness for chasing the mean boys around on the playground. I held them down with a knee to the windpipe, while Kari lectured them on behavior expectations and how to get along well with others. Kari's personality is a perfect fit for teaching. She has more patience than my brother Craig does while bow hunting. He can sit up there in that deer stand for hours on end, not making a sound, just waiting for Bambi's unsuspecting male relatives to come along, waiting for the perfect shot. I tried deer hunting in a stand once. Within ten minutes I was ready to swing upside-down from the branches and scratch my armpits.

Kari is getting married in December, and I am her maid of honor. This terrifies me. I have a very bad track record when it comes to weddings. At Craig and Kimmie's, Rick Townsend's baboonery relegated me to the back in all the wedding pictures due to the trail of barbecue sauce down the front of my bridesmaid dress. He goosed me when he discovered me sampling the appetizers a bit early. And we won't even talk about my encounter with the ice sculpture. Or Kimmie's greatuncle Graham, who, come to find out, is a bit of a groper.

Kari always works the fair for a few days, too. She's an old pro, having worked for Uncle Frank for as many years, if not as many hours, as I have. Her fiancé, Brian, is a Physical Education teacher at one of our four elementary schools. His only flaw is that he hangs out with Ranger Rick Townsend way too much. Kari and Brian make a really cool couple. His black hair and athletic build is the perfect foil for Kari's pale skin and dark blond hair.

Kari and I were scheduled to pull the day shift at the Emporium together. Brian would be up that evening, and the two of them would hang out then.

"Hey, Kari," I said, and Gram and Aunt Reggie

greeted her, too. "We're having instant cappuccinos. You're welcome to join us. They're actually not terrible."

"Yeah, if you put in ten tablespoons of cappuccino," Gram said. "And I miss all that foam on the top, like you get at the convenience store. Although you have to be careful with those. I burned my lip once and went around for a week looking like I had this hideous cold sore."

I raised my eyebrows at Kari. "Partake if you dare," I said.

"I think I'll pass." She laughed, dropping the copy of the *Grandville Gazette* I'd asked her to pick up for me on the table. I like to take a look at what I've written to see how much Stan has changed it.

"Besides," Kari continued, "it's hot when you hoof it up that hill. You got anything cold?"

"There should be pop in the fridge," I answered.

"And there's sun tea in there, too," Aunt Reggie said, "but you'll have to sweeten it."

Kari went into the RV, and Gram unfolded the paper. "Wonder who died I don't know about yet," she said. "I hope if it was somebody I knew, they don't think I'm rude for not sending flowers or a card."

I patted her hand. "I think it's safe to assume the dearly departed will not think ill of you, Gram."

She swatted my hand. "I was thinking about their kin, girl. I have a reputation for being on top of all the births and deaths in the area," she said.

"So you're in charge of the comings and goings?" I asked. I gave a wink. "Good to know."

Gram shook her head. "Anybody ever tell you you're a character?"

Kari returned, carrying a glass of tea and one of Uncle Frank's day-old donuts. Brave girl. She asked, "Does cartoon character count?"

Gram went back to the paper.

"Check for my fair feature promo," I told her. "Kari and I have to take off for work in a few minutes, and I want to see what kind of hack job Stan performed on it so I know how ticked to act the next time I e-mail him."

"Hold your horses, I'm looking," Gram said, turning another page. "It's not in here," she said after going through the entire paper.

"Whaddya mean, it's not in there?" I roared. "I worked long and hard on that preview piece!" Okay, so I hadn't, but that's beside the point.

"Well, it isn't here," Gram said, closing the paper. "And apparently everyone had the decency to hold off dying 'til I got back home," she added, "'cause there's no obituaries either."

I took the paper from her. "I don't get it. Why didn't Stan run it?" I asked, and caught a look at a front-page headline. "Wait, here it is. He put it on the front page! How cool is that?" I said, staring first at the content to check for Stan's handiwork. I took a sip of my cappuccino while I perused the article. Stan had made a few changes, mostly for economy of space, but not his usual butchery. I took a look at the accompanying picture. I blinked my eyes a couple of times to make sure lack of sleep wasn't playing tricks with my vision. I opened my eyes. Then crossed them. I felt all kinds of really naughty words form in my subconscious, each vying to be the first one out of my recently reformed mouth.

"Holy sh-moley!" I jumped to my feet, taking the newspaper with me. "Would you look at the time?" I said. "We'd better hit the road, Kari. We open in less than half an hour."

She gave me a startled look. Yep, she's got that expression down pat. Lots of practice.

"Uh, yeah, sure. Okay, Tressa," she said. "Just let me finish my tea."

"We've got to go now!" I said, my voice taking on the

same urgency young children use when they've just polished off a Big Gulp drink and their parents have passed the last rest area for thirty-five miles.

"Leave that paper here," Gram ordered. "I want to see what bargains I'm missing at the meat market." She yanked it out of my hand.

"Why beat yourself up?" I grabbed the paper back and stuck it under my arm. "You'll just stew over them."

"Do you know something I don't?" Gram asked. "They got them breaded tenderloins on special? Nothing I like better than a big old tenderloin with mustard, pickles, and onion. Think that's what I'll have for lunch today. 'Course I'll belch onions all afternoon. Hm. I'd better remember my Tic Tacs."

I turned to leave.

"Give me that paper!" Gram pulled it from under my armpit before I could stop her, and swatted me with it.

I grabbed Kari's arm and pulled her to her feet, trying to slink away.

"Hell's bells! Will you looky here! Frank's made the front page!"

"Damn!" I said, and stopped.

"What are you talking about, Hannah?" my Aunt Reggie asked.

"Your husband. He's front-page news. And he's drinking beer with some woman."

You've heard of being ripped from the headlines, right? Well, my usually placid, even-tempered, takes-a-lot-to-rile-her Aunt Reggie ripped this headline from my grammy like it was a buy-one-get-one-free offer on coney buns.

"Let me see that!" she said, poring over the picture of Uncle Frank and Lucy Connor like I examine my dogs for wood ticks.

"Isn't that Lucy of Trinkets and Treasures?" Gram

asked, peering over my aunt's shoulder. "The one who smokes like a chimney?"

"Lucy Connor," Aunt Reggie growled.

"That's right. What's she doin' sharin' a pitcher of beer with Frank? I didn't think he cared for beer all that much."

"Neither did I," Aunt Reggie said in the same tone my mom uses with clients who bring in their tax receipts in shoeboxes and Tupperware. "Where was this taken, anyway?" she asked.

"My guess is the corner table at the Bottoms Up," Gram said. I stared at her.

"How do you do that?" I asked, wondering how my gammy can account for everyone else's whereabouts and activities but manages to forget she's not supposed to answer my mom's business phone and pretend to be her secretary and has difficulty remembering to bring along her checkbook when someone takes her shopping.

She shrugged. "It's my curse," she said. "I didn't think Frank hung out at the Bottoms Up."

"Neither did I," Aunt Reggie said again. "You took this picture, Tressa?"

I shook my head. "A friend did," I said, not wanting to get Rhonda involved. It was sure to be ugly.

"It wasn't me!" Kari joined the group perusing the paper. "I didn't do it."

"It was a friend at the Bottoms Up," I elaborated. "She was just fooling around and shot a couple of pictures. I totally forgot they were on the camera when I downloaded the images for Stan. I'm so sorry, Aunt Reggie. But, honest, nothing happened between Uncle Frank and Lucy. He was just thanking her for helping him suck up cockroaches. I took pictures of Taylor and Townsend for Stan to print. I can't imagine why he picked this one of Uncle Frank."

"'Frank Barlowe takes a break from the steamy temps at the State Fair,'" Kari read.

"Hmph. How nice that Frank has time to take beer breaks," Aunt Reggie replied.

"With lady friends," my grammy added.

"Gram!" I scolded. "She's Uncle Frank's, uh, business associate," I pointed out. "They've run their businesses next to each other for the last ten years."

"Yes, they have, haven't they?" Aunt Reggie said, her scary guess-who's-gonna-be-audited tone giving me the willies. "You know Frank never did tell me how Lucy came to be at the Emporium the night the roaches were let loose," she added. "Did Frank ask you to go get her to help out, Tressa?"

I'd never wanted to lie so badly in my whole life. Well, except for the time when I was fifteen and I pilfered my grammy's wine coolers and my dad found me in the hayloft singing "California Dreamin'," and asked me if I'd been drinking. Or the time the local cop asked me if I was responsible for the horse manure left in the car wash, or when I had that stiff in the trunk and the deputy asked why I couldn't get to my spare tire. Okay, bottom line here? I wanted to tell a doozy of a whopper.

"Not exactly," I said, shifting my weight from one foot to the other.

"Tressa?" Aunt Reggie pressed.

I rubbed the back of my neck, as if trying to remember. "As I recall, Mrs. Connor was already there, so I didn't have to go get her, but I'm sure Uncle Frank would've asked me to if she hadn't already been there, as she has the biggest bug-sucker vac this side of the fairgrounds. But she offered that shop-vac right away and it worked like a charm. Sucked those mothers right up. *Thuuuup!*" I made a long, loud suction sound.

My aunt shook her head. "But you told us the Emporium was dark when you got there. So, where did Lucy come from?"

I felt my wiggle room start to slip away. I put a hand on my chin. "Hmm. Let's see. Uh, Townsend was behind the counter chasing bugs, and I was sweeping up a pile on the floor with the broom, and . . . um, oh, yes, I think that was when Uncle Frank walked in, and I'm not sure, but I think I seem to remember vaguely that he might have had—"

"Oh, spit it out, girlie. You caught Frank and Lucy in flagrante delicto," my gramma interrupted.

"Huh?" I said, no clue what she'd just said. "What?"

"In flagrante delicto. You know. Caught in the act. Clinch-time," she explained.

I shook my head. "The only thing Uncle Frank had in a clinch was a glass of beer I'd have given my graduation savings bonds for," I said. "It was Lucy who had a hold of *his* arm—tighter than Uncle Frank's hands on his wallet," I said; then saw Gram's pupils dilate and Aunt Reggie's shoulders stiffen. I clasped a hand to my mouth, then covered it with my other hand for good measure.

"Like yesterday, at the emporium with Luther Daggett," Aunt Reggie said, and she slowly stood, her back as straight as the temporary flagpole Uncle Frank always erects at the campsite. She took the newspaper and carefully folded it. "You girls better run along now. You don't want to be late opening up," she added, turning and heading for the RV.

"Well . . . that wasn't very tactful, girl," Gram said, rapping my knuckles with her spoon.

I did a double take. "You were the one who told me to spit it out," I reminded her.

"That's because I didn't know there was anything to spit out!" she said. "I was just being dramatic. Adding a little spice to the dialogue."

"You mean adding fuel to the fire." I groaned. "Aunt Reggie is really upset, isn't she?"

"I dunno," Gram replied. "Is not blinking for five minutes normal?"

I shook my head. "I am in so much trouble. Uncle Frank is gonna think I'm responsible for that photograph."

"Well, technically, aren't you?" Kari asked. I gave her a dark look.

"You're a big help, friend," I said.

"Well, this is turnin' out to be one lollapalooza of a fair. First our Oscar Meyer disappears, then the pranks. Now we have a real-life love triangle in our midst. You remember that rumor I heard, the one about the two concessionaires getting it on? Well, I'm wondering if that talk was about Frank and Lucy."

"Frank and Lucy are only getting along, not getting it on, Gram," I snapped. "Uncle Frank loves Aunt Reggie."

"Maybe." Gram made a *tsk*ing sound. "But you know that sayin', 'Don't come a-knockin' if the trailer's a-rockin'?'" I nodded. "Well, let's just say that's gonna take on a whole new meanin' tonight when Mr. Front Page gets back."

"Uncle Frank must be going through a midlife crisis," I thought aloud.

"I know something about midlife crises," Gram replied. "It tested the bounds of your grandpa Will's and my matrimony," she admitted.

"That's *bonds,* Grammy," I said. "But do tell. What did Paw Paw Will do? Did he have a passionate affair? Did he gamble your life savings away? Did he buy a bright red sports car or have a tummy tuck?"

"Yes, Hannah," Kari joined in. "How did your husband's midlife crisis manifest?" I gave her a sideways look. "Being a bride-to-be, it's nice to know these things," she explained.

"What are you two chattering about?" Gram got to

her feet. "Paw Paw Will never had a midlife crisis," she said, and headed for our trailer. "Now, should I wear the lavender or the hot pink today?"

"She's scary," Kari said.

I agreed.

Uncle Frank was already at the emporium making coffee and those yummy little breakfast burritos with the sausage, cheese, and egg that only the Emporium serves on the fairgrounds. At a buck-fifty each, they were a big seller, and Uncle Frank made a respectable profit.

"You're up and at 'em early," I greeted him, wondering how on earth I was going to break the news that he was on the front page of the hometown paper sipping beer with a woman other than his wife. I pulled an apron on over my white tank top and tan skort. (You know, a cross between a skirt and shorts. I wonder who ever thought of *skort* in the first place. It's so clever.)

"I had a breakfast business meeting," he said, and I looked over at Kari, who shrugged. What kind of business did Uncle Frank have to conduct without Aunt Reggie around to translate for him? Let's face it: Uncle Frank was not the brains behind the business, although his talent in the kitchen was the basis on which the Barlowe empire was built.

Bravely, I asked, "Oh, yeah? That's strange: Aunt Reggie was still up at the campgrounds. Did she know about your business breakfast?"

"It came up at the last minute," Uncle Frank answered, a certain gruffness to his voice that didn't encourage further discussion.

"Uh, guess what, Uncle Frank?" I said, joining Kari in the kitchen, where she was wrapping burritos in white plastic paper. "You got some free advertising in the *Gazette*," I told him. "Front-page photo and the works."

Uncle Frank followed me into the kitchen. "How'd you sneak that by Stan?"

I concentrated on rolling my next burrito. "It was all Stan's doing," I said, making sure he knew where to lay the blame when the time came. "You remember he's running a fair feature at the end of the fair and I'm supposed to send him pictures and small write-ups? Well, he ran a preview in the paper, and out of the selection of possible photos I sent him, he ran one of you. It says 'Frank Barlowe, local businessman' and everything! Totally cool."

Uncle Frank was still frowning. Not an encouraging sign. "When did you take my picture?"

"Well, actually, I didn't," I said. "Someone else was fiddling with my camera and took one. But, trust me, it's a keeper." For sure Aunt Reggie would be keeping it. Forever and ever.

"Where was this photo taken?" he asked, and I caught myself overfilling a poor tortilla.

"Taken? Let's see. I could be mistaken, but I think I recall it being taken at a local establishment where they serve various appetizers and, of course, drinks to wash them down. But remember, it's free advertising, so it's all good!"

"What local establishment?" he asked.

Dang. Why did he have to choose today of all days to show an interest?

I looked at Kari, who looked back at me with a should-I-seek-cover look. "Uh, the picture was taken the other night at Bottoms Up. But now that I think of it, I doubt very many people will notice. After all, it's not like they care about seeing Frank Barlowe on the front page, having drinks with some strange woman or anything. Right?"

"Strange woman?" Uncle Frank's face was redder than his homemade salsa.

"Did I say strange? I meant unknown. As in unidentified. For all anyone knows, it could be your sister."

"I don't have a sister."

"But not everyone knows that," I pointed out.

"Did you bring the paper to the fair?" Uncle Frank asked Kari.

"Tressa told me to," Kari responded, and I gave her a dark look.

"Do you by any chance have it with you?" Uncle Frank asked. I could detect a hopeful look in his eye.

I shook my head. "Sorry. But you'll be seeing it later," I said, " 'cause Aunt Reggie has it."

Uncle Frank nodded. Then kept nodding. "Great. Just great. Things just keep getting better and better. You know, I've half a mind to just throw in the towel and go ahead and retire. It seems to be what everyone wants."

Not me. I still depended on the Dairee Freeze as steady, secure employment.

"What do *you* want to do, Uncle Frank?" I asked.

"Depends on what day you ask me," he said.

"It's been quiet the last couple days, so maybe the prankster has pulled his last prank," I suggested.

"You ever heard that it's always quietest before the storm?" he reminded me.

I nodded. I'd found that to be true, myself.

"I'll be back later. Hold down the fort, would you, girls?" my uncle said.

I nodded, but suspected it was Uncle Frank who would need to fortify his defenses.

Kari and I ran through the burritos quicker than my grammy goes through her secret stash of M&Ms. By ten we'd sold out, and were already preparing the beef burgers and taco meat for our two main lunch staples.

I was in the freezer grabbing another container of tin roof ice cream (okay, so this is a particular flavor favorite of mine—what of it?) and was carrying it back to the front when I spotted Townsend sitting at the counter, looking gorgeous as usual. He was clearly off-duty today, as he had on a white Nike T-shirt with blue trim. I couldn't tell what he had on from the waist down, but suspected it was probably khaki shorts and his Nike tennies.

I maneuvered the ice cream into the refrigerated display case out front, feeling self-conscious and not a little flustered. After our romantic interlude of the previous night—stymied only, I feared, by a case of *clownus interruptus*—I felt myself slipping back into my own confused version of the Safe Mode. I was backpedaling from our earlier overheated overtures faster than the unicyclist who followed the horses in the annual state fair parade.

The Rick Townsend I knew and wrangled with had a reputation for playing the field—while I suspected I was more apt to play for keeps. Which led to the obvious question: Once the Grandville slugger hit a couple grand-slam homers off me and rounded my bases several times, would he decide I was—er, *baseball* was—too restrictive a pastime? And where would that leave me? High and dry with the Great Bobo. That's where.

"What'll ya have?" I said, pulling my order book and pencil out of my front pocket, opting for a businesslike demeanor. "It's a tad bit early for lunch, but we've still got some donuts back there."

"Donuts instead of lunch? If I didn't know better, I'd say you were tryin' to do me in, Calamity," Ranger Rick said. "Or get me out of the way by sending me off to the dentist."

I frowned at him. "Why would I want to get you out of the way?"

"Oh, I can think of a couple of reasons," he said. "And they all fall under the I-don't-want-to-go-there category."

"Oh, really? What do you think you know?"

"I know *you*. And I foresee big trouble ahead if you continue playing Sherlock Holmes and Dr. Watson with Frankie."

"Uh-oh! Sonya the Seer better watch out, or all-knowing, all-seeing Ranger Rick will put her out of a job!" I said, gratefully seeking the safe refuge of righteous indignation from emotions that flip-flopped more than my gammy's boobs when she went without her foundation bra. "I'll have you know, I'm making headway on this case as we speak. I've got several suspects identified and am getting a better handle on their motives, and even now I'm formulating a plan to bring the guilty party to light." Well, actually, I had no plan, but since Townsend really wasn't psychic, he couldn't know that.

He busted out laughing, far more than I thought appropriate. "Geez, do you hear yourself? You even sound like Holmes! 'Even now, my good Watson, I'm formulating a plan to bring the guilty party to light.'" He grabbed a napkin from a nearby dispenser and wiped his eyes.

"I'm glad you find this so amusing," I told him. "I assure you, Uncle Frank isn't getting any jollies from this, and neither is Aunt Reggie. Their marriage may even be in jeopardy."

Townsend finished wiping his eyes and nodded. "I heard about your little fair preview piece. Nice," he said.

"How'd you—? Who told you?" I asked, knowing the answer as soon as the question left my lips. "Oh, I get it: Joe told you, and Gram told Joe."

"Bingo," Townsend agreed.

It wasn't my fault!" I complained. "Ronnie took the picture and I thought it had been deleted. I meant to have Stan run a picture of you and Taylor."

Townsend looked at me. "You took a picture of Taylor and me? Why?"

I shrugged. "You're both cover-model caliber, so why not?"

He shook his head. "I don't think I'll ever understand how that brain of yours works," he said.

"But you're not giving up. Right?" I asked, a pitiful edge to my voice that I'd not consciously put there.

"Lucky for you, I'm known for my stamina," he said. "In more ways than one," he added with a wink.

The bell sounded. The door opened, and Gram and Joe walked in.

"I prefer them Tucks pads," my gramma was saying. "No mess. Just wipe and toss."

I looked at Townsend and made a face. "Yep," I said, "I'm a lucky, lucky girl."

"Well howdy-do, you two!" Joe helped Gram onto a bar stool and took the one beside his grandson. "Imagine finding you two here. Together. Talking real friendly-like."

"Not so unusual," I told Joe. "I work here, and Ranger Rick likes to eat."

"You got any breakfast burritos left?" Gram asked.

I shook my head. "Had a big run on 'em. But if you wait a few minutes, we'll have beef burgers." I didn't tell her about the tacos. Sometimes Gram and tacos don't get along.

"What? No tacos?" Gram asked, pronouncing it tackos. Sometimes I think she needs to come up with her own dictionary.

"Uncle Frank's belly burners? You sure you want one?" I asked. "The mood he was in this morning, he probably went heavy on the hot sauce."

Gram looked at Joe. "I'm game if you are," she said.

Townsend frowned. "I think you better stick with the beef burger, Pops," he said to his grandfather.

Joe looked at Gram. "Maybe he's right, Hannah. We got us a lot to do this afternoon, and we may not have time for pit stops."

"What do you two have on tap for the afternoon?" Townsend asked, a slight tremor in his voice. I felt the same anxiety.

"Yeah, Gram, what's on the agenda?" I asked, thinking that these two let loose on an unsuspecting fair crowd could qualify for changing the country's terror alert status to orange.

"Oh, we were hoping to take some photographs of the fair," Gram said. "You know, one never knows when it will be their last. Look at poor Dottie: She keeled over in her donut batter one day and *puufftttth*, she was gone. We thought it would be kinda nice to have pictures. We figured we'd take photos of ourselves at the fair enjoying various activities, and maybe make a scrapbook or photo album for you kids."

I looked at her. A scrapbook? Photographs? All her family pictures were still in shoeboxes in a basement closet. "You don't even own a camera, Grammy," I told her.

"No, but you do. You have that digital doohickey. We could use that, couldn't we?"

I shook my head. "I need it. I've really been lax about getting pictures for Stan at the *Gazette*," I said. "I'm behind, big time."

"We could snap a few fair attractions while we're out and about," Joe suggested. "You know, the old favorites. The butter cow. The big boar. The big bull. A shot of the sand sculpture—I hear you're not real welcome there anyway, since that time you destroyed the Statue of Liberty. The midway. We'll shoot all the general-interest stuff. All you'll have to do is write a few blurbs to go with the photos."

I nodded. The old guy had a good idea. With all the

extra time I was giving Frankie in the stakeout department, I really could use the help. "I suppose you could take a few pictures for me," I said.

He slapped his thigh. "Well, go fetch the camera for us, girl," he urged, "and give us a crash course in digital photography."

I went into the back room and got the camera, then gave them a quick overview of the basics. "You'll have a few seconds to look at each pic before it's saved automatically," I told them. "If you want to look at your shots, turn the camera on and press review. The delete button is here. You really shouldn't need to use the menu if all you're doing is pointing, shooting, reviewing, and saving or deleting," I explained.

"Looks simple enough," Joe said. "Smile!" He pushed the button, and a second later the flash followed. "Why, looky here, Hannah, there's Tressa! She doesn't look too happy, does she?"

"She looks like she needs some Tucks medicated pads," Gram said. They both laughed. I shook my head.

"I'll get your burgers," I said.

"Here." Kari brought up two beef burgers on foam plates with a dill spear and chips on the side. "I heard the conversation. What can I get for you, Rick?" she added.

"I'll have the same," he replied, "but hold the onions." He looked at me. "I'm a considerate kind of guy."

"That's nice. I'm having the belly burner," I told him.

The door opened, and another customer stood in the doorway. In fact, he took up the entire doorway. I stared as he entered the ice cream place and took a seat by my grammy.

"Manny!" I said, still not believing what I was seeing.

"Hey, Barbie," he said. He leaned forward and acknowledged Townsend. "Yo, Rick the Dick," he growled.

"What on earth are you doing here?" I asked.

"Manny's here to meet somebody."

I frowned, thinking that Uncle Frank would be rather upset if Manny starting bringing a certain clientele into his shop. "I see," I said, imagining his face as he walked into an Emporium full of biker types.

"Yo, you two wanna move to a table?" Manny asked.

To my total surprise, he addressed the question to my grandma and Joe.

"You're here to meet *them?*" I asked.

Joe nodded. "Let's move over to that table in the corner, Manny," he suggested. I noticed Manny helped my grammy off her stool and picked up her meal to carry it for her.

"What would you like, Manny?" Joe asked. "It's on me."

"Manny's not very hungry," he said. "Just bring three burgers, fries, and a tall diet cola, and Manny's good to go."

I nodded, still stunned by the fact that Manny, the biker I'd bailed out of jail several months earlier and who had been in the lock-up at the fair police station, was having burgers with my grandmother and her friend.

I imagined Townsend was even less enthusiastic about his granddad rubbing elbows with a guy who sported some pretty graphic tattoos and referred to him as Rick the Dick. I braved a look at Townsend. His constipated look confirmed my hunch.

"What is that all about?" Kari asked.

"I think it's called old-timer's," I said, attempting to explain away the unexplainable. I scurried away to fill the giant biker's order before he started chanting, "Fee, fi, fo, fum."

CHAPTER 18

Kari and I pulled a long shift at the Emporium. It was close to six and the mid-supper rush when Uncle Frank returned to relieve us.

"Where's Aunt Reggie?" I asked, certain that both had been scheduled to close that night.

"She's got a headache," Uncle Frank said, but I noticed he was wincing.

"Is she all right?" I asked. Aunt Reggie was never one prone to physical ailments.

"She'll live," Uncle Frank said. The impression was, the same could not be said of him.

"I'll hang around for a while," I told him.

He shrugged. "I think Taylor was planning to come over from the mini-freeze and help out," he said. "But you can help out through the supper rush."

Kari excused herself, planning to hit the campgrounds to wash the burger smell off before she met Brian. I watched her leave and wondered how our relationship would change after she was married. I suspected Brian would frown on girls' night out. At least with this particular girl. Over the years, Kari's friendship with me had landed her in more than a few dicey situations, and I had a hard time picturing Brian Davenport advocating a continuing supporting role for his wife as Calamity's sidekick.

By seven-thirty, Taylor still hadn't shown up, but the dinner crowd had been served, so Uncle Frank assured me he could handle the remaining customers and herded me out the door. I told myself I was going to bed early that night, since I still had to work from two to five watching the emporium, so I decided to head for the trailer, take a few twists in the shower, and go to bed.

I was tired enough that I opted to catch the campground shuttle rather than hoof it up the hill, feeling no shame at all in wimping out. I climbed onto the trolley and sank into a bench in the front, taking in the sights and sounds of the fair as we pulled out. Tiny tots squealed and pointed at the cotton candy stand. An old couple shared a funnel cake on a bench in the shade. A mother of triplets struggled to push a triple stroller over the rough grass. Rick Townsend embraced my sister, Taylor, at the corner of the pizza-by-the-slice booth.

I jerked my head to the side as the trolley lumbered by. As we moved past, I slowly got to my feet and walked down the narrow center aisle of the trolley, keeping pace with the hugging couple until I got to the back of the transport. I hung over the back rail and watched their hug go on longer than my grammy used the bathroom facilities after ordering and consuming the Mexican sampler at the South of the Border Restaurant on the square back home. When the twosome was out of sight, I removed my fingers from the rail (this almost required surgical tools) and plopped down into a seat.

We'd traveled through the entire campground and were ready to head back down to the fairgrounds when the driver turned and looked at me. "You miss your stop, young lady?" he called to me. I shook my head.

"No," I answered, "but I may have missed the boat."

I settled back in my seat for the return trip to the fairgrounds, one part of me hoping the cozy couple had disengaged by the time we made another pass, but the rowdy cowgirl in me was primed for a catfight. How could the reptilian cad go from sweet-talkin' me at noon to striking a romance cover-model pose with my little sister at dinnertime?

Upon our return, the couple was nowhere to be seen. What to do? What to do? I finally resorted to an activity that always consoles me when I'm feeling down.

"Drop me off near the Steer, driver," I told him, thinking there had to be a nice, fat, born and slaughtered in Iowa, medium-well T-bone steak with my name on it browning on the Steer Grill. Add a baked potato with butter and sour cream, a side salad, and Texas Toast, and by the time I was finished, the stomach discomfort I'd suffer would override any pain I'd experienced seeing my sister and the guy I lusted after in each other's arms. Well, it was a start. There was always cotton candy, taffy, caramel apples, and funnel cakes, too.

I thanked the driver, who put his fingers to his Deere hat and bade me a rather somber farewell.

I stepped down and decided before I put any more food in, I'd better make some room, so I headed back to the horse barns to use the facilities. I'd just stepped out into the narrow alley behind the barns (I can never visit the horse barns without taking one walk-through) when I was grabbed from behind.

"Your uncle give any more thought to retirement?" a voice I now recognized asked. Well, halfway recognized. I still couldn't distinguish between Tai or Chai, but I knew it was a Li.

I pivoted. Sure enough, the two brothers stood there,

eerie duplicates down to their blue jeans and black T-shirts with Asian symbols. "I don't know what Uncle Frank's plans are, guys," I said. "He doesn't discuss stuff like that with me."

"But you did relay the benefits of early retirement. Right?" one brother asked.

I shuffled my feet, not too proud to admit that I was more than a little nervous about being in a deserted alley behind the horse barns and near the Dumpsters with two rather volatile personalities who hadn't seemed to take a shine to me.

"Uncle Frank knows all the ins and outs relating to retirement. After all, his sister-in-law is a CPA. I'm sure he'll know best when he's ready to make the leap. Personally, I think the idea of Uncle Frank retiring scares the heck out of my Aunt Reggie." I snorted, thinking I'd try to keep it light. Easy. Non-confrontational. Especially considering it was two against one, and last week I'd finished a mystery where the murderer stuffed the murder vic in a Dumpster outside a construction site. I sure didn't want the authorities having to make up a grid at the local landfill to figure out where to start picking through the garbage to find my body. That's really gross.

"I'm disappointed. Aren't you, Chai?" Tai said. Okay, so now I knew which was which. Tai was on the left. "I thought you'd be more helpful in convincing your uncle to sell."

"Maybe she could disappear like her cousin did," Chai suggested. "If family members start disappearing, that might make Frank realize what's important in life."

"Disappear?" The quaver in my voice was more pronounced than Grammy's limp when she wanted sympathy. "I don't think that would work with Uncle Frank. Aunt Reggie says his middle name is Contrary. It's really Joseph, but you get the idea."

"Word has it you don't think your cousin's behind the stunts targeting your uncle and you aim to prove it," Tai (the Li on the left) said. "How's that workin' out for you? You makin' any progress?"

"I have come up with a few suspects with both motive and opportunity," I said, thinking the two standing right in front of me were at the top of my list.

"You've been spending time with a representative of the law enforcement community, too, I hear. You been supplying him information on this case? Maybe giving him your short list of suspects?" Tai pressed.

I shrugged and started to back up, taking no shame in a strategic retreat. "We've discussed the case in general terms," I conceded.

"Did the Li name come up?"

Shoot. Why *hadn't* I mentioned the troublemaking twins to the trooper? Or even Townsend? Or Uncle Frank? Or Frankie?

"Uh, yeah, your names came up in the conversation," I lied, thinking that, if they thought I'd given their names to the cops, they might be less likely to do me any bodily harm. "After all, your behavior has been a little extreme."

"Extreme? You'd be extreme, too, if you had to suck in the fumes from the shitter two weeks a year for fifteen years," Chai growled, clearly not the diplomat of the two.

"That's not my Uncle Frank's fault," I told them. "He doesn't have anything to do with where they place concession stands—or restrooms, for that matter."

"People who are handed opportunities on a platter can't understand how those who have to work like dogs feel when they are continually disenfranchised," Tai said. "It's very painful to watch," he added. Chai cracked his knuckles.

"It's very painful," Tai went on, and I felt like I'd had

one too many strawberry daiquiris and was suffering double vision. The two Li boys took up positions on either side of me.

"We could send her on a short vacation for the rest of the fair," Chai—or was it Tai?—suggested. Now that they'd changed positions, I wasn't sure who was who.

"That's kidnapping!" I told them.

"That's an unpleasant name," one of the twins told me.

"I could use a vacation," I conceded. "Where did you have in mind? I've always wanted to go to Scotland. I have ancestors who came from Scotland. I think I may even have a connection to William Wallace. You know— Mel Gibson played him in *Braveheart*. Excellent movie, but disturbing. I mean, that drawing and quartering thing? Ugh." I looked at their dazed expressions and realized I was in full babble. I do that when I'm nervous. Or feeling threatened. Or both. "Or, you could send me to Arizona. I have relatives all over out there, and it's been a while since we got together. My dad's sister, my Aunt Kay, lives in Flagstaff. It's up by the Grand Canyon. Have you ever visited the Grand Canyon? It's awesome. From what I've seen of it. I couldn't seem to get the image of Thelma and Louise driving off the rim out of my head. Have you seen that movie? *Thelma and Louise*? It's disturbing, too."

"Would you shut up?" the brothers shouted in stereo.

"Okay, so set me up at Motel Six," I said. "Pay Per View and a vending machine down the hall is all I need."

I noticed I was no longer the focus of the Li brothers' attention. Their gazes drifted down the alley to a point near the back entrance to the horse barn.

"Who's that?" one brother asked.

The other brother shook his head. "I've never seen him before. Jesus, he's a mountain."

I expelled my breath in a noisy gust that made the brothers look back at me. "And he's *my* mountain," I said, knowing of only one ultra-large person who could elicit the reaction these two small-time thugs were showcasing.

"Yo, Barbie doll! You need a hand?" Manny's greeting was as welcome and beautiful to my ears as "Yes, we have those in a size nine."

The brothers gave me an uncertain look. "You know him?" they asked.

I nodded, and put up two crossed fingers. "We're like this," I said, and was rewarded when the twins' Adam's apples bobbed in time.

"Yo, Barbie. What's the deal? You cool?"

I managed to slide out from between the brothers grim and jogged toward Manny, grabbing hold of one massive arm and clinging for dear life when I reached him. "Uh, actually, I think those two might have been thinking of detaining me unlawfully," I told him. "Then again, maybe they just like to play gang bangers."

Manny walked toward the pair, and I continued to cling to him. (Okay, so there are times when the clingy female persona is appropriate. This just happened to be one of those times.)

"You got business with Barbie, here?" Manny asked. The Li brothers' eyes grew bigger than my eyes do when I see my credit card balance each month.

"Barbie?" the Li boys asked.

Manny nodded toward me. "Blondie. You got business with her?"

Have I mentioned yet that Manny is a man of few words, and that he always refers to himself in the third person? I admit it struck me as a little weird at first, too, but, hey, you don't walk up to a guy who makes Governor "Ahnold" in his prime look like Danny DeVito, and tell him he talks funny.

"We were just havin' us a conversation," the twin I took to be Tai said. "Like you said, conductin' business."

Manny took a couple more steps toward the twins. "Your business is concluded," he said. "Permanently," he added, crossing his arms so the tattoos displaying such warm titles as HELLRAISER and DRAGONSLAYER, complete with black and purple dragon, and another tattoo I'd never been able to make out, took on epic proportions.

The Li brothers looked at each other. "You can't be everywhere, my friend," Chai said. (Or was that Tai? Oh, who cares? You get the point.)

"Then maybe Manny'd better kick your asses now," the biker said, and I flinched at his matter-of-fact response. Probably the two brothers sensed this signaled trouble, because they looked at each other, then backed away.

"You remember what we said," they told me. "Retirement can be a beautiful thing."

"So can chewing your food as opposed to sipping it through a straw," Manny said. "Remember *that*."

Hands balled into fists at their sides, the Li boys turned and fled, giving Manny one last look before they disappeared around the far corner of the barn.

"Barbie attracts trouble like horse shit attracts flies," Manny observed.

"All sh—manure attracts flies," I said, still shaking but not wanting Manny to know. As if my fingernails taking up permanent residency in his arm wasn't a giveaway.

"Thanks, Manny," I told him. "You know, I really think those two could be the culprits. They clearly don't want me continuing my little investigation and conducting any more stakeouts. Since Frankie and I set up our surveillance, the two haven't been able to proceed with their next move."

Manny looked down at me and gently removed my hands from his arm. "You think a little person like you could stop those two from their mischief?" he asked. "Where you livin', Barbie? In your Fantasy Dream House?"

I looked at Manny and wondered how he knew about Barbie's Dream House, and whether he knew about the cool pink convertible she drove, the RV, and Barbie's stable, complete with Palomino horse (of course) with real synthetic-hair mane and tail so you could groom it. Barbie toys are the best. I remember the Christmas Taylor got the Barbie Primp and Polish Styling Head. She spent hours with her Barbie head, making it up red-carpet glamorous. Then, I'd sneak in and add my own special touches, and her Barbie Primp and Polish would end up looking like Barbie Pimp and Polish. Ah, memories.

"If I'd had my camera," I told Manny. "I'd have nailed them with hard evidence."

Manny almost chuckled. At least, I thought it was a chuckle. I'd never seen Manny smile before, let alone laugh, so I wasn't real sure. "Camera versus blade," he said. "You're funny, Barbie."

"Blade?" I gulped. "What blade?" Since my run-in with that murderer, I had issues with knives and the people who wielded them. "Knives aren't allowed on the fairgrounds!" I told him. "It's posted at all the gates!"

Manny shook his head. "What knife?" he repeated. "The knife sharp enough to slide in and out between your ribs before you can say, 'Knives aren't allowed,'" Manny elaborated. "That's what knife."

I grimaced. Manny didn't mince words.

"Barbie needs to be more careful," he went on. "Or start packin' serious heat," he suggested.

I shook my head. "Firearms aren't allowed either," I told him with a long sigh.

"'Zzat right?" Manny replied, rubbing his chin. "Huh."

I stared at him. "You aren't packing now, are you?" I looked him over but couldn't see any bulges that didn't have a physiological reason to be there.

"So, your great-grandpa was a cop," Manny said, completely changing the subject. I tried to catch up.

"How did you know that?"

"Your grandma," he said, and started to walk away.

"About that," I said, hurrying after him, having to run to keep up. "What kind of business exactly did you have with Gram and Joe? I get kind of nervous when the two of them collaborate. You remember what happened to you when the two of them decided to work together?" I saw him wince, but he kept walking. "Just tell me if they're into something that might give Joe the chance to indulge his fantasy obsession with crime-fighting."

"Seems harmless enough," Manny responded.

I frowned. "That's what I thought the time you ended up being Maced," I told him. I grabbed his elbow and was carried along with his powerful stride. "You gotta tell me what they're up to, Manny!"

He stopped suddenly, and I was left dangling on his arm. "They wanted some expert advice on how to get the goods on a cheating spouse," he said.

I stared at him. "Cheating spouse?"

"Your uncle."

"Uncle Frank?"

"Guess so."

"They plan to get the goods on Uncle Frank? What else did they say?"

"They talked a lot about leverage," Manny said.

"Leverage?"

"Proof of infidelity to use in court. Dates and times. Photos."

I slapped my head. "My camera! Those . . . those stinkers! Like they were ever gonna take a picture of the big boar for me. Ha!"

Manny looked down at me, one eyebrow slightly raised above the other. "Big boar, Barbie?"

"Never mind," I said. "I need to track down those two crackpots before they do even more damage to an already shaky marriage." I rubbed my forehead, all thoughts of thick juicy steaks and buttered taters ripped asunder by two senior citizens who thought they were running the Cheatin' Heart Detective Agency.

Lord have mercy.

CHAPTER 19

I decided the best place to waylay my grammy and read her the riot act was the trailer; she'd have to return there sometime, so I planned to lie in wait. I took the trolley up to the campgrounds (thank goodness it was a different driver this time) and found the trailer unlocked and unoccupied. I wouldn't want this to get around, but we often leave our RV unlocked. We've never had a problem with break-ins. Folks who pull their trailers or set up tents in the fair campgrounds are either retired persons or folks raising families, and generally low-risk when it comes to burglary. At least, that's what we tell ourselves. Besides, with so many people coming and going, it's impossible to issue enough trailer keys.

I jumped in the shower and hosed off, donned an oversized Cyclone T-shirt and shorts, took a long swig of cranberry juice from the container (please don't tell my mom), and then decided I'd sack out and try to get some sleep before Gram got back. I flopped down on the sofa, stuffed a pillow under my bed, and grabbed the maroon throw that took my grammy ten years to complete and represented her solitary foray into needlework that couldn't be completed on her ancient Singer sewing machine, and hoped I wouldn't dream about switchblade knives that could slide between my ribs like butter or nosy nellies who got picked up on criminal trespass charges for sticking their cartilage where it didn't belong.

I dreamed instead of creeping vines: long green lengths of foliage that curled around my ankles and slid up my leg to wrap themselves around me. In my dream I reached out to pull the clinging flora away from my body only to find it creeping back to ensnare me. I finally woke to a dark room, with light from the campground outdoors shining through the window near the sofa. I yawned and punched the button on my watch to read the time.

Ten P.M., and still no Grammy. I frowned. Where was everyone? I wondered, deciding I might as well continue to veg out on the couch for a while; the family would be draggin' in any time.

I had just closed my eyes when I felt myself slipping back into the coiling plant dream. I could feel it twirl around one ankle ever so slowly. I shook myself out of the dream and opened my eyes. I lay there staring at the ceiling, thinking how weird it was to fall back asleep and into the same dream so quickly, when I suddenly felt something slide against my ankle. I frowned. I *was* awake, wasn't I? I sat up and looked down at the outline of my afghan-covered torso. I felt something slip around my ankle, and flipped on the built-in wall lamp. Slight movement between my feet made faint ripples in the covers. Curious, I pulled the blanket off and threw it to the floor. There, curling around the bottom of my right leg was a thick, dark ankle bracelet. And it was moving.

The scream that ripped from my lips was loud enough to wake my grammy from a sleep after she'd polished off three margaritas (without my parents' knowledge, of course) and was just a tad above the decibel range that recommended ear plugs, but not yet to the shattering-glass stage. I'm not sure, but I think I may have broken a record for the longest scream not part of a *Chainsaw Massacre* movie, too, but since there is no way to verify that, I guess we'll never know.

I catapulted to my feet and frantically shook my right foot, trying to dislodge my serpentine ankle adornment from hell. I hopped up and down on one leg like a psycho pogo stick. I finally managed to fling the long, butt-ugly snake to the floor and onto Grammy's prized, one-of-a-kind, crocheted blankie.

I watched as the uninvited trailer guest recovered, far more quickly than I did, and headed again in my direction. I screamed, but resisted the temptation to jump up on the sofa, thinking that if I didn't corral the cunning creature before it slithered out of sight, it would be the very devil to find. And if the reptile wasn't removed from the premises, this here good ole girl wasn't about to step another foot in the trailer ever again—even if I was wearing chest-high waders and carrying a ten-foot electric cattle prod.

Frantic, I stared at the dark, reddish-brown, blotchy rope that moved swifter than a lightweight adolescent did going down the giant fair slide, and wondered how on earth I could contain the speedy serpent—and yet not come within arm's length of it. I spotted the Swiffer mop thingy that my mom uses to clean the linoleum in the kitchen and dining areas. It's so handy: You just stick a pad on the bottom, push it into the slots, and take off. Dust and dirt stick to it like Hillary sticks to her hubby at social functions. Then you pull off the pad and pop that in the trash. Ah, the benefits of good old American ingenuity!

I grabbed the mop and quickly clobbered the snake

on the head a couple of times. Garnering an evil hiss in return, I clobbered it again, praying my handy little moppy thingy didn't snap before I stunned the snake into submission. He flipped over, exposing a cream-colored belly with dark markings, then quickly recoiled. I could swear I heard a rattling sound.

It suddenly tried to change direction on me, heading for the bedroom, and I raked it back onto grammy's blanket, thumping it a couple more times for maximum stun effect, then quickly brought the edges of the blanket together in a makeshift bag, trapping the still-squirming creature inside.

"That will teach you to invade my space," I told the writhing bag, which I held at arm's length while praying my grammy's handiwork was stronger than it appeared. I was heading for the outdoors to release my captive when the door burst open and Rick Townsend filled the doorway. Behind him I could see my grammy and the brim of a goofy, bright yellow hat that I knew could only belong to Joe.

"We heard screaming. What the hell are you doing?" Townsend said, stepping into the trailer with Gram and Joe on his heels.

I shoved the sack of snake at him. "Your job," I said. "The good ranger will have one sack of five-foot squirming serpent to go," I told him, and he continued to stare at me. "Snake!" I yelled, pointing to the bag and jumping up and down.

He took the makeshift bag. "What the hell?" He started to open the top to look in.

"Not in here!" I yelled, pushing him past Grammy and Joe and out on the tiny porch.

"What the heck is Townsend doing with my afghan?" Gram asked. "It took me almost a decade and ninety-two calluses to crochet that thing."

"He's releasing a snake from it," I told her. "At least I

hope he is. Knowing Townsend, he'll be playing with the damn thing." Now that I'd faced my fear and vanquished my foe, my legs were like Slinkies. I wanted to sit but wasn't ready to trust the couch. Where there was one snake . . .

"What the Sam Hill was a snake doin' in my blankie?" Gram asked.

"Scaring your granddaughter out of what little wits she has left," I told her.

"How'd it get in here?" Gram asked. She looked at me. "Did you let it in?"

I stared back at her and started nodding. "Yeah, Gram, being such a longtime fan of the snake species, I saw this one passing by and decided to invite him in for a spell. Hello! I have no clue how he got in."

I flicked on the outside light. "Is it poisonous?" I asked, looking on from a safe distance as Townsend examined the occupant of the makeshift enclosure.

He shook his head. "It's a bull snake," he said. "They're harmless—actually, one of the most beneficial snakes in the Midwest. They consume a huge number of rodents."

I wrinkled my nose. Beneficial or not, a varmint crosses my threshold and it's snakeskin-boot time. "How did it get in?" I also wanted to know.

Townsend shrugged. "In hot weather, they sometimes feel the air conditioning escaping from the bottom of a screen door and will crawl up on the porch to curl right underneath the door's edge. If a person isn't paying attention, it would be simple for it to slide right in after you." I shivered at the idea of possibly stepping right over a snake and not knowing it.

Townsend knelt and took another look in the bag. "What the hell did you do to him? He looks like he went a couple rounds with a hawk."

"I used the Swiffer thingy on him," I explained,

pointing to my weapon of choice and wondering why the home invader was getting all the attention and the victim was left to defend herself. "I had to subdue him somehow," I told the ranger, who was now holding the snake and examining him more carefully than I did my checkbook math.

"First my one-of-a-kind blanket, and now your mom's Swiffer broom. What next?" Gram asked.

"You'd prefer I left him there in the bed with you for the night?" I asked. "I'm sure that can be arranged. Oh, Townsend, it appears my grammy has developed a soft spot for Mr. Bull Snake. Do you suppose you could release him to her custody for the night?"

Gram grunted. "Now, I wasn't complaining about the way you handled the situation, Tressa Jayne." My grammy backpedaled quicker than a politician after he's been elected. "Just making observations."

I nodded. "You two are good at that, aren't you?" I said, remembering what I'd wanted to discuss with them earlier.

"What are you talking about, girlie?" Joe said, lighting up the night in his yellow shirt and matching hat.

"Observing. Manny tells me you two asked his advice on how best to . . . observe and document your observations."

"What's she talking about, Pops?" Townsend said, getting to his feet, snake still in hand. "Tressa, what are you talking about?"

Joe gave me a panicked look and made a slashing motion across his throat. "You remember, Rick," the old man said, "Hannah and I were going to take some fair photos for Tressa, since she's been working such long hours for Frank."

"Yes, I remember. But what does an ex-con biker have to do with taking fair photos? Does he have a hidden talent I don't know about?" Townsend asked.

I nodded, thinking how he'd supported a traumatized, dangling blonde of average height and weight (hey, now, be nice) with one meaty arm while sending two young yahoos packing without breaking his stride or breaking a sweat. That made him a pretty gifted individual.

"He, uh, has had prior experience with photography," Joe explained, pulling a hankie from his back shorts pocket and wiping his brow.

"What kind of experience?" Townsend asked. "Mug shots?"

Joe looked at Gram, then at me. "Actually, he really wanted to know about Tressa here," Joe said. I looked at him.

"Me? What would he want to know about me?"

Joe looked at Gram again and seemed to have difficulty with what came next. Not too hard to understand when you were spinning a yarn more tangled than the threads in my grammy's maroon afghan.

"He wanted to know if you and Rick had an understanding," my grandma said, looking pleased with herself.

"An understanding?" I repeated, my brain still slow to recover full function after being forced to face my very own *Fear Factor* challenge. "An understanding about what?"

Gram patted my cheek. "A relationship, my dear," she said. "Don't be obtuse." This coming from a woman who, to this day, still doesn't understand why Rock Hudson and Doris Day never married.

"Well, what did you tell him?" I asked, not believing the little cover-their-tails bit of fiction the two had concocted.

"Yes, what did you tell him?" Rick asked, much to my displeasure still coddling Mr. Swiffer.

"What could we tell him?" Joe asked. "We know squat. Except that you two set off sparks hotter than

Frank's belly burners." He stopped and slapped a hand to his mouth.

"Did you go ahead and eat one of those after you promised me you wouldn't?" Townsend said, placing the bull snake gently back in the middle of the blanket and then tying the ends together.

"He absolutely did not," Gram interjected. "He split one with me," she said, making me once again eternally grateful that Taylor would be the one with the pleasure of our grammy's nighttime company.

"What are you doing with Mr. Swiffer?" I asked Townsend, watching him pick up the wriggling bag.

"I'm gonna take him down to the DNR snake display, and put him in with another bull snake we have down there. Give him a chance to recover a bit before I release him."

I sighed. "Ranger Rick, reptile rescuer," I said.

"Care to join me?" he asked. I considered it, snake notwithstanding, until I remembered the hug I'd witnessed between the snake charmer here and my kid sister.

I shook my head. "I'm beat. Since your friend there kind of disturbed my nap, I think I'll turn in early."

He looked at me and seemed to want to argue, then nodded. "Have it your way," he said. "You heading back to the trailer, Pops?" he asked Joe.

"I'll be along," his grandpa answered. "But don't wait up for me." He gave Gram a big wink and she giggled like a schoolgirl.

I waited until Townsend was out of earshot before I cut loose on the maniacal meddlers.

"What were you two thinking, following Uncle Frank around like friggin' paparazzi?" I said after I sat them down on the couch like two recalcitrant kids. "Are you trying to submarine that marriage or what?"

"We're trying to *save* that marriage," Gram said. "That fool Frank is so dense when it comes to women, he don't see when a woman is makin' a play for him—though why any woman would want him is one of them mysteries that will probably never be solved."

I paced back and forth in front of them. "Explain to me again how taking pictures of Uncle Frank in semi-compromising situations is going to help his marriage."

"When a perpetrator is confronted with the evidence against him, he either comes clean, repents and reforms, or he chooses to continue the activity until he's brought into a court of law and that same evidence convicts him," Joe explained. That sounded way too law and orderly for my comfort.

"What court?" I asked. "Having a fling isn't illegal last I knew." Unless you did it in the Oval Office and then lied about it under oath.

"*Divorce Court*," Joe said. "As in, proof of infidelity where the injured party gets the house, the car, and beaucoup alimony."

"Uncle Frank and Aunt Reggie aren't going to get a divorce," I told them.

"Not now," Gram said, giving Joe's hand a squeeze. "Frank Barlowe would be a fool to file once he got hold of the dirt we've got on him. You know the saying a picture paints a thousand words? Well, our pictures speak volumes."

"Hand over the camera," I told them, holding out my hand.

"But we're not done. We still have five more days to photograph!" Gram objected.

"Hand it over," I repeated. "Or I tell Mom you switched the fat-free cream cheese with the regular kind," I told Gram.

"Oh, all right, here it is," Gram said, pulling the camera out of her less-than-fashionable fanny pack and handing it over. "But don't you delete those pictures! They're evidence, you know."

"Evidence that you two spend too much time watching *Unsolved Mysteries* reruns and reading whodunits," I replied.

"I'm gonna call it a night, Hannah," Joe said, getting to his feet. "If your granddaughter is done chewing my back end, that is," he added.

I nodded. "Go ahead," I told him, making a point of looking at his backside. "You're lookin' a little lean there, so I'm cutting you some slack." I looked down at the camera, too tired to view their handiwork. "I suppose you two were so busy shooting pictures of Uncle Frank not having an affair, you didn't get any for my fair feature," I said.

"Oh, we got your pictures, dear," Gram said, getting to her feet. "And that giant bull . . ." She shook her head, "I swear, his testicles are the size of cantaloupes. Aren't they, Joe?"

I made a face. "You didn't get that in the picture, did you?" I asked.

Gram looked at Joe, and he shrugged.

"Well, it was kinda hard to miss 'em, if you know what I mean." And saying that, he left.

Half an hour later, tucked in my tiny little crypt at the front of the trailer, I thought about the snake and again wondered how, of all the gin joints in all this campground, it had found its way into bed with me.

Townsend's explanation about the snake crawling in unnoticed was possible, but in view of the events leading up to the snake scare my gut told me this was one of those *Jaws* moments. You know—as in, "This was no accident!"

I fell asleep about midnight, thinking that never, ever again would I complain about having the bed in the nose-bleed section of the trailer.

CHAPTER 20

I ended up sleeping right through my wrist alarm and didn't awaken for my hoot-owl shift at the Emporium until nearly four. I finally woke, took one look at my watch, said a few really bad words in my head, and slid off my bed. I threw on a blue Country Chick T-shirt I'd laid out that featured an adorable, fluffy yellow baby chicky, and pulled on a pair of blue jeans, shoving my feet into my walking shoes. I quickly gathered my keys, my camera, a cell phone, and a penlight flashlight. Hands full, I prepared to depart.

As I was leaving, I caught a glimpse of Gram's pink fanny pack draped on the coat hooks by the front door. It had been kind of nice to have my hands free, I thought, and that might well prove exceptionally handy if the need to defend myself arose. Or, say, I wanted to eat a slice of pizza bread and wash it down with a diet soda at the same time. I looked back at the sleeping occupants of the sofa bed, ready to leave the pack hanging if they woke before I'd pilfered it. (Hey, I have a reputation to uphold that doesn't jibe with hot-pink fanny packs, folks.)

I lifted Grammy's pack off the hook and was out the door and down the hill before I let my breath back out. I jogged up to the Emporium and stopped. The front door was standing wide open. I looked around for a friendly trooper-type patrolling the fairgrounds, or even a hardworking sanitation technician picking up trash but didn't see either. I moved to the door and side-stepped my way into the darkened restaurant, crouched in a defensive posture, hoping I looked like I was ready for action. I probably looked more like the Hunchback of Notre Dame. I sucked in my breath when I detected movement behind the counter. I could make out the weak beam of a penlight at the cash register. Holy shine-oly, a robbery in progress!

I smacked myself around mentally for a moment, telling myself it was my fault the criminal had had the opportunity to break into the Emporium in the first place, and that it wouldn't have happened if I'd been there, but I finally made up with myself after I realized I'd probably have slept right through the break-in if I had been on the floor behind the counter. And how totally lame would that have been if I'd been stepped on by the perp?

I heard some whispered swear words that seemed kind of wussie for any hard-boiled felon type, and decided the element of surprise was a great advantage in a situation like this. Of course, so was a nine-millimeter, but with my luck, I'd shoot a hole clean through my Skechers and obliterate a big toe. (I'm kinda partial to having two big toes. Face it: You're limited in footwear choices when you're minus a big toe. No open-toe shoes ever again, no way.)

I reached out and grabbed a heavy metal napkin dispenser from the counter to my right, got a good grip on it, and hurled it at the figure by the register, putting enough cheese on it to drop a moose.

Whack, pow, thump, crash! The dispenser hit the guy near the top of his head, and he dropped like the price of sidewalk salt in late March.

I grabbed the push broom—hey, the Swiffer sweeper had done all right as a weapon—flipped on the lights, and crept around the end of the counter, poised to pummel the person with the broom if the need arose.

The first thing I saw was a set of feet—large ones, and brightly colored, but not those of a clown. These feet were orange. Shiny latex orange, complete with three long digits, the biggest positioned between two shorter ones, and a wee little digit on the inside of the foot. The claws were painted a brilliant white. I peered at the things, trying to figure out how human-sized fowl feet had ended up in the Emporium. I crept to the end of the counter, broom poised, and peeked around the corner . . . and still couldn't figure out what the heck I was looking at.

A fully dressed chicken ("dressed" as in attire, not as in bread crumbs and sage seasoning) was sprawled out on the floor below the open cash register. The prone pullet, I had to admit, was rather remarkable. The polished plastic fowl feet climbed to knee-level on this human, and from that point on up came a blindingly white, shaggy and thick furry material constituting poultry feathers. The head of the chicken, slightly askew, was totally radical: an imposing, large, yellow-orange beak, complete with large black beak nostrils and flanked by ketchup-red wattles and a dramatic shiny red comb. Very striking. Large, eerily pale turquoise-colored eyes were surrounded by a bright yellow ring and traced in black, and I have to confess here, their penetrating gaze made me a bit uneasy.

I jabbed the hen with the brush end of the broom, but

it didn't move. I wrinkled my brow. How did one wake a chicken? With a cock-a-doodle-doo?

I prodded the horizontal chicken again and finally got a response. It moaned, and the latex-crowned head moved slightly. One red latex-trimmed wing reached across and rubbed the forehead. Another soft moan escaped the beak.

Realizing that the chicken might be seriously injured and having a difficult time breathing inside the heavy head unit, I decided I'd have to remove it. And once I did, I'd snap a couple of shots of the culprit just in case he flew the coop before the cops arrived. (Now *that's* a legitimate pun.)

I ran to the Emporium kitchen, grabbed a filet knife—I was dealing with poultry, after all—and hurried back to my feathered friend. Knife in my right hand, I reached out and slowly removed the chicken head from the body with my left.

"You have got to be kidding!" I hissed as I exposed the identity of Foghorn Leghorn, our pillaging poultry perp. I ran to the kitchen, grabbed a glass of water, some ice, and a dish towel, and returned to the semiconscious chicken.

Wrapping some of the ice in the towel, I gently pressed it to the faux fowl's forehead, where an egg-sized knot was already forming.

"If I've killed you, Frank Barlowe, Jr.," I said, "I'm gonna kick your feathered fanny all the way to the funeral home." I felt tears trickle down my cheeks. "You hear?"

"Oh, ow! Hello? Hello?"

"Frankie!" I said, relief that he was conscious rippling through me. "Can you hear me? Open your eyes, Frankie!" I instructed.

"Tressa? Is that you?" He opened one eye.

I nodded, saying heavenly thanks that he could recognize me and was still able to see and speak. "Yes! It's me, Frankie."

He opened both eyes. "You look like hell," he said, and I grinned.

"Well, since that comes from a real cock-up, I'll consider the source," I told him. "What on earth are you doing here? Why were you at the cash register? I thought you were a burglar."

My words drew a vigorous response from our chicken man, not unlike the one a chicken might make when a predator sneaks into his henhouse. Frankie sat up, put one wing on the counter, and extended the other to me, and between the two of us, we managed to get him to his shanks and then to his feet.

"We've been robbed!" Frankie said, one hand holding the ice bag to his head, the other rifling through the cash drawer. "Cleaned out! Shit, shit, shit. They hit us again!" He kicked out with his large, orange latex foot.

I gave Frankie a real close look. He almost never used fowl (uh, I mean foul) language.

"Where the hell were you?" He turned to me, accusation apparent in his voice. "You were supposed to be watching the place!"

"I'm sorry!" I said. "I slept through the alarm. But don't take that tone with me, Chicken Boy. You have no idea what I've been through tonight."

"Well, it can't be any worse than being knocked out with a blow to the head. What did you hit me with, anyway?"

I bent over and retrieved the stainless-steel napkin dispenser and handed it to him. "If it had been the thief I interrupted instead of you, his goose would have been cooked," I told Frankie. "I didn't play four years of high-school softball for nothin'. So, did they really clean us out?" I asked.

Frankie nodded.

"How did you come to be here?" I asked. "Who's minding the mini-freeze?"

Frankie hesitated, rearranging the ice in the kitchen towel and pressing it back on his forehead. "Dixie," he said.

"You left our biggest competitor to guard our other concession stand? Isn't that like leaving the wolf to guard the henhouse?" I asked, making a face at the inadvertent poultry reference. Frankie didn't seem to notice the play on words.

"I trust Dixie," was all he said.

"You never did say what you were doing here. If I'd been on the floor behind the counter and you came in, no telling what I would have done to you," I told him.

"Something worse than knocking me out with the napkin dispenser?" he asked. He dabbed at his forehead again. "How bad is it?"

He looked like he had a goiter growing out of his forehead, but I wasn't about to tell him that. "Head bumps always look worse than they are," I told him. "You can barely notice it." *With the chicken head on,* I didn't add. But it begged the question: "Why on earth are you wearing a chicken costume?"

Frankie moved to one of the benches along the far wall and eased into a seat—not an easy thing to do when you're wearing yards of white feather fur. "Hello. I'm still working UC," he said.

"UC?"

"Undercover."

More likely under the care of a physician, I thought, but reminded myself I'd been in lockstep with Frankie in this asinine adventure since day one, so what did that say about my mental faculties?

"Why a chicken?"

"I have to mix it up. You know, rotate between disguises. Change my UC character so as not to attract attention."

Yeah, nothing to notice about a six-foot chicken. Keep tellin' yourself that, Frankie, I thought.

"But why a chicken?" I asked again.

"It fits in with the fair. Kids love me. You should see them smile and come up and shake my hand when I walk around the fairground. It's so neat."

"Where on earth did you find the costume?" I asked.

"I got it from Dix," he told me. "You remember when they used to call their business Cluck 'n' Chuck?"

I nodded. I used to call it Cluck 'n' Up-Chuck, which had truly endeared me to Dixie and her daddy. "Yeah. So?"

"They kept the mascot costume. Dixie told me about it, and I figured it would be the perfect way to blend in. I thought, Who's gonna hassle a chicken? And boy, was I right. They love me down at the Egg Council booth."

I felt a brain aneurysm coming on. "So, why did you come to the Emporium again?"

"I was starving," Frankie said. "I figured I'd get something to eat before the morning shift arrived."

"Couldn't you just chew on your wing or drumstick?" I asked with a snort.

"Funny," Frankie snapped. "So, what have you learned so far?"

"Well, I've been threatened by the Li boys, who desperately want me to jump ship and try to convince your father to sell—to their father, naturally," I said, filling him in on my encounter with the two hooligans. "And there's always Luther Daggett and his cantankerous—" I stopped, remembering that Frankie had professed his love for Luther Daggett's daughter, a development I was still trying to get my head around.

"Dixie is not involved," he told me. "I know she isn't." Oh, great. Yet another psychic, I thought.

"But sometimes I feel like someone is following me," Frankie added.

"Are you sure it's not Colonel Sanders?" I asked, performing another unladylike snort and enjoying the idea of chicken jokes, as opposed to blonde ones, for a change. Okay, so I was still a tad traumatized over the fact that I'd almost killed my cousin, and that made me a bit loopy.

"We may have more trouble," I told Frankie, snapping back to our conundrum. "Your folks aren't getting along, and there may be another woman in the wings to be the springboard to the old my-wife-doesn't-understand-me breakdown." Wings? I winced at my inability to keep from mentioning poultry parts.

"Another woman? What are you talking about?"

"Who, not what," I told him. "And the who is Trinkets and Treasures's Lucy. She and your dad have been spending quite a bit of time together. And Gram and her old friend Joe have made it their pet project to . . . er, protect your folks from her. They tailed your dad like two Keystone cops all day yesterday. I may have to devote some time to keeping the two of them out of trouble, or all heck may break loose."

"Is it that bad?" he asked. "Are Mom and Dad really struggling?"

I nodded. "It's a tough time," I said. "But I know they love each other, so they'll get through this."

He looked at me. "Sometimes it takes more than love," he said, and I knew he wasn't thinking about his folks.

"You'd better get out of here," I told him. "No telling how early your dad will get here.

Frankie got to his feet. "I could use some shut-eye," he said.

"By the way, where do you roost?" I asked, curious now that he'd been assigned the mini-freeze surveillance.

Frankie blushed redder than his shiny red wattle.

"Uh, I'm . . . uh, staying at Dixie's," he said.

"You're sleeping in the Daggetts' RV?" I yelled. "Isn't that a bit awkward? And, as much as I'm sure Luther Daggett would be thrilled to have Dixie bring someone home to meet the folks, I gotta think even Luther is gonna question a six-foot chicken on his daughter's arm."

Frankie handed me the towel with the now-melted ice. "Luther is gone most of the day," he said, and his blush deepened.

"You are being careful, aren't you, Mr. Leghorn?" I asked. "You don't want to hatch any baby chicks before you're ready," I warned.

Frankie gave me an angry look, grabbed his chicken head from the counter, and marched to the back door. "Cluck you!" he said, and put on his head and slammed the door behind him on the way out.

Wow! Beneath the ruffled feathers of Sir Cluck-n-Up-Chuck beat the heart of a hawk—well, a chicken hawk.

Who knew?

CHAPTER 21

Sheesh. I needed the State Patrol on speed dial. After I'd alerted the troopers to the latest break-in and theft, I woke Uncle Frank with my next phone call. It wasn't a long conversation. As a matter of fact, I'd barely hung up and he was on the doorstep. He must've really had his little white golf cart flying. Good thing no troopers were running radar at that hour. Is there a speed limit for golf carts?

I explained to Uncle Frank what had happened, and finally decided to come clean with him before the cops got there—though I had to two-step around the truth for Frankie's sake. Admitting to the authorities that he'd been at the scene of yet another hit on his father's business would point the finger of guilt right in his direction.

"He's been working deep UC to catch the culprit in the act," I told him.

"UC?" Uncle Frank raised an eyebrow.

"Undercover. With disguises and everything. The cowboy I got stuck with on the Sky Ride? Frankie. The insulting clown? Frankie." I decided not to mention the chicken. I wasn't all that comfortable with that particular personality, so I could only guess at Uncle Frank's reaction.

"I thought you said the clown was the bad guy," Uncle Frank said, clearly trying to get a handle on the situation.

"The horn-tooting trolley clown was," I explained, remembering that horn in the Emporium with some unease.

"So, there are two clowns?"

I nodded. "And one cowboy."

"And the two of you have been staking out my businesses, trying to catch the crooks?" he asked. "You know, I did kinda wonder what brought you down to the fairgrounds the night you caught the Daggett girl, but I sure as heck didn't expect this. By the way, why is this the first I'm hearing of it? Last I knew, I was the owner of record."

I nodded. "I wanted to tell you, but Frankie convinced me that if anyone else knew, chances were the bad guys would hear about it, too, and back off, leaving him high and dry." I smiled, thinking of Frankie's little routine in the dunk tank. "Frankie desperately wants to clear his name, Uncle Frank," I went on, "and he feels this might well be the only way to do it. I'm sorry we kept you out of the loop."

"Stakeouts, huh?" Uncle Frank rubbed his chin. "Wonder why I didn't think of that? Guess I've had a lot on my mind. So, who was supposed to be staking out this establishment last night?" he asked.

I hung my head. "Me," I admitted, disappointment that I'd let him down making my stomach hurt. "I slept through my alarm. I got down here a little after four, and that's when I found Frankie."

To my shock and surprise, Uncle Frank put a hand on my shoulder and a finger on my chin and tilted my head up so our eyes met. "Don't you be putting that hangdog look on," he said. "You put yourself out there for me and my family, niece, and don't think for a minute you let me down. You hear?"

I felt my nose sting and my eyes begin to burn and water. I could take a lot of things from Uncle Frank— *had* taken a lot from him—but gratitude and gentleness? Well, this was a first. Mr. Sensitive, Uncle Frank wasn't.

"Thanks, Uncle Frank," I said.

"Thank *you*," he said, and gave me a big bear hug.

I pulled away and looked up at him. "Now you remember, you can't tell a soul about our little covert operation," I told him. "We've only got four days left to catch the UNSUB and clear your son's name."

"UNSUB?"

"Unidentified subject."

"I will have to tell your Aunt Reggie, though," he said, and I nodded.

"I know," I agreed. "I think it will do her a world of good, knowing her only son is alive and well." Though he's living a life as a chicken franchise mascot.

"I'll handle stakeout duties here tonight," Uncle Frank told me. "You've earned a night off."

"Are you sure? Frankie and I usually put a bedroll down behind the counter. That way, no one can see us from either window and won't even know we're there until they're busted. But that floor is still pretty darned hard."

Uncle Frank frowned. "And you did this on your own, without backup or a weapon of any sort?"

"I had my camera and the cell phone," I said. "And the ability to scream really, really loud."

He shook his head. "No more solo stakeouts," he commended. "You recruit someone you trust of the male persuasion to stay with you or you're benched," he told me, ever the sports fan.

"But—"

"No buts, young lady. Find a partner or I pull the plug."

I nodded. "Okay," I agreed, resigned to the fact that I would have to ask the Don Juan of the DNR to partner up with me the following night. It would be strictly business between us, though. No kisses, no hugs. No hanky. No panky.

"I'll get a message to Frankie that you're in the know and will be covering the Emporium tonight," I told Uncle Frank.

Uncle Frank's eyes widened. "You've got a system in place to relay messages to each other?" he asked.

"Yup. We're not a bunch of hillbillies here," I told him. "We use s*oo*phist*ee*cated technology to communicate."

He gave me a funny look.

"We pass notes," I explained, and he nodded.

"Would you tell him something for me?" Uncle Frank asked. I detected a certain huskiness in his voice. "Tell him Mom and Dad send their love."

I felt the weepies coming on again, and since an undercover operative really can't be seen with a case of the weepies, I excused myself to blow my nose before the authorities arrived.

And they came. They saw. They rolled their eyes and shook their heads. I requested Trooper Dawkins, telling them he was familiar with the case (all right, all right, and because he's so danged cute), but I was advised he wouldn't be on until eight. I was surprised when Uncle Frank made me tell the cops that Frankie had actually been there, too, so I wouldn't be in hot water if it came out later; however, we both felt it was best to leave out the particulars relating to our nightly temp security jobs and Frankie's various theatrical disguises.

I'd stuck as close to the truth as I could, telling the cops that Frankie had gone to the Emporium to get something to eat and to use the restroom, and that I had no idea where he'd gone from there. Which was true, although I had a pretty good idea it was straight into the arms of Dixie Daggett, so she could kiss his boo-boo and make it all better. Even the mere thought of that particular picture in my head gave me the willies.

It was close to eight A.M. by the time the troopers left and Aunt Reggie arrived. Uncle Frank shoved me out the front onto the sidewalk, shut the door, and stuck a CLOSED sign in the window. I figured he wanted uninterrupted time with Aunt Reggie to explain things. I wondered how that conversation would go.

I headed for the campgrounds and some much-needed rest. Craig and Kimmie would take over at the Emporium at three, and Taylor was at the mini-freeze until Mom relieved her midafternoon, so I actually had a day off. That realization almost made me giddy. I could get some sleep, then venture out and take some fair photos and just enjoy myself for a while.

Remembering the camera, I unzipped the fanny pack pouch and pulled it out and switched it on. The low-battery indicator flashed, but nothing else happened. Dang. I should have stuck it in the charger last night. Sticking it back in the pack, I climbed the hill to the campgrounds, feeling the pull on my leg muscles as I ascended. I really did need to start that fitness program. And I'd do it. I would. Right after the fair. I frowned. Uh-oh. Wasn't that when the Halloween candy arrived in the stores?

As I approached the trailer, I saw the picnic table under our pull-out awning was inhabited by two senior citizen sleuths, one ranger from Jellystone Park, and one brother who was still in the doghouse with me.

"Heigh-ho!" I greeted the group, knowing I looked like I'd been sucked through a wind tunnel backward, but too tired to care. Townsend and his granddad got to their feet, but my cloddish brother remained sitting.

"Crikeys! It's the snake huntah back from down undah!" Craig called out. " 'Lo, mite. Beat up any harmless reptiles today?"

I felt my lip curl. It was way too early, and I was way too tired to put up with 'tude from my big brother. "No, but I could be persuaded to knock some sense into a six-foot, loud-mouthed ass," I said.

He frowned.

"Bad night?" Townsend asked.

"You have no idea," I said. "Where's Kimmie?" I asked Craig, receiving only a terse jerk of his head toward the trailer in response.

"You look at our pictures yet?" Joe asked, reaching out for a fat blueberry bagel. I smiled when I spotted the fat-free cream cheese container. Right.

"Battery conked," I said. "I'm gonna stick it on the charger now. I'll take a look at them later."

"You been down to the see that big bull?" Joe asked the other men at the table. Both shook their heads. "It's worth your time—isn't it, Hannah?" Joe said. "Although, for a male, it's a bit of a humbling experience."

I started to giggle.

"What's so funny?" Gram asked. "Did I miss something again?"

I shook my head. "I'm just tired," I explained, "and when I'm tired everything strikes me as funny."

"Even five-foot-long bull snakes?" Craig asked with a smirk.

"How is the repugnant little trespassing vertebrate, anyway?" I asked Townsend. "Recovering nicely, I suppose, given all the TLC you lavished on him last night after my brutal beating. What an insensitive durfwad you must think me not to have welcomed Mr. Swiffer into my bed with open arms."

Townsend gave me such an intense look, it made me think back on what I'd said. I blushed when I rewound to the "welcoming into my bed with open arms" part.

"He'll live," Rick said.

"To invade someone else's living area, no doubt," I grumped. "He'd better be careful. Next time someone will use a hoe instead of a Swiffer sweeper thingy."

"Am I gonna get my afghan back?" Gram asked. "I crocheted that myself. Only blanket I ever finished."

Townsend shrugged. "It's got a little snake blood on it, but since the blanket's maroon you probably won't even notice. If that doesn't bother you, you're good to go."

I gave a shiver. "I'll replace the blanket," I told Gram.

"Can you replace ten years of swollen joints and finger cramps?" she asked.

I looked at Townsend. "Give her the blanket," I said.

Gram considered her options for about a tenth of a second. "I'd like a nice cornflower blue throw," she decided, and Townsend smiled and sat. "Not one of those cheapos you sell at Bargain City, Tressa, but a nice one, with fringe on the borders. You'll have to take me with you when you get it. If I don't go, you'll come back with a horse blanket."

I nodded. "Gotcha, Gram," I said, noticing an open atlas sitting on the table amid various printed sheets of paper. I picked it up. It was open to Northern Ontario.

"Someone planning a vacation?" I asked, shuffling the papers around on the table. "'Wild Goose Family Resort,'" I read. "Are you and Kimmie planning a little getaway?" I asked Craig, who started gathering up the loose pages. He grabbed the atlas from me and stuck the loose papers inside.

"I told her she was welcome to come, too," Craig said, and I looked down at him, making one of those faces that dermatologists warn you not to do or you'll give yourself forehead furrows.

"*Too?*"

"Yeah. Rick and a couple other guys and I are planning to take a fall hunting and fishing trip to Canada. I told Kimmie she could come along. The cabins are big enough, so there would be more than enough room. We want to be there for the moose hunts. Bow, that is," he clarified.

My eyebrows raised. "You invited your wife along on a moose hunt with three other men?" I asked. "Are you insane?"

"There's shopping twenty minutes away," Craig asserted.

"Near a golf course," Kimmie inserted from the doorway.

I nodded. "I get it now. You're going off on a sports vacation with the guys and you want to pacify Kimmie, here, with a lame offer to invite her to come, knowing full well no woman in her right mind would tag along with a carload of men bent on hunting moose with a bow. Give me a break, Craig."

Craig stood. "I work hard at the dealership," he said.

"And I work hard at the courthouse," Kimmie replied, coming to stand between her husband and me. Probably a good idea. "And you don't see me taking off for two weeks and leaving the country with you home alone."

"So go," Craig said. "Do it. Nobody's stopping you."

"I don't want to take my vacation time and spend it away from you," she told him. "We're married. Husband and wife. We should share our vacations. You know, be a family."

"Ah, I see what this is," Craig said. "There it is. The *F* word again: family. You're just annoyed because I'm not ready to have a family yet. Admit it."

I saw tears pool in Kimmie's eyes.

"When do you plan to be ready, Craig?" she asked. "When? After one more Canadian vacation? After one more NCAA championship? After one more Superbowl? When? When will you be ready to become a father?"

"I don't know!" Craig yelled, running his hand through his hair. "I don't know. But I'm not there yet. Okay?"

"No, it is not okay," Kimmie said. "You've got to grow up, Craig, and stop spending your life with your head in some game or contest or sport. And it better happen soon, because I won't wait forever." She spun around and entered the trailer, sliding the door closed with a snap.

Selfish ass, I said under my breath, though from the look Craig gave me, it might've slipped out. My brother gathered up his flyers and stomped off toward his pickup, which was parked alongside the trailer.

"Well, you were a big help, Townsend," I said, taking the seat Craig had vacated.

"Me? What do I have to do with this?" Rick asked.

"You saw the tension between those two and the serious unresolved issues—like, why can't my brother stop his game-playing obsessions and attain adulthood? Why didn't you say something? Tell him you think he should reconsider and cancel the trip? Stay close to hearth and home and all that?"

Townsend rubbed a tanned jaw. "Because I don't intend to insert myself into a highly personal matter that is clearly between a husband and his wife—and I suggest you do the same, Tressa."

I rolled my eyes. Townsend was always full of s . . . suggestions.

"All this marital discord has put me off my bagel," Gram said and got to her feet. "How about you, Joe?" she asked. "You put off, too?"

"I confess I'm having a difficult time chewing mine," Joe admitted. "But I could go for a warm cinnamon roll. If you're up to it. We covered a lot of ground yesterday."

"I'm fine," Gram assured him. "I'll just go grab my fanny pack."

I made a face when I realized her fanny pack was still strapped around my gut. I emptied it with one hand and unhooked it with another, sliding it along the picnic bench until it was a safe distance from me.

"Here it is, Grammy. You must have left it outdoors." I handed it to her.

"Thank you, dear," she said, and patted my arm. "You're a good granddaughter. I need to tinkle, then we'll be off," she told Joe. He stood.

"Come to think of it, I'd better make a quick stop, too. The prostate ain't what it used to be."

When they were gone, I smiled at the ranger across from me. "Did you hear my grammy, Townsend? She said I was a good granddaughter." I did a dimple thing with an index finger on each cheek. "That's me. A good girl."

Townsend snickered. "Yeah, right. A good girl who pilfers from her grandmother, then lies about it. A good girl who plays detective and then plays fast and loose with the truth when questioned about it. A good girl who has more secrets than the CIA. You're good, all right," he said.

I looked over at the guy I called such things as carp cop and bass buster, and with whom I'd made an outrageous raccoon tattoo bet earlier this summer and sighed. Someday I really needed to sit down and figure out when *I* was planning to attain adulthood. But for now I shrugged. I was still several years behind Craig; I'd worry about it when I was his age.

"This good girl has a favor to ask," I told Rick. "And it involves one of those secrets you just referred to."

"Go on," Townsend said slowly, as if not quite sure he really wanted to hear.

I told him about the break-in at the Emporium that morning and how I'd run into Frankie, adding that he was in disguise at the time and that was why I'd beaned him.

"Was he hurt?" Townsend asked.

"There was an egg-sized lump forming," I admitted, wincing at yet another fowl joke. "But he seemed okay."

"He should have seen a doctor," Townsend said, and I could only imagine how the attending physician would have reacted if I'd walked in with a tall, lanky chicken in hand.

"And your uncle is cool with this?" Townsend asked.

"Probably he knew I'd go ahead and find a way to watch the joint anyway," I said. "He got all huggy and friendly when he found out we'd been watching his places." I shivered. "It was creepy."

"So you're gonna do this with or without my help, right?" Townsend asked.

I nodded. "I have to," I told him. "For the family."

He looked at me for a second. "What's in it for me?" he asked.

"Apart from the pleasure of my company all night?" I batted my eyes at him.

"Yeah. Apart from that," he replied. I stopped the eye thing. Apparently, compared to Taylor, my flirting was more closely read as dry-eye syndrome. "What's in it for me?" he asked again.

I chewed my lip. "Food. Conversation. We could play poker."

Townsend's eyebrow did an up-the-flagpole move. "Strip?" he asked.

"In your dreams," I told him. "Oh, but I'll throw in one promise to butt out and let Craig and Kimmie try to handle their own marital issues."

Townsend considered the package I'd put on the table.

"Pinky-swear?" he asked, cocking his little finger in my direction.

I stuck my finger out and we locked digits. "Pinky-swear," I said, feeling the heat from the paltry contact as if someone had lit a sparkler way too close for comfort.

I made the mistake of looking into Townsend's eyes and imagined I saw my own heat reflected there, even magnified. I suddenly remembered the night Townsend had wanted to be alone in the Emporium and had to wonder if planning to spend the night with him there the following night was such a hot idea after all.

I'm a good girl, I am, I reminded myself.

Keep tellin' yourself that, Tressa.

CHAPTER 22

I spent the remainder of the morning and a good chunk of the afternoon dead to the world. My mother insisted I take the back bedroom to catch up on my rest, and one doesn't argue with my mother. Besides, I wasn't crazy enough to refuse a queen-sized bed for one the size of an army cot.

I roused around three and padded to the bathroom, then out into the living area, but no one was about. I decided this would be an ideal time to get some additional photos for the fair insert for the *Gazette*. I sure didn't want to have to end up running a picture of a bull with melon-sized male parts. I wasn't sure what kind of reaction I'd receive from the older readers in my small town, but the youngsters would have a field day.

I took a quick shower, secured my hair in a French braid down the center of my back, and dressed in denim shorts and a white T-shirt with a pair of Indian pink and turquoise Tony Lama boots on the front. Way cool boots. Though, like, four hundred and fifty dollars or so beyond my present means. Still, the T-shirt only cost nine-

ninety-five, so I was okay. I pulled on some white socks and slipped into my boots and was ready to go.

I raided the refrigerator and found a container of ham salad and some bread, and made a quick sandwich. I washed that down with a bottle of water, then collected my camera and keys and sunglasses and stood trying to figure out how I was going to carry everything with me. I found myself thinking that a fanny pack wasn't all that horrid of an invention. It beat a backpack hands down.

I rifled through the tiny closet, trying to find something that would transport my valuables efficiently. On tiptoes, I reached up on the closet shelf and found two umbrellas, a Hawkeye baseball cap, and, to my amazement, pulled out a bright red fanny pack, the one that Gram had worn at last year's fair and had sworn Abigail Winegardner had pinched at the Labor Day parade. I searched through it and discarded a couple of toothpicks wrapped in clear plastic, a really old package of Spearmint gum, three plastic-wrapped star mints, and eight dollars and twenty-seven cents.

I wrote a quick note for Frankie to let him know his dad was now on board and tucked it in my back pocket. I strapped on the tomato-red fanny pack with almost no degree of shame and filled it with my necessities. I'd just meander through the fair and snap whatever jumped out at me, I told myself, sticking on a khaki visor and fairly dancing out the door, happy to finally have some time to enjoy my surroundings. I'd call it a night early, I told myself, as I might not get much sleep the following night, bunking up with Rick Townsend. All alone. All night. Just the two of us. I stared down at my feet. Geez, my toes were curling already!

I waved to the shuttle riders as I headed down to the fairgrounds, content to walk, my stride light and bouncy. Next I skipped to the horse barn, located my cousin's private little message board, lifted the poster, and discovered a note from Frankie. I replaced his with mine, then skipped back out onto the sidewalk. Life was good.

I opened Frankie's note and scanned it.

Olde Mill Stream. Nine sharp. Come alone.

I rolled my eyes. Who'd Frankie think he was, anyway—Deep Throat? I seriously hoped he wouldn't come dressed as a chicken to the Tunnel of Love ride. A chicken escorting a cowgirl wearing a bright red fanny pack was bound to attract attention.

I spent a delightful afternoon on my own, with a quick stop at the mini-freeze to say hi to Mom, then was back on my mission to find photos for Stan. I snapped more than a few equestrian events. (Okay, so I'm biased—tell me the mainstream media isn't.) I shot some really disgusting pictures of the pie-eating contest and one of my old friend, the Tooterville Trolley. I got the neatest photo of a kindergarten-age girl with long blond pigtails, her face stuck in a big pink mass of cotton candy, and one of the talent show in progress, where a high-school girl decked out in cute cowgirl attire sang—or rather, tried to sing—the "Boots Are Made for Walkin'" song.

I found myself outside Lucy's Trinkets and Treasures, and I wandered through the stalls, handling the assorted mood rings, different-colored bike horns, and fiddling with the crepe-paper fans and tiny little dream catchers.

"Well, look who's gracing my humble stand," I heard, and noticed Lucy near the back of one of her larger tents on a stool near the cash register. "Find anything of interest?" she asked.

"Lots of interesting things, but no money," I told her. "How's business?" I asked. Every concessionaire always wants to know how others' businesses are faring so they know if a downward trend is "due to the economy, stupid," or their stupid concession.

"Fair to middlin'," Lucy said. "The weather has cooperated so far, so that helps. Everything settling down over at Frank's?"

I shrugged. "Sure, yeah, everything is back to normal," I lied, thinking that if Lucy thought she was going to pull any information about Uncle Frank from me, she was living in La La Land. A tiny toddler grabbed a cowboy hat from a table down a piece and stuck it on his head. It dropped over his eyes and made his cute little ears stick out. I took my camera and snapped a picture.

"So, you're picture-taking," Lucy said—stating the obvious, I thought. "Isn't that the same camera your grandma had yesterday? She said she was taking pictures for a scrapbook or something."

More like for a civil action.

"Gram wants to capture some memories," I explained. Or manufacture some.

"Funny. Everywhere I went, Hannah and her friend turned up. If I didn't know better, I'd say they were following me." She laughed. I joined in with a fake laugh of my own.

"For folks of a 'certain age,' they do get around," I said. "But they're basically harmless." It was a lie. The pair was about as harmless as termites in a new construction project. "Well, I still need to snap a couple more photos for this fair article I'm putting together," I told her, "so I'll see you around." I walked away, thinking that the private eyes hadn't been private enough if Lucy kept spotting them.

I spent a leisurely afternoon wandering the fairgrounds. At eight-thirty I stopped in at the Emporium to see if Craig and Kimmie were getting along any better.

I entered and took a seat at the counter. Craig was

handling the food orders and Kimmie the customers. The place was still pretty busy, and I considered helping out until I realized most everyone had been served and was at the consuming stage.

"You want something?" Kimmie asked. I shook my head.

"No, but thanks for asking," I said. "I feel like a real patron."

She smiled. "Thanks for, well, you know," she said, casting a look over her shoulder at her hubby.

"Think nothing of it," I replied. "I fully enjoy each and every opportunity to hassle my big brother that presents itself. After all, Craig never misses a chance to diss me."

"So I've noticed," she said. "And I'm sorry I was a bit insensitive when we spoke earlier in the week. I didn't realize until later how what I said about having Taylor talk to him must have sounded. It's just that you and Craig have a much more volatile relationship."

"That stems from years of abuse at the hands of Caveman Craig and his Neanderthal sidekick, Rick Townsend. Of course, I always retaliate in kind," I assured her.

She laughed. "Family dynamics are so—"

"Sucky?" I suggested, and she laughed again.

"Exactly."

I spent a few minutes giving Craig a hard time over his grill cleanup skills—or lack thereof—used the restroom, and then headed out to the Olde Mill ride to meet Frankie.

Located off to the right of the entrance to the midway, it was one of the oldest rides at the fair. I remembered Gram telling how she and Paw Paw Will had made whoopie during the ride. I'd thought it was so cool to think of them as young lovers exploring and acting on those potent emotions.

Until I'd learned they'd both been nearly sixty.

I stood for a moment and looked around, wondering when Frankie was going to show and if he was going to strut and scratch the ground, walk bow-legged and with a gimp, or ride up on a unicycle.

"Pssst!" I heard, and looked over to see Frankie the clown get on one of the boatlike carts that moved through the ride. He motioned for me to follow.

"Oh, good grief," I said, handing the ticket-taker my fare and taking a seat next to Frankie. The car moved forward and took us into the darkened interior of the romantic ride, which featured glowing depictions of a shore at night.

"This is like really lame," I told Frankie. "Why all the Serpico stuff? Did you get my note about Uncle Frank? Did you read his message?"

One minute Frankie sat there looking at me and the next he was all over me like Joe Townsend on a sticky bun.

I pushed him away. "Frankie! What are you doing?" I asked. "Have you lost your mind?"

I struggled with him for a few more seconds before he lunged for my torso again. "Stop it, Frankie!" I yelled. "Get your hands off me!"

It took a few more seconds for me to realize that he wasn't after my beauteous bod but rather after my gaudy red fanny pack. On the heels of that light-bulb moment came the realization that the groping clown was not Frankie.

The clown reached out and grabbed at the strap that ran around my waist and attempted to curl his fingers around it. I raked my fingernails across his hand and he hissed and grabbed hold of my braid and yanked. Hard. I pulled at the other hand grabbing at my gut area and managed to throw a strategically placed elbow (completely by accident, I assure you) that made harsh contact with the cartilage of his nose. He howled and released me just long enough for me to propel myself out of the moving cart, landing in the gross water filling the ancient attraction. I picked myself up out of the murky depths of the water ride and ran toward the entrance, water filling my boots and soaking my socks. The realization that my boots were probably ruined made me almost turn and face the Looney Toon, but I recalled a story I'd read about an evil clown that turned out to be a spidery creature thingy the size of a house, so decided to keep running.

I heard splashing behind me and knew the clown was in wet pursuit. I hoped he ruined his big old clown shoes. Those had to cost a pretty penny to replace, too.

I sprinted out of the Olde Mill ride and did one of those things that always makes me want to yell and throw popcorn at the movie screen in the theater. Or I would if I was ever willing to part with my popcorn. I looked back. Yeah, I know, another one of those, if-she's-that-dumb-she-deserves-to-die moments. I confess, I did it. I think it must be instinctive. When you're being chased, you naturally want to know how close your pursuer is, so you turn around. Which of course always slows you down. Like, how fast can you run in one direction when your head is turned the opposite way?

Which brings us to the next opportunity to yell at our heroine. She falls. Like you knew she would. She's lying there on the ground, and the serial killer is getting closer and closer, and she's crawling along the ground on her hands and knees and you're yelling, "Get up, you moron! He's gonna eat your liver with fava beans and a nice Chianti," but she's all sniveling and pathetic.

Anyway, long story short, I looked back, crashed into a helium balloon concessionaire inflating a dinosaur for little Johnny, and knocked him clean over, landing on top of him. T. Rex went sailing off into the cosmos. Little Johnny started wailing "My balloon, my balloon!"

and reached out and kicked me with his tiny tenny. Behind the endearing toddler, Mom and Dad gave me dual what-have-you-done-to-our-little-Johnny looks that, truth be told, were so unfriendly I figured I was safer in the hands of the Great Bobo.

I apologized, patted little Johnny on the head, and looked back to see Bobo rounding the snocone stand, so I took off again. I spotted the Giant Slide and flew past the ticket-taker, bolting up the stairs as fast as my soggy, water-logged boots would take me, figuring I'd just remain along the top of the slide and wait for the ticket-taker to alert the troopers that he had a problem patron, and all would be well.

As I was pacing on the metal walkway across the top, the two boys I'd passed on the stairs on the way up gave me dirty looks, put their mats down, jumped on them belly first, and took off. Their screams could be heard over two speakers attached to poles on either side of the slide.

Microphones? I looked up and, sure enough, above me were mikes designed to pick up the screams of sliders on their descent. If screams could be heard . . .

"Uh, hello out there! Yoo-hoo!" I heard my words bounce out of the dual speakers. *"Uh, my name is Tressa Turner, and, uh, I need your help. I'm being chased by Bobo the insulting clown, so if you could please get the troopers over here, I would appreciate it. Hello? Did you get that?"* I addressed my remarks to the ticket guy, a scruffy-looking young man in a black Pink Floyd T-shirt. *"Yoo-hoo! Did you get that? I need the police. Now!"*

I stood there a few seconds, and stiffened as Bobo appeared around the corner.

"That's him!" I yelled toward the microphone. *"That's the clown who tried to steal my fanny pack!"*

I waited for the kid to take action and alert the cops, but to my disbelief, he merely exchanged a few words with the clown and nodded. In total amazement—and with no small sense of anxiety—I watched Bobo walk right past the slide concessionaire and head for the stairs. And me!

I began yelling in earnest, calling for help; then I remembered I'd been told that "Help!" didn't work (ya think?) and started yelling "Fire!" instead. That *did* attract attention. But still no action. A small crowd had gathered at the bottom of the slide, and Bobo the insane clown was getting closer with every step.

He ascended the final stair and was at the opposite end of the walkway. He smiled, and not a happy here's-some-candy-and-a-pat-on-the-head clown smile. An *It* smile.

Bobo moved toward me. The crowd below had grown to include the dude on stilts who walks around the fair, the vampire boy from the freak show with real honest-to-goodness fangs, Tattoo Teddy from the same freak show, little Johnny, a new T. Rex balloon clutched in one chubby hand, and his two unforgiving parents.

Bobo took a couple more steps in my direction. He was only about five feet from me. I looked down the long slide, accurately assessed that it constituted my only avenue of escape, sat down, and thrust myself forward. Of course, I'd completely neglected to allow for the no-mat factor, or the fact that I was wearing short shorts. The slide seared the back of my thighs like a hot iron as I whipped down it, slowing my speed and hurting like heck. I put my knees up so only my T-shirt and denim-clad butt made contact with the slide and my speed increased. I flew the remainder of the way down.

I didn't need to turn to ascertain that Bobo was still giving chase. The reaction of the crowd and chants of "Bobo!" were enough to convince me to pick myself up as fast as I could and keep on truckin'.

I got to my feet and ran toward the crowd, hoping to

lose myself in it. As I flew through the people, my fanny pack caught on the string of little Johnny's new dino balloon, ripping it out of his hand.

"My balloon! My balloon!" Little Johnny screamed, but I didn't take time to look back. (I do catch on eventually.) I cut through the back of the midway rides, trying to head for the back side of the Emporium.

I bobbed and weaved and darted in and out of concessions and tents, but for the life of me (ho, ho, ho) I simply could not lose Bobo the psycho. He stalked me more efficiently that I stalk the shoe-store shelves after getting my income tax refund.

I ran past the kiddie cars and the swings. Flew past the airplanes and octopus. I sprinted out of the midway and ended up by the restrooms in back of the frontier town and Old West Show. Music was playing, and the last performance of the show was in progress. I caught my breath for a second, thinking I'd finally lost Bobo, when I saw him step out from a row of cars parked near the carnival trailers. I frowned. With his tracking skills, this guy should be with a government security agency.

"Look, Mommy! T. Rex!"

I stared at a little blond girl with two front teeth missing who had just come out of the restroom with her mother, and followed the direction of her pointing finger. There, above my head, was little Johnny's dinosaur balloon bobbing and bouncing like a blinkin' beacon for all the world—and any psycho clowns—to see—and follow. I pulled the string from the latch of my fanny pack and handed it to the girl.

"Here," I said, patting her head. "You take it."

She looked up at her mother, who nodded and then took the balloon.

"Thank you," she said. And I smiled, praying the little girl and her mum didn't run into little Johnny and his folks before they left the fairgrounds.

Bobo, meanwhile, had not given up. He picked up his pace now that the girl and her mother had moved away, and so I took off again, deciding that the john wasn't a real safe place to hide. I ran toward the back of the stage, where the Wild West Show performed a goofy version of a gunfight each year. I hadn't had the opportunity to take in this year's production yet.

Bobo was gaining on me, my last lengthy run having been prompted by the discovery of a dead guy some weeks back. The fair foods I'd indulged in didn't help matters. I noticed a short set of stairs with a door at the top, and took them three at a time. I yanked the door open and stepped onto the front porch of the Last Chance Saloon. Talk about prophetic.

"And I'm tellin' you, she's my woman!"

"She's mine! And I'll kill the varmint who says otherwise!"

I walked straight from a horror novel into a Wild West romantic triangle. Out on Main Street, a cowboy in white—presumably the good guy—faced a mustachioed outlaw in black. The "she" they were presently fighting over was leaning on the rail outside the jail. The woman was wearing a veil, and I suspected an interrupted-wedding plot. It was as overdone as the cowboy-and-the-baby stories you see in romances. (All right, all right, I admit it. I'm still a sucker for those baby books. They just tug at your heartstrings, don't they?)

"If that's what it takes," the guy in the white hat said.

"Whenever you're ready," the outlaw replied. "If you got the guts." Personally, I was rooting for the outlaw. He was the hotter of the two.

The cowboys circled each other for a moment before the veiled lady suddenly ran by me and down off the stage, pausing briefly as she swept by. She threw herself between the two cowboys.

"Please!" she begged the outlaw. "Please! I love him." She moved to the hero and put her head over his heart. "If you kill him, you'll have to kill me, too."

Mesmerized by the play in spite of its over-the-top hokeyness, I failed to hear the creak of the back stairs until it was almost too late. I shoved my back against the door and grabbed the knob so the clown couldn't gain access. I braced myself against the door, my fanny pressed flat. He pushed. My butt and I resisted. He twisted the doorknob. I held firm.

It was only after several minutes passed that I realized the actors out front had stopped acting and, along with their audience, were looking expectantly at the door.

Somebody on the other side pounded on the door.

"That's my cue! Let me in!" I heard.

I looked over at the hunky cowboy, and he nodded his head urgently at me.

I hesitated, then opened the door a slit, and it burst open. A hillbilly-type, shirtless, with bib overalls and a long beard, with a hayseed stuck in his mouth, gave me a dirty look and bellowed, "She cain't marry either of you! 'Cause she's already married to me!"

All three actors out front performed an exaggerated gasp, and the hillbilly moved down the stairs. I followed him to stand at the top of the steps, wondering how this romantic coil was going to work out.

"Come along, Sadie. The carnival sideshow is fixin' to move to the next town."

"Carnival?" Sadie's two suitors replied as one.

The hillbilly nodded. "Sadie here is their biggest attraction. Aren't you, Sadie?"

The hillbilly husband reached out and yanked the veil from her head. "May I present my wife, Sagebrush Sadie!" he announced.

The cowboys acted stunned.

Sadie rushed to her hillbilly husband and into his arms. "Take me home, Harold," she said. "Home to our sideshow."

Music started to play and the four actors out front began to sing and square dance to the tune of "Sagebrush Sadie," the famous bearded lady.

Before I knew what was happening, the outlaw actor grabbed my hand and pulled me down the stairs, twirling me around like I was one of the actors. Good thing I know a little Texas two-step. I was whirled and twirled and passed between the hero and the outlaw like a hot potato in a church picnic contest. Finally the music wound down and the finale was over. Or so I thought. Just as the last of the music faded, the outlaw grabbed me and hauled me over his shoulder.

"This little filly's mine," he said, with a loud yee-haw and a firm swat on my behind.

"What the hell is this?" I asked him from my perch on his shoulder.

"Improvisation," he replied. "Improvisation."

I shook my head. Actors.

CHAPTER 23

I awoke around seven A.M., staring at a ceiling not all that far above me, and thought about the events of the night before. I'd managed to make it back to the trailer unmolested, choosing to attach myself to a group of folks my parents' age who were returning to the fairgrounds from the rock 'n' roll concert. I tried to visualize my folks giggling and crooning "My Boyfriend's Back" to each other, but only got static and white snow.

After taking bows for my not-ready-for-primetime acting debut the previous night, I'd hung with the crowd until I was safely at the State Patrol headquarters, where I spilled my guts, along with the contents of my fanny pack, to the officer on duty.

"I can't imagine what Bobo wanted," I'd told him.

The same sergeant who'd been unfortunate enough to process me the time before looked across the counter at me. "Cash, maybe?"

I snorted. "I've got eight dollars on me and it's not even mine," I said. "Besides, this guy lured me to the Olde Mill on purpose. He wanted something only I have."

The sergeant seemed to give my less-than-bountiful chest a once-over and apparently decided that wasn't the source of Bobo's interest.

"And you're sure it wasn't your cousin?" the officer asked again.

I nodded. "I've hit Frankie in the nose before and heard his grunt of pain. This was definitely not the same nose—or the same grunt. Besides, from what I've heard they employ a passel of Bobos in order to fill three shifts of insult-hurling and episodic dunking. So, who's to know how many Bobos are running around at one given time and who they all are?"

"I see you have a key ring. Is it possible that the individual was trying to get your keys?" He fingered the keys that were clearly marked for the Emporium and the mini-freeze. "Perhaps to facilitate a break-in?"

"Wow!" I said. "You're good!"

The cop rubbed the back of his neck. "I'll file an attempted-assault report," he said, "but the best advice I can give you, since it appears you are a target, is not to go anywhere by yourself. If you *must* work alone, have a phone handy to call for help. Be aware of your surroundings."

"I don't suppose you have any troopers who would hire out as off-duty security for the rest of the fair and agree to be paid in ice cream bars and beef burgers?" I asked.

The sergeant looked at me over the top of his glasses.

"I didn't think so," I replied, and left.

I thought about the officer's advisory not to work alone if possible, and knew I was scheduled for the mini-freeze from opening 'til three today. Who could I count on to baby-sit me for those seven hours who wouldn't drive me so crazy I'd want to get the Swiffer sweeper out and club them?

"Tressa, get up! Frank wants to know if you want a

ride to the mini-freeze on his golf cart. He says to tell you he's taking off in fifteen minutes, and if you don't want to get soaked, be ready."

I sat up and hit my head. "Soaked?"

"It's rainin' cats and dogs and earthworms," Gram stated. "I knew it was fixin' to rain last night. My knee joints gave me fits. Thank goodness I brought my Gay Ben."

I chuckled. Apparently, the joint pain reliever was now officially Gay Ben. My family is so weird.

I slid to the floor below and stretched. "It had to rain sometime. It's held off so long, the midway was starting to make an armpit smell good," I said.

I cleaned up, dressed, braided my hair quickly, and grabbed the camera off the charger and my keys from the counter and the red fanny pack.

"Where on earth did you get that?" Gram asked, seeing me secure the pack to my waist. The waistpack had proven its worth to me the night before, and we were now joined at the hip—in a manner of speaking. "Has Abby Winegardner been sneakin' around up here without me knowin'?"

I shook my head. "I found it in the back of the closet," I told her. "Aren't you sorry you accused Mrs. Winegardner of taking it?"

Gram looked at me and then walked over and bent down to look. "That's not my pack," she said. "Mine was a lighter red. More of an apple red than a tomato," she said.

"What's the difference?" I asked. "And this is too your fanny pack, because I found your spearmint gum and mints in it. Plus eight dollars and odd cents."

"I tell you that is not my fanny pack," she insisted. "I should know my own fanny pack when I see it."

I raised my eyebrows, reminding myself that someday my own granddaughter would have to deal with me.

"Okay, Gram. It's not yours. That's cool. I wouldn't want to take it if it was yours. Not to mention the eight bucks."

I could see the battle within her: admit it was her pack and pocket the bread, or continue blaming her enemy, Abigail Winegardner?

"Thank you, Tressa. I know I'm old, but I do recognize my own property." Old animosities won out, and I was the richer for it.

I grabbed a poncho from the coat hook, headed next door to fill in Uncle Frank about Clown Chase Part Two from last night, and told him I needed to make one more short stop before we headed down to the fair. Next I found myself rapping on Joe's trailer, wondering if asking Townsend to come along was like asking Lester the Molester to baby-sit for your kindergartner. I hoped it wasn't too early and the two men were dressed. Well, at least Joe. Townsend could be in dishabille and that would work for me.

The door opened, and I about fell off the porch.

"Taylor?" My sis peered at me through sleepy eyes and swept her silky brown hair over one shoulder. She looked as if she'd just gotten out of bed. "What are you doing here?" I asked, rain pouring down my poncho and into my leather sandals.

The door opened wider. "Tressa? Get in here. You're soaked." Rick Townsend, shirtless and also looking like he'd just woke up, reached around my sister and opened the screen door.

I felt my insides twist and turn like the taffy makers outside the air-conditioned industry building.

"No thanks!" I hissed, adding as much *screw you and the horse you rode in on* to my voice as I could, and hoping it was enough for Taylor and Townsend to split evenly. "Is your granddad home?" I asked.

Townsend frowned. "What do you want with him?"

"That is none of your business," I snapped.

"He's my grandfather," Townsend replied, his jaw suddenly rigid. "That makes it my business."

"Well, howdy-do, Tressa!" Joe said, walking out of what I figured was the bathroom. "What brings you here today?"

"I was just asking her that same question myself, Pops," Townsend said, "and I'm still waiting for her answer."

I crossed my arms under my poncho, wanting instead to encircle his two-timing neck with them.

"Joe," I said, completely dismissing Townsend and my dear sister, who had moved across the room to sit in a chair, "I was wondering if you'd care to earn a bit of money today."

"What the hell?" Townsend said.

"You see, we've really been doing some booming business at the mini-freeze, and I could use some extra help there," I told him. "Just until three or so. And you can take breaks whenever you need them."

"Sold!" Joe said. "Hannah and I've been itching to help out, but no one has asked," he admitted. "We may not be in our prime, but we've got lots to offer."

I made a face, realizing that very shortly I was going to reap what I'd sown with my big, fat mouth.

"Great!" I said, my smile as phony as Townsend's ethics. "Uncle Frank is going to run us down on his golf cart. We'll swing by and pick you up. Don't forget your raincoat and umbrella." I turned to head down the slippery stairs.

"Tressa!" Townsend stuck his head out the door. "About Taylor—I can explain."

I looked at the water trickling down over his head and face. I shook my head. "You're all wet, Townsend," I said, and left.

* * *

"And then Victor was married to this blind gal—what was her name? And there was the deranged blonde who tried to kill him. She left and came back again. Just when you think they're dead, they come back. I remember one soap star who died three times and came back from the dead every time. Couldn't make it in films, I guess."

I had listened to my grandmother and Joe discuss everything from the best gas reducer on the market to how many plastic surgeries a pop star had undergone to betting on when his nose would finally fall off. They were currently collaborating on how many soap opera vasectomies hadn't taken. I was actually beginning to wish the clown would appear and put me out of my misery.

For the last several hours, I'd whipped up sundaes and splits and floats, and fumed about Taylor and Townsend. How dare they . . . what? Have a relationship? They were both adults. Great-looking, smart, sexy adults. One just happened to be four years younger than the other, who was old enough to know better. I looked over at Gram.

"What time did Taylor come to bed?" I asked her. "I was so tired, I didn't hear her come in."

Gram shrugged. "She was there one minute and gone the next. All I know is that when I was up at midnight to use the pot the first time, she was gone. And she didn't come back."

Joe looked in my direction but couldn't meet my eyes.

"Joe?" I asked.

"I don't know nothing. Honest. I was out like a light by eleven."

"Where does your grandson sleep?" I asked. "With you?"

He shook his head. "Says I rub my legs together too much. Bothers his sleep. He uses the pull-out in the living room."

I nodded. "Do you have any other beds?" I asked.

Joe nodded. "We got the same setup as your folks. And one of the chairs in the living room converts to a small bed."

Dang. I should have stepped in to check out the chair.

"Was the chair pulled out when you got up this morning?" I asked.

"Why the big interest in Joe's sleeping arrangements?" Gram asked.

"She wants to know if my grandson and your granddaughter slept together last night," Joe said. "That's why all the interest."

"Wouldn't Tressa know if she'd slept with your grandson?" Gram asked. "Unless she was drunk. You didn't tie one on, did you?" Gram asked me.

"Not yet," I answered, mentally penciling in a time and date to tie one on. And soon.

"Not this granddaughter, Hannah," Joe told her. "Your other granddaughter. Taylor."

Gram looked at me, and even she couldn't keep eye contact. "Oh," was all she said. "I remember on one soap opera, this girl was slipped a mickey and ended up sleeping with the brother of her husband, and she never knew it until she got pregnant and the DNA test came back."

I opened the ice cream spigot and let ice cream pour into a large cup, then ladled on a generous amount of hot fudge, followed by a handful of nuts.

"Who's that for?" Joe asked.

I sat down and dug in.

"Oh," was all he said.

"You wouldn't let me explain, Tressa." Townsend paced the confines of the emporium near midnight. At first I'd had no intention of accepting the ranger's help with the stakeout, but ultimately decided that the least he owed

me was to make good on his promise. And I was rarin'
for a showdown with the Conservation Casanova.

I pretended I was busy cleaning the grill. (Actually,
Uncle Frank had left it so clean you could see your re-
flection in it).

"There's really nothing to explain. You and Taylor are
both adults beyond the age of consent." I stopped for a
minute, as if counting in my head. "Yeah, yeah, Taylor is
definitely over the age of consent, despite the difference
in your ages," I went on.

Townsend shook his head. "You are the most exasper-
ating person on the face of the planet," he said.

"You do say the nicest things, Townsend. I can see
how Taylor was beguiled by that sweet-talking tongue
of yours."

"Shit!" Townsend said, and dropped onto a stool at
the counter.

"I hear you're signed up for the demolition derby
again," he said out of the blue. I guessed my grammy
had gabbed again. I've been a competitor in the powder
puff division—the female class of the demo derby—
since I first got my driver's license. It's one of the few
places where crashing into other people's cars is not
only acceptable, but applauded. Even bet on. Like, what
could be cooler?

Unfortunately, I also knew Townsend's opinion of the
sport he called, "Rock 'em, sock 'em, real-life bumper
cars."

"We don't have a car lined up yet, but Uncle Frank always comes up with a jalopy," I said. "It's tradition."

Townsend shook his head. "I thought after last year
you'd hang up your helmet and goggles for good."

At last year's event I'd ticked off the Maluchi cousins,
whose family ran several alcohol-free daiquiri stands.
The cousins had tag-teamed me, turning my car into a

squeeze box. It took two hours and the jaws of life to extricate me.

"That was nothing," I said. "Besides, it's great PR for Uncle Frank." We always slapped a bunch of signs and ads all over the derby car each year. "It's a total hoot and perfectly harmless," I added.

Townsend grimaced. "Fun or not, it's unnecessary risk-taking," he said.

I turned and folded my arms. "Like moose-hunting in Canada maybe?" I asked.

"Apples and oranges, T. J.," he said. "Apples and oranges."

I made a face. "Yeah, right," I said, then picked up a broom and started to sweep the spic and span floor. "Because it's you, not me, that's why. You hunt. That's who you are. You keep a reptile ranch. That's who you are. And I do—well, I do what I do—because maybe that's who I am. Why can't you accept that?"

Townsend looked at me for a long moment. "I don't know," he finally said. "I really don't know."

How convenient, I thought, and put the broom away and grabbed my sleeping bag, too crabby to do much of anything other than call it a night.

"Where's your bag?" I asked.

He frowned at me. "You didn't tell me to bring a sleeping bag. And why would I have a sleeping bag when I sleep in an RV?"

"So, like, what are you gonna sleep on?" Even for a hardhead like Townsend, the floor would be uncomfortable.

He crossed his arms. "We'll share," he said.

"Like hell," I responded.

"Just unzip it, and it should be big enough for us both to lie on."

"Maybe. In your fantasy world," I told him.

"Oh, for God's sake, Tressa," he said, crossing the floor, unzipping the bag, and unfolding it to full length. "I'm not going to jump your bones on the floor of your uncle's ice cream shop," he said.

I raised an eyebrow. "Too tired from last night's exertions?" I said, tapping a sandaled toe.

"Too tired of your insecurities," he retorted, lying down and putting his arms under his head. "Are you going to turn the lights out so we can get this over with or what?"

"Ah. Mr. Romance," I said, giggling, thinking that was more what a tired wife would say to her sex-seeking hubby after a day chasing the kids.

He grinned. "I could be, you know."

"I'll take your word for it, Mr. Ranger, sir," I said. Then I flipped off the lights. "I'll just take your word for it."

I settled down on the side nearest the counter and lay there, listening to the whistle in Townsend's nose.

"I never noticed it before, but did you know you have a nose whistle?" the ranger asked.

"I do not!" I said.

"Do too."

I flicked on my penlight and shot the beam right in Rick's face.

"What the hell?"

"Just making sure you haven't migrated to my side of the bag," I said, turning the light off. "And I don't whistle."

I heard a big sigh from next to me, and could feel the heat of Townsend's body sink into the sleeping bag and work its way over toward me. I turned on my side, realized I was facing Townsend, turned to my other side, and then flopped onto my back.

"I need to change sides," I told Townsend.

"What?"

"Sides. I need to be on that side."

"Why?"

"Because I like to sleep on my left side," I told him.

"So? Sleep on your left side."

"But that would be facing you," I explained.

"So?" he said again.

"I can't sleep when I'm facing someone."

"Oh? What are you gonna do when you get married? Turn your back on your poor spouse all night if he insists on taking the wrong side of the bed?"

"My dearly beloved husband will insist that I take whichever side I am most comfortable with," I told him. "*He* will be understanding and considerate of my feelings. He will be loyal and devoted and loving . . ."

"Sounds like your mutts, Butch and Sundance, back home," he said.

"Don't be ridiculous," I snapped. "My dogs are hardly considerate. Have you seen my sofa? But my husband, my life partner, will be gallant and tender, and always put me first. He will indulge my every whim and place me on a pedestal—"

"In other words, he'll be pussy-whipped."

I sat up. "That's not true! Sensitive doesn't mean wussie," I told him. "Anyway, you're not a woman," I pointed out. "You don't know what women want."

He laughed. "I know that once you got your tender, gallant, indulgent, pussy-whipped husband, you'd be bored out of your gourd," he told me. "You, Tressa Jayne Turner—Calamity—need a challenge. Someone who isn't afraid to butt heads with you, or put up with your line of BS; who'll love you unconditionally and deeply enough to tell you 'no' and mean it when it's in your best interest, and who knows you enough to know you don't tolerate 'no' easily and, therefore, to follow through in order to save you from yourself if necessary. In other words, a warrior."

I tried to think of a pithy comeback, but his words knocked the pith right out of me.

I lay back down. "Okay, all right, I was just making small talk. You know, daydreaming at night. Sheez. I didn't expect a detailed analysis of my marital horoscope in response," I said. "But thanks."

Townsend let out a long, loud gust of air. Suddenly, I was grabbed and physically moved from my side of the sleeping bag, across Townsend's body and to the other side. His residual body warmth in the fabric seeped into me like I'd just reclined on a full-body heating pad. Against the light coming in the window I could see Rick's silhouette. He lounged on his side, looking down at me.

"There's nothing going on between your sister and me," he said. "Other than friendship," he added.

I waited for him to continue.

"She couldn't sleep last night with your grandma having leg aches, so she asked if she could bunk at our place. Pops was already asleep. She slept on the pull-out, and I took the single."

I still didn't say anything.

"Your sister just needs someone to talk to. I don't know why she picked me—"

I did. Who wouldn't choose to confide in the hottest guy in Knox County?

"But as I said before, we're just good friends."

Why wasn't that reassuring? Probably because every guy who'd said it to a wife or girlfriend ended up sleeping with the "good friend" at one time or another.

"What about the clinch?" I finally asked.

"Clinch? What clinch? What the hell are you talking about?"

"I saw you two," I found myself saying, my voice really tiny and so unlike the way I'd imagined informing him he'd been caught—what was it Gram called it: in flagrante delicto? In my mind's eye I'd seen me announcing it on banners trailing behind planes, transmitting it via the cable news networks, or broadcasting it from the studio of the Iowa radio station that set up shop at the fair each year, the fifty-thousand-watt voice of the Midwest. Instead, I sounded more like Oliver Twist asking for more gruel.

"What do you mean, you saw us?"

"Tuesday. Sevenish. I was on the trolley on my way back to the campgrounds and it was then I witnessed—the clinch." I could see Townsend's head move back and forth.

"I'm still not clear on this clinch thing. What do you mean, clinch?"

I rolled my eyes. Men are so clueless sometimes.

"A hug," I said. "No, not a hug. More like an embrace. But not just an embrace, a romantic embrace. An embrace with romantic underpinnings—i.e., a clinch."

Townsend shook his head again, and I saw one hand go up to his forehead. Not a good sign.

"Listen, Tressa, what you saw might have been an embrace, but it had no underpinnings other than friendship. Your sister is going through a difficult time. I'm just being her friend. That's all."

I sat up. "You've said that before. About Taylor having a difficult time. What's going on? Is she all right?"

Townsend lay back. "I'm sorry, Tressa, I'm not free to discuss her business."

"But I'm her sister!" I told him. "Maybe I can help."

"No, it's not that kind of problem," he said. "It's something she needs to figure out for herself."

Exasperated and propelled by nosiness out of control and, of course, out of concern for my sister, I decided I'd do whatever it took to get the truth out of Townsend. No matter how difficult and unpleasant the task.

I leaned over the prone ranger and let my breath fan his cheeks. I was glad I'd popped one of Gram's star mints earlier, after the onion rings. "You do know I want to support my sister, don't you, Ranger Rick—Rick? But how can I support her if I don't know what the problem is?" I put a hand out and touched his jaw. "She wouldn't mind if you told me."

He laughed, a deep, husky laugh. "She specifically told me not to tell you," he said. I frowned.

"She needs her family at a time like this," I said, reaching down to kiss his cheek, then jerked back. "Ohmigosh! She's pregnant, isn't she?" I yelled. "My baby sister is going to have a baby! What will this do to my parents? And my grammy! And wait 'til the congregation at Open Bible hears about this—"

"Oh, for God's sake, Tressa! She's not pregnant. She just wants to drop out of college!" Townsend said.

"Yes!" I said, raising a fist. I still had it. "I knew I'd get it out of you!"

"What the—? Why, you little—"

"Now, now, now, Mr. Ranger, sir. You don't want to be saying something you might later regret," I cautioned, blown away by Townsend's news. So, honors grad and full-ride scholarship recipient Taylor Turner wanted to drop out of college. The you-know-what was gonna hit the fan. And you-know-who wanted a front-row seat.

"I have no intention of doing anything I'll regret later," Townsend said, sitting back up, an edge to his voice that wasn't exactly comforting.

"I'm beat," I said, preparing to roll to my left side and away from the ranger.

"Oh, no, you don't. Now that you've educated me on clinches," he said, "let me show you what a real clinch is, Calamity." He took me in his arms, and I felt the heat of his body and the warmth of his breath on my face. He covered my mouth with his.

I gave myself to the exquisite feelings Rick Townsend set off within me. I felt my toes curl as he slid his hand down my thigh, and back up to the area of my left breast. With each kiss and each caress I grew hotter and hotter. Townsend reached beneath my T-shirt to caress my stomach, which I naturally sucked in as much as I could. Oh, come on, you gals do it, too. We learn to hold it a long time, too. With our tight jeans, sucking in our gut is the only way to get them fastened and keep them fastened.

"I've waited a long time, Tressa," Townsend said. "But I think you're gonna be worth the wait."

Ya think?

He kissed me again, and I forgot his typically male, totally doofish comment as his arms and heat enveloped me. Oh, buddy, was it hot tonight.

"Fire! Fire!"

I frowned, wondering if I'd yelled that aloud like some women yell "Yes! Yes!" during intimate moments, but Townsend had taken a break in exploring my tonsils, too.

"Fire! Fire! Tressa! Are you in there?"

Townsend and I jumped up and, to my horror, saw the back door of the Emporium ablaze. The curtains of the back door caught and started to burn, and I raced to grab the fire extinguisher. Townsend took it from me and started spraying the flames.

The back door suddenly crashed open, and there was Frankie, in his chicken costume, calling my name.

"Are you all right, Tressa?" he asked, as flames began to ignite his white fur.

"Frankie, you're on fire!" I screamed, not wanting to see my wiener cousin become chicken fricassee. "Stop, drop, and roll!" I yelled. "Stop, drop, and roll!"

Frankie ran out, flopped down on the grass, and began to roll. I followed him outside, prepared to douse him with the garden hose, but saw somebody else had already beaten me to it.

"Mr. Daggett?" I said, totally confused.

I ran back inside to see how Townsend was faring

with the flames and was thankful to see he'd gotten most of the fire out. I beat at several tiny flames with wet towels, trying save Aunt Reggie's curtains.

"Bet that was the hottest clinch you've ever had," Townsend said, looking over at me, wiping sweat and soot from his face.

I walked over and handed him a wet towel. "Yep, I admitted, laying my head on his chest. "But, if anyone asks, I'm pleading the fifth," I told him.

He folded me into his arms and I didn't resist.

CHAPTER 24

It was nearly closing time Friday night, and Gram and I were the sole occupants of the emporium. Every year Gram and I spent the last Friday night of the fair together. It was the one night of the year when Gram could enjoy a cold beer and not have my mother hassling her. We'd go to the Bottoms Up, sit at a table up front, and listen to the country-western band. In years past, Gram would get up and "show the young'uns how it's done" and dance a dance or two; but this time, with an ankle injury from a fall earlier in the year and everyone's general funk over the earlier fire, my guess was that our evening would be pretty low-key. If we went out at all.

I know I was still trying to process everything that had happened since the fire in the early hours of that morning. Police and fire services had arrived to secure the scene, but the fire—and Frankie—had both already been put out. Frankie was fine, but the Cluck 'n' Chuck mascot would never recover.

The troopers had escorted us down to headquarters

and called Uncle Frank to verify we were all who we said we were, and that we were at the Emporium at that time of night with his permission. When it came to okaying Frankie, however, Uncle Frank surprised us all.

"I want him arrested for criminal trespass," he'd said, pointing to the soaking wet and scorched birdman. "He had no reason to be at my place of business at that time," he said. "Unless he was up to no good."

"Uncle Frank!" I said. "Frankie probably saved our lives!"

"Or risked them, when he didn't know you were in there until too late," Uncle Frank argued.

I stared at my uncle F and then walked over to put my arm around Frankie. I resisted the urge to hold my nose. He smelled just like the fuzzy hood of my parka did when it had caught fire two winters ago when I was burning papers out back in the incinerator and got too close. We all would have preferred Frankie remove the suit, but he'd refused to, since he was only wearing boxers beneath the hot costume.

"I know you're not to blame, Frankie," I'd told him.

The police had also questioned Luther Daggett but released him. Interestingly enough, the Li brothers had been in the area that night as well, but they had taken off before they could be questioned.

As Gram and I sat in the empty Emporium, Frankie was either still in the holding cell down at fair headquarters awaiting transportation to the county jail, or already at the jail. That was, if Uncle Frank hadn't changed his mind about filing charges.

"You can't blame your uncle," Gram said. "He's just trying to do the right thing."

I nodded. "I know. But it's so unfair. Frankie was the hero here."

"That fire was started deliberately."

"I know, but not by Frankie."

"He was there. In a chicken getup, no less. I don't think he'll ever live this down."

"He's got a lot more to worry about than being seen in a chicken suit," I told her. "And don't forget, Uncle Frank's biggest competitor was there, too," I said. "And I don't buy his story that he was looking for his daughter either. And what about the Li twins? They took off as soon as the cops got there. I know from experience, they play rough."

"Guess we'll just have to wait and read all about it in the papers," she said. "If them reporters don't know how it ends, they make something up."

"Hey! I'm a reporter, too, Gram. Kinda. Sorta," I reminded her.

"Speaking of which, did you ever look at Joe's and my fair pictures? We spent a lot of time and effort taking those."

"You spent more time taking pictures of Lucy Connor and Uncle Frank," I said. "But you're right, I could look at them now. I got quite a few really good ones the other night, too, but haven't had time to check them out."

I grabbed the red fanny pack out of the back room, removed my camera, and placed it on the front counter and turned it on. Then I ran through the early shots and deleted the dopey one of me that Joe had taken.

"Hey, don't delete them until I look," Gram ordered. "I might want a copy of something you'd just delete."

"Okay, okay," I said, "but there better not be any more shots of me."

I was just about to take a seat by Gram, so we could view the pictures together, when the front doorbell sounded and Lucy Connor walked in.

"Good evening, you two," she said, taking the seat next to Gram. "So, how are you all doing?" she asked. "How are Frank and Reggie holding up?"

Gram snorted. Ah, so *that's* where I got that nasty habit.

"Figures you'd ask about Frank first," Gram said.

I tried to shush her. (What was I thinking, right?)

"I'm on to you, you know," Gram went on.

"Gram," I said again.

"I don't understand, Hannah," Lucy said.

"Sure you don't," Gram sneered. "Sure you don't."

Lucy shook her head. "Am I missing something here?" she asked.

"It's been a long and difficult day, Lucy," I said. "We're all just trying to deal with things in our own way."

"You don't miss a thing, missy," Gram growled, and I grabbed one of her favorite ice cream bars and slapped it down in front of her in an attempt to keep her lips occupied. She picked it up and unwrapped it. Phew!

But the ploy wasn't successful for long.

"Don't think we don't have the goods on you, Miz Lucy," my grammy said, " 'cause we do. Isn't that right, Tressa? It's like I told Tressa: A picture may paint a thousand words, but—"

"I know, I know, your pictures speak volumes, Gram," I finished. "Now just eat your ice cream!"

I looked at the clock on the wall by the window. "If you want to order something, better speak now, Mrs. Connor; we're fixin' to close. Gram and I always stay out late on the last Friday of the fair and get a little crazy—right, Gram?"

My grammy nodded. "Don't suppose I should've had the ice cream if I'm gonna have beer," she said, but she kept eating.

"No, thanks," Lucy replied. "I just wanted to see how everyone was doing, and see if I could help out in any way." She stood. "I also thought I'd better warn you that the Li twins are still out there, and I understand from their father that they aren't happy he was questioned by the cops. Just thought you might keep that in mind. I hear there might be some hard feelings between you and the Lis."

"Thanks. I'll keep that in mind," I said.

"Take care," Lucy said, and she left.

"Guess I told her," Gram said.

"Guess you did," I replied. "Now, let's see if your photographic skills are as good as your skills at running off customers." I flipped on the camera and ran through the pictures, standing to Gram's left as we looked at them together.

"There's Frank and that S-L-U-T at the turkey stand. Oh, and there they are at the ag building." Gram recited locations where Lucy and Uncle Frank were together, but there weren't all that many, and all appeared completely innocent.

"I don't see any incriminating caught-in-the-act stuff here," I said. "But I bet Uncle Frank will think twice about keeping company with another woman once he sees these," I said. "You did a nice job centering your subjects," I added.

"Joe took most of the pictures," my gram said. "He has a nice, steady hand."

I looked over at her. "And how would you be knowing that, young lady?" I asked. She winked.

"I'll never tell," she said.

"Oh, look! You've got one of Frankie!" I realized.

"Frankie? We never took a picture of Frankie," Gram said.

I smiled at the large chicken surrounded by children in the background of the picture. "That's okay, Gram. You wouldn't have recognized him."

We ran through the remainder of the pictures, including the big boar and the super-sized, super-virile bull.

"Told you he had a set on him," Gram said, and I stared at the picture. No way could I run this picture in the fair feature. I'd be the laughingstock of Grandville. Again.

I hit review and looked at a few more of their pictures, then stopped on one. I stared at it and frowned. I hit the zoom button to get a better look.

"Holy cannoli!" I said, staring at the picture on the tiny screen in front of me. "Geezalu, Gram! Forget what I said about you not getting an incriminating picture; you got the friggin' motherlode here!"

"Huh? You still lookin' at them testicles, Tressa?" she asked. "That's not healthy, you know. It will build up an unrealistic expectation on your part—"

The bell on the door jingled again.

"We're closed!" Gram snapped.

"That's right," I heard a rather familiar voice say, and looked up to see a white, latex-covered hand flip the OPEN sign to CLOSED and bolt the door.

"Hey!" Gram said, "What are you dressed up for?"

I felt the mucus in my throat thicken. My stomach felt like it had been sucker-punched by Ali in his prime. Figuring I had precious little time left, I slipped the memory card out of the camera and pressed it into the napkin dispenser on the counter.

"I'll take that," our worthy adversary said.

Damn. I hadn't seen this coming. Not at all.

We sat, hands and feet bound, in the semidarkness of the Emporium, the fountain drink machine and jukebox lights the only illumination.

"So, what about them?" The bad guys seemed to be at a loss as to what to do with Gram and me. I wasn't sure whether to be relieved or concerned.

"We can't just let them go. They know who we are. Know what we did. We might make a case that the old one here is senile, but that one's not just a dumb blonde anymore. Since she stumbled onto those stiffs earlier this summer, she's gained some credibility."

Despite the imminent danger I found myself in, I got

a warm, fuzzy feeling inside at the unintended compliment. *Not just a dumb blonde anymore.* Sweet.

"That's too bad. For her. Things would've been a lot less messy if she was still an airhead. As it is, she's a loose end."

I wanted to speak up and tell them there was still a lot of space cadet in this here cowgirl but thought the less attention I brought to myself, the better. Especially considering the gun pointed at my left boob.

"It has to look like an accident."

Someone in the room snorted. "Shouldn't be too hard with her reputation. Remember when she fell into that sand sculpture in the cultural center? Man, was that guy pissed! He'd spent three weeks sculpting Lady Liberty and had to scrap it in favor of John Wayne."

I raised my eyebrows. Personally, I thought I'd done the viewing public a favor. His Statue of Liberty had looked an awful lot like Hillary Clinton.

"What about the golf cart race down the concourse that time?" Our captors continued their litany of Tressa's State Fair Antics. "And just last year she locked herself in that freezer."

An uncomfortable silence preceded four sets of eyes roaming to Uncle Frank's freezer, then back to Gram and me. They wouldn't, I thought. Would they? I looked over at Gram, wondering just when it would dawn on her the nature of the demise these two had in mind for Hellion Hannah and Calamity Jayne. The gruesome-twosome looked at each other, smiled, and then cast their fiendish eyes back on me.

"You can't be serious," I said. "Nobody would find us until morning. We'd be human Popsicles. Last time I was only in there for two hours and I had icicles hanging from my nose. And trust me, it's not a good look for me!"

They nodded at each other.

"What's going on? What did I miss now?" Gram asked.

"Listen, we can talk about this," I said, struggling against my bonds while keeping an eye on the revolver clutched by a hand that was shaking more than my own terrified limbs. "My credibility isn't all that good, you know. Why, just yesterday I asked the lieutenant governor if she could direct me to the restroom in the ag building. And what about the giant slide and the Wild West Show? I'm a legend now—and not in a good way!"

I could tell my little speech wasn't having much effect on the two desperadoes. At least, not a positive one. They moved toward Gram and, hog-tied to the chair as I was, the only thing I could do was throw myself sideways, chair and all, and hope I didn't hit my head and pass out on the way down.

"Grab her!" Ben said to Jerry.

I tried to roll away from them and toward the door—not an easy thing when you're strapped to a chair.

"Help!" I managed, before a dirty dishrag was stuffed in my mouth. The flavor brought to mind the soy burgers Gramma grilled on July fourth.

"Tressa!" Gram got out just before she, too, was silenced.

I found myself being dragged, chair and all, to the entrance of the walk-in freezer. I made a really lame attempt to foil their progress by wedging myself sideways in the doorway. The deadly duo quickly righted me and shoved me to the floor of the cold storage area, then they went back for my grandma, picking up her chair and hauling her into the freezer like ancient royalty being conveyed through a procession upon a litter. I guess the ancient part fit.

Working as a team, the partners in crime quickly untied Gram and turned their attention on me, releasing my bindings and grabbing the chair before they rushed out, slamming and locking the heavy freezer door behind them.

Inside the freezer, the cold, tomblike darkness settled quickly around me like a heavy, damp cloak. I thought about refrigerated morgue tables and chilly, dank mausoleums, and shuddered. *Patooey!* I spat the offending cloth from my mouth and gulped in several deep, openmouthed breaths. The cold air hit my bronchial passages like an ice ball in the kisser. (I've been on both sides of those puppies in the not-so-distant-as-you'd-think past.) I moaned and shifted my weight, wincing when my elbow impacted with the hard floor, sending pain shooting up the length of my cramped arm.

"Tressa, are you okay, dear?" I heard ahead and off to my left.

I groped around in the dark for the only other person in the family with a mouth bigger than mine. "I can't complain," I remarked. "Who'd listen? How about you, Gram? Did those bastards hurt you?"

"Hell's bells, no!" Gram's voice came to me from where I sat trying to come up with a game plan to extricate the two of us from this latest predicament and foil the bad guys. "I wouldn't give them the satisfaction."

"Atta girl," I said, trying to figure out if the coast was clear outside our dark little igloo. I squinted at the wall of black around me. This was not going to be the piece of cake I thought. My heart began to pitter-patter, and not in a good way. The freezer was getting colder—or maybe it was just me. I realized if I was going to pull off a Houdini-esque escape for my grammy and me, I'd better get to it. If I waited much longer, I'd be stiffer than Gramma is after a three-hour car ride, and she'd be able to do a stint as a backboard.

"I think you'd better get up and move around, Gram," I said. "Do jumping jacks. Run in place. Anything to keep the blood circulating," I suggested, getting to my feet and wishing I'd worn jeans and tennis shoes that day rather than the shorts and sandals I had chosen. I pulled off my T-shirt and handed it to her. "Here, wind this around your head, Gram," I instructed. "We lose more heat through our heads than anywhere else, you know." I'd picked that up from some mountain-climbing-expedition-gone-bad movie.

"What about you, Tressa?" she said. "Won't you get cold quicker?"

"I'll have us out of here in no time," I said, hoping I spoke the truth. I stuck out my hands in front of me and shuffled forward slowly. I felt like one of the living dead. "Brains," I whispered. "Brains . . ." Then decided that was not what I wanted to be thinking of in a cold, airtight room where I couldn't see my hand in front of my face.

"Of course you have brains," Gram said. "You're my granddaughter."

I let my fingertips do the walking over the shelves filled with tubs of flavored ice cream and frozen yogurt. I found the various bins piled high with frozen novelties (at least we wouldn't starve) and felt my way over to where I thought the door was located. With both hands, I made like Helen Keller and traversed the length and width of the wall, shuffling slowly along, until I located the doorway.

"Think. Think." I prodded my memory, trying to recall exactly where Uncle Frank had installed the interior light switch so I could locate the unlocking mechanism—you know—the one the bad guys didn't know about. The one that was going to save our frozen giblets. If I ever located it, that is. "Where was that switch?"

"What switch?" Gramma asked.

"The one Uncle Frank installed so nobody would get locked in the freezer again."

"You mean the one he installed so you wouldn't get locked in again," Gramma replied. Nice.

I pawed around some more, shivering from the intense cold that transformed my fine motor skills into palsied movements, and began to think I really was going to end up a corpus delicious, when I finally found the light switch. I gave frosty thanks and flipped on the light. Then I proceeded to pound on Uncle Frank's freezer door that would probably require a bunker buster to take out.

"Help!" I hollered. "Help! We're in the freezer! Please, let us out!" I figured if our cold-storage specialists were still out there, they would expect some pounding and screaming and yelling, and who was I to disappoint? I thought I was pretty convincing as a damsel in distress. Okay, okay, so I've played the "Perils of Pauline" before and brought hands-on experience to the role. Or on-the-job training, maybe.

"What the devil are you doing, Tressa?" Gramma had got to her feet and was chewing on a Nutty bar.

"I'm acting like a helpless, hapless female," I said, "just in case the bad guys are still out there."

"And you think that they're going to open the door and let us out?" Gram asked.

I shook my head. "Of course not! I just don't want to open the door and walk out there and find they're still sitting out there, gun in hand, waiting for us."

Gramma's eyes got bigger. She dropped the ice cream bar on the floor and hauled ass to the door and started beating on it. "Help!" she screamed. "Help! Get us out of here! I'm old and frail and have osteoporosis and a touch of rheumatoid arthritis and my joints just give me fits when the cold settles in them. Help! Let me out!" Gram turned to me. "How was that for acting?" she asked.

I raised an eyebrow. "Don't give up your day job," I told her. After a few more minutes of beating up on Mr. Indestructo Door, the novelty had worn off—and the cold was really beginning to seep in. I was starting to feel like Jackie Frost, and imagined Gramma was feeling much the same. My face was so cold, if I remained in the freezer much longer I'd have the same array of facial expressions as Dorothy's Tin Man, or an aging actor after too many Botox injections.

I took a deep breath, saw it leave my body in a white fog, and decided to heck with it. I wasn't about to let my grammy come down with a case of pneumonia. Joltin' Joe Townsend would never forgive me.

"We need a weapon," I said, looking around for anything I could use to defend myself and the golden girl beside me. "See what you can find."

"How about a frozen pig?" Gram asked.

I stopped looking through boxes of ice cream bars. "A pig?"

Gram nodded. "Frank always has a hog roast at the end of the fair to thank everyone for helping out. He's probably got the pig in here somewhere. That would make a pretty impressive dent in someone's skull," she added.

I nodded. "I'm just not sure I'm up to wielding a two-hundred-pound hog, Gramma," I told her. "We need something easier to handle. More compact. Less—ugh." I gave a pronounced shiver.

"What about turkey legs? I bet he has some of those around here, too. He always buys a bunch of them from Pearson's Poultry every fair season. If we could locate those suckers, you could inflict some serious damage to someone's noggin."

"Turkey legs." I nodded. "That might just work," I said. "Just don't tell the PETA people."

Several minutes later, killer turkey legs raised and kick-ass attitudes firmly in place, I, Calamity Jayne, and her rusty—I mean trusty—sidekick, Hellion Hannah, let go with our family's traditional war cry and flung open our frosty prison door, our loud chant echoing throughout the darkened Emporium.

"Dead meat!"

CHAPTER TWENTY-FIVE

"So, when do we jump out again?" Gram asked, pulling on my arm.

"We don't jump out," I explained for the tenth time. "Uncle Frank opens the freezer door and discovers us. Then we simply walk out."

"We don't get to jump? How about a stumble? Or we could scream. You know, like we did when we thought the crooks were still waiting outside the freezer for us. When we used the turkey legs as weapons."

I shook my head. "We don't need to jump, stumble, or scream," I told her. "All we need to do is show up alive."

"That's it? I gave up the yodeling contest for this?"

Gram and I were again huddled in Uncle Frank's freezer, but this time the temperature wasn't how-low-can-you-go low. We were bundled up like two Midwestern bag ladies in January.

"Yodeling. Since when do you give a flip about yodeling?" I asked. "Besides, the police already told you you didn't have to be here. Apparently, all they needed was one of us alive."

"I still don't get it. We pop out: 'Hey, we're alive!' Then what?"

"They're hoping when confronted with the evidence of their crimes—you and me being exhibits A and B— the guilty party will break down and make some kind of admission or react in an otherwise guilty manner." I wasn't too clear on this alternative to a confession but figured the pros were up to speed.

"In other words, we're messin' with their minds. I like it," Gram said. "Wish I'd thought of it."

I nodded. "Me, too." If all had gone as planned, outside in the Emporium our family would be nervously waiting for word regarding our disappearance. The State Patrol and Division of Criminal Investigation would be on hand to interview family members and concessionaires who last had contact with us—er, the missing women. At some point, when everyone was assembled and the time was right, Uncle Frank would open the freezer and out we'd pop.

"What's taking them so long?" Gram asked. "Even with all this paraphernalia on, I'm getting frostbit."

"It's only thirty-two in here, Gram, and you've only been in here forty-five minutes."

"Seems longer. And they should have a chair in here."

"In a freezer?"

I rolled a large ice cream bucket over to her. "Here, Your Highness," I said. "Your throne."

She took a seat, asking, "What about that trooper out there? You gonna see him again?"

I blinked. Gram changed subjects so frequently, I needed a scorecard to keep track. "Huh?" I said.

"Trooper Dawkins. He's quite the stud muffin. Do

they still say stud muffin?" she asked. "I wouldn't want to be outdated."

I shrugged. "Stud muffin's cool. And, for the record, Patrick and I are really just friends."

Gram was silent for a second. "What about Rick Townsend?" she asked. "Are you two really just friends?"

I thought about it. "Only time will tell, Gram," I said. "Only time will tell."

She was just about to make another comment when we heard the click and slide of the latch.

"This is it!" I said, and Gram and I stood, ready to spring the Turner trap.

"Now remember," I told her, "don't yell. Don't scream or jump. Just walk out there nice and calm. Then let the police officers do their jobs."

"All right," she said. "But after all I've been through, I should at least be permitted an 'Aaaggghhh!' or a 'Boo!'"

"Remember, Joe will be out there. You don't want to embarrass yourself in front of him," I told her.

The door opened slowly, as if the person on the other side was hesitant to find what he thought he might find. I could just make out Uncle Frank's face.

"Oh, my God!" he said in a distressed and horrified voice. "Oh, my God!"

"What is it, Frank?" I heard Aunt Reggie say. Damn, these two were good.

"Oh, my God, how could this happen again!" Uncle Frank sank to his knees. I was blown away by his performance.

I saw Uncle Frank nod to me. Apparently, that was the extent of his acting ability.

I took Gram's hand and we exited the freezer arm in arm.

"Aaaauuugghhh!" The scream, when it erupted,

came not from Gram but from me. Honest, guys, I don't know what happened. One moment I was content to walk out all cool, calm, and collected, and the next moment I was jumping up and down and waving my arms and yelling like a banshee.

To my left, Gram gave an exaggerated "Hmpf" and jabbed me in the ribs. "Over-actor," she snapped.

"Oh, my God. They're alive?" Lucy Connor looked like she'd just been given the news that she had six months to live—and had to spend the whole time watching *Bozo the Clown* reruns. Her mouth flew open and her face became the color of Uncle Frank's vanilla soft-serve. She looked around wildly. The officers had someone stationed at the front door but had neglected to post anyone at the scorched and damaged back, since that door had been out of commission since the fire. And, of course, that was the door little Lucy headed for: She shoved the deadbolt back and threw it open, and was out and on her golf cart before anyone moved.

"Get her!" Gram yelled, but I was already out the back door and on Uncle Frank's golf cart. I heard the hum of a vehicle behind me and turned to discover Trooper Dawkins in hot—well, lukewarm—pursuit.

I bounced along behind Lucy as we sped past the dollar root beer place (now *that* root beer is flat) and the gyro shop. (Note to Tressa: Haven't had a gyro yet.) We proceeded down Rock Island and past a stage, where someone was trying to play "America the Beautiful" on an accordion. We blew by one of the three foot-long stands located on the fairgrounds and proceeded past the horse pavilion.

"Watch out! Move!" I yelled, trying to avoid hitting innocent pedestrians. Instead I took out a trash bin, sending it careening down the sidewalk behind me, garbage spilling everywhere and, from the subsequent clattering I suspected, right into the path of the state trooper. I winced. "Sorry!" I yelled back. At least the sanitation technicians would have steady work.

"Stop that cart!" I called out, not stopping to think just how someone might do that. I heard sirens and wondered if State Patrol golf carts were equipped with red lights and sirens.

Lucy suddenly made a right turn and drove right into the horse barn. I cringed but followed behind her, wondering if Dawkins was still mobile or out of service. Lucy proved to be an adept driver, squeezing through the narrow aisles, getting hung up on a large, fresh mound of horse manure, but managing to get going again. She sped out of the west end of the horse barn, where 4-H entrants were walking their mounts preparing for competition, then suddenly left her cart, ran to a stocky buckskin nearby, jerked the reins out of the surprised horse owner's hands, and jumped into the saddle.

"Hey, that's my horse!" the boy of about ten, with a black hat and pants and a white shirt with a horse show entrant number pinned to his back yelled. "Hey! That lady stole my horse!"

I looked around, hoping for similar luck in the mount department, but the only available horse I saw belonged to the fair security person who was chatting up a blonde with a nice figure, but who had turned to look at the boy with the stolen horse.

"Uh, I really need to borrow your horse, Officer," I said, whipping the reins out of his hand and throwing myself into the saddle. "Don't worry, son," I reassured the young cowpoke. "Nobody steals a horse with Calamity Jayne on the scene and gets away with it."

"Huh?" both the kid and the officer replied. I slapped the horse's rear and dug my heels into the sorrel's belly, and the race was on.

*Little Lucy Connor is the first out of the gate on a
magnificent buckskin quarterhorse with two white
socks and a brilliant star. Four lengths back and on a
borrowed mounted reserve officer's leggy American
saddlebred sporting four white stockings is our very
own Calamity Jayne. And they're rounding the turn
beside the flea market and circling back around the
United Methodist Church's Sit-a-Spell Sandwich
Shoppe. Little Lucy is still in the lead, but Calamity
Jayne is gaining. They've passed the First Baptist Pie a
la Mode booth and are heading north on Rock Island,
by the big clock at the administration building.
They're taking the turn onto the Grand Concourse,
and it's the quarter by a nose! The riders are at the
northwest corner of the grandstand and they've hit the
dirt of the grandstand track and they're neck and
neck. . . .*

In true Triple-Crown tradition, I called the race in my
head as if I were watching the Derby as well as running
in it. A crowd was assembled in the grandstands to
watch a tractor pull in progress. Cheers and whistles
erupted from the stands, and I looked around to see
what they were all so excited about. And then I realized:
They were cheering us on. How bizarre was that?

I could see Lucy's quarter tiring. Quarters are great
speedsters at short distances, but the leggier saddle-
breds have a clear advantage in the mile. This beauty
was just hitting her stride.

"Give it up, Lucy!" I hollered at her over the roar of
the crowd and the tractors. "It's over!"

"It's over when I say it's over!" she yelled back, and
kicked the buckskin cruelly, slapping it on the rear with
her reins as she headed into the first turn.

By then I sensed that Lucy was already around the

bend, and remembered my pledge to bring the young cowboy's horse back to him safe and sound. I pulled a rope from its place behind the saddle and fashioned a clunky lariat. It had been a while since I'd thrown one. Last time I'd roped anything it had been Rick Townsend during one of his jackass moments.

The crowd was still screaming and whistling as I grew closer to the fading buckskin. Its flanks were lathered white, and bubbly white foam spewed from its mouth. I was just about to toss my rope when, slicker than snot, another white rope loop fell neatly over Lucy's shoulders. I threw my loop, anyway. My throw wasn't pretty. In fact, it wasn't really a throw at all. I basically rode up behind Lucy, tossed the rope over her head, and slid it down her chest. Both ropes tightened. The next second Lucy was in midair and sailing toward the dirt track.

I kept just enough tension on the rope so she wouldn't hit the ground too hard but hard enough to maybe knock some sense into her, then finally took the opportunity to check out who had snared Lucy with the first rope. Sitting across from me on a palomino that could've been kin to Trigger was Trooper P.D. Dawkins. I shook my head. Men.

I secured the end of my rope around my saddle horn, jumped out of my saddle and hurried over to the lady outlaw. Dawkins dismounted as well, and we met at Lucy's prone figure. Rodeo queen that I am, I grabbed P.D.'s right hand and raised our joined hands in the air with a shrill whistle and a good ol' girl "Yeehaw!" Dawkins removed his trooper hat and held it aloft.

And the crowd went wild!

"Nice throw," I told Dawkins. "You've been keeping secrets from me, Mr. Smokey," I said.

He grinned. "I did tell you my grandparents had a farm," he reminded me. "And I felt I owed you one for those so-called games of 'chance' on the midway the other night."

"We'll talk," I promised. "And as for you, Lawless Lucy," I said and knelt down next to the prone prankster, feeling one of those corny classic country lines springing to my lips. "Horse-stealin's a hangin' offense in these here parts," I drawled, wagging a finger. "And even a city slicker like you should know you don't come between a cowboy and his horse."

I stood and waved to the noisy crowd again. Calamity Jayne versus Lawless Lucy was one for the record books.

What now, you ask?

Can you say, "It's Miller time!"

EPILOGUE

The last day of the fair had arrived, and not a minute too soon. I was looking forward to reuniting with my animal family back home—as opposed to the traveling circus I'd spent the last two weeks with—and the opportunity to enjoy the final dog days of summer.

A large crowd of us were assembled inside the grandstand, and the Powder Puff Derby, that non-politically correct demolition derby for drivers of the female persuasion, was scheduled to begin shortly. A cluster of television reporters flanked by their respective camera personnel thrust microphones at Gram and me, peppering us with questions like, "How did it feel to be put on ice?"

"How do you think it felt?" my gammy responded. "It was colder than a witch's tit in a brass bra," she said, garnering a general consensus that this eyewitness observation probably wouldn't make the ten o'clock news but would almost certainly end up on some bloopers show down the road.

I'd phoned Stan Rodgers shortly after my heroic

horse race and lassoing of Lucy had ended, and had filled him in on the excitement. By the time Lawless Lucy was cooling her fake moccasins in the same Port-A-Cell Manny had previously occupied, Stan was on the scene putting together a special edition of the *Gazette*, hitting the wires with an exclusive that other print-media types could only grumble about and pick up—with appropriate credit, of course.

"I understand you were actually responsible for exposing Lucy Connor as the person behind all the incidents targeting Frank Barlowe's businesses," a reporter said to Gram. "How did that come about? How did you figure out it was Mrs. Connor?"

Gram looked over at me. "How *did* we figger that out?" she asked.

"Why, by brilliant detective work, of course," I said with a wink. Actually, it was Joltin' Joe and Hellion Hannah's brilliant Cheatin' Hearts detective work. While following Lucy around trying to get the goods on her and Uncle Frank, the dynamic duo snapped various shots of Lucy. And there, in living color, was a photo of Lucy and the great Bobo. And how did I know it wasn't Frankie, you're wondering? Glad you asked. In earlier photos Gram had inadvertently got a couple of Garth Wayne, Frankie's country-western alter-ego. Judging from the date and time of the photo, it was impossible for Frankie to have been the Bobo in the picture with Lucy, which nailed Lucy as the villain. The Great (or Evil) Bobo, as it turned out, was Lucy's boyfriend, Alberto Munoz: a wanted felon who for obvious reasons couldn't easily show his face at an event a million people attended, and where you can see a trooper every hundred yards or so. The Bobo character had provided both a terrific disguise for Munoz and a little added income from the dunk tank booth.

"And what was Lucy Connor's motive?" another reporter asked.

"The oldest one, of course," I said. "Greed."

Gram looked at me. "She wasn't hot for Frank's body?" she asked, and I shook my head.

"She was actually hot for the Emporium," I explained. Lucy wanted to expand her Trinkets and Treasures from her hot, uncomfortable tent location, and felt the best way was to appear as if she wasn't interested in acquiring the building at all. Meanwhile, every chance she got, she fed Uncle Frank's suspicions about Luther Daggett, throwing in just enough uncertainty about Frankie and the Li boys to make her the obvious choice if and when Uncle Frank decided to sell. From the clown horn left at the Emporium to whispered innuendoes in Uncle Frank's ear, Lucy worked both sides of the fence. She even got her old pal, Sonya the Seer, in on the act, feeding her enough information so her readings would point to disaster for the family if Uncle Frank didn't sell his fair holdings.

"What about the freezer incident? I understand there was a similar incident last year? Can you speak to that?"

"There was an unfortunate incident last year that left me in the freezer for several hours. However, after that Mr. Barlowe upgraded the walk-in freezer with a new safety latch inside, so I knew we would be able to get out if they put us in there, and was actually relieved when they did."

I'd actively lobbied for the freezer confinement by doing my best Brer Rabbit and the briar patch performance. Thankfully, it worked like a charm. It was just fortunate that, in his tête-à-têtes with little Lucy, Uncle Frank had failed to mention the new safety latch he'd installed, or Gram and I might still be defrosting on a slab somewhere.

"And what about those charges against Frankie Barlowe Jr? I understand his father had his son held at the jail," the reporter asked.

I smiled. "My Uncle Frank is a lot more conniving than he lets on," I said. "And I gotta say, I'm impressed." After the fire at the Emporium, Uncle Frank realized these weren't pranks anymore, but posed a very real danger not only to his family but to his customers as well. He convinced the authorities that, in order for the incidents to stop, they had to pretend to hold Frankie on those charges. With Frankie cooling his heels in police custody, the real perpetrators couldn't very well move ahead with another incident and blame Frankie for it. Of course, Uncle Frank had no way of knowing that two senior citizens with more time on their hands than should be legal were following him and his supposed mistress like a pair of past-their-prime bloodhounds, and had snapped incriminating photos of the culprits. But Lucy and her felon had realized it, and that explained their pursuit of me and my fanny pack. They wanted those pictures. Bad.

"What about your uncle's biggest competitor, Luther Daggett? I saw where he was at the scene of the fire. Was he exonerated?"

I nodded. "Luther and his daughter, Dixie, were in no way involved in the crimes against my uncle's property." Which had surprised the heck out of Uncle Frank. Come to find out the most serious crimes the two Daggetts committed were ones of mistrust. When Uncle Frank's businesses were initially hit, Dixie Daggett had been certain her father was behind the mischief, and took steps to catch him in the act before things got out of control. That explained her being at the mini-freeze the night we'd tangled. Luther, on the other hand, had suspected his daughter might be trying desperately to help him win the bet with Frank Barlowe, by hook or by crook, and that was why Luther Daggett was out and about the night of the fire. He was actually expecting to catch his daughter in the act. Oh, what a tangled web we weave . . .

"I've also heard references to an Asian gang element. Can you address this?"

"I have no information on that," I said. "I suspect that is pure fiction." Fiction, indeed. They had just been two misguided sons who'd seen too many gangsta movies and desperately wanted to move their father's stand to a more advantageous location. When their father found out how hard they had been leaning on me to help persuade Uncle Frank to sell, including letting a giant bull snake loose in our trailer while I slept, Mr. Li went bonkers, or whatever the Chinese equivalent of that word is. Both boys were put on permanent egg roll duty.

And in a surprising move, Uncle Frank decided to go ahead and let Mr. Li have his coveted space on the Grand Concourse, saying he reckoned it was time to downsize. He'd apologized to Aunt Reggie, finally opening up to her and acknowledging that the stress of running three businesses coupled with not enough time off, plus his disappointment that his only child wasn't interested in taking over a livelihood he'd sunk his heart and soul into, had begun to take a toll. He'd been wrong to seek solace in drink rather than confiding in her, he told her, and assured her at no time did he have an interest in Lucy Connor beyond that of a convenient drinking partner. Uncle Frank and Aunt Reggie were planning a trip to Vegas come fall. I looked over at Frankie standing with his folks and Dixie and Luther Daggett. I expected Uncle Frank and Aunt Reggie would need a getaway once their son introduced them to their prospective daughter-in-law, Dixie the Destructor. Or maybe therapy.

And Lord only knew what they would say when

Frankie told them he'd decided on a career as a police officer and wanted to begin taking criminal justice courses in the fall. Or what my own folks would say when Taylor finally dropped her own bombshell and informed them she wanted to decline a full-ride scholarship and drop out of college. And whether Kimmie would convince Craig he was ready for fatherhood and if next year at this time I might be Aunt Tressa.

As for me—I'm just thrilled Mr. Li has added lo mein to his fair menu for next year!

Gram and I concluded our three minutes of fame and the media moved away to pester Trooper Dawkins for a statement.

"So that psychic lady was a fake, huh?" Gram asked.

I shrugged. "I guess."

"Guess this means I won't be going on the Love Boat after all," Gram said. "And you won't be having sex in the near future like she said."

Like I needed to hear that.

"It seems every time I happen upon you two lately, you're discussing sex," Rick Townsend said, joining us and putting an arm around my grammy. "So, who's getting it—or not getting it—this time?" he asked. His eyes were on my face.

"Who the heck knows?" Gram replied. "Now that Psychic Sonya is a fake, who the heck knows? Sonya predicted some serious sexual conflict and hot, steamy climaxes for Tressa there, but now, well, it's anybody's guess." My grammy gave Rick a sideways look. "What about you, Rick?" She pointed a finger in my direction. "What do you foresee for Tressa?"

Townsend gave me a hard look. His gaze slid past me to rest on the pink-and-white Uncle Frankmobile that was this year's Dairee Freeze derby entry, and the hot pink helmet I had clutched in one hand. A muscle jumped in a tanned cheek.

"This soothsayer predicts a bumpy ride, Hannah," he said. "One very bumpy ride." Townsend walked away.

"Is that anything like rough sex?" Gram asked.

I shook my head. "More like tough love, I imagine," I said. And tough luck for Tressa.

The Powder Puff Derby was about to begin. The stakes were higher than ever. This was for all the marbles. Whoever's car was left moving the longest would be the victor. And to the victor would go all the spoils— in this case, bragging rights only, as Uncle Frank and Luther Daggett had already agreed to end their thirty-year sales competition and jointly refurbish the horse-shoe pitching venue. The next day Uncle Frank would co-host his traditional pig roast along with Luther Daggett.

Dixie Daggett and I stood toe-to-toe.

"You know, I still don't like you much," Dixie said.

"Ditto," I replied.

"We're never gonna be bosom buddies," she told me.

"Good. Dodged that bullet."

"And I'm gonna kick your ass out there on the track."

"You can try."

"*To your automobiles, ladies!*" I heard over the loud-speaker. I found myself searching the sidelines for, and finding, Townsend. He stood beside Taylor, his arms crossed, a grim look on his face.

"Your head protection, milady." Dawkins held my helmet out to me. I paused.

"Is there a problem, Tressa?" P.D. asked. "Second thoughts, maybe?"

Was there? The sudden, sobering irony that a guy I'd just met accepted me for who I was without question, foibles, flaws and flakiness notwithstanding, while a guy who'd known me when I'd made and consumed real mud pies still refused to do so was not lost even on me.

I looked over and saw Uncle Frank and Aunt Reggie, arms around each other, and Uncle Frank gave me the thumbs-up sign. I caught sight of my folks, my father standing just behind my mother, one hand on her shoulder. Kimmie stood beside my mom and Craig was next to my dad. Kimmie smiled and waved. Gram and Joe were hunched over the digital camera, no doubt trying to remember how it worked.

"Are you okay, Tressa?" P.D. asked.

I thought about it. And do you know what? I decided I *was* okay. Not perfect. Nowhere even close. But for now? Okay.

"I am okay," I told Trooper Dawkins. "And I yam what I yam."

"For the record, just what are you, Popeye?" P.D. asked.

I grinned. "Why, the winner of this year's Powder Puff Derby, of course, Mr. Super Trooper," I replied, securing the helmet on my head and hurrying to my ancient pink Oldsmobile. I resisted glancing in Townsend's direction for fear I'd find he'd left the grandstand.

"Ladies! Start your engines!"

I cranked the key and the motor fired like there was a jet-propulsion engine under the hood. I frowned. Knowing Manny and the car he'd gotten me . . .

"Good luck, Tressa," P.D. told me, and he tapped the driver's door with his palm. "Make 'em eat dust," he said.

"Thanks, Patrick," I said, and waved him off. Dawkins saluted and backed away. The horn sounded to signal the start of the contest.

I popped the clutch on the Olds and shoved the stick-shift into reverse. I hit the accelerator and released the clutch and shot backwards toward the vulnerable front end of the Daggettmobile, laughing maniacally as dust billowed and rocks flew.

Boys had their toys. Men had their moose hunts. And me? I had Dixie Daggett's vulnerable front end dead in my sights.

Don't ever say cowgirls don't know how to have a good time.

Wondering what happens to Tressa, Rick and the Grandville gang, and what Calamity strikes next?

Don't miss:

GHOULS JUST WANT TO HAVE FUN

Kathleen Bacus

October 2006!

FROM THE AUTHOR

I have always loved fairs—from the times I blew my allowance tossing ping-pong balls and plastic rings for a chance to win a stuffed animal at the county fair, to the time I first strutted my stuff around the state fairgrounds as a rookie Iowa State Trooper. Oh, the tales I could tell! For the purposes of this particular story, I have taken certain liberties with the fairground proper and the names, locations, and descriptions of certain attractions or venues. What I hope the reader gleans from this work, however, is my great fondness for and genuine enjoyment of this one-of-a-kind annual Midwestern celebration. Our state fair *is* a great state fair!

KATHLEEN BACUS

CALAMITY JAYNE

Tressa Jayne Turner has had it up to *here* with the never-ending string of dumb-blonde jokes and her long-time nickname. Crowned "Calamity Jayne" by Iowa Department of Natural Resources officer Rick Townsend, Tressa's out to gain a little hometown respect—or die trying. She's just been handed the perfect opportunity to get "Ranger Rick" to finally take her seriously. How? By solving a murder no one else believes happened.... No one, that is, except the killer.

Yup, Calamity Jayne is in it up to her hot pink snakeskin cowgirl boots. Tressa would tell you her momma never raised no dummies, but the jury's still out on that one.